# SAVAGE COLLISION

## A HAWKE FAMILY NOVEL

### BILLIONAIRES OF NEW ORLEANS: THE HAWKE FAMILY
### BOOK 1

## GWYN MCNAMEE

SAVAGE COLLISION
by
Gwyn McNamee © 2016

Cover Design: Michelle Johnson at Blue Sky Designs
Cover Model: Assad Shalhoub
Photographer: Christopher Correia at CJC Photography

❀ Created with Vellum

*To my wonderful husband, who puts up with my crazy on a daily basis and still manages to love the hell out of me.*

# ACKNOWLEDGMENTS

First and foremost, I need to give a HUGE thank you to my beta readers—Dawn, Kim P., Jennifer W., Janice, Renee S., Diane E., Rachael F., and my super-betas, Star and Christy—without all of you, this book would have remained dormant on my laptop for another two years. I also need to thank Donna and Lea, who are always 100% behind everything I do and love all my crazy ideas. The same is true of my Pirate Wenches, the wonderful group of writers who are always there with support, to bounce ideas off of, or to listen to me rant when I lose my mind. Finally, thank you to Kim G., who stepped up and helped me at the last minute to make sure this book got finished on time. Everyone's support and encouragement has been absolutely essential to getting me where I am today. I love you all!

# 1

SAVAGE

*N*aked women gyrate on stages—asses, tits, flesh on display—their images covering three-quarters of my computer screen, but they are merely blurs in my peripheral vision.

My focus is on the top right corner, where one of my vendors is unloading his truck on the loading dock, and taking his sweet-ass time doing it. He's no doubt using it as an excuse to gawk at the girls. Byron is in heated discussion with him about something. Hopefully, my club manager is reaming him out for taking up so much of our damn time with an unload that should take only minutes.

*Why are people so fucking lazy these days? What happened to work ethic?*

Mom and Dad made damn well sure all their children understood the importance of a hard-day's work and always giving it one hundred percent. I guess that kind of thing just isn't instilled in people anymore. It shouldn't surprise me really, the degradation of society, not when I see the degenerates who always manage to find their way in here, despite my best efforts to keep the club clientele upscale.

Byron and the vendor move to the back of the truck and start unloading several handcarts-full of cases of beer at a time. At least I can always rely on Byron to get the job done.

I return to the paperwork on my desk but barely have time to regain my train of thought before my office door flies open, slamming against the wall.

Instinctively, I reach under my desk, wrapping my hand around the grip of the Sig Sauer 1911 Scorpion I keep mounted there. I look up, expecting to find one of Domenico Abello's thugs, because, surely, that would be the only person capable of making it past both Gabe and Byron to end up in my office unannounced.

My breath catches in my throat when, instead of a burly threat, my eyes land on what I can only describe as a Victoria's Secret model. An enraged one.

She is furious—the fire in her stormy blue eyes and her scowling red lips are a dead giveaway. With a toss of her long, wavy blonde hair behind her shoulder, she thunders into my office as if she owns the place.

I track her progress across the room, taking in her polished appearance—from her French-manicured nails, thousand-dollar bag, and Burberry trench down to the four-inch Louboutin stilettos that make her long, elegant legs extend beyond comprehension as she clicks across the wood floor with purpose.

My cock hardens instantly and, despite my surprise at my body's reaction to her, I steel my expression and shift uncomfortably in my chair.

*Damn. This woman is livid, and hot as fucking hell.*

I doubt she's a threat, though—to anything but my libido—so, I remove my hand from the gun and surreptitiously slide it to my crotch to adjust my erection before reclining and watching her speculatively. Despite this being my office, my domain, I wait patiently for her to say something. A hint of uncertainty and maybe discomfort surface from beneath her diamond-hard demeanor.

"Are you the owner?"

She stops several feet short of my desk, props her hands on her shapely hips, and huffs in defiance. Her voice is level and steady when she asks the question, but her eyes give her away. They roam over me with blatant interest, and the slight flush on her neck and cheeks only confirm my suspicion—she's checking me out.

I relax in my chair and school my features, trying to hide my amusement. I answer her question with a nod. "I am, and you might be?"

"Danika Eriksson." She tosses her name at me like a poison dart, and her bravado impresses me despite my uncertainty about her purpose here.

*Do I know her? Should I be recognizing her name? No, I would remember a woman like her.*

Movement in the open door catches my attention. Gabe eyes Ms. Eriksson with concern. I wave off my best friend, right-hand man, and business partner with a look, and he nods his understanding before disappearing down the hall.

"What can I do for you, Ms. Eriksson?"

She crosses her arms over her chest in a huff, which only succeeds in pushing her abundant breasts higher.

*Not helping the raging hard-on situation, lady.*

"You can tell me where the hell you get off tricking young, innocent girls into selling themselves like slabs of beef in your disgusting club." She spits the words at me, completely, unabashedly unafraid to insult me and my business, while standing right in front of me and looking me in the eye.

I struggle to withhold a grin at her audacity as I lean forward, resting my elbows on the edge of the desk.

"I can assure you, Ms. Eriksson, that none of my employees are 'tricked' into doing anything."

She scoffs and shifts her weight, drawing my attention back to her impossibly long, shapely legs. The woman must be at least five foot seven without those heels on. With them, she towers over me in all her elegant glory.

"Bullshit..." She searches my desk for a nameplate, then looks at me again when she doesn't find one.

The corner of my mouth quirks up before I can stop it. "Savage, Savage Hawke. But please, call me Savage, and just what is it you think you know about my employees?"

"Savage?" Her eyes narrow, and then, she rolls them. "Your parents honestly named you Savage Hawke?"

This isn't the first time someone has questioned my name, or that my name has left me the butt of some joke. "Yes, they did. It's a family name."

My gaze naturally drifts to the framed photo on the corner of my desk. It was my father's second-to-last fight. He's standing in the center of the ring in Madison Square Garden, the WBA heavy-weight championship belt around his waist, and I'm hoisted above his head, both of us smiling in his victory. I was ten.

She follows my stare and when she sees the photo, her eyebrows pop up in recognition. "Wait, your father is Sam 'The Savage' Hawke?"

Stunned doesn't even begin to describe how I feel, hearing my dad's name from her. It takes me a moment to shake off my surprise, but eventually, I manage a smile and nod. "I'm surprised you recognize him." I lean forward to grab the photo and turn it around so she can see it more clearly.

In my thirty years on this planet, I don't think I've ever met a single woman who knew who my father was. Men, on the other hand, gape in awe when they find out my lineage. I guess it just goes with the territory of being the son of a heavy-weight champ, and one who died the way he did.

She takes a step closer to me, bending down slightly to get a closer look at the photo. "Holy shit! I can't believe you are 'The Savage's' son! Of course I know who he is. My dad was a huge boxing fan. I grew up watching your dad's fights from my old man's lap."

"That's great." And very unexpected. I'm not quite sure what to say. Talking about my father is always bittersweet.

Her smile and astonishment fade, and she glances at me apologetically. "Shit, I'm sorry..." Before she finishes her thought, she seems to realize she's been sidetracked from her intended purpose. She straightens herself, squares her shoulders, and I can tell she's ready to get back to business.

"Well, Savage," she says my name like it's a four-letter word, "I would very much appreciate it if you kept your sleazy hands off my baby sister."

*Bingo!*

She isn't the first, and she certainly won't be the last, person to find their way into my office on their high horse, accusing me of taking advantage of some innocent little sister, cousin, or friend.

"And who is your baby sister?"

Her face scrunches in disgust at my inability to immediately make the familial connection.

"Nora Eriksson, she started shaking her ass and tits for you almost three weeks ago."

The way she throws the words "ass and tits" at me, I have to cover my mouth with my hand to hide my grin. This woman is all attitude, and it is sexy as fuck, although I have no idea why. She definitely isn't my usual type, although, I'm not sure if I even know what my type is anymore. Certainly, she's about as far from Becca as one can get, yet my cock is still straining against my pants.

I clear my throat before responding, hoping to give myself a second to regain my composure. "Ah, yes, Nora. My manager, Byron, hired her. I've only had the pleasure of meeting her on one occasion, but I can assure you, Ms. Eriksson, she was in no way 'tricked' into taking her position here."

She glowers at me, and her hands ball into tight fists at her sides. "I know my sister, *Savage*, and there is no way in hell she just up and decided she wanted to be a fucking stripper. She was tricked, or forced..."

I barely manage to contain an eye-roll. "If I didn't have such thick skin, I might be insulted by the way you throw your words at me like daggers." I sit back and enjoy watching her distress at my ability to maintain my cool. The color in her cheeks flares, and her blue eyes flash at me.

*Who knew angry could be such a fucking turn on?*

---

## DANIKA

My blood is boiling and this man—Savage Hawke—has grated my last nerve. I can barely contain my desire to climb across his desk and smack him across his handsome, smug face for acting so high and mighty. He is a pussy peddler. A goddamn sleazebag who preys on young, impressionable, desperate girls in order to make a quick buck.

*Savage Hawke.*

He even has a porn star name. It wouldn't surprise me if he was shooting them in some back room.

It's too bad he's so fucking gorgeous. He runs a hand back through his thick, wavy black hair and focuses his Caribbean-blue eyes on me with a calm that makes me want to throw my purse at him.

My traitorous body reacted to him instantly, heat churning

deep in my belly the moment I walked into his office and saw him dominating the space behind his large, wooden desk.

The longer we talk, the worse it gets, and I have to press my thighs together to stop the dull ache there.

*Damn, it has been way too long since I had a good fuck. What? Twelve days?*

I'm so busy fuming and trying to rein in my runaway sex drive, I completely forget to respond to him.

"Ms. Eriksson," he continues, giving me a smug smile, "I have a very rigorous interview process established to ensure none of my employees begin work here under any duress..."

I lift my brow in speculation and to ensure he's aware of my disbelief. *Bullshit!* I bet their "interview process" involves lap dances and blowjobs in the champagne room.

"...Byron conducts a very thorough interview with each girl, including a complete background check to determine if they are under any serious financial strains. If I find they are, I typically offer them a personal loan, to be repaid at standard interest rates, to ensure they aren't tempted to engage in pursuits some of the other clubs are often known for. We also do weekly drug testing and nightly breathalyzers, as our girls are forbidden from engaging in any illicit drug use and cannot perform while under the influence of any alcoholic beverages."

I don't believe him for a second. No damn strip club operates like that. He must think I'm some dumb, naïve, bimbo blonde to believe I'll fall for his line of horseshit.

He reclines back in his chair and waits for me to say something.

*What does he expect me to believe? That he's a pussy peddler with a heart of gold?*

"Surprised I'm not a total scumbag?" His amusement is evident in the slight turn at the corner of his luscious mouth. "There are a hundred trashy strip clubs in New Orleans a man can go to if that's what he's looking for—drugs and easy women. I wanted to offer something different. People are always a bit shocked to learn how I run my business. But when I built The Hawkeye Club, I wanted it to be an upscale and supremely classy gentleman's club and established a very strict set of rules and regulations to ensure that both my reputation, and the reputation of my girls, remains pristine."

I huff and take a step closer to his desk. "My sister was the goddamn valedictorian of her high school class and had a full ride to Tulane for pre-med. Then, this morning, out of the blue, I find out from one of her roommates that she has dropped out of school and started working here. She's twenty years old, for Christ's sake! Clearly, you can see why I'm concerned. I mean, why the hell would she do that?"

He offers me a small, understanding smile and leans over his desk, toward me. The fabric of his dress shirt stretches across his broad shoulders and strains against his massive biceps. My mouth salivates, and I fight the flush I'm sure is creeping up my neck. The worst thing about being fair-skinned is the complete inability to hide my reactions, especially to men like Savage Hawke.

"I do understand, Ms. Eriksson, but I don't have the answer for you. Have you tried asking your sister?"

*Shit. I should have seen that question coming.*

I shift uncomfortably and twist my hands in front of my body. "No, she's been avoiding my calls. That's why I finally went to her apartment today, to make sure she's okay."

He almost looks sympathetic.

*I wonder how long it took him to perfect this nice-guy act.*

"Well, I think you need to talk to her. I don't think she's on the schedule tonight, but you can ask Byron downstairs, and, if she's here, he will gladly show you to the changing rooms in the back so you can speak with her."

Casting an uncomfortable glance toward him, I move my purse from one shoulder to the other and turn to leave without a word. Absolutely no good will come from me spending any more time in this room with this man.

Savage Hawke is precisely the type of man I always end up getting myself into trouble with: dark, strong, passionate...

I almost stumble when a vision of him slamming me back against the wall and yanking up my skirt to gain access floods my mind.

*Jesus—I bet he takes absolute control in the bedroom, and I bet he fucks like a complete animal. Men like that don't do things slow and sweet.*

"I don't even get a 'thank you' or a 'goodbye?'"

His sultry, deep voice stops me halfway to the door. I look over my shoulder at him.

*Deep breaths, Dani. Keep it together.*

*Don't let him see how he affects you. Don't let him see you rattled.*

"I don't have anything to thank you for." I raise my head high and strut out the door, not bothering to close it behind me. I punch the button on the elevator and tap my foot impatiently.

I need to get out of here.

I need to get as far away as possible.

I need to find Nora.

I need to find something to prevent me from racing home, grabbing my Rabbit, and spending the rest of the day fantasizing about that man.

I need to find something to prevent me from racing straight back to his office, climbing over his desk, and straddling his lap.

An angry fuck can be supremely hot—ripped clothing, hair pulling, strong, groping hands—but having an angry fuck with my stripper sister's deviant boss would be an epically bad life choice.

## 2

---

SAVAGE

*T*he instant she disappears around the doorjamb, I grasp my rock-hard cock and adjust it away from under the zipper of my jeans. That woman is walking attitude and sex. I can already smell the trouble she will cause me, mixed with the heady blend of lilacs and rain she left in her wake. I haven't reacted to a woman this way in, well, ever.

I pick up the phone and press the extension for the downstairs bar, waiting impatiently as it rings several times. "Yep." Byron answers, slightly out of breath.

"A very angry, very beautiful blonde is on her way down from my office. She's looking for her sister, Nora Eriksson."

"Your office? Shit. I'm sorry, Savage. I stepped out back to take care of a delivery. She must have slipped in when I was gone. I'll take care of it."

As much as I want to ream him out for letting someone get up here unannounced, I know he was busy out back, and it really isn't his fault. It does get me wondering about better security, though. I thought we had things covered—Gabe is kind of an expert when it comes to assuring things are locked down—but if a woman like that can waltz right up here, so can anyone else.

"Please do, and track down Nora if she isn't here. See if she can come in and meet with me as soon as possible." I drop the phone back into the cradle and relax back into my chair.

My cock is still pressing uncomfortably against my jeans, but there isn't anything I can do about it now. So, I take a deep breath, close my eyes, and make my best attempt to center myself.

*Deep breaths, Savage. Deep, cleansing breaths.*

There's work to be done, phone calls that need to be made...

"What the hell was that all about?" Gabe struts into my office and drops unceremoniously into one of the leather arm chairs facing me. "Was she here for a job? Please tell me you hired that fine piece of ass!"

His lecherous grin makes me smile despite my disgust at his constant dehumanization of females.

"No, sorry, Gabe, she wasn't here for a job interview. She was here to tell me off because I hired her sister, Nora Eriksson."

Gabe's eyes widen, and his jaw drops. "*That* is Nora's sister?"

I nod, and he chuckles, dropping his head against the back of the chair.

"You know what she does, right?"

"No," I shake my head, "should I?"

He pulls his head up and gives me a look I've seen way too many times over the last twenty-plus years of our friendship—the "you're a fucking moron" look.

"Should I?"

His grin tells me I may be in more trouble than I realized.

"Uh, yeah, man. She's a goddamn investigative reporter for the *Times*. If you cross her, you're liable to end up being the cover story."

*Shit.*

I knew she looked familiar for some reason. I've seen her photo at the top of her column every fucking morning.

"Fuck, you're right...but I don't think she was here for a story. This was personal. This was about her sister. I gathered that the last thing she would want is for the world to find out her little sister is now a stripper."

Gabe barks out a laugh. "Why do you say that with such disdain? You own the place, Savage. You employ these strippers."

"That doesn't mean I would necessarily want any of my baby sisters doing it."

That gets Gabe absolutely rolling, doubling over in the chair and wiping tears from his eyes. "God, I can just imagine if Storm or Skye tried to become a dancer. You would completely lose your shit."

I glare at him. "Not funny. Stop picturing my baby sisters in thongs, you pervert."

"They are hardly babies anymore, Savage. They're what, twenty-seven and twenty-nine? Storm is married and has a child, for Christ's sake."

*Not the fucking point!*

My big-brother blood boils and, if Gabe weren't basically my other half, I might act on my urge to punch him in the fucking jaw. I love the guy, but he should know better when it comes to the Hawke girls.

"Still, you're practically family, and they will always be my baby sisters, so, just stop."

He holds his hands up in surrender. "Fine, fine." He relents, standing and stretching out, the tips of his fingers almost hitting the ceiling. "You ready to get outta here for the day?"

"No, I asked Byron to try to get a hold of Nora. I want to talk to her and make sure nothing else is going on. Her sister seems to genuinely think she wouldn't be here unless it was because of some sort of outside forces."

Gabe looks concerned for the first time since he entered my office.

"You think Byron missed something in the interview?"

"I doubt it." I shake my head. "But I have to ask, just to ease my own mind."

He shrugs. "All right, just let me know when you're ready to bail." He disappears out the door, tossing a half-wave over his shoulder before closing it behind him.

I return to the paperwork on my desk and try to lose myself in the numbers and contracts in front of me. At least my dick has finally calmed down.

My reaction to Danika unnerves me yet has me considering things I haven't thought about in a very fucking long time. If I spend any more time thinking about her, I won't get anything done today. I try my best to push her to the back of my mind.

After an hour of phone calls and staring at the tiny print in these one hundred-page contracts, my head pounds and my eyes are starting to burn.

A soft knock at the door breaks the concentration I finally managed to find. I look up.

"Come in." I drop the papers in my hand onto the pile accumulating on my desk. No matter what, I'll head home as soon as whoever this is leaves. I am fucking exhausted.

Nora appears, barely popping her head into the cracked door. "Sir? Byron called and said you wanted to see me?"

*Sir. Christ. I can't be more than ten years older than her and she's calling me sir?*

"Yes, hello, Nora. Please, come in."

She pushes the door open and steps in, all five foot three inches, one hundred pounds of her, timidly making her way to my desk. The sisters must really take after different parents, because I would have never known they are related based on meeting them. They have the same blue eyes and blonde hair, but where Danika was all confidence and legs, Nora is petite and carries herself more like someone walking the plank.

"Um, am I in trouble, sir?"

*Shit. Of course she thinks she's in trouble. I must have scared the crap out of her, asking for this meeting.*

"Oh, shit, no! Come, sit, please...and for the love of God, stop calling me 'sir.'"

She hesitates briefly before slowly lowering herself into the leather chair across from me. I can sense her nerves. She's barely able to make eye contact with me, and her leg bounces up and down in an anxious rhythm.

"Ms. Eriksson, please, you aren't in any trouble. It's just, I received a visit from your sister earlier today and wanted to discuss it with you."

She closes her eyes and mumbles something under her breath before shifting forward to the edge of her chair. "Oh, God, what did she do? What did she say?" She drops her face into her hands.

Her reaction shouldn't be funny, as she's clearly distressed, but after my encounter with Danika today, I understand her concern. I bark out a laugh as I lean forward in my chair. "Yes, well, she certainly is...opinionated, isn't she?"

Her head snaps up, and her eyes meet mine. She frowns. "That's a nice way to say it, sir. She tends to be a little... overzealous at times." She offers me an apologetic smile.

*There's the sir, again.*

I don't correct her, because it doesn't really matter, and she clearly has bigger concerns at the moment than trying to stroke my ego by not making me feel so fucking old.

*When did thirty become "sir" territory, anyway?*

I understand being respectful to your elders. As children, Mom and Dad always made us call people "sir" or "ma'am," but in this situation, it just makes me wonder what happened to the last ten years of my life to suddenly make me an "elder" without me even realizing it.

*Christ, I wonder how old Danika is and if she saw me the same way Nora does.*

At least she didn't call me "sir," although, I'm sure she had a few choice names for me in her head when she stormed out of here.

Nora shifts in her chair, and I realize an uncomfortable silence has settled over the room. *You aren't making this any easier on her by daydreaming about Danika instead of just telling her what's up.*

"Yes, well, she seemed very concerned about your employment here, and what your motives for working for me might be."

She lets out an exasperated sigh and relaxes back into the chair. "Look, I'm sorry you had to deal with her. She's just used to looking out for me, but I can assure you, I'm here because I want to be here."

I never doubted it, but hearing it from her does ease the tension in my neck and shoulders and make me feel like slightly less of a scumbag. What Gabe said was true. I've never regretted my choice in business, and I've never been ashamed of what I do, but every time a big brother—or sister—shows up here raging, I get that niggling feeling deep in my chest that feels a lot like shame and guilt.

"I'm sure that's true, Nora. Otherwise, Byron would have found out."

Nora stands and paces in front of my desk. "I've been avoiding her ever since I dropped out of school. I didn't know how to tell her..."

Her distress tugs at my heartstrings. I can picture Skye in this position. My youngest sister has a habit of getting herself into unsavory situations, and I'm constantly forced to play white knight, riding in to her rescue. She shares that trait with our baby brother,

Stone. Things have only gotten worse with Skye in the last three years. Sometimes, I wonder how she has managed to hold down her job at the hospital. She's a great nurse, but with everything going on, she just hasn't seemed to be able to keep her shit together.

"Look, your relationship with your sister isn't any of my business, but she seems genuinely concerned about you. I think it might be a good idea for you to talk to her, sooner rather than later."

She nods in agreement. "I just want you to know, I really love working here. Danika won't understand, but, I've been busting my ass my whole life in school, in work, trying to please my mother and Danika, but none of it made me happy and I just needed a break. Being here, dancing, that makes me happy. I feel like I can be free and just be myself."

I nod my understanding and offer her a smile. A lot of the girls tell me the same thing. Something about being completely free on the stage...I can't understand it, but if they love it, that's all I care about.

"Thank you for coming in on your day off, Nora. Again, I don't want to involve myself in your family relationships..."

"No..." She holds her hands up to stop me. "I really appreciate you letting me know she was here."

"Of course. I'll see you later."

She turns and disappears out of my office, closing the door behind her.

*At least she has some manners, something that apparently doesn't run in the family.*

The difference between the sisters is striking. Danika came in like a whirlwind—a finely dressed, heavily-attituded whirlwind—and let me have it. She wasn't intimidated by me or by being on my turf. She stood her ground and managed to walk out with her head held high, despite the blush I caught more than once during our meeting. Nora, on the other hand, dances naked for a living but dealt with me in a mild and respectful manner. She doesn't possess the same fire as Danika; that much is clear.

*Why the fuck am I attracted to the difficult one?*

---

## DANIKA

He presses his body against mine, chest to chest, and his hot breath fans my ear as he kisses his way up and down my neck. Large hands cup my ass and jerk me forward to meet his grinding hips, and his massive erection presses against my engorged clit, eliciting a moan from me against his cheek. I push myself even closer to him, pulling away from the wall. He growls and shoves me back, making it clear who is in control, and reaches one hand around to tear off my soaked panties, letting them fall to the floor.

"Please, Savage..." The words fall from my lips before I can stop them, and I want to smack myself for sounding so needy and desperate. That is so not me. But I am on fucking fire! I need release like I need my next breath, and he isn't giving it to me. Instead, he's teasing me, using his wicked mouth and body to push me to the brink of insanity.

"Hello? Earth to Danika?"

I jerk awake, almost falling out of my chair when Caroline grabs the back and spins it around to face her.

"What the hell, girl?" She stares at me intently. "What is going on with you today? This is the third time you've totally zoned out since you came back from lunch."

Since I came back from "lunch"—since I came back from seeing Savage fucking Hawke.

I've been a complete basket case all afternoon, and I have only myself, and that man, to blame. Well, that's not true. I can also blame Robert, my former fuck buddy who decided to up and move, leaving me utterly bereft and needy as hell.

It's inhumane to leave a woman hanging like that. I always get like this when I don't get laid. It's been over a week—almost two. Twelve long, lonely, agonizing days, and now I can't stop fantasizing about the first man I've been attracted to since Robert left.

*Get your shit together, Eriksson. You have a job to do. Put your libido away until you get home and can spend some time with BOB or find someone else who can take your mind off Savage.*

"I'm fine, Caroline, relax. I'm just distracted thinking about this story." It isn't a complete lie. I've been trying to nail Domenico Abello since I started this job almost four years ago, but all I've managed to do is meet with brick walls of silence.

Abello is dirty—the kind of dirty that makes Tony Soprano look like Mr. Clean.

Everyone knows his reputation, but I only recently got wind of some very unsettling information. Paul, my source, a low-ranking henchman of Abello's, heard I had been asking around, trying to tie Abello to anything that could actually get him sent away. When he first approached me outside my apartment, I'll admit, I thought I'd end up with a bullet in my head, but it turns out Paul wants out of the organization, and he's smart enough to know Abello won't let him just walk away.

Paul confirmed something I've long suspected and feared— Abello doesn't just control New Orleans' underworld. He controls the government, too, through a seedy connection to Mayor Dunne.

Many of the people who stood in the way of Brian Dunne's political advancement over the years have disappeared or been in questionable accidents. Once he reached office, a lot of his opposition seemed to back off quite unexpectedly from vehement resistance to certain projects. Quite a few contracts have also ended up going to businesses with hidden connections to Abello.

According to Paul, Dunne's success is, in large part, due to this "assistance" from Abello. The only question is, can I prove it?

If I can verify and document that the head of the biggest

crime syndicate in New Orleans has unsavory ties to the mayor and has not only been receiving special consideration on projects in exchange for not even remotely legal favors but may be going so far as to commit murder for Dunne, my career will be made.

"You still trying to get that source to get some documentation for you?"

"Yeah." I spin around to check my email, "he keeps hedging. I've only been able to get him to tell me about the shit he's heard or seen, but no actual hard evidence of anything yet. No way I'm publishing this story until I have iron-clad documentation and the source's allegations are backed up."

Diligence is important in this business, and I won't risk losing my job, or my reputation, on someone who may just have an axe to grind. Not that I really think that in this case.

"You don't believe his story?"

Spinning back around to face her, I shake my head. "That's just it, I *do* believe his story but there is no way I am putting my neck out there and exposing the people I plan to until I have everything I need."

It would be career suicide to publish a story like this without one hundred percent confirmation. It wouldn't be fair to my source, either. I know he's putting his neck on the line for me, with no benefit to him other than the potential opportunity to get out from under Abello's thumb. I can't risk his safety.

Caroline drops down into the chair opposite my desk and frowns. "You still won't tell me what this is all about?"

I sigh and run my hands back through my hair, which only reminds me of a hair-pulling Savage fantasy I had earlier this afternoon. *Shit.* I release my hair and let out a deep breath. Caroline is my best friend, and I would love to be able to share my Abello story with her, but I refuse to spill anything until I have the story wrapped up with a pretty bow around it—it's just too dangerous.

"No, Caroline, but it has nothing to do with you, or me not

trusting you. It's just better if no one else knows this information. It's safer that way."

She gives me a leery look. "You know, when you talk that way, it makes me hella nervous, girl."

I wave her off and bend to grab my purse and briefcase. I toss them over my shoulder, and she follows me out of my office. "You don't have to worry about me, Caroline. My dad taught me how to take care of myself."

Before he died, Dad ensured his girls knew basic self-defense skills—as much as you can teach that to a five and a twelve year old. Thankfully, I've never needed to use them. But, getting on the wrong side of a guy like Abello was probably not what Dad contemplated when instructing me.

Still, I refuse to back down because of some potential perceived danger. That wouldn't be doing my job, and I would feel like utter shit if I let my suspicions go. Maybe it's because Dad was a cop and spent his whole life trying to put douchebags like Abello away, or maybe I have some innate moral compass compelling me, but either way, I can't just let this get buried. If I did, I feel like I'd be letting myself, and Dad, down. He died protecting people from Abello's type of scum, and I'm not about to let him continue his control over this city.

"Your bravado is exactly what concerns me, Danika."

I smile at her, grabbing her arm and tugging her toward the elevator with me. I definitely need to get some drinks tonight, and I know Caroline is always up for whatever, so I try to steer the conversation away from her unfounded fears. "I'll be fine. I know what I'm doing."

*Mostly.*

## 3

**DANIKA**

*A*fter three days of agonizing Savage fantasies and frustrating non-movement on my story, I walk into my office and immediately see an over-the-top bouquet of at least a dozen white roses occupying the center of my desk. Glancing up and down the hallway, I check to see if the person who left them might be lingering nearby, but the entire office is empty. I'm almost always the first person in, and it's barely seven a.m.

*How did these even get delivered?*

My bags slide down my arm and onto my chair. I don't know why, but finding this in the middle of my desk in the deserted office is making me more than a little nervous. I refuse to acknowledge it might be related to my current investigation; that means admitting Abello can get to me.

A small, white envelope is nestled in the petals, and I reach in and pull it out. I slip my finger under the seal and open it. I'm half-expecting it to be from my sister, as an apology for all the shit she put me through in the last couple weeks. She knows I love white roses, and there aren't really any other possible senders.

*Except maybe Max.*

I met him the same day I met Savage. Caroline and I went out for drinks, and it wasn't like I was looking—okay, maybe a little bit—but he was there, and so damn hot with his dark hair and flashing blue eyes. He reminded me of Savage, a little too much. We had amazing sex that night, but I just couldn't get there. I've never *not* been able to orgasm. Talk about fucking frustration!

I would have stayed with him longer and continued to try, but I kind of ruined the mood by accidentally whimpering Savage's damn name when Max had me pinned against the wall, his cock buried deep inside me.

*Smooth, Dani, real smooth.* Just remembering the look on his face and the tensing of his body makes me cringe.

Pulling the card from the envelope, my heart races when I see the elegant, sloping scrawl of the writing in the note, certainly *not* Nora's handwriting.

*Ms. Eriksson –*
*Dinner.*
*Friday.*
*Angelo's.*
*8:00 p.m.*
*Savage (504) 202-5555*

*That pompous bastard!*

I throw the card onto my desk, knock my bags down to the floor, and drop into my chair in a huff.

*That arrogant prick!*

Who the hell does he think he is? What makes him think I would ever even consider going to dinner with him? He didn't even ask. He just demands with a goddamn four-word note?

*Presumptuous fuck!*

A litany of curses spew from my mouth as I stare at the beautiful flowers taking up the majority of my desk. As if it isn't bad enough I haven't been able to stop fantasizing about him since I met him, now he's demanding my presence at dinner?

*I won't go. He can sit there, alone, waiting for me. That will teach him a lesson about how he treats women—damn pussy peddler.*

And Nora defended him! Thinking back to my conversation with her earlier this week, I find it hard to believe we were talking about the same man.

"He's not as bad as you think," she'd insisted.

"Yeah, right. He pays women to shake their asses and tits for pervs. I'm sure he's an angel."

She'd sighed and rolled her eyes at me. "Really, Dani, he's not a perv, at least, not with us. He's really a good boss and doesn't ever cross the professional line with anyone."

The way she told it, he's some kind of fucking saint, acting like an overprotective big brother to all the girls working for him and taking care of them whenever they get into any kind of trouble. If she had her way, he would win a fucking Nobel Peace Prize.

"Professional? You call parading naked women across a stage for men to gawk at professional?"

She glowered at me, and I knew I said something I shouldn't have. "Look, Dani, I get that you don't approve of me dancing, but it's my decision, not yours. I'm happy doing it, so why can't you just leave it alone? Savage is a good boss who takes care of us. He always thinks about the girls' well-being. I'll be okay."

Well, she may have full confidence in her boss' motives and glowing character, but my experience with Savage couldn't have been more different. The man is self-centered, arrogant, holier-than-thou...and fucking beautiful. How the women at the club are immune to his good looks and radiating sexuality is beyond me.

I haven't been able to stop thinking about him since the

second I saw him sitting regally behind his desk, the master of his pussy universe. He doesn't belong in an office. He belongs in the movies, preferably a porno, where I can see what he has under those clothes. His broad shoulders and the fabric straining across his biceps had me practically begging to touch him.

I shake my head.

*No, fuck him. He can sit and wait for me, forever. I am not giving in to his arrogant demand.*

The card goes into the garbage can under my desk, and I turn to my computer and pull up my email. I barely have time to read the first one when I hear a familiar squeal from behind me and drop my face into my hands, letting out a groan.

*I should have trashed the flowers, too.*

"Ho. Ly. Shit! Who the hell sent you roses? Have you been holding out on me, girl?" Caroline grabs the back of my chair and spins me around to face her. She glares at me momentarily before she begins digging around in the flowers.

"What the hell are you doing?"

"Looking for a card so I can find out who sent these, since you have obviously been keeping important information, like the fact that you have a new fuck buddy, to yourself. Oh, my God, is it that guy from the bar the other night? Max?"

I surreptitiously push the garbage can further under my desk with my foot while Caroline is still nose-deep in the long stems. The last thing I need is her finding the card and asking all sorts of unanswerable questions.

"There isn't a card. There isn't a fuck buddy. They're from my sister." The lie slips out so quickly and so easily, I'm confident she'll buy it.

Turning to face me, she props her fists on her hips and gives me the "you have got to be fucking kidding me" look. "Your sister? Nora, broke college student, Nora, sent you two dozen white roses that probably cost over a hundred bucks?"

*Shit. Maybe I should have thought out that great lie a little better.*

Caroline doesn't know about Nora stripping yet. I hate keeping things from her, but Nora asked me not to say anything, and I can't rat out my own sister, even to my best friend.

"Yeah, she got a job and wanted to thank me for all of the support I've given her recently."

Caroline laughs and sits on the edge of my desk. "Girl, I don't know why you don't want me to know who really sent these, but you can drop the act. You're a terrible liar."

She's right.

I know any other attempts at deception will be pointless, but that doesn't mean I have to give her the whole story. I let out a sigh of resignation before dropping my head down onto my desk. "Ugh, fine, they're from this guy I met the other day, and no, before you ask, we haven't fucked. He's my sister's new boss."

I don't have to be able to see Caroline to know her mouth is agape and her green eyes are bulging out of their sockets at the prospect of a new man in my life.

"And just how did you come to meet Nora's new boss?" The sing-song tone in her voice makes me curl my fists at my sides.

There isn't any point in continuing to keep it from her. She knows me too well, and she's the queen of poking and prodding until she gets what she wants. The only thing she *hasn't* been able to get out of me is the subject of my big story.

"I went to make sure she was being treated right."

"Ha! I bet you a million dollars you went there to give this poor guy a hard time."

I lift my head and throw my best death glare at her. If I didn't love her so much, she might be the recipient of a cunt punch.

"You telling me you didn't?"

*Crap. I did.* I push back from my desk, stand, and pace around my office, glancing quickly between the flowers and Caroline.

"Okay, so I kinda gave him a hard time. To be honest, I have no fucking clue why he sent these." Maybe actually talking about it with Caroline will help me work through my strange obsession with him.

"Was there a card?" She smirks, and I know she knows there was one and that I probably disposed of it.

"In the garbage, under my desk."

She leans down, grabs the can, and pulls the small, white card from the top. As she reads it over quickly, I watch her eyebrows rise. "Holy shit, he's asking you on a date!"

"No, no, he isn't. He's demanding my presence at a certain place at a certain time. He isn't *asking* me anything."

*Fucking beautiful arrogant asshole...*

"Aaand that's a problem because...?" She circles her hand in front of her in an incredibly condescending gesture.

"Because, I am not one to let a man dictate when, or if, I do something."

Caroline doubles over in laughter, tosses the card on my desk, and makes her way toward the door. "That's a good one, Dani. Just remember, I know all about you and what you let men dictate."

She disappears around the corner, and I collapse back into my chair, the offending card mocking me from the desk.

*Fuck. What now?*

---

## SAVAGE

"You don't think it was maybe a tad bit overkill?" Rick raises an eyebrow.

*What? Two dozen white, long-stem roses to a woman I only met once?*

I stare up at my trainer as I recline on the bench in the gym and try to look more confident than I really feel. "No, not at all."

He smirks at me. "Dude, two dozen roses? I don't even get my wife two dozen roses on our anniversary." He reaches down to grab another twenty-five pound plate to add to the bar.

Sweat drips down the sides of my face and onto the bench under my head. I grab my towel from the floor and do my best to mop it off, even though I know I'll just have to do it again in a couple minutes. "Maybe that's why you never get laid, my friend."

He laughs as he adds another plate to the other side of the bar, making it three hundred fifty pounds. "Whatever, dude, let's bust out this last set."

I re-center myself under the bar and try to get back to concentrating on my workout instead of Danika, but I can't help but wonder about her reaction to the card.

*I bet she is fucking pissed, and I bet it's fucking hot.*

A laugh escapes me and Rick looks at me like I'm insane. Thankfully, my cock stays in place instead of inflating to nut-busting proportions like it so often has every time I think about meeting Danika. The flashing anger in her eyes and the way she stood up for her sister have me under some kind of spell.

There's just something about that woman that stokes a fire in me I didn't even know still existed. God knows I don't have a clue what to do about it anymore. The "invitation" seemed like a great idea at the time.

I grip the bar tightly, raise it up off the rack, and then slowly lower it down to my chest. My muscles strain and burn as I push it back up, raising my arms to full extension. After repeating the process five more times, I gasp in relief when I finally rack it and finish.

Rick is in my face immediately, grinning like an idiot. "Way to go, man! You rocked that! I can't believe you did six reps at three-fifty!"

I wish I could be more excited about the accomplishment, but my mind is elsewhere.

"Thanks, man." I wipe my face with my towel. I slowly sit up and look around the gym, searching for Gabe so we can get out of here.

I finally locate him talking up a petite redhead near the treadmills. I catch his eye, and he winks at me with a knowing grin.

*He is such a dog sometimes. Okay, well, all the time.*

She hands him her cell phone, and his fingers fly across the screen, no doubt giving her his number. I swear, I see more women coming and going from Gabe's condo than I would from a gynecologist's office.

I wait until he glances up at me again and roll my eyes, making it clear I don't appreciate waiting for him just so he can line up another booty call. He shrugs at me and says goodbye to little red before making his way over to where Rick and I are waiting.

"You ready to go?" Gabe asks it like he doesn't already know the answer. We have a routine and we rarely, if ever, break it. Gym in the a.m., early, like really fucking early sometimes, then we head to the office, then the gym again in the afternoon on days one of us really needs to let off some excess steam, and then we head back to our condo building so he can clean up before one of his lady friends arrives and I can relax and unwind from what lately have been excruciatingly stressful days.

We're opening several more restaurants and bars under the Hawke umbrella, and it appears it may not have been such a good idea to try to do so many at once. Gabe and I are constantly on the move—examining potential locations, interviewing potential managers, dealing with contractors and the city to arrange permits—and it's enough to cause constant migraines and sleepless nights.

"Yeah, I was ready five minutes ago, but you were too busy shaking your dick at that redhead to notice."

"And you completely missed his badass bench set," Rick adds. Gabe rolls his eyes, clearly unimpressed with my weightlifting skills. "I'll be sure to catch it next time. I was more worried about getting her digits."

I scoff and wipe myself again with my towel. "Shocking."

"Oh, you can't talk, my friend. You've been brooding and distracted since you met a certain feisty blonde last week, and you don't see *me* sending two dozen roses to someone I barely know and who already hates my guts."

"She doesn't hate my guts." I offer the retort a little too quickly.

*Shit. I hope she doesn't hate my guts. What if she does?*

*No, she doesn't.*

That blush creeping up her neck during our confrontation was a dead giveaway—she was just as attracted to me as I was to her. Rage may have been simmering in her veins, but it was mixed with a burning desire she couldn't hide. I have to believe that. Otherwise, I really will feel like the utter and complete asshole she probably thinks I am.

I say goodbye to Rick and turn back to Gabe. "Let's just get the fuck outta here."

By the time we get to the club, I'm confident I made the right decision in sending the flowers. I've never been one to second-guess my decisions when it comes to women. At least...I wasn't before Becca, but it has been a long time since I asked a woman out on a date, and even longer since I went on a first date, let alone someone who wasn't exactly thrilled to meet me in the first place.

I could debate myself in a circle about this. Part of me wants her to decline my invitation, but the bigger part of me needs her to accept. The way she stormed into my office and didn't give me an inch, despite my somewhat condescending attitude toward her ethical conflict with her sister's profession and my business... I've never been with a woman like that, someone who exudes confidence and doesn't back down from someone like me.

It intrigues me; *she* intrigues me. She makes me question

what I've been doing the last thirty years with women who were meek, easy, happy to appease. Something about her "take no shit" attitude made me instantly hard, and *that* truly is a feat. It terrifies me as much as it excites me.

Waiting two more days to see if she shows for dinner is going to do a real fucking number on my psyche, and my dick.

# 4

SAVAGE

$\mathcal{T}$he back corner booth at Angelo's is usually more comfortable. Tonight, sitting and waiting for Danika, my usual table just doesn't have the same feel. I swirl the Chianti in my glass and take a long sip, letting the thick wine slide down my throat and praying it helps calm my nerves.

*Nerves. Jesus Christ, I haven't had nerves about anything since I was in middle school. In the last week, I've somehow reverted to my insecure ten-year-old self.*

My watch does nothing to assuage my fears. When I see it's already 8:15, I shift uncomfortably as the once-delicious wine begins to sour in my stomach.

*She's late. Hell, I don't even know if she will show.*

Maybe I fucked up?

Maybe the flowers *were* overkill? But, what girl doesn't love roses? And two dozen of them, at that? I thought they were the perfect accompaniment to my dinner invitation.

I guess I expected she would call to let me know one way or

the other if she was going to show up tonight, but since I spend most Friday nights here anyway, I figure it can't hurt to hold out some hope.

But, then again, maybe it can. My hand begins to shake, and I set down the wine glass so my anxiety isn't quite so obvious. If she shows up, she can't see me this way. A strong, confident woman like her would do a stiletto-heeled one-eighty if she found me here shaking like a leaf.

What the fuck do I do if she doesn't show up? I haven't been able to stop thinking about this girl. How will I ever get her out of my mind if I haven't at least tried?

Staying busy at work hasn't done the trick, nor has beating myself up at the gym. Gabe keeps telling me I'm working myself too hard, but he's smart enough not to press it with me. I may not be my father, but I can still kick his ass and he knows it.

Across the main room of the restaurant, Michael catches my eye. My regular waiter approaches the table with a half-hearted smile.

"Is there anything else I can get you, Mr. Hawke?"

"No, Michael, not right now."

He refills my wine glass and gives me a small bow before retreating to the kitchen.

*How long do I wait here, alone, before I order dinner or go home? Shit, being stood up right now would be a real kick to the nuts.*

I reach for my glass, put it to my lips, and take another long pull at the red liquid, thankful I have it to keep me company. In my peripheral vision, I see a flash of blonde and turn to find Danika making her way toward my table. Her long hair is twisted up and pulled back, away from her face, and she's decked out in a fantastic knee-length black dress with a plunging neckline that shows just a tasteful hint of cleavage.

My lips twitch up in the first smile I've managed all night, and I try, probably unsuccessfully, to hide my delight at her arrival. Jumping up and down like a middle school kid who just received his first kiss would probably not be a huge turn on for her right now.

"Ms. Eriksson, I am so glad you could join me this evening."

She returns my smile, drops her purse on the bench next to her, and settles in the seat across from me.

"Thank you for the invitation." Her cool reply floats over to me.

My smile fades at her tone, but she's here, so I'll consider that a win.

Michael appears at the table and gives me a knowing grin. "Ma'am, would you like some Chianti?" He presents the bottle to her, and she nods, glancing over the table at me.

The moment our eyes meet, she blushes and shifts in her seat, fidgeting with the linen napkin on the top of the table. Throwing her my best panty-dropping smile, I'm helpless to keep myself from chuckling when her blush deepens and spreads down her neck and into her cleavage.

*And just what is causing that blush, Danika?*

*She's nervous.*

*Good.*

*That means I affect her just as much as she affects me.*

And affect me she does. I'm forced to reach down as inconspicuously as possible to adjust my throbbing cock.

*Less than a fucking minute with this woman and I am already hard as granite. This could be a very long dinner.*

Michael retreats from the table.

She clears her throat, barely glancing up at me before looking back to her hands while I take another sip of wine. "Thank you for the flowers. I have to admit, I was surprised to hear from you, and certainly don't deserve them after the way I acted in your office the other day."

I almost spit out my wine. *An apology?*

She doesn't seem the type to apologize for anything. That I'm getting one tells me it's a nudge in the right direction.

"You mean when you stormed in like hell on wheels and tore me a new asshole?" Her head snaps up, and I grin at her, making sure she understands I'm just messing with her. "Relax. You didn't offend me. In fact, I haven't been able to stop thinking about you for the last week."

*Obsessing might be a more accurate term.*

"Really?" She shifts forward in the booth, her eyes never leaving mine. I'm glad she's apparently gotten over her initial reservation. "Thinking about ways to get back at me for my horrible behavior?" She picks up her glass and tilts it back.

I grin and lean forward across the table, close enough so I'm sure she'll be the only one able to hear me.

"No, thinking about how much I want my face buried between your legs and my tongue in your pussy."

---

## DANIKA

I sputter, and the wine I'm about to swallow sprays across the table, barely missing Savage's smug face. He settles back into his seat, laughing as I cough and try to regain some semblance of control.

"You all right?" His right eyebrow quirks up in a way that makes me want to climb across the table to ride him and smack him simultaneously.

*Shit. This is definitely not what I was expecting when I got his dinner invitation.*

I was sure he was baiting me just to get me here so he could convince me to leave him and the club alone. And maybe to tempt me more with his sinful smile and come-hither bedroom eyes.

"Yes." I clear my throat one last time and take a sip of water as nonchalantly and confidently as I can. "I'm just fine."

*Lie.*

I am most definitely *not* fine. How could I possibly be fine while looking at this man? His arms bulge under his fitted, perfectly-tailored suit jacket, and I suck my bottom lip under my teeth to keep from moaning. A handsome, muscular man in a well-fitted suit is fucking porn for me.

"I'm sorry. I didn't mean to shock you."

*Yeah, right.*

I roll my eyes at him and take another drink of my wine. "Bullshit, that's exactly what you meant to do. I bet you get a real kick out of fucking with women like that."

He chuckles and takes another drink of his wine. "No," he smirks, "only you. And I wasn't fucking with you. I'm dead serious. I haven't been able to stop thinking about you. You got under my skin."

He says the last part with such sincerity, I'm forced to rein in my smartass comeback.

*Is this guy for real?*

I study his face as he holds my gaze. His strong, stubble-covered jaw sets off his cerulean blue eyes, and his lightly tanned skin gives him an almost exotic look. He must have women throwing themselves at his feet, especially in a club like his. He probably fucks a new girl every day of the week.

*PUSSY PEDDLER! Don't forget who he is and what he does!*

Just because Nora defended him doesn't mean I have to forget his profession.

"While I appreciate the compliment, Savage, I have to be honest when I tell you I'm not the least bit surprised to hear your motive for asking me here."

He looks surprised. "What motive is that?"

I scoff and roll my eyes at him. "To fuck me."

He bursts out laughing, throwing his head back while his whole body shakes. When he looks at me again, his eyes twinkle with amusement. I have to bite my lip again to stop the smile that tries to creep out. He's so damn sexy when he laughs like that, and it goes straight to my clit.

"Danika, I did not invite you here to try to fuck you. You asked me why I had been thinking about you, and I answered you, truthfully. I'll always do my best to respond honestly to everything you ask, but that doesn't mean my motives in inviting you here were not pure."

"Pure? I doubt you know the meaning of the word."

He flinches slightly at my retort, and I cringe inwardly.

*Okay, maybe that was a little harsh.*

He searches my face, contemplating something before he replies. "Did you speak with your sister?"

*Okay, hadn't expected him to go there after I just insulted him...again.*

"Yeah, actually, she showed up at my apartment the day after I came to see you."

"You two talked?"

I nod, and he watches me, waiting for me to elaborate.

"Look, she told me she spoke with you, so thank you for getting her to come talk to me."

Being beholden to him for anything irks me, but after chasing Nora for weeks, he was the one who finally got her to actually stop avoiding me. I have to give him credit for that, at least.

"You're welcome. I can only imagine how worried you were for her. If I didn't hear from my sisters for a couple weeks, I would be worried, too."

"You have sisters?" I hadn't intended that to come out so coarse, but for some reason, the thought of a strip club owner having sisters seems unthinkable.

He grins and sips his wine. "Yeah, I have three younger sisters and one younger brother."

"And they know what you do for a living?"

*Damn, there I go sounding like a judgmental bitch again.*

He doesn't take the bait, barely reacting to my snide comment. "Yes, they know, and so does my mother."

I scowl at him. "And they are okay with it?"

Before he can answer, the waiter returns and asks if we're ready to order. I scramble to open my menu and review it. Glancing up at Savage, I see he doesn't even bother to open his. He must come here a lot.

"Everything looks so good." I focus on the waiter. "What do you recommend?"

"If you don't mind, I would love to order for you," Savage interjects. "I eat here all the time and I think I know what you might enjoy."

I eye him skeptically for a moment before closing my menu and handing it to the waiter. Letting him make the decision for me feels like giving in to him somehow, and I've already done that just by coming here tonight. Still, I have a feeling he may be right about knowing exactly what I want.

"Good, Michael, we will both have the *fra diavolo*."

"Very good, Mr. Hawke." He retrieves Savage's menu and backs away from the table.

I haven't looked away from Savage once as I wait for an answer to my last question.

"My family understands that my business is just that, a business. I opened my first bar, Hawkeye's Pub, after college, and now, eight years later, I have several bars, restaurants, and the club. The club seemed like a logical step a few years back, and I took it. I run it tight, and I keep it legit. I don't involve myself with my girls, and they know they will be gone immediately if I find out anything is going on behind the scenes."

*Doesn't involve himself with the girls? Does that mean he doesn't sleep with them? Was Nora right?*

The question is on the tip of my tongue but, with some effort, I manage to bite it back. I really need to rein in the bitchiness tonight.

"Well, it certainly sounds like you run the club differently than most, but I still can't imagine having a son, or a brother, running a strip club. You have to admit, it's a little seedy."

He smirks and leans back. "I guess you're right. I just hope you can put aside what I do for a living and will make up your mind about what kind of man I am based on facts, not prejudices."

*Shit. That was a real chastisement. I must be acting like more of a bitch than I thought.*

I drop my gaze to my wine glass momentarily before I look back at him, unwavering. "I will be the first to admit that I may have misjudged you. After talking with Nora, I know you treat your employees well and everything you told me is true."

A pleased grin spreads across his face. "And what did you find out when you researched me?"

I try to hide my surprise but sputter momentarily trying to answer him, "Uh, I...what makes you think I researched you?"

"Because I did the same thing, and you're a reporter. Frankly, I would be disappointed if you hadn't done some research on the scumbag your sister was shaking her ass and tits for."

# 5

## DANIKA

*L*aughter bubbles up, and I cover my mouth with my hand. I watch Savage glance down at my chest and shift in his seat.

*He's uncomfortable. Good. It's only fair he be in the same position I am.*

"I'm sorry I said that." I have no doubt my face reddens with my embarrassment. "I did research you, but I couldn't find very much information. You seem to keep a pretty low profile for someone in your business."

He grins at my observation but offers no explanation for his mysterious ability to stay out of the papers.

I've never seen anything like it. There are articles about his father that mention Savage and his siblings when he was a child —crap, now I remember the sisters being referenced—including quite a few from the weeks following his father's death in the ring. But, as an adult, other than mentions of the opening of his restaurants and the club and a few other business dealings, there was *nada*. It's as if he disappeared from public view and intentionally stayed that way.

The need to dig and probe further has been eating away at me since I hit the dead end, but I don't think it would be appropriate to do that here at dinner. Especially not when I've already insulted him many, many times in the few minutes we've spent together.

*Wait, did he say he did research on me?*

"You researched me?"

He chuckles and picks up his wine glass, swirling the maroon liquid around and around. I can't tear my eyes away from his strong hand and long fingers wrapped around the stem.

*Fuck. Even his hands are orgasmically beautiful.*

Flashes of him doing things—dirty, nasty, sinful things—with those hands race through my mind, and my clit throbs just imagining his touch. I cross my legs under the table, pressing my thighs together as tightly as I can in a vain attempt to ease my need. There's no doubt in my mind I'm blushing, and Savage's focus on my cleavage assures me I'm correct.

*Arrogant prick knows he's causing this and is getting off on it.*

"Yes, I researched you. I like to know all I can about people who come storming into my office with murder in their eyes."

"Murder? Oh, come on, I wasn't that bad!"

*He's such a drama queen!*

His eyebrow quirks up, and the corner of his mouth moves into a sexy half-smirk. "Weren't you?"

*Was I?*

Thinking back, maybe I was a bit overzealous in my advocacy on behalf of Nora, but I never would have hurt him. At least, not without his permission. Just thinking about digging my teeth into the side of his neck and shoulder while he pounds into me has me shifting uncomfortably again and chugging half my glass of water.

I take a cleansing breath before I even bother trying to speak again. "Savage, I'm sorry..."

His smile fades, and he leans forward, looking me directly in the eye and holding me captive with his blue gaze. "Danika, stop apologizing. I told you, if I was offended by anything you did or said, I wouldn't be sitting here with you right now."

A flood of relief washes over me.

I nod my understanding but, truthfully, the fact that *nothing* I have said has offended him is a bit of a mind-fuck. It makes me wonder what it would take to actually insult him and how he got such a thick skin.

The fact that he did research on *me* is a little disconcerting, too. It's not that I have anything to hide, but a man like Savage Hawke knowing things about me, things I didn't divulge, makes me a little shaky. "So, what did you find out in your digging?"

"Well," he sets down his glass and leans back into his seat, "your father was a cop and died in the line of duty when you were twelve. Now, it's just you, Nora, and your mother, who lives in Harahan."

*I bet he even knows our social security numbers.*

"Stalker, much?" I smirk.

He grins back, and I wish I had brought an extra thong with me tonight. Sitting in wet panties with a throbbing clit is worse than medieval torture. I would much rather be stretched out on a rack right now than sitting across from Savage practically dripping with need. Sometimes, my libido can be such an inconvenient bitch.

"You graduated with your bachelor's in journalism from Loyola and almost immediately went to work at the *Times*."

"All that information is very easy to find. I would have expected a deeper probe from you."

Savage's eyes widen slightly, and he drops his head back, roaring with laughter. My skin heats, and I bite my tongue to prevent further sexual innuendos from slipping out unbidden.

When he finally recovers, he leans his elbows on the table and locks his gaze with mine. "Oh, Danika, believe me, I always ensure a very deep probing."

*Fuck.*

I completely lose it, dropping my face into my hands in a fruitless attempt to hide my beet-red face and bone-deep embarrassment. Savage is something else, that's for sure. His response only endears him to me while making me even more aware of my constant verbal diarrhea, which only seems to happen around him.

Thankfully, before he can say anything else, our food arrives. I'm able to down the rest of my glass of water while our plates are set on the table.

"Is there anything else I can do for you right now, Mr. Hawke?" The waiter refills our wine and water glasses.

"No, Michael, thank you."

Michael disappears, and I'm left staring at a plate of *fra diavolo* with linguine and shrimp piled high. I grab my fork and twist it in the pasta, trying to get a manageable bite so I don't end up shoveling dangling pasta and spraying red sauce all over myself.

Just as I am about to slide my first bite into my mouth, Savage clears his throat. I look up at him and melt under his wicked grin.

"I hope you like things spicy."

*You have no fucking idea, Savage. No idea.*

---

## SAVAGE

Our dessert arrives, and we both dig in, my hard cock throbbing when she moans at her first bite of tiramisu. She wraps her lips around her fork and pulls it out slowly, her eyes closed and head tilted slightly back. "Oh, my God, this is absolutely amazing."

*She's doing it intentionally. She has to be. No woman can be this overtly sexual without trying.*

I clear my throat and take a sip of water to wet my suddenly parched throat. "I'm glad you like it."

Dinner has been both exhilarating and excruciating. Every word out of her mouth has me more convinced she's absofuckinglutely perfect for me. She's brilliant, sarcastic, funny—even when she isn't trying to be—and sexy as hell. Watching her lips while she eats and talks is like watching porn two feet in front of me.

The constant hard-on I've had for the last two hours will definitely need some attention later, but it's worth it. Asking Danika to dinner is the best decision I've ever made—even if my cock might not currently agree. It's like I stepped back in time to freshman year of high school when every look, smile, or giggle from a girl had me sporting wood. Under any other circumstances, I might be embarrassed by my body's reaction to her, but I'm not. I just wish there were a way to control my raging hard-on so I could make it through dessert a bit easier.

Three bottles of wine aren't helping me keep my desires in check. I've barely been able to restrain myself from pulling her onto my lap and letting her ride me right here in Angelo's. I've never been into public sex, but with her, I can't even imagine the restraint it would require to sit next to her in a car all the way home before getting her naked and plunging into her.

Danika drains the last of the wine from her glass and sets it on the table before looking around the restaurant. I follow her gaze. The rest of the place has emptied out; we're the only table left.

Her eyes meet mine, and that adorable blush races up her neck from her chest. "Damn, I didn't realize it was so late."

"I don't mind." I smile at her and reach out to take her hand in mine across the table. I gently run my thumb across her knuckles, and she shudders, sending quivers down my arm and straight to my already-strained cock.

She bites her bottom lip and glances away. "I hope you don't have to get up early. I would feel awful keeping you up."

*Christ, if she only knew.*

"Actually," I pull her hand to my mouth and press my lips to her knuckles, "I do. I have to catch a plane to San Diego in the morning for my brother's law school graduation ceremony. It isn't until next Friday, but my whole family will be flying out for it, and we have a lot planned this week."

"Oh." She casts her eyes down, then away again.

*Yes!*

As horrible as it sounds, I'm pleased to see the disappointment in her eyes at learning I'll be gone for the next week. That's a really fucking good sign, the best I can really ask for right now.

I wait for her eyes to return to mine. "But, I would love to see you when I get back. I get in late Friday night, so maybe dinner on Saturday?" I brush my lips over her hand, and she shudders again.

She smiles at me and squeezes my hand gently. "Yeah, that sounds great."

"Good." I release her hand and motion for Michael to come over to the table. "Michael, can you please tell Gabe I need him to drive Ms. Eriksson home?"

Gabe usually joins me for dinner on Friday nights, but tonight, he spent his time at the bar talking with Stephanie, one of his go-to girls. I'm sure I'll be seeing her leave his condo tomorrow morning while I'm on my way to the airport.

*Lucky bastard.*

Danika glances around in confusion. "Oh, no, I can take a cab. I took one here."

"Please, it's no trouble at all. I insist. Gabe is already here anyway. This way, I know you got home safely and won't be worrying about you all night."

The thought of her taking a cab, alone, dressed like that makes my skin crawl. I know exactly what every man who sees her will be thinking; the exact same thing I am. And while I may have some self-control when it comes to Danika, I don't trust any other man to get within ten feet of her, except Gabe. He may be a player, but he's also loyal as fuck and would never do anything to interfere with a woman I'm interested in.

Letting out a reluctant sigh, she nods her agreement and stands when Michael returns from speaking with Gabe.

She turns back toward the table and offers me a smile, and my heart flip-flops in my chest.

*Be careful, Savage. This one will hurt you.*

"Goodnight, Savage. Thank you for dinner." She leans down and kisses me gently on the cheek, her warm breath lingering against my skin before she pulls away. Goosebumps spread down my arms and my already painfully hard dick twitches against my pants.

I want to grab her and yank her down into my lap so I can devour her mouth, but I restrain myself, instead smiling at her, telling her how much I enjoyed our evening with as much composure as I can muster.

I track her progress across the restaurant to the bar, where Michael introduces her to Gabe. He tosses me a wave over his shoulder, and she glances back at me before disappearing out the front door. The moment she vanishes from my sight, my heart sinks and I bite out a curse.

This woman could break me—easily—and I am more than willing to let her.

I lean back in my seat and run my hands through my hair with a groan.

Angelo drops into the seat Danika just vacated and raises his eyebrows. We've known each other for years and our post-dinner, closing-time chats have usually been very lighthearted and relaxing. Tonight, the look on his face says this one will be anything but. Probably because she's the first woman I've brought here in over four years.

"What?" I ask before draining my wine glass.

"How did it go?"

Twirling the empty glass in my hand, I give him the play-by-play of the evening, including Danika's slips of the tongue and adorable blushing incidents. "So, great, I guess."

"You guess?" His brow furrows skeptically. "It sure sounds like it couldn't have gone better, so what am I missing?"

I let out a deep sigh and place the glass on the table before dropping my face into my hands—anything to avoid looking him in the eye when I tell him. "She doesn't know."

I knew she wouldn't find anything when she researched me. I pay my lawyers a lot of money to keep my personal business out of the papers.

He releases a long breath and whistles before he gives a humorless chuckle. "Then, my friend, you have a major problem."

*Understatement of the fucking year.*

# 6

## DANIKA

$\mathcal{I}$ lie in bed staring at the clock on my nightstand, mentally counting back two hours to figure out what time it is in California. 2:00 a.m. here means midnight there.

*Fuck. Do I call him?*

Not if I don't want to look desperate.

It's only been two days since I saw him last.

*Calm your tits and give it a little time.*

I roll onto my back, sprawling across the bed, and stare at the ceiling fan, watching the paddles spin round and round until I get dizzy and have to clench my eyes shut. Sleep has been elusive since my dinner with Savage. If I get any at all, it's fitful and short, and I end up having to bust out BOB to fulfill my middle of the night needs the Savage sex dreams create.

After his buddy, Gabe, dropped me off at my apartment on Friday night, I tried to go to bed immediately. I figured after three bottles of wine, I was wasted enough to crash right away. But, instead, I spent most of the night replaying every word we said to each other and thinking about every heated look he threw at me. Mostly, though, I thought about how his eyes and his mouth looked when he told me he wanted to bury his face between my legs and stick his tongue in my pussy.

*Who the fuck talks like that? Savage Hawke, apparently.*

My pussy clenches and my clit throbs just remembering that look when he said it. I have no doubt that man would know *exactly* what to do if I ever let him between my legs. I press my thighs together, but it's no use. Two nights of masturbating thinking about Savage have not been enough to ease the deep ache he put there.

Work hasn't helped either. I thought maybe concentrating on my story on top of my daily assignments—really exhausting myself and staying late—would help keep my mind off that man, but it was futile. Flashes of his smile, his strong hands, the brush of his lips against my skin, the smell of his cologne when I kissed him goodnight, they just kept coming until I finally gave up and gave in to the fantasy.

I glance at the clock again—2:09 a.m.

*Nine minutes? Fuck. It felt like nine hours.*

Mentally slapping myself, I reach out and grab a pillow, pressing it over my face to muffle my frustrated scream.

*Don't give in. Don't give him the power.*

Who the fuck am I kidding? I love men who display their power. Strong, powerful men are a fucking drug to me, and I am a hopeless addict...as long as they don't want more than a hard, fulfilling fuck. The whole relationship thing is just not in the cards. Not after seeing what losing Dad did to Mom. I can't ever rely on someone like that for my own happiness.

Once I get Savage out of my system, I'll move on, like I always do. He doesn't seem to be the type who will be willing to just be friends with benefits so it may be a one-time thing, but something tells me it will totally be worth it.

Admitting that helps any reluctance fly out the window, and I grab my cell phone off the nightstand along with the card that came with the roses he sent—the one with his cell phone number scrawled neatly along the bottom.

*You are probably going to regret this.*

The beeps as I press the numbers into my phone are exceedingly loud in my silent bedroom. I enter it as a new contact, but instead of hitting "Call," I open a message box and type the first thing that comes to mind.

< Hey! What are you doing? >

*Jesus, that was lame.*

I wait, not so patiently, and within seconds, those three little dots appear, and my stomach does somersaults. The three dots are slow torture. Whoever invented them knew exactly what they were doing to people.

*Oh, crap! I never gave him my number! What if he doesn't even know it's me?*

> I was wondering when you were going to use that number I left you. I'm just getting into bed. <

The image of Savage, naked, sprawled across a huge bed, assaults my brain, and I clamp my thighs together again with a frustrated whimper.

*Goddamn this man and what he does to me.*

Finding release has never been a problem for me, nor has finding a partner to do it, but ever since I met him, *nothing* seems to satisfy my soul-aching need for him. My dalliance with Max was wholly unfulfilling and after going through a Costco-sized box of batteries in the last two weeks, I'm surprised my poor, abused BOB is still functioning.

But I need to keep cool. I can't let him know what he has done to me, how much I've been obsessing over him the last two days, and every single day since we met.

< How is your trip? >

> It would be a lot better if you were here. <

I grin as I consider my response. Flirting via text message isn't usually my thing. Usually, I'm direct and just ask where we can meet to get down to business, but with him two thousand miles away, what other choice do I have?

< What would be happening if I was there? >

Almost immediately, my phone rings in my hand, startling me and making my heart jump in my chest.

*Fuck, it's him!*

I can't not answer it, but now I feel a little stupid for texting him in the middle of the night. *Shit.* I take a deep breath and hit "Accept." Trying to sound nonchalant is impossible at this point, but I give it a shot anyway, "Hey."

"Hey, yourself." His deep voice sends chills down my spine and does nothing to disperse the annoying throb between my thighs.

"What's up?"

*What's up? Really, Danika? Are you ten? He's in bed at midnight, what the fuck do you think is up, besides maybe his dick?*

He chuckles softly. "My dick."

Moisture pools between my legs. God, I bet his cock is hard and thick just like the rest of him.

*Is he touching himself?*

*Jesus Christ...*

Watching a man stroke his own cock is just about the sexiest thing I've ever experienced and imagining Savage doing it has my body begging for it, despite knowing he's hours away.

I slide my hand down between my legs and find my wet core. I've been practically dripping since meeting Savage, and with the visions in my head right now, it's more like a tidal wave.

The slow glide of my finger over my clit has me biting back a groan. He doesn't need the ego boost of knowing what I'm doing right now. For all I know, he's just joking about having an erection.

*If it is a joke, he is one sick bastard.*

## SAVAGE

I grip my cock in my right hand while I hold the phone to my ear with my left. It was rock hard the second she texted me. There is only one reason someone texts you after midnight—because they are horny and thinking about you.

*Score one for Team Savage.*

Her sharp intake of breath lets me know she heard me and that she's still there. I patiently wait for her response. Is she going to bite? Or will she pretend to ignore the invitation I've just offered her?

I'm a phone sex virgin and have no fucking clue what I'm doing here. Not being in control, not being able to anticipate her response, throws me off-kilter. Waiting for her reply is killing me.

She clears her throat, and I smile, imagining her flushed face and breasts. I've already come to love seeing the spread of that red, and knowing I'm the one who put it there. I only hope my words had that effect on her. Given the way she reacted to me at dinner, I would place my money on yes.

"Really?" Her voice comes quiet and breathy.

*She took the bait!*

"Uh-huh." I stroke my cock slowly, desperately wanting her to join me in what has become my nightly activity since I met her. "What's up with you? Why are you still awake at 2:00 a.m.?"

*Shit, that wasn't sexy at all. Way to shoot yourself in the foot.*

Her chuckle echoes through the phone, and I picture her beautiful smile, directed at me.

"I couldn't sleep."

"Oh, and you thought talking to me might bore you enough to render you unconscious?" I lace my comment with sarcasm, hoping she'll understand I'm only joking.

Silence meets me. Maybe I've stepped too far. *Shit, Danika, don't disappear on me.*

"Oh, shut the fuck up, you arrogant prick. You know what I meant, and you know damn well you are the reason I can't sleep."

*Yes!*

My heart lurches into my throat at her confession, and the throb in my cock resurges. "Actually, no, I didn't know that. I can hope, but..."

She huffs, and I can practically see her rolling those gorgeous blue eyes at me.

"Oh, come on, look at you..." She trails off, and I close my eyes, wincing slightly, because she has no idea what her words actually mean. She can't know, because I haven't told her.

*Switch topics.*

"I'd rather look at you, or at least think about looking at you."

"Yeah? Why's that?" Her voice is breathy, and I can't help but hope her heart is racing in anticipation the way mine is. It's almost beating out of my chest.

"Because just picturing the way you looked when you stormed into my office that day gets me hard as a fucking rock."

She doesn't respond, but I can hear her heavy breathing over the line, which tells me she at least hasn't hung up on me yet.

*Take the leap, Savage, just tell her exactly what she does to you.*

"You have no idea what you do to me." I make the confession while I resume the slow glide of my hand up and down my length. "I've jerked off too many times to count thinking about you over the last two weeks, and it's only gotten worse since our dinner."

Another agonizing pause has me questioning the sanity of being so honest. I barely know this woman. I should keep my damn mouth shut. It's one thing to casually joke about it and flirt over dinner, but this is very real. Maybe I took it a step too far.

"I'm glad to hear I'm not the only one." Her words are quiet but clear, and blood rushes in my ears at her admission. "I haven't been able to stop thinking about you, either."

*Ding! Ding! Ding! Round one to Savage.* Getting her to admit she feels something other than disgust for me is a major win as far as I'm concerned. Her body may have given her away at dinner, but to hear the words out of her mouth confirms everything I've hoped for.

Now, I just need to ease into this. "What do you think about?"

No way I'm jumping off this cliff unless she takes the lead. I'm not going to scare her away now, but goddamn, I hope she's ready to leap because I sure as fuck am.

She lets out a breathy sigh, and a rustle of covers comes through the line.

*Dear God, please let her be touching herself under those sheets.*

"You...touching me."

*FUCK YES!*

I struggle to swallow against the sudden dryness of my throat. "Touching you where?"

"Everywhere."

Images of her swollen breasts, impossibly long legs, and pale white skin against the darkened skin of my hands has me ready to come quicker than any porn I've ever watched.

"Tell me what you're doing." I make the command while my hand sets a steady, slow rhythm up and down my cock. The brush of my own skin against my needy flesh does in no way compare to how she would feel wrapped around me, but if I think about that too much, I'll blow my load right now.

"Touching myself."

The visual of her, sprawled out naked on her bed, her hand between her legs, her pussy glistening with her arousal, has me groaning into the phone.

"I wish I was there. I would bury my face in your cunt and lick you slowly before sliding my tongue into you and sucking on your clit until you scream my name, come all over my face, and beg me to stop."

A moan floats out from the phone at my words, and her breathing becomes more of a desperate panting.

*She's close already. Good, because I won't fucking last much longer.*

My hand continues to pump my cock in a rhythm designed to keep me dangerously close to the edge. I don't expect her to respond. Her throaty moans, gasps, and pants are enough to make me want to blow my load.

"I wish I was sucking your cock right now." Her words stun me momentarily, and my hand stills on my cock before returning to a more intense motion.

*FUCK!*

"Me, too. Sliding my cock into your hot, wet mouth right now would be fucking paradise."

She moans, and her breathing picks up. It's time to take her over the edge.

"When I pull my cock from your sweet mouth, I won't waste any time sliding it through your wet pussy and slamming into your tight, wet cunt."

A strangled cry alerts me to her release, and I picture her body bowing up off of the bed while her finger swirls around her clit. "Fuck..."

Her breathy curse pushes me over the edge, and I roar as I come, shooting my cum all across my stomach and chest.

"Did you come?" she asks a moment later, after I've finally descended from the heavenly high.

"Uh, yeah, Danika, I have the evidence all over my stomach right now."

She responds without hesitation, "Show me."

I grin and hang up so I can access the camera on my phone. If she wants it, I'll show it to her.

After hitting "Send," I wait a few seconds to give her time to examine the photo. I know what she's seeing—my chest and abs coated in cum and my still-hard cock jutting out from the edge of white sheets, resting against my stomach.

*This will either scare her off or make her come running.*

I call her and wait for her to pick up.

"Fuck, I am in so much trouble."

There's no stopping my grin at her response. I'm glad she can't see me right now because if she really knew how much that meant to me, she would probably run screaming for the hills. Although, that's probably just a matter of time anyway.

## 7

## SAVAGE

*T*he rest of the week in San Diego attending family gatherings and activities planned by Mom being her usual over-zealous self dragged slowly. Just about the only thing that was even remotely bearable was the entire day we spent at the world-famous zoo.

Seeing the look of enjoyment and wonder on three-year-old Angelina's face made me really appreciate what I have in my family, even though they were relentless in questioning me about who I was texting with all day and why I had "that shit-eating grin on my face all the time."

I guess I'm not very good at hiding my feelings. I always thought that was a good thing. I've always prided myself on being an open book. Like I told Danika at dinner, I always endeavor to be honest with people about everything.

That's precisely why my heart is currently in the pit of my stomach and I can't seem to stop my hands from shaking as I prepare dinner and clean up my condo before she arrives.

*You're an idiot for not telling her. You know she couldn't have known without you telling her and still, you said NOTHING.*

I stop stirring the sauce on the stove and drop my face into my hands for the thousandth time since I met her. Not telling her the moment we met, or at the very least at dinner, was probably the most gigantic mistake I could ever make.

Waiting to tell her is like waiting for a nuclear bomb to go off. When she finds out, there's a strong chance she will storm out of here just like she did my office that fateful day.

"Fuck!" I run my hands back through my hair and curse myself again and again for being such a selfish, fucking idiot.

When Mom and the girls were harassing me endlessly about the reason for my mental state this week, I somehow managed to avoid revealing anything about Danika to them. It's not that I have anything to hide, there's just no reason to get their hopes up that I might have some sort of a relationship with her.

That would truly be a miracle once she knows, and I'm not sure I believe in those.

Eventually, after my repeated refusal to discuss what was going on, the family was, thankfully, more than happy to turn their attentions to Stone, which is how it should have been in the first place, considering he was the one graduating.

As the baby of the family, Stone has always managed to get away with just about everything and coast through life by the skin of his teeth. Despite being my only brother, he and I have always been the least close of any of the siblings. I would blame it on the age gap, but frankly, Stone and I are just two completely different people.

He's a genius—an honest to God, MENSA member, genius— yet he always manages to make the stupidest fucking decisions. The fact he was able to graduate law school, let alone college, is something I would never have believed possible. His complete inability to control his own behavior or make adult choices has me worrying about him even now, but he has a great job lined up at a prestigious firm, so I guess I can hope he finally came to his senses and is using his God-given gifts in a productive manner. I guess only time will tell.

Spending time with him always makes it so much more evident what missing out on having Dad around really did to him. Stone was only five when Dad died and, despite my best efforts to step into the role of father-figure, I could just never do enough. He chose to look to other, less savory, individuals for role-models, which certainly did nothing to help him develop a good pattern of behavior.

Stone is exhausting, even more so than Skye. Fuck, the entire family is exhausting. After the long week with them and then a late night flight, I'm worn out, physically and emotionally. Maybe seeing Danika tonight was a bad idea; maybe I should reschedule.

*You're just trying to put it off.*

*Shit.*

It's been a whole week since my dinner with her, but, even after as much time as we've spent texting and talking on the phone each night, it feels like an eternity has passed since I last saw her.

Not that I haven't *seen* her...

The graphic pictures and videos we've exchanged almost every night have only heightened my desire for her. It's the thought of potentially seeing the real thing tonight, however remote that possibility, that's preventing me from calling her to cancel.

Unsurprisingly, my cock is winning out in this internal struggle even as my head is screaming that things are about to go up in flames.

I look at Princess lying in her bed near the couch. The tiny Yorkie tilts her head and examines me before slumping back down. Apparently, my absence wasn't felt too strongly. She got to spend the week with Gabe, who is probably her favorite person in the world, so I'm sure she didn't give a rat's ass where I was.

She did her usual jumping and bouncing last night when I got home, but this morning, she was back to her usual semi-interested mode, preferring to sleep and be completely aloof. I was never much of a dog person. Mom and Dad always refused to let us have one growing up because they said none of us were responsible enough to take care of it and they would end up doing it. Probably a valid point, but now that I have one, I can't imagine living in this place without her.

Being alone as much as I am is probably not very healthy, and it only adds to the anxiety I feel about having Danika here, in my space.

I thought getting back to my normal routine today might help, but my trip to the gym and my usual Saturday morning basketball game did nothing to ease the tension or apprehension about Danika's arrival tonight. All it did was physically exhaust me. After a quick trip to the grocery store, I came home and started all the prep for tonight's dinner.

*If it even gets that far.*

Cooking usually relaxes me, probably because I spent so much time doing it with Mom growing up, but not today. Today, I found myself forgetting what ingredients I already put into things and had to taste them a hundred times to make sure they were right.

Even now, with everything ready in the kitchen, my body is quivering with tension.

*Calm down!*

Taking a deep breath, I look around my place, making sure nothing is out of order. Everything looks perfect, but because of my need to be exceedingly organized, it rarely does to me. The book on the far left of the shelf next to the fireplace is sticking out a half inch farther than the rest of them in that row and I quickly shove it back in line. If I truly took the time to look, I'm sure I'd find a thousand little things like that to correct, but I need to change and prepare for Danika's arrival.

I need to make the best impression possible the moment she sees me, just in case she leaves in ten seconds flat like I'm anticipating.

Princess follows me down the hall to my bedroom, and I close the door behind me. I told Danika to let herself in when she gets here, and I don't need her accidentally wandering down the hall and into my inner sanctum without me ready for it.

I'm just sliding on my shirt when the doorbell echoes through the condo. Princess scampers away from her bed and is stuck at the bedroom door, jumping and barking wildly.

"Shh, knock it off, Princess."

She rang the bell despite my instructions.

*Maybe she's just as nervous as I am?*

Doubtful. A woman like that doesn't get nervous. I may keep her on her toes and embarrass her a bit, but nervous? Not Danika.

Now me, on the other hand, I'm practically shaking trying to button my shirt. The front door slams shut. Thank God for the extra minute to try to get my shit together before I have to see her and watch everything I've accomplished with her in the last week vanish in a millisecond.

I check myself one final time in the closet mirror before heading to the bedroom door.

*No matter what happens, just stay calm. You can't control her reaction and trying to will only make things worse.*

I scoop Princess up and turn her tiny face to meet mine. "You be nice to Danika." She licks my face, and I drop a kiss on her nose before returning her to the floor.

*At least I'll always have her.*

The second I open the door, Princess takes off, sprinting down the hall at full speed to see our visitor, her nails clicking on the hardwood floors.

I follow her slowly, hoping to delay the inevitable despite my desire to see Danika. That scene from *The Green Mile* where John Coffey is walking down the hallway on his way to the electric chair flashes through my head.

This will probably be a death sentence for our budding relationship, but I just need to nut up and do it.

I hear her moving around in the living room, her heels making that damn clicking sound just like they did that day in my office. My throat is dry, and I struggle to take a deep breath.

It's out of my hands now.

*Jesus, this is going to be harder than I thought.*

------

## DANIKA

I stand in the middle of his living room, in total awe of the sleek, modern design of the condo, or should I say, penthouse—thirty stories up in one of the most sought-after buildings in the city.

*I wonder how he managed to snag this place. I guess the pussy business is very lucrative.*

It's absolutely stunning, and it's clear that either he, or his decorator, has exquisite taste. A long, low, sleek, black leather couch sits directly in front of me, with two matching chairs all facing a low, stained black wood coffee table. A large fireplace dominates the wall, with enormous slate tiles reaching all the way up to the cathedral ceilings. The built-in bookshelves on either side are filled with books, not the usual chachkies.

He's a minimalist, and it is breathtakingly beautiful. I hate to admit I'm jealous but compared to my tiny, second-floor studio apartment, this place is a Taj Mahal. He probably has an enormous king-sized bed with silk sheets while I'm on my queen with Egyptian cotton every night. The floors alone in this place probably cost twenty thousand dollars.

No one gets into journalism for the money, but seeing this place really makes me question my choice in profession. Not seriously, I love what I do too much to do anything else, but there's that tiny voice in the back of my head telling me I could have done a thousand other things that made better money. Right now, my entire paycheck goes to my designer shoe fetish and to the essentials, like a roof over my head and food.

When I picture my closet, the *Sex in the City* episode where Carrie adds up the cost of her closet only to determine she had forty thousand dollars' worth hits a little too close to home.

I look down at my feet. My Sergio Rossi pumps look freaking fantastic but guilt creeps up my bare legs thinking about the half-paycheck that went to buy them. If Savage has a shoe fetish, it will all be worth it. Wrapping my legs around his waist and digging these heels into his back while he fucks me would certainly justify the thousand dollar price tag.

*Cool it. You can't jump on his cock the second he appears. That would look desperate. Maintain some dignity.*

Glancing around the room, I'm drawn to the large windows making up the entire left wall. I wander over to them and find a large patio with chaise lounges and a magnificent view of the Mississippi. The smell in the penthouse is mouthwatering— garlicky and sweet. I hope the wine I brought goes with whatever he made. The bottle in my hand has me picturing sitting out there with Savage and enjoying the warm evening air after dinner and a few glasses, and then partaking in other activities in full public view.

Naked skin against the night air is such a fucking turn on. The way it cools the sweat-slicked body...

I shudder and press my free hand against the glass to stabilize myself on my suddenly wobbly legs.

*Damn. This isn't helping.*

Not that anything would. This past week has been seven days of foreplay and one giant clit tease. Who would have thought phone sex could be so fucking hot? I've always needed the real thing—skin-scratching, sweaty, hot, raunchy sex. But watching Savage touch himself on video? Holy shit...there are just no words.

Big, strong hands wrapped around hard flesh. It's hotter than anything I could have imagined or found in any porn. I haven't come that many times solo since...well...never.

And I need to do something about this because I can't go on at work with my mind somewhere else—mainly on Savage's dick. Somehow, I've managed to get my articles done, but I've gotten nowhere on my investigation into Mayor Dunne and his sketchy dealings. Paul has cold feet and no matter what I say, I haven't been able to convince him to get me what I need on Abello.

Anyone else would have given up on this story a year ago, but not me. Sometimes my stubbornness hurts more than it helps. I just hope this won't be one of those times. My skin crawls just thinking about Abello. That man is depraved. There's just no other word for it. The sheer number of bodies desiccating out in the bayous—bodies that can be attributed to him—is staggering. The only reason he isn't in prison for the rest of his life is the loyalty of his subjects—a loyalty that is making this investigation damn near impossible.

But someone has to crack eventually. I just hope I've found that person. If not, I'm back to square one, and the notebooks full of rumors, innuendos, and theories I have at my apartment become nothing more than kindling for the fire I can't have in my non-existent fireplace. Maybe Savage will let me borrow his?

A nice roaring fire in that thing would set quite the mood. I could watch my career go up in smoke as he fucks me on the floor, and the couch, and the coffee table, and the chairs. That familiar throb starts between my legs, and my only consolation is that I'll see Savage any minute and, hopefully, this night will end with our clothes off and our needs fulfilled.

I look down at my dress. I may have overdone it for a dinner at Savage's place. The red sundress looked casual and flirty when I examined myself in the mirror before I left, but now, now it feels like I'm overdressed and begging for something. The plunging neckline and high hem are practically an open invitation to him.

*Who am I kidding? He has an open invitation to anything and everything he wants.*

A door down the hall opens, and a strange, fast clicking noise races toward me. I turn and the most adorable dog I've ever seen appears from around the corner.

*I don't remember Savage ever mentioning he had a dog.*

My love for animals is only rivaled by my love of shoes, so I'm more than happy to welcome the little one. A pink bow on the top of her head alerts me it's a girl, and I crouch down to greet her.

"Oh, hi!" She jumps up, her front paws barely reaching my knees, and wiggles so hard I think she might fall over. I laugh and run my free hand over her soft, fluffy head, reaching down to find the dog tag on her collar. "Princess, eh? What kind of man has a Yorkie named Princess?"

"One who's a total fucking sap."

I jerk, surprised to hear his voice. I hadn't noticed him enter the room. I glance up with a smile and lose all control of my body and senses when I finally catch sight of him. A barely-audible gasp escapes my mouth, and the bottle of wine falls from my hand, crashes to the floor, and shatters, sending glass and dark, red wine spraying across the wood.

Princess yelps and bolts away, disappearing down the hall.

*Shit.*

*Oh.*

*My.*

*God.*

*What did I just do?*

Looking down at the mess on the floor, I avoid his eyes and, instead, watch the dark red liquid spreading across the floor.

*Say something!*

"I'm so sorry." I whisper the apology, still keeping my eyes firmly planted on the mess I've made.

"It's okay." His voice is calm and understanding, but I just can't bring myself to look at him, not after how I just reacted.

*Why didn't he tell me?*

I hear him leave the room and look up as he disappears into what I assume is the kitchen. My knees give out, and I grab the back of the couch and lean against it while I stare down at the wine on the floor.

He re-enters the room and stops in front of me without a word. I glance up and reach out, taking a handful of towels from him before dropping to the floor to sop up the wine.

"Be careful, don't cut yourself."

Tears well in my eyes at his concern.

*Christ, I am such an idiot.*

Savage uses a small vacuum to suck up the broken glass as I push it to the side. When the floor is finally dry, I hand him the wet towels without making eye contact.

A loathsome combination of embarrassment and disgust at myself has my stomach churning. The desire to leave while he's out of the room is one I have to fight—hard. I can't leave now. That would really make me a thoughtless bitch. I may be a lot of things, but I'm not that.

Instead, I make my way around the couch and drop down into the corner with my back to the kitchen. I rest my elbows on my knees and drop my head into my hands, closing my eyes and cursing myself for the millionth time.

I sense his approach, and his feet appear in front of me. His black shoes are gleaming, almost as if he's had them professionally shined recently.

Every single moment I've spent with Savage runs through my head—our meeting at his office, our dinner, the late night phone calls and videos—and I try to figure out what I missed.

*Why didn't he tell me? Why didn't I realize?*

"I'm sorry I didn't tell you." His voice finally breaks the tense silence between us.

I'm thrown by his calm reaction to my not-so-adult response to the new information.

*How can he be so fucking calm right now?* The longer I avoid looking at him, the more the apprehension builds and the shittier I feel.

Pulling myself together, I shake my head and glance up at him, finally meeting his sympathetic blue gaze. He smiles at me, and it seems genuine, but it does nothing to ease the tension in my body or the situation.

"I didn't do it intentionally...not tell you.... It just...never came up. I knew you probably couldn't see in my office, and I beat you to Angelo's the other night, so..."

He trails off and watches me expectantly.

*Say something! Don't leave him hanging like this.*

I manage a tight smile and wring my hands together in front of me. "I guess it's a good thing I didn't invite you to go dancing."

# 8

## DANIKA

*a*s soon as the words come out, I clamp my hand over my mouth, wishing I could take them back. My verbal diarrhea has reached epic proportions, and heat floods my face and neck.

*Did you really just say that to a guy in wheelchair, Dani? Really?*

His eyes widen slightly, and I want to crawl into a hole and die. I look away and am tempted to get up and run out of here as fast as my Sergios can carry me, but then, he bursts out laughing, his entire body shaking, and he reaches out to pull my hand away from my mouth.

I dare a quick glance at him and find him grinning at me. "Wow, look at you, already making jokes, huh?"

*What the fuck kind of a reaction is that? Why the hell is he laughing?*

He pulls my hand up to his mouth and presses his lips to my palm.

"Relax, Danika, just because I can't walk doesn't mean I can't appreciate a good joke. And, for the record, I would have said yes."

"Huh? Said yes to what?"

He smiles again and squeezes my hand. "To dancing. I play basketball. I'm sure I could figure out the dancing thing, too."

His reaction helps me release the breath I've been holding, and I try to calm the churning in my stomach. I look into his unfairly handsome face and just can't avoid asking it. "Why didn't you say anything?"

He sighs and releases my hand before running his back through his hair. "I don't know, honestly. It didn't come up at my office, or at dinner. I knew you couldn't see my chair from where you were standing in my office, and I beat you to the restaurant and was already in the booth. It isn't really something you tell someone in a text message." He pauses and drops his hands onto his lap. "And, frankly, I was worried about what your reaction might be. This is the first time I've been interested in someone since the accident."

*Accident.* The word sends chills down my spine before I even know what happened. Whatever it was, it must have been violent and awful for him to end up like this. "What happened?"

When he closes his eyes and drops his head back, I fear he isn't going to answer me.

*Shit, maybe I shouldn't have asked.*

Just as I suck in my breath to apologize for being so intrusive, he drops his head forward and meets my eyes again.

"Car accident...almost three years ago. I was in Europe, skiing with my sister, Star. I took her there as a graduation gift. She had just finished getting her nurse practitioner license. Skye, her twin, was supposed to come with us but she ended up ditching the trip to be with some guy. Our third day there, we were driving back to our lodge and a semi jackknifed on the road. I couldn't swerve to avoid it. We were on a mountain pass, and there was a giant cliff on the other side."

A picture forms in my mind of a dark, narrow, winding mountain pass—those roads are terrifying enough without envisioning a giant semi-trailer barreling at you. I try to hide my reaction, but a shudder runs through me.

He notices because he winces slightly. "The trailer hit our SUV and pushed it through the guardrail. We rolled down into the ravine. I lost consciousness at some point and don't remember much, which is probably a good thing." He glances down at his hands clenched in his lap.

My eyes burn with tears, but I refuse to cry right now.

*Pull yourself together!*

I shake my head and wipe at my eyes while he's not looking at me. When he glances back up, I notice a sheen in his eyes too, and it makes my stomach lurch into my throat.

"I was in a coma for almost two weeks. When I woke up, I was in a hospital in Germany..." He takes a deep breath and lets it out slowly. "...and my whole family was there to tell me my sister was dead."

A gasp escapes me before I can stop it, and the tears that have been threatening finally fall. He gives me a sad smile, and I can only imagine how much talking about this must rip his fucking heart out. I want to climb onto his lap and hold him but that would probably be inappropriate, given my actions today.

"I'm so sorry." I manage to eke the words out in between sobs and when I wipe my eyes again, I find tearstains on his face, too. He nods, never taking his eyes off me.

"In addition to lots of broken bones and lots of cuts and gashes, I underwent several back surgeries while I was there. I won't bore you with all the medical shit. My spine was partially crushed, but because it wasn't severed and the injury was so low, I'm actually pretty lucky."

"What do you mean?" How can someone call themselves lucky when they're paralyzed?

"I have what's referred to as an incomplete spinal cord injury, and it's at the base of my spine, which basically means I still have some feeling in my legs and have very minimal movement of them, but not enough that I can really control them and I'll never walk again. I work with a personal trainer who is also a physical therapist almost every day to help keep myself in the best shape as I can."

Just thinking about all that sounds horribly painful. "Holy shit. How long were you in the hospital for?"

"Almost six months. The hospital I was at is one of the world's leading treatment centers for spinal cord injuries. I let them do everything they could for me before I came home."

*Jesus. I can't even imagine what he's been through.*

"That is a long time to be away from home."

He nods and smiles, but it doesn't touch his eyes. "It was. Before the accident, I was engaged."

My inner green-eyed monster appears out of nowhere at the thought of him marrying someone. My lunch tries to make an appearance, and I clench my hands into fists on my lap.

"Were? What happened?"

He shrugs. "I guess it was all just too much for her. We had been together almost four years and were supposed to get married that spring. We had a house, and a dog," he looks at Princess, who has made her way back over to us and jumped up on the couch next to me, "and she flew over to see me immediately after the accident. She stayed for a week, but had to go back for work. She made it over a couple more times in the next two months, but somehow, I knew she wouldn't be back when she left that last time. Things had changed between us, and she didn't know how to deal with everything. Hell, I didn't either. At least I got to keep Princess."

At the sound of her name, she leaps down off the couch and jumps up into his lap. A true smile appears on his face for the first time in this conversation, and seeing him doting on that damn tiny, girly dog has me smiling, too.

*Jesus, he's a total softy.*

He turns that killer smile on me. "So, are you ready to run screaming yet?"

My smile must falter because his expression changes rapidly. "I was just joking," he places Princess back on the couch, "but seriously, if this has all been too much for you and you want to skip dinner, I totally understand. It was kind of an asshole move for me to spring this on you when I'm on my home turf."

Flustered by his directness, I shake my head while I try to collect my thoughts. This is a truly gorgeous, funny, sweet, filthy-mouthed man who wants to cook dinner for me.

*Of course you're staying! What the hell is wrong with you for even considering leaving?*

"No, I don't want to leave. You promised me dinner."

Grinning at me, he turns toward the kitchen. "If you are staying, I'm putting you to work."

---

## SAVAGE

Following me into the kitchen, the click-click-click of her heels on the hardwood floors is hard to ignore. I have a feeling she may be taking those off soon. I glance over my shoulder to find her leaning against the doorframe, her eyes wide and jaw practically on the floor as her eyes sweep the room.

"Holy shit. This looks like a professional restaurant kitchen... if all the chefs were children." Her eyes flicker to mine, and she slaps her hand over her mouth again.

I want to fuck with her and pretend her comment offended me, but I can tell she's really worried about it. In all truth, I find her apparent inability to process what she says before she says it refreshing and endearing. It means she's always pretty honest, and she doesn't take the time to create a lie in her head before words tumble from those pouty lips. That will be important if this relationship is going to go anywhere.

*You're just lucky she's still here. Not telling her was a real dick move, and she has every right to be pissed.*

Grinning at her, I run my hand along the island countertop. "Yeah, I had this whole place custom built for me. I knew I couldn't return to my house when I came back to the States. It would have cost a ton, been a pain in the ass, and who knows if I would have even wanted to stay there—too much history. Gabe had already acquired the other half of this floor, so he made some calls and made sure I got this place quickly so work could start making it completely accessible. I spent a few months at my mom's before I moved in here."

She visibly relaxes when I fail to react to her comment and leans her hip against the counter that is way too low for her.

I motion to her four-inch fuck-me pumps and smile at her. "You know, you would probably be a lot more comfortable in here if you took those things off."

She glances down at them and raises her eyes to me, embarrassment on her face. "Sorry, I have freakishly long legs as it is, but with these on, I am more like a giraffe. I should really stay away from heels." Reaching down, she slides them off and sets them down near the doorway before turning back to me.

"I couldn't disagree more. You look hot as hell with those on. They make your mile-long legs look even longer; I can barely take my eyes off them."

Blushing, she eyes me curiously. "How tall are you, anyway?"

I'm busy filling a large pot with water at the sink, but I glance over my shoulder and shrug. "Six-threeish."

*At least I used to be.*

"No fucking way! Well, I guess your dad was a pretty big guy."

"Yeah, he was almost six-five and weighed nearly two-eighty when he was fighting." Dad was a beast. He dominated his weight class in two different boxing leagues and probably would have kept going if the aneurysm hadn't killed him. It came out of nowhere. One minute, he was pummeling his opponent in the ring, and the next, he just stopped and dropped to the mat. He never got up again.

"What can I help with?" She watches me move around the kitchen, getting the things I need.

"In the bottom drawer of the fridge is stuff for a salad. You want to pull it out and make it?"

"Of course." With an adorable little skip, she moves to the fridge and bends down to slide out the crisper drawer, her already-short dress riding up until I almost glimpse the sweet dip of her ass cheeks.

*Damn! This woman has a body that won't fucking quit. Down, boy!*

I return my attention to the sauce that has been simmering on the stove for several hours and give it a stir. She sets something down behind me on the counter and then, in my peripheral vision, I see her grab a knife from the butcher block. Anticipating her next question, I turn around and reach into one of the cabinets below the island, pulling out a cutting board and setting it on the counter in front of her.

She grins at me, and I see some of the tension and unease leave her body. My heart thuds irregularly in my chest, and I have to turn back to the stove and unnecessarily stir the sauce again so she doesn't see how much she affects me.

"What are you making?" She begins chopping the salad ingredients.

"Chicken parm. I hope you like it."

"Oh, I love chicken parm. It's one of my go-to orders whenever I go out for Italian."

"Well, I hope mine stands up." I pull the glass baking dish that contains the already breaded and pan-fried chicken breasts from the fridge and set it on the counter next to the stove. I can feel her eyes on me, following me as I move around the kitchen. She isn't saying much, and that worries me.

*What's she thinking? Does she want to leave and is just too polite to tell me? Should I push her into talking to me about what she's feeling about all this?*

I top the chicken with sauce and cheese and slide it into the oven before turning back to see how Danika is doing on the salad.

"How's it coming?"

She drops sliced tomatoes into the large wooden bowl and smiles at me. "Done."

"Good, let's open a bottle of wine while we wait for it to finish cooking."

"Okay."

By the time the food is ready and we're at the table, we've almost finished a bottle. I'm not a big drinker. I enjoy a whiskey, or beer, or glass of wine, but tonight, just like at Angelo's, drinking seems to ease some of the tension between us. Tension I caused.

*Shit. I have some serious making up to do.*

# 9

## SAVAGE

*S*he picks at her food, complimenting me on how good it is but barely eating anything. Her eyes flicker over to me every couple of minutes but she doesn't say much, and I can sense her unease returning.

It's only natural, but it's so different from the last time we had dinner. It saddens me to know I caused this. I'm the only one to blame for her discomfort and confusion, and I wish I could kick myself for not just telling her from the beginning. I might have saved both of us some heartache, and from having a really uncomfortable dinner tonight.

An awkward silence settles over the table, and she fidgets with her napkin and glass, avoiding eye contact again.

She's thinking. She's making her list of questions she's too afraid or embarrassed to ask.

"Why don't you take another bottle of wine and the glasses out onto the deck, and I'll clean up and then join you?"

Her eyes flicker up to mine, and the corners of her mouth turn up into a half-hearted, fake smile.

*Shit. She is really uncomfortable. What the hell did you expect, dropping it on her like this?*

She slides her chair back from the table and approaches me slowly. Stopping in front of me, she pauses as she reaches for my wine glass. "Are you sure you don't need any help cleaning up?"

"Nope, I got it." I give her a reassuring smile and hope it helps her relax, but she grabs my glass and the bottle of wine quickly and disappears toward the living room without even glancing back.

*Double shit.*

I clear the plates from the table and load them into the dish-washer with the baking dishes and pots before I head out to the deck. When I reach the sliding glass door, I stop and watch her.

She's lying on one of the chaise lounges, soaking up the last of the waning light of the sunset. Her eyes are closed, face turned up toward the sky, hair blowing in the light breeze. She's a picture of pure beauty. To anyone taking a quick glance, she might even look relaxed and peaceful; but, I know better. I see the crinkles around her eyes as she squeezes them closed, the lines around her slightly-frowning mouth, and the way she's gripping her wine glass so hard her knuckles are white.

*She doesn't know what to do, what to say. You've put her in an impossible position. You're a selfish asshole. You should have told her from day one.*

Dinner sits like a lead weight at the bottom of my stomach. I take a deep breath to avoid it coming back up and open the door before moving out onto the deck.

Her eyes fly open, and she turns her head in my direction. When she sees me, she looks almost panicked, and the tension in the air is so thick I can feel it weighing down on me like the late summer humidity. I want to wipe the trepidation from her face, the reservation from her stare, but I don't know how.

"Why don't you pour me another glass?"

She nods and reaches for the bottle, slowly pouring me a glass of wine while I move from my chair onto the chaise lounge parallel to hers. I feel her eyes on me the entire time, and I know she must have a million questions by now.

Once I settle in, she hands me my glass and returns to other chaise, her body turned slightly toward me.

*That's a good sign, right?*

"Ask." I watch her shift anxiously in her seat.

Her head whips up, and her eyes widen in surprise. "Uh, ask what?"

I smile at her and take a long sip of my wine, never looking away.

"Ask the million and one questions I know you must have but are either too afraid or embarrassed to ask. I promise you, I've already answered them a hundred times for other people, and you won't offend me with anything you have questions about. I brought you into this without giving you all the information, and that wasn't fair of me. I'm sorry. So, ask. I'm an open book."

She takes a deep breath and pulls her bottom lip between her teeth, chewing on it in a way that has me wishing it was my teeth there. I watch patiently as she struggles to come up with her first question.

*Don't push her. She has to do this on her own.*

I take another drink of my wine, never taking my eyes off her, as she stares alternately between her bare feet and my hand wrapped around my wine glass.

"Um, so, you live alone and don't need any help with anything?"

*That isn't the question you want to ask.*

"No, I don't need help with anything. Like I said, this place was specifically built to be handicap accessible so I wouldn't need help. I do have a cleaning lady who comes in once a week, but, otherwise, I do everything myself."

She seems to consider that for a moment. "What about Gabe? He drives you."

"Yes, but that isn't because I can't drive. I have several cars that are modified so I can drive them. It just happens that Gabe is with me most of the time anyway, so it's easier if he drives."

"Oh." She stares at her wine before taking a long drink. Her hand shakes slightly as she lowers it from her lips.

It fucking breaks my heart to think I'm making her that nervous.

I like her nervous, just the kind of nervous she was at our Angelo's dinner, nervous because of the sexual tension between us.

*Do something about it!*

My wine glass clinks down on the table between the chaise lounges, and I extend my right hand out to her. "Come here."

She looks at my hand, considering it for a moment before she slowly sets her glass down on the table and places her palm against mine. I gently tug her across the space between us until she falls lightly onto my lap, her bare legs dangling off the side of the chaise.

"Why are you so nervous?" I brush her hair back behind her shoulder and cup her cheek to turn her face toward me.

Her eyes meet mine, and I'm momentarily lost in the silvery blue of her irises and the glint of the setting sun off her flawless skin.

"I'm not," she whispers.

"Yes, you are." I cup her face between my hands, refusing to let her look away from me when I say this. "And I'm sorry you had to find out this way. It isn't fair to ask you to take me, and all this, on. We said, and did, things when you didn't have all the information. I wouldn't blame you if you choose to walk away right now. But, before you do, I need to kiss you, because I haven't been able to stop thinking about doing it since the second you walked into my office."

Her eyes flash with heat, and her tongue slips out over her bottom lip, wetting it, making it even more irresistible.

Pulling her to me, I pause when our lips are a mere hairsbreadth apart. "Last chance to run," I whisper.

She doesn't even flinch, and I strike, pressing my lips against hers in a scorching kiss. My cock hardens beneath her, and she responds, groaning and sliding her tongue along my bottom lip, begging for entry. I oblige and our tongues tangle, thrusting against each other wildly. It is exactly everything I had known it would be.

When we finally come up for air, I know there is no way I can let her go after that kiss. "Danika, you have no reason to be nervous with me. I'm still the same person I've always been with you, and I know exactly what you want to know."

Her lips part slightly, but she sucks back the words, glancing down at her hands pressed against my chest. "You do?"

I nod and slowly brush my thumb down her cheek before lifting her chin so she's facing me again, her buttery-smooth skin like velvet under my fingertips, and I long to know if the rest of her body feels the same. "You want to know if I am paralyzed, how can I possibly have sex, right?"

She freezes against me, going so stone still, her chest barely moves with her shallow breathing.

*Bingo.*

---

## DANIKA

*Shit. How the fuck did he know that? Am I really that transparent?*

I sigh and drop my forehead against his chest, my face probably turning many brilliant shades of red to match the sunset behind me. He chuckles and captures my cheeks in his palms, pulling me up to face him again, a smirk on his lips.

"Yes, some paraplegics have issues with sexual function. I, thankfully, don't have trouble getting hard." Leaning forward, he kisses my cheek, then brushes his lips against my ear. "What? Do you think I somehow faked those pictures and videos?"

*Yes.*

"No." I hope my blush doesn't give me away again.

*Why do I have to be such a horrible liar?*

He laughs again and pulls back, pressing his lips to mine gently. "Baby, you can feel the evidence of how I feel about you pressing against your beautiful ass right now—proof that those pictures were very much real."

He pushes his cock up against me, and a groan slips from my lips.

The constant buzz of electricity that has been sliding across my skin since I fell onto his lap arcs between us, and he captures my mouth again. Cradling my face in his left hand, he devours my lips and slowly skims his right hand from my knee up my thigh to the hem of my sundress.

Instinctively, I shift on his lap, grinding down against his rock-hard erection. He moans into my mouth as his tongue glides effortlessly along mine.

*Fuck, he tastes like wine and sex. My two favorite things. I'm a total lush, and I desperately need to get fucked. By. This. Man.*

His hand slips up under the hem of my dress, searing a line of fire along my sensitive skin. When the tips of his fingers brush against the silk fabric of my thong, a shudder rolls through my entire body, and I push against him, urging him further.

*Touch me!*

It has the opposite effect. His hand stills momentarily, and I want to scream at him, but instead, a desperate whimper escapes my lips, and he groans in reply, redoubling his assault on my mouth as he finally slides my panties to the side.

I turn into him, giving him a better angle and gasp when he drags his fingertips slowly through my drenched folds. My body vibrates with need—the need for him to shove into me with his fingers, his tongue, his cock, hell, anything at this point.

He slides his fingers up until he finds my throbbing clit, and he coats it in my arousal, making me bow up off his lap. He doesn't relent, instead slipping two fingers into my needy pussy as he continues to roll against my clit with his thumb. I close my eyes and drop my head back; he follows, his mouth and tongue moving in time with his fingers.

*Holy shit. I'm not going to last.*

Bright lights flash behind my eyelids as I roll my hips against his hand, keeping time with the demanding rhythm he has set. I clutch at his shirt, my fingers tugging on the crisp fabric, desperate for anything to keep me from flying apart.

He pulls away from my mouth, and my eyes flutter open, searching his face for a reason why. His blue eyes are ablaze with desire.

His swollen lips are slightly parted as he groans. "God, you are so fucking beautiful, Dani. I want to see your face when you come for me."

All I manage in reply is a whimper when he curls his fingers up and finds my G-spot. A fire roars through me, and the world disappears as my orgasm eliminates any possibility of cognizant thought.

"Oh, fuck, Savage..." My hips buck and roll against his hand and he covers my mouth with his, sucking my tongue in rhythm with my orgasm and devouring my scream.

When the splintering pleasure finally ebbs, his thumb slows, and he eases his fingers out before capturing my face between his hands for a bruising kiss.

"Fuck, you have no idea how incredible it was to see you fall apart like that." He drops his forehead against mine.

My breaths are still coming out in short pants and the world seems a little hazy around the edges, but his cock is still very hard beneath me. I would love nothing more than to yank the zipper of his pants down and sit down on his dick, but a realization hits me.

*I can't fuck him. Even if I want to, even if he wants it, I can't do that. Not when I have no idea where this is going between us. Not when he clearly isn't just looking for a fuck buddy. Not when he can't give me what I need.*

Reluctantly, I pull my head away from his, and I glance down at my dress, now shoved up almost to my panties. I yank it toward my knees, clear my throat, and quickly stand, turning my back on Savage.

"Danika?"

I peek back at him as I straighten my dress. He hasn't moved an inch, but recognition that the mood has shifted is written all over his face.

"Um, I have to go. I'm sorry. I have to finish an article before tomorrow morning."

*LIAR!*

With a quick turn, I make a break for the sliding glass door and immediately beeline for the kitchen to grab my heels before dashing toward the front door.

*Shit. This isn't me. I don't get ashamed or shy after sex. I never run. What the fuck am I doing?*

My stomach roils, and I flatten my hand over it, taking a deep breath before I stop by the front door to bend down and slip on my shoes.

I see him approaching in my peripheral vision, but keep my eyes on the floor. This man has me so off balance, I don't even trust myself to look at him right now.

*Because you know running is WRONG!*

As soon as my shoes are on and I grab my purse from the table near the door, I'm out of excuses. Turning to face him, I plaster on a smile I hope is convincing.

He smiles back, but I see the question and disappointment behind it.

*Cold-hearted bitch.*

I step over to him and bend down to place a kiss on his cheek. Pulling back, I smile again.

"Thank you for dinner. I'll talk to you tomorrow."

He nods but otherwise doesn't respond.

I turn my back on him and slip through the door and out into the hallway. The second it clicks shut behind me, I slump back against it, dropping my head into my hands.

*What the hell is this man doing to me?*

## 10

SAVAGE

"Ｗhat crawled up your ass today?"

I cast my death glare toward the other end of the table at Skye.

"Skye!" Mom's chiding of the youngest girl Hawke only grates more on my already tortured nerves.

"What?" Skye throws her hands up. "It's not like you aren't all thinking the same thing."

I glance around the table at Storm, her husband, Ben, and their daughter, Angelina, then at Mom, who gives me a sympathetic look.

"Well, honey, she does have a point. You have kind of been out of sorts today."

Tossing my fork onto my plate with a clank, I drop my elbows to the table and run my hands back through my hair, tugging on the ends and looking to Storm for help. She's the most level-headed of the Hawke kids, and she always tends to be the mediator. She purses her lips and frowns slightly.

*Shit, I really have been a dick today.*

"Savage, come on, what's going on?" She pushes her empty plate away from her and focuses her eyes on me. I don't move or say anything. I really don't need the entire family involved in my love life. I don't know why I'm stupid enough to think they will just let it go.

"Well?" she probes. "Come on, Savage, last week in California you were happier than I've seen you in years, and now you are biting everyone's head off anytime we talk to you and sulking around like your dog ran away or something. So, what the hell happened?"

*She's too perceptive for her own good sometimes.*

I huff out a resigned sigh and lean back in my chair.

"It's a woman."

"Ha!" Skye yells. "I knew it!"

I glare at her again. "Shut up, Skye."

The little brat sticks her tongue out at me and goes right back to eating. For a twenty-seven year old who constantly complains we treat her like a child, she certainly doesn't do much to change our perception. Sometimes, I swear she's intentionally childish because she knows she can get away with more that way.

Lord knows, we have been letting her get away with a lot since Star's death.

"A woman, huh?" Mom's question holds a ton of weigh in it.

I look to her, reigning over our Sunday dinner from the head of the table with a glass of red wine in her hand. "Well, that would certainly explain the change in moods." She gives me a small smile before taking a sip and setting her glass on the table. "You never mentioned you were seeing anyone."

"That's because I wasn't. I'm not. Hell, I don't know what the fuck is going on."

"Savage!" Storm yelps. "Watch your language in front of Angelina."

I look over at my niece, but she has her eyes glued to the iPad on the table in front of her and isn't paying anyone an ounce of attention.

"She didn't hear me."

Storm rolls her eyes and gives an exasperated sigh.

Skye chimes in from the other end of the table. "Tell us about the girl."

*Fucking nosy women. I almost miss Stone.*

"We met because her sister works for me at the club. She's an investigative reporter for the *Times*. We went to dinner the Friday before we all went out for Stone's graduation."

"And it was good?" Storm's genuine interest makes her turn her back to Ben and Angelina and lean toward me on the table.

I think back to the dinner and how amazing it was once she loosened up. "It was spectacular, actually. We talked and texted the whole time I was in Cali."

*And did a whole fucking lot more than that, but that isn't for anyone else's consumption.*

"No wonder you were in such a good mood the entire time we were there." Storm smiles at me.

Skye snorts. "So, why are you being such a douche now? She get wise and dump your ass?"

"Skye Marie Hawke!" Mom snaps. "Shut your trap."

I chuckle at Mom's ridicule of her. Skye has always been the sassiest of the Hawke children and the one who tests Mom's patience and temper the most. Mom has given her a lot of leeway since Star's death. Losing your sister is gut-wrenchingly painful, but losing your twin sister, that's another form of misery I can't even begin to fathom. Skye hasn't been handling it well, anyone can see that, but she keeps everyone at arm's length and has adamantly refused to talk about the accident, or Star's death, with anyone, as far as I know.

Maybe I shouldn't talk. I haven't exactly been forthcoming with the family about everything either, and I was a total dick to the psychiatrist who tried to talk to me in the hospital. We

Hawkes are known for our stubbornness and need for control. I guess it shouldn't surprise me she would react the way she has.

"No, she didn't dump my ass. At least, I don't think she did. I guess that's the problem. I have no idea where we stand right now."

"What happened?" Mom asks.

Sighing, I drop my head back and stare at the popcorn ceiling of the dining room for a minute. I know they aren't trying to pry —they're genuinely concerned about me—but sometimes I wish my family didn't care quite so much. It might leave me some space to breathe.

Returning my eyes to the table, and finding them all staring intently at me, I know I won't get out of this without telling them.

"Well, she came over to my place for dinner last night, and things didn't exactly go smoothly." I glance around the table, hoping that will be enough to satisfy them, but they all urge me on with their eyes.

"Why not?" Skye finally sounds like she really gives a shit instead of just asking to goad me.

I drop my head into my hands and grit my teeth. "Because she didn't know."

"She didn't know what?" Skye continues.

I look up at her just in time to see her take another drink of her wine.

Storm glares at her, then turns her attention back to me with a sympathetic smile. I don't have to say it. Everyone, except Skye apparently, knows exactly what I'm talking about. "How did you manage that?"

"It wasn't intentional. It just kind of happened that way. When she came to my office I was behind my desk, and when we had dinner at Angelo's she came late. I was already at the table."

Storm groans and leans back in her chair. "And you didn't think to maybe mention it to her?"

I growl and slam my palm against the table, garnering a look of reproach from Mom. "Of course I thought to mention it, but things were going so well, and it's not like it organically comes up in conversation."

Skye scoffs. "No shit."

"Seriously, Skye?" I snap at her.

She holds her hands up in surrender. "Sorry. Shutting my mouth now."

Storm laughs at her. "Yeah, right, that'll last ten seconds, tops."

"Stop it," Mom barks. "Savage, what happened?"

"Well, when she saw me, she dropped the bottle of wine she was holding and it shattered all over the floor." Everyone, including me, cringes and I debate how to tell them the rest while keeping it PG. "Then, I told her about the accident and we had dinner. I thought it went well...but, after we were done, she high-tailed it out of there like her ass was on fire and told me she would talk to me later."

"And?" Storm stares at me intently.

"And, it has been almost a full day, and not a single word from her." I can't remember the last time I sat around waiting for a phone to ring.

*Adults don't do that, do they?*

"Shit." Storm reaches out and downs the rest of her wine. "That really sucks. Have you tried calling or texting her?"

"No, I'm not going to push her into anything she isn't ready for. She knows how to get a hold of me. I just wish I knew what the hell she was thinking."

---

## DANIKA

"Are you just going to sit on your ass drinking wine all night?" Caroline drops down into the couch next to me. She leans forward and grabs the almost-empty bottle off the coffee table and tips it back, emptying what's left into her mouth. "What is that? Bottle five in the last twenty-four hours?"

"Don't exaggerate." I take a long drink from my, thankfully, full glass. "It's more like four."

She bursts out laughing and snatches the remote off my leg, pressing pause on that damn rain scene in *The Notebook*. "It might help if you stopped watching all these damn romantic chick-flicks and got your mind off of it. Since when are you a sappy movie girl, anyway?"

*Since I met Savage Hawke.*

I set my glass on the coffee table before turning my back to the arm of the couch and pulling my knees up to my chin. "I just don't know what to do, Care."

My brain has been a maelstrom since I left Savage's last night. All I can think is what a total, absolute, complete fucking bitch I was to run out of there like that, especially after he gave me an incredible orgasm.

"I know, sweetie, but sitting here drinking isn't going to give you any of the answers you are looking for."

*I beg to differ.*

"What will?"

*Seriously, what will?*

I've been living the last day in a nightmare of indecision. One part of me wants nothing more than to fall into his arms and enjoy the sweet taste of his kiss again, while the other part of me wants to run as far and as fast as my legs and my will can carry me.

Savage Hawke is my greatest desires and my greatest fears all rolled into one. He is precisely the kind of man I've always known would capture my heart and actually be able to hold onto it— something I've managed to avoid my entire adult life—and now I know he might not be able to give me what my body needs.

*Sometimes having a sex drive like a man really, really sucks.*

Caroline smiles sympathetically and rubs my knee. "Honey, I don't know. What do you want me to say? From what you have told me, he's stupid hot, kind, funny, rich. It doesn't seem like there's much not to like. I get that you are worried about how his, uh, condition will affect things between you, and believe me, I get it, but you are the only one who can make this decision."

Letting out something resembling a groan and a sigh, I drop my head back on the couch and close my eyes. "I'm so glad Doug is sending me to D.C. tomorrow. I need an assignment to occupy my mind right now." Although, politics isn't the most exciting area of my job, getting away for a couple days can only be good right now; anything to take my mind off my inability to make up my mind.

"What's going on with that big story you keep teasing Doug with? You ever gonna tell me what it is?"

I reach for my wine and return my gaze to her. "No, not until I know where it's going. This contact I have sounds promising, but he still hasn't delivered on any of the stuff he says he can get me. I'll let you, and Doug, know when I have something solid."

"Well, take the time you have in D.C. to figure your shit out, girl, 'cause you can't leave that poor guy hanging like that."

Downing the rest of my wine, I savor the cool liquid sliding down my throat and resign myself to the fact that Caroline is right. What I did was awful, and I can't leave things like that, even if I decide I am too big of a chicken-shit to pursue things with Savage.

Savage, who, even now, sets my body on fire. The videos, his words, his damn hands...

I climb up from the couch, surprised when I don't wobble after the drinks I have already consumed. "Hey, it is still early... ish. Let's go out."

She eyes me and points at the clock. "It's almost 8:30, on a Sunday. Where the hell do you want to go?"

Pulling my shirt off and walking toward the bedroom, I glance over my shoulder and wink at her. "It doesn't matter, anywhere but here."

"I don't have any clothes here," she whines, looking down at her sweatpants and t-shirt.

"You can borrow something!" I call from the bedroom as I yank off my sweatpants and step into the bathroom.

*Ick. I look like crap.* I guess that's what happens when you sit on your ass drinking all day and don't bother with makeup, or a curling iron, or anything else normally used to make yourself presentable.

"Fine." She appears behind me in the mirror and leans against the doorjamb while I start applying my eye makeup. "You know, I think The Garage has a band on Sunday nights."

"Excellent!"

I need to lose myself in something, something other than Savage. Maybe music would do the trick.

Music.

Dancing.

Men.

Booze.

All the things that normally put me in that blissful state of "I don't give a fuck" and just let me be.

At least, they did before I met Savage. I let myself get way too involved with him way too quickly. The phone calls and videos lured me into this semi-relationship status when I barely knew him—clearly—and when the last thing I need in my life right now is the complication of a full-time man.

I need quick and easy. Well, not necessarily quick.... There is definitely something to be said for slow, torturous, unhurried sex. Sometimes that is exactly what I need, but more often than not, a rapid, hard pounding is just the ticket.

I'm sure that's all I need to get Savage out of my head for good.

# 11

## DANIKA

Staring out the cab window at the rain-soaked streets, buildings, and people of D.C., I'm barely able to contain my annoyance at the cabbie's choice of route to the hotel. We're at a dead standstill in some roundabout, and I'm ready to bite his head off after a long four days of interviews and writing. All I want to do is get back to the hotel, yank off my heels, throw on my sweats, and down about half a bottle of bourbon.

*At least this asshole isn't blasting music in here. The last thing I need is a headache.*

I hate politics, and I hate politicians and lobbyists even more. These people are the true scum of the Earth. I honestly think my version of Hell would be living and working with these people and having to hear them spew their nonsensical horseshit all day.

Four days of it already has me at my boiling point. I thought Mayor Dunne was a scumbag, but he pales in comparison to some of these people. I need that story done, just like I need to figure this Savage situation out. Both have been weighing heavily

on my mind. One, the Abello/Dunne story, is out of my control—
I'm at the mercy of Paul and him getting me what I need. But the
other—my indecisiveness about Savage—is completely on me
and I need to suck it up, be a big girl, and figure out what I'm
going to do.

I pull out my phone for the millionth time during the trip to
check my messages. My heart sinks when I see nothing has
changed.

No texts.

No voicemails.

No videos.

None from Savage, at least.

For the millionth time, I open our text conversation. The last
one we had, the Friday before my disastrous performance at his
condo. He was still in San Diego, and I was still blissfully
unaware of the fact that a relationship with him would be, well, a
little complicated.

> I can't wait to get my hands on you. <

< I can't wait to have your hands on me. >

*Shit. He was good with his hands, so damn good.*

A shudder rolls through my body as I remember his hand
blazing a trail of fire drifting up my thigh. His fingers sliding my
panties to the side and gliding through my slick folds...

I have to clamp my thighs together to help ease my throbbing
clit at the memory.

*Damn.*

I quickly close out the message screen and check my emails.
Doug—wanting to know when I will be sending him the notes
from today. Mom—wondering when I'm going to visit her. They
can wait. I slip my phone back in my purse and refocus on the
rain outside as we finally start moving again.

Five minutes later, I'm slamming the cab door outside my
hotel and racing in through the rain. As I walk through the lobby,
I focus on the bar. Any other trip, I would be spending my night

in there, hoping to meet a guy who would bang the ever-loving shit out of me in his room or mine, and not even bother asking my name.

Hot.

Rough.

Hard.

That's what I need.

I am hornier than a goddamn teenager, and I have absolutely zero desire to find my usual business trip bang buddy. I wasn't even able to seal the deal when Caroline and I went out to the club the night before I left for this trip. I tried—boy, did I fucking try, anything to forget about the Savage situation—but when the beautiful man I had been dancing with all night kissed me, it felt all wrong and I couldn't suppress the rotten feeling in my stomach.

After slipping into the empty elevator, I lean back against the wall and close my eyes, trying desperately to let the synthesized version of some pop song being piped through the speakers lull me into some semblance of relaxed.

Just as the ding sounds, alerting me I've reached my floor, a familiar ringtone sounds in my purse.

*Caroline. What the hell does she want?*

I dig in my purse for my phone and stumble out of the car, making my way down the brightly lit hallway toward my room.

"Hey, what's up?" I pull my keycard from my wallet and slide it in the door.

"Hey, girl, what are you up to?"

"Nothing." I toss my bag onto the chair next to the small table in my room and kick off my heels before dropping back onto my bed. "I just got back to my room."

"Are you alone?"

*Fuck.*

I hate that she knows me so well. "Yes, I am alone, thank you very much."

"Well, that's a first."

"Bitch."

She chuckles, and I flip on the television, praying there is something on tonight I can completely lose myself in. No more chick-flicks. My heart can't handle it anymore.

"Does this mean you've made a decision about Savage?"

I let out a deep sigh. "No, it doesn't. It just means I didn't want company tonight. It has nothing to do with Savage. He's not the only thing I think about, you know."

"Oh really? So, you aren't interested in the single white rose that appeared on your desk today or what the nice little card attached says?"

I bolt upright.

*Savage. It has to be from him.*

"Bitch, don't fuck with me. What does it say?"

She laughs, and I hear the brief rustle of paper. "Danika, I'm sorry about the way I handled things. I don't blame you for running. I hope you are all right. Please, take care of yourself. S."

"Shit." I turn on speakerphone and drop my face into my palms.

"Shit, indeed. Girl, this guy has it bad for you, but he's still willing to let you go. The ball is in your court. You won't be able to hide from it in D.C. any longer. You're coming home tomorrow and need to put this poor man out of his misery."

"I know."

I need to put myself out of my misery, too. This week has been agonizingly painful, and not just because I'm hornier than I've ever been in my life. I never thought I'd have to make a decision like this, and five days of thinking haven't gotten me anywhere closer to final judgment.

It can't go on any longer. It's not fair to me, and it's especially not fair to Savage.

## SAVAGE

"You sent her more flowers?" Gabe quirks his eyebrow at me, and his lips twist into a grimace.

"Yes, well, one flower." Leaning back in my chair, I stretch my arms and twist, trying to loosen up to the tight muscles after this morning's workout.

"You think that was a good idea?"

"At this point? I don't think it matters much what I do. What did you come in here for, anyway?"

He drops down into a chair across from me and leans forward, his forearms on his knees. "You aren't going to like it."

"Oh, good, bad news. My favorite kind."

Nothing has been going right this week. Ever since I returned from San Diego, anything and everything that *could* go wrong *has* gone wrong.

First, my epic crash and burn with Danika. I'm still trying to recover from it but find myself pathetically reviewing our old text conversations and pining like that's going to change anything about this shit situation.

Then, one of the dancers got chicken pox from her kid and managed to infect three of the other girls, leaving us short-staffed during our peak season. Spring means weddings, and weddings mean bachelor parties.

And, if that wasn't bad enough, the manager at one of my other bars up and disappeared, taking over ten grand out of the safe when he left. So, I got to spend two days talking with the police and trying to hire another manager. "What is it? Just lay it on me."

"We are almost out of beer."

"What do you mean we're almost out of beer? There should have been a delivery this morning." I open the supply management program on my computer and scroll through it. "We ordered enough to last two weeks, and it was supposed to be delivered before noon today."

Gabe leans back and shrugs. "Maybe it was supposed to be, but it wasn't. Byron and I have tried calling the supplier all afternoon, and we can't seem to get a straight answer from them about where the shipment is or when it's coming."

*This has to be some kind of fucking joke.*

"Jesus, we have four bachelor parties tonight and five tomorrow."

"I know," he says, eyeing me speculatively. "You know what you need to do."

"No. Hell no." I shake my head and rack my brain for *any* alternative.

"Savage, come on. You need to call Dom."

"I said, hell no." I slam my palms against my desk. "I'm not going to owe that guy any more favors."

*Never again.*

"I get it, I do, but he's also the only one who is going to be able to get us what we need before the tidal wave hits tonight."

Dom Abello is the last person in the world I want to call for help.

My unfortunate connection with him was forged even before I was born. Mom grew up on the same street, and Dad went to school with him. Then, years later, Dad did some "work" for him from time to time.

Growing up, he had always just been Uncle Dom to us. Mom either didn't know or chose to ignore what he did for a living—the murders, drug dealing, corruption. None of it was ever mentioned or acknowledged in my home. I never really understood who or what he was until I was well into high school. By then, it was hard to untangle myself from him due to the family connection.

I've tried my best to steer clear of Uncle Dom and his associates, but when I couldn't get financing for the first bar after college, he helped me out. The problem is, getting help from Uncle Dom always comes with a price.

Almost a decade later, I'm still paying for his "generosity" with favors I would rather not do.

"Shit." I drop my head into my hands and groan in frustration. "Why can't anything go right this week?"

"I don't know, man. One of us really must have done something to piss off the big guy upstairs."

*No shit.*

"Well, given your track record, I'm betting it was you."

He grins and flips me off.

Unfortunately, Gabe's right. Dom is the only one with connections to get us what we need fast. I reach for the phone and reluctantly dial. It rings three times he picks up.

"Well, well, well...Mr. Hawke, to what do I owe the pleasure?" There's a knowledge and a smugness in his voice, knowing I'm calling him because I need something. The man revels in holding things over people, and it frankly wouldn't surprise me if he had orchestrated the beer shortage just so I would need his help and would therefore owe him a favor. Of course, I will never call him out on it, even if I knew it to be true. I don't have a death wish.

"Hey, Dom. I'm hoping you can help me out with something. I am in a bit of a jam."

I can practically see his grin at knowing I'm about to ask for another favor.

"Of course, son, what do you need?"

I despise when he calls me "son." It is as much an insult to Dad as it is to me but I need his help, so I bite back my anger before I answer.

"Beer, lots of it. Our supplier flaked on us this afternoon and we're almost out with a busy weekend fast approaching."

Dom laughs on the other end, and I can picture him, his head tipped back, smug smile on his face knowing I will owe him big time after this. "No problem, Savage, I can have it there within the hour."

Relief washes over me at the averted disaster, but my gut clenches at his next words.

"You'll owe me."

Being told "you'll owe me" by a man like Dom Abello doesn't mean you'll give him a ride to the airport, or pick up his dry cleaning for him. No, "you'll owe me" from a man like that might as well mean "I own you." And, I've already heard it way too many times to be comfortable with it.

"I know, Dom. I always do. Thanks." I drop the phone into its cradle and return my gaze to Gabe.

He chuckles and grins at me. "You just sold your soul to the devil for some beer."

*Asshole.*

"No, I sold my soul to the devil for our business, which just happens to require beer."

He laughs, tossing his head back before he stands and walks toward the door. "I'll make sure the guys are ready for the delivery. You need anything else?"

*Lots of things.*

"Not that you can give me."

## 12

SAVAGE

*I* stare at the computer screen and take another long drink of my bourbon. It is almost 9:00 p.m., and things have gone surprisingly smooth for a Saturday night. Usually, there's at least one asshole trying to climb the stage to get to the girls, or one inappropriately grabbing at the waitresses. But tonight, things are quiet. It certainly makes my job a lot easier.

Clicking on the screen to enlarge the image in the far left corner, I zoom in on the bar where Byron is helping Clarissa and Jamie with the flood of customers seeking drinks.

Busy is good.

Busy keeps my mind occupied.

Busy keeps it off Danika.

*Yeah, right...*

The shrill ring of the phone on my desk tears me away from the camera feed. "This is Hawke."

"Savage, son, it's Dom."

*Shit. That was quick.*

"Hey, Dom, to what do I owe the pleasure?" I toss his phrase back at him, though I doubt he knows I'm mocking him. He may be brilliant at running a criminal empire, but he isn't the brightest bulb in the shed when it comes to anything else.

"I need a favor."

*And there it is.*

My chest tightens, and my stomach turns imagining all the depraved things he may ask me to do. "What do you need?"

"I have an associate who's in town tonight and would really enjoy a visit to your club. I need the champagne room."

We have five private rooms in the club, the champagne room being the largest and most luxurious. We also have five bachelor parties here tonight, and a very wealthy lawyer and his friends are currently enjoying the benefits of the champagne room before they send him off to the altar.

"I'm sorry, Dom. I can't. I have a bachelor party in there tonight." The silence on the other end of the line is deafening, and I wonder if I've just dug myself into a hole I can never get out of. I take a deep breath and pray that he doesn't get even more offended. "I'm happy to set up a private area in the main club for him. It would give him a better view of all the girls, anyway."

Dom lets out a deep sigh and clears his throat. "Savage, I am asking you to do me a favor here, in return for the one I did for you earlier this week. I don't think I'm asking much of you."

I knew there would be a price. I guess in the grand scheme of things, I should be thanking God it's all he's asking for. At worst, it's just some pissed off patrons. "Okay, I'll talk to Byron and get them moved out of there. Give me at least a half hour."

"Thank you, Savage, you are truly a prince among men."

An eye roll seems appropriate at his comment. After hanging up with Dom, I immediately call down to the bar.

Byron answers and I watch him on my screen. "Hey, boss,

what's up?" He looks into the camera as he talks to me, knowing I always keep an eye on things.

I explain the situation quickly. He grumbles but disappears to break the bad news to the bachelor party.

Slumping back in my chair, I drain the rest of my bourbon and pour myself another glass. I'm going to need this tonight to deal with all the complaints this will cause.

*Fuck Dom!*

The bump of the music from downstairs thuds through the floor. I drop my head back and close my eyes, willing the headache starting to form at the base of my neck to hold off until I can get home and slip into a hot shower.

I hear the door open, and I'm hit with a familiar scent, one I will never forget.

Lilacs and spring rain.

*Danika.*

My eyes snap open, and I find her standing near the door, looking as beautiful as the first day she stormed in here. Her flaxen hair floats around her shoulders in waves, and she sucks her red, plump bottom lip between her teeth as she eyes me warily.

I scan her, checking to make sure she's physically okay. After not seeing or hearing from her for a week, even after sending the note, I've been secretly terrified something happened to her.

She's sporting her usual four-inch stilettos and a skirt so short it leaves very little to the imagination. Then again, I don't need my imagination after what happened on my patio. Her skirt is paired with a shimmering tank top that exposes the tops of her breasts in a way that is practically begging me to touch them.

*Holy. Hell.*

Finally, her lip slips from between her teeth, and she takes a tentative step toward me. "Hey."

"Hey, what are you doing here? Are you okay?"

She cringes, and I regret my choice of words; she probably thinks I'm pissed and don't want to see her.

"Um, Gabe said it was okay if I came up."

I move around my desk and approach her slowly. "Of course it's okay. I've been worried about you."

She hangs her head and looks to the floor, shifting uncomfortably in her heels. "Yeah, I'm sorry. I just...needed some time."

*Needed some time? Time to figure out how to tell me to fuck off? Time to accept the situation and roll with it?*

I stop in front of her and look up into her eyes. "But...you're okay?"

She nods at me, her blue eyes flashing with emotion. What emotion? I don't have a fucking clue, and isn't that a fucking bitch?

"Then, what's wrong?"

A single tear falls, sliding down her cheek and dropping from her chin. "I'm sorry." She wipes at her eyes. "I didn't mean to make you worry."

I reach out and grab her hand, squeezing it in mine. "Don't worry about me. Just tell me that you are okay."

"Yeah, I'm fine."

*Crying isn't fine. A woman crying is absolutely never fine.*

"Come, sit down."

She nods, and I release her hand, letting her follow me over to the couch in the sitting area of my office. She drops down onto it, and I settle in front of her.

"You want a drink?"

Relief floods her face and she smiles. "Yeah, please."

I grab the bottle of Blanton's and my glass off my desk and stop at the bar to grab another glass for Danika. I give each of us a strong pour before setting the bottle down on the side table.

*I have a feeling we're both going to need this.*

Handing her a glass, I lean in and catch her eyes. "Tell me what's going on."

She takes a sip of the bourbon and seems to relax instantly. After staring down at her glass for several agonizing moments, she finally clears her throat. "I needed to see you."

*That's it.*

My heart tightens in my chest, and my mind immediately jumps to the obvious conclusion—she's here to tell me she's done.

"Why did you need to see me?" I set my drink down on the end table so I can take her free hand in mine.

She looks up at me from under impossibly long black lashes and flashes a shy smile. "Because I haven't been able to stop thinking about you since I left your place."

Her repetition of the almost exact words I spoke to her on our first date makes my heart flutter with hope.

*Is she trying to tell me something? Why can't she just say it?*

I take a fortifying breath and steady myself. "What have you been thinking about?" I rub my thumb in circles over the palm of her hand.

She squeezes my hand gently. "How badly I want you to do what you did to me on your patio again. How badly I want you...us."

---

## DANIKA

I pause, waiting for his reaction, searching his face as he hears the words I have been dying to say to him for days but kept denying.

His eyes glimmer with concern and then heated lust, the blue darkening as they flick from my eyes down to my mouth. I lick my lips, and he groans.

"Shit, Danika, you have no idea how happy I am to hear you say that." His words come out in a rush, and he visibly relaxes, his tense shoulders dropping slightly as he brings my hand up to his mouth and presses his lips to the center, letting them linger there, his warm breath spreading across my palm.

My clit throbs, remembering how that hand, those fingers, felt between my legs. I shift uncomfortably on the couch, trying to press my thighs together. He grins at me and takes my drink from my hand, placing it next to his on the end table.

*Shit! I need that!*

"What are you doing?"

"Get on the table." He points to the long conference table behind the couch.

It takes me a second to process what he's saying, but the heat in his eyes leaves no question about what he wants. Moisture floods between my legs, and I shakily stand and make my way around the couch to the table.

He follows closely behind me, stopping and watching intently as I turn and stare him down while I boost myself up onto the table and let my legs dangle over the edge.

A lecherous grin spreads across his face. He moves in, using his broad shoulders to press my thighs wide open.

*Boy, am I fucking glad I wore this skirt, so much less fabric to deal with.*

"Come here." He pulls on my arm so I bring my head down to him.

I'm so used to men just taking what they want; that one of a kind alpha-dog confidence is precisely what I have always craved. But, with Savage, his inability to be physically assertive makes him all that more demanding with his words, and having him tell me what he wants, what he needs, is getting me just as hot as any other man who has slammed me against a wall to fuck me.

He captures my mouth with his, a searing kiss that blazes and stamps me as his. I know this is just the start of us, but I already feel a tiny piece of my heart slipping away to him.

Reluctantly, he releases my mouth, lingering for several short, hard kisses before finally letting me go.

"Lie back."

I comply with his order, reclining back and leaning on my elbows so I can watch him. After this week of agony, I don't want to miss a moment of the looks he's giving me. I need to see him, his face. I need this.

He leans forward, pushing my thighs open even wider as he slides his hands up and slips his fingers around the thin strip of my soaked thong. My heart races, and my breath comes out in pants. His eyes find mine, and he winks at me.

*Fuck! Why is that so hot?*

I squirm under his heated stare. His eyes locked on mine, he yanks on my panties, ripping them apart. I don't give a single fuck about them. All I want is his mouth, on me, this very second.

His eyes sparkle with wicked intent as he leans even further in, and his breath flutters across my wet flesh, causing my hips to instinctively arch into him. He groans, never taking his eyes off mine, and uses his thumbs to spread me open.

"I've been desperate to taste you since the second you stormed into my office." His calloused thumbs slowly slip up and down, touching, but not where I want it, where I need it.

I don't even care how it sounds.

I can't wait.

I beg. "Please, Savage, just..."

He chuckles, and, without any preliminaries, slides his thick tongue through my folds, from my ass to my clit, flicking it with the tip before plunging it into my dripping cunt.

I bow off the table, dropping my head back, and rocking against him.

He devours me.

Digging my hands into his hair, I pull him closer while he swirls his tongue around my clit in a figure-eight motion that has me making sounds I don't even recognize as human.

He slides one, then two fingers into my pussy, and I clench around him, desperate for something to grip. He moans against my flesh, sending my entire body into sensation overload. I chase my orgasm, the week of pent-up frustrations coiling deep in my core, about to reach a breaking point.

He curls his fingers into my G-spot as he sucks my clit between his lips in a pulsing rhythm that has me spiraling out of control. I finally break, splintering and crying out his name as wave after wave of pleasure roll through me.

*Fuuuuuuuuuccccccccccccccccckkkkkkkkkkkk.*

When my orgasm finally ebbs, I shift up onto my shaking arms and watch as he lifts his head from between my legs, a smug smile on his face.

"Come here." He tugs on my hand until I slide to the edge of the table and lean down to him. He captures my mouth, and tasting my release on his tongue is sexy as fuck.

But, I want nothing more than to know what he tastes like in my mouth right now.

Just as I'm about to slide down off the table and return the favor, the phone on his desk lets out a shrill ring.

"Fuck." He pulls away from me with an apologetic smile and turns to his desk, yanking up the phone. "What?" He barks at whatever poor sap is on the other end. I almost feel bad for him, until my clit throbs and I remember what was interrupted.

His eyes darken, and he turns his computer monitor toward him before glancing over at me. "I'll be right down."

He returns the phone to its cradle before moving quickly to the door. "Danika, I have to go take care of something. Lock this door behind me and don't open it for anyone but me, Gabe, or Byron. Got it?"

I slide off the table onto shaky legs, and my stomach churns. "Savage, what's going on?"

With a quick tug, he yanks the door open, glides through it, and turns back to pull it shut. "Danika, please, just do what I ask."

The concern I see in his gaze makes me shut my mouth when all I want to do is chase after him and find out what's going on. It's not in my nature to sit on the sidelines, but I nod my understanding. He closes the door without another word, leaving me half-satisfied and more worried than I care to admit.

# 13

SAVAGE

*Hurry the fuck up!*
        The elevator seems to take an hour while I wait impatiently, unable to stop myself from looking back toward my office, and her.

I can still taste her in my mouth, and the sounds of her gasps and moans are echoing in my ears. The fantasy I had worked up in my head was nothing compared to the real thing.

But I can't think about that now. Shaking my head, I try to get myself in the game. The shit is hitting the fan downstairs, and I can't be distracted by my dick when I get down there, no matter how hard it is.

When the ding finally sounds and the doors slide open, I move in, punching the button for the main floor and waiting impatiently for the doors to close.

*Jesus, I should have known something like this would happen.*

Things have been going way too smoothly today, and my luck is never this good. It was only a matter of time before my "favor" for Dom was going to bite me in the ass. I just hadn't imagined it would come this quickly.

The ding sounds, and the door slides open to the main floor and the melee ensuing by the main stage. Quickly taking stock of the situation, I see Nora clinging to the center stage pole watching the ruckus as Byron and Gabe try to pull people from the top of the pile.

*Where the fuck are Tubbs and Rocky?*

I can't see my door security guards over the throngs of people. Being so low to the ground has distinct disadvantages. I push my way through the crowd, ordering people back, but don't make it very far before a wall of patrons block my path.

*Shit, I will never get to Byron and Gabe from here.*

A hand lands on my shoulder, and I grab the wrist, twisting my torso to flip the assailant onto their back, but, thankfully, I catch a flash of familiar blonde hair in my peripheral vision and recognize Nora. She somehow made it to me from the stage.

"Savage!" She leans in, pressing herself to my side. "What should we do?"

"You need to get the fuck out of here, go back to the dressing rooms where it's safe, and make sure all the other girls are back there."

Anger flares in her eyes, and she pushes past me and then turns to face me. "Hell no! I may look like a fucking princess, but I'm not helpless. Gabe and Byron need help, so we're going to help them."

I growl at her, but she ignores me, turning back to the crowd and pushing people out of the way, making room for me to get through.

*Maybe Nora is more like Dani than I realized. Nora and I will definitely be having a talk later.*

We finally make it to the epicenter of the melee, and I find Byron and Gabe, each with a choke hold on guys in expensive-looking clothes while another asshole is doing some serious ground and pound on some poor soul on the floor.

Byron catches my eye and nods down to the MMA-wannabe.

I nod my understanding and reach down, grabbing his arm as he brings it back for another swing and twisting it backward. He screams, turning toward me, frantically trying to get the pressure off his shoulder and elbow.

"Fuck! Let go, you motherfucker!" The wannabe thrashes wildly, striking out at me with his free hand, but his fist only grazes my right cheek.

*Damn, that actually kind of hurt. All this time away from the ring must have turned me into a real pussy.*

Byron steps in and wrestles him away from me, and I turn to find Rocky and Tubbs escorting the other two guys toward the front door.

"What the hell, man? That asshole started it!" Mr. Wannabe screams, pointing to the bleeding kid on the floor.

"I don't give a fuck who started it. I don't tolerate this bullshit in my club. You're all banned from the premises, permanently."

More cursing and grumbling comes from various directions, but I push my way through the crowd to the bar. Clarissa and Jamie are waiting for me, wide-eyed and visibly shaken.

"Everything's fine, girls. Did you see what happened?"

Jamie nods. "Those guys were all part of that bachelor party that started out in the champagne room. They were really being assholes, then Byron moved them out here and they just got worse."

I cringe. I knew it would come back to my Dom favor.

*Selling your soul has repercussions.*

"So, what started the fist portion of the evening?" I glance over to see Byron and Gabe shoving the last offender out the door.

"The bachelor grabbed Crystal's leg while she was at the end of the stage. One of his buddies got real pissed and started screaming something about his sister. I have a feeling he is the future bride's brother."

I don't blame the guy for reacting, but this stuff absolutely cannot happen in my club. Ever.

Glancing around the main room, I find things are slowly returning to normal. My employees are doing their jobs, wrangling the clientele and getting the girls back on the poles. I run a tight ship, and I don't let things like this ruin the evening for everyone, at least I try not to.

This is going to cost me.

"Have the waitresses tell their sections the next round is on the house. I will help you man the bar until things calm down." They nod and disappear to tell all the waitresses just as Gabe and Byron make it back to the bar.

Gabe gives me an "I told you so" look.

"Don't you fucking start with me." I grab a bottle of Glen Livet and pour us all a shot. We raise our glasses in unison and down them in one gulp.

"Gabe, go check on Danika. I left her in my office. Keep her company until I'm done down here."

His look holds a thousand questions that I have no plans to answer right now, or maybe ever, but he keeps his mouth shut and walks toward the elevator, leaving me and Byron to get things back to normal.

---

## DANIKA

I down my second glass of bourbon and pour myself another one as I sit at Savage's desk, my eyes glued to the footage of the club on the screen. My heart hasn't stopped racing since Savage disappeared behind the door.

*How the hell does he think he can just bolt out of here like that without explaining what's going on to me?*

I raced to his desk to see what was happening and found myself watching Nora push her way through a throng of men to get Savage to the middle of the crowd. My heart may have stopped when I saw that asshole throw a punch at him, but another glass of bourbon has somewhat steadied my nerves. That, and seeing Savage is okay.

Now, on glass three, my heartbeat is finally returning to normal as I watch him behind the bar. A knock at the door startles me, and I almost drop my glass. Setting it on the desk with my shaking hand, I stand to open the door but wobble on unsteady legs. Maybe I shouldn't have poured that third drink. I kick off my heels and, with a little more balance, make my way to the door, Savage's parting words echoing in my head.

"Who's there?" My voice shakes slightly. Shit, adrenaline does weird stuff to your body.

"Danika, it's Gabe, open up."

I recognize his voice and turn the lock, then open the door and let him in. He offers me a kind smile and closes and locks the door behind him.

"Why isn't Savage back?"

He walks to the bar and grabs a glass, glancing around for something. He finally sees the bottle of Blanton's on the desk, and they flicker to me. He grins. "Bourbon girl, huh?"

I nod and walk over to the desk, scooping up my glass and taking a long pull while I take a seat.

*This night is becoming a hell of a lot more stressful than I had anticipated.*

"Savage has to sort some stuff out at the bar." He grabs the bottle and gives himself a generous pour before dropping down into the chair across from me.

"And you or Byron couldn't do it?" It comes out with a little more snipe than I had intended.

*There goes your mouth again, girl. Rein it in.*

He grins at me. "If you haven't noticed yet, Savage likes to be in control, especially of his business. Getting him to delegate isn't easy."

I sigh and slouch back into the chair I dragged over after Savage left. "Has he always been like this?"

"More or less, but it definitely got worse after the accident."

I glance at the picture frame in the corner of the desk. It's Savage and a young, female version of him smiling widely at the camera with snow-capped mountains in the background. "Did you know her well?" I turn the picture around to face Gabe.

His gaze falls on it, and his smile falters. He takes a long drink from his glass. "Yeah, I did. I grew up with the Hawkes. They're like family to me."

The sadness in his voice rips at me.

I probably should just leave it alone, but the opportunity to delve deeper into Savage with his best friend and business partner is something I can't pass up. "Did you go to school with Savage?"

His eyes flicker to mine, and his smile returns. "We met in first grade. My mom died giving birth to me, and my dad was always so focused on work. I was basically raised by nannies and babysitters. Savage's mom found out my situation and kind of adopted me into the Hawke clan. We only lived two blocks away, so I ended up spending almost every day and night there."

While I don't know much about Savage's family, being adopted into the Hawke clan sounds like it would be pretty amazing.

"What was she like?" I know he knows I mean Star without me saying her name. He returns his stare to the photo, and the corners of his mouth turn up in a sad smile.

"Star was quiet, reserved, brilliant...kind of a perfect angel."

"Is Skye a lot like Star?"

He bursts out laughing, tossing his head back and wiping at

his eyes. "Fuck no. They couldn't be more different. Don't get me wrong, Skye is brilliant, too, but their personalities couldn't have been more opposite. Even if they tried to trick someone by switching places, they always gave themselves away the second they opened their mouths."

"So, Skye is what? A troublemaker?"

He scoffs and drains his glass. "Troublemaker is an understatement." His hand tightens around the now-empty glass, his knuckles turning white as a muscle along his tense jaw flutters.

"What about the other two? Stone and Storm?"

He shakes his head and grins at me. "Boy, aren't we inquisitive?"

I feel my face flush and grab my drink, draining the glass to cover my embarrassment at being busted. "You have something else you want to talk about?"

He leans and sets his empty glass on the desk before reclining in the chair. "I'd rather hear about what's going on with you and Savage." His smirk returns, and he watches me squirm.

*Shit.*

"Well, *that* certainly isn't happening, so, why don't you tell me about them instead?"

He grins. "Fair enough. Storm is kind of the responsible one in the family. She married Ben Matthews several years ago, and they have a little girl, Angelina. She's an architect, and he owns a construction company. She actually designed this building, and Ben's company built it."

I look around the room, taking in the tray ceiling, crown molding, and built-in shelves. "It is a beautiful building."

*For a pussy palace.*

"I know."

"What about Stone?"

He huffs out a laugh. "Well, he is a shining example of youngest child syndrome. Savage's father died when Stone was pretty young, and his mom really babied him. She let him get away with a lot that never would have flown with the big guy around. He's a bit of a loose cannon, but, in the last couple years, he has more or less straightened himself out. I mean, he managed to graduate top five in his law school class."

A knock at the door has me practically jumping from my chair.

Gabe laughs and stands. "Relax, I'll get it."

I glance at the computer screen and don't see Savage anywhere the cameras cover. It must be him. My stomach flip-flops, and my heart practically breaks my ribs as I wait to see him.

Gabe unlocks and opens the door and Savage enters, his eyes immediately searching the room until they find me. I try to stand and wobble as the room spins.

I grab the edge of the desk to steady myself and close my eyes, fighting the churning in my stomach making me feel like I just got off the Tilt-a-Whirl at the State Fair.

*Crap. I'm drunk.*

I vaguely hear Savage say something to Gabe about drinking and a car, but I'm more worried about not falling over right now.

When the room finally stops spinning, I open my eyes to find Savage in front of me, watching me intently, concern written all over his face. His cheek is slightly puffy, scratched, and starting to discolor. He actually did get hit.

"Oh, my God! Are you okay?" I reach out to cup his cheek and brush my fingers gently over the abraded skin.

He captures my hand, pulls it to his mouth, and presses his lips to my fingers. "I'm fine. I'm sorry I had to leave you." His eyes wander behind me to the desk, and I follow his gaze to the almost empty Blanton's bottle.

Turning back, he quirks his eyebrow at me and grins. "Are *you* okay?"

I step toward him, wobbling slightly, and nod, my eyelids suddenly feeling very heavy. He grins and tugs on my arm, pulling me down onto his lap. "You look like you're about to fall over."

*Probably because I am.*

Even though I know I should be an adult and stand up and walk out of here on my own two feet, I settle against him, burying my face in his neck and my fingers in his shirt. He presses his lips to my forehead and murmurs another apology for leaving me.

"Let's get you to bed."

I'm too tired and too drunk to care about the fact that he doesn't know where I live.

Instead, I let the warmth and comfort of his embrace lull me into a contentment I haven't felt in a very long time, if ever.

# 14

SAVAGE

*G*abe returns to my office a few minutes after I arrived. "Is she out?"

I glance down at her, even though I don't need to confirm she's out like a light. She must have drunk half the bottle while I was downstairs. "Yeah, she's gone."

*But she's fucking here! And that's all that matters.*

He laughs and walks over, leaning down to check her face, currently snuggled into my neck, her hot breath teasing my skin. "You want to drop her off at her place before we go home?"

I know where she lives. My deep probing turned up her address easily, but the thought of leaving her after this week of indecision and torture, wondering where we stand, has my stomach leaping into my throat. I shake my head and cuddle her closer to me. "No, I'm not leaving her alone tonight. We're going to my place."

She manages to sleep through the elevator ride to the car,

Gabe transferring her into the back seat, and the entire ride to my condo, her head resting on my lap.

By the time we arrive at my door, I'm convinced I may not be able to wake her up. Gabe holds the door open for me and follows us in, greeting Princess as she jumps at me, trying to climb onto my well-occupied lap. Gabe scoops her up and waits at the threshold.

"You need help with her?" He nods toward Danika.

I glance down and brush a strand of her white-blonde hair back behind her ear. She stirs, snuggling closer to me and tightening her arms around my neck.

"No, we'll be okay. Thanks. You got Princess, though?"

He nods before disappearing and pulling the door closed behind him.

*I don't think I have the energy to concentrate on two girls tonight. I'm glad Princess thinks Gabe is her knight in shining armor and won't even miss me.*

I retreat to my bedroom and into the closet where I manage to reach around her to grab one of my t-shirts and head to the bathroom. Stopping just outside the open door, I cup Danika's cheek, brushing my thumb along her smooth skin and down to her lips, slightly parted with her slow, even breathing.

*Fuck, she's beautiful.*

"Danika, babe, wake up."

She stirs, but her eyes remain sealed and her lips curl down slightly into an adorable frown. A smile spreads across my face.

*She is so damn cute.*

I press my lips to hers softly, trying to wake her the gentlest way possible.

Moaning, she reacts to my kiss, pressing her body into mine and pulling her arms from behind my head to cup my face and tug me to her.

*Guess she's awake now.*

What started out as a tender kiss quickly becomes more, her

tongue slipping against my lips, demanding entrance and response. I capture her face in my palms and slowly pull away, ending the kiss with several slow, sweet presses of my lips. She sighs, and her eyes flutter open, her lazy, alcohol-soaked gaze roaming my face.

"Hey," she murmurs before pressing her lips to mine again and offering me a wide grin.

I grin back at her. "Hi."

She leans back and looks around the room. "Is this your bedroom?"

"Yeah." She takes in the room—the large, low king-sized bed in the center, the black lacquered nightstands and dresser along the walls, the bank of windows on the far wall. When those hazy blue eyes find mine again, I hand her the shirt. "Here, you can sleep in this. There is a new toothbrush you can use in the second drawer on the right. Let me know if you need anything else."

She grins at me, grabs the shirt, and slides off my lap, wobbling on unsteady legs. I reach out and grasp her hip, steadying her. She giggles and glances back at me. "Shit, how much did I drink?"

*Too much.*

"Half a bottle."

Her eyes bug out, and she covers her mouth with her hand. "Fuck, I'm sorry. I don't normally drink that much, at least not liquor."

I laugh and gently squeeze her hip. "Don't apologize, you probably needed it."

She barks out a laugh. "Probably."

She slips from my grip and stumbles into the bathroom. Grinning, I return to the front door and lock it, shutting off the lights as I make my way back to the bedroom. The bathroom door is closed, and I can hear the water running in the sink.

I return to the closet and change into a pair of long, silk pajama pants and a t-shirt.

By the time I emerge a couple minutes later, she's opening the bathroom door. She looks around the room until she sees me and she smiles. My 30 Seconds to Mars t-shirt hangs off her full breasts and stops just south of the spot between her long legs that I am dying to taste again.

*God, she was fucking sweet, and so fucking wet.*

My cock responds, and I hope she's too drunk to notice it straining against the thin silk pants that do nothing to hide it.

She glances down at herself and tugs on the end of the shirt before smiling up at me. "Great shirt, by the way. I love Jared Leto." Turning, she wobbles her way over to the bed, pulls back the duvet and slides in, snuggling down with a giant sigh.

Somehow, even in her drunken state, she managed to figure out what side of the bed I sleep on, though I guess the alarm clock, bottle of water, and stack of books on the right side night-stand kind of makes it obvious.

I get ready in the bathroom and when I exit, I find her face down in the bed, a light snore filling the room. It should be gross, a huge turn off, yet, it isn't. It is fucking adorable.

*I am so screwed.*

This is somewhere I never thought I would be a week ago, joining her in bed. After getting my legs under the covers, I pull my shirt off and toss it onto my chair. I can't stand sleeping in shirts, and she's already passed out, so it's not like she will be looking.

I lie back against my pillow and reach out with my right hand, running my fingers through her soft, blonde hair, which cascades over the pillow behind her. She mumbles something unintelligible and rolls over toward me, settling her head against my chest and wrapping her arm around my stomach.

*Whoa.*

I hold my breath as she snuggles even closer to me, eliminating any space from between our bodies and throwing her leg over mine, my cock hardening again at the brush of her skin.

No one has touched me in over three years.

Well, that's not entirely true. The doctors, a lot of doctors have, and my family, they are huggers, but, not a woman, and not in my bed, and certainly not below the belt.

She settles, and her breathing returns to the rhythmic sound of deep sleep. I slowly release the breath I'm holding and wrap my arms around her, keeping her impossibly close.

Pressing my lips to her head, I inhale and take in the clean smell of her shampoo and the faint lilac scent that always surrounds her.

She smells like summer, and having her here, wrapped around me in my bed, makes me crave everything I never thought I could have again.

*Just don't fuck it up.*

---

## DANIKA

I wake to a wall of heat and hard flesh—under my cheek, my right arm, my hand, between my legs. The crisp, cool scent I've come to associate with Savage invades as I take a deep breath and snuggle in closer to him.

The steady rise and fall of his chest under my cheek is soothing, and I drift toward sleep again.

*Shit. How did I get here?*

Sitting up abruptly, my head spins and a stabbing pain pierces my temples. I wince and scrunch my eyes closed, pressing my palms against my head and praying it stops.

*Shit, what the hell happened last night?*

*What the fuck did I do?*

The splitting pain finally fades to a dull ache, and I open my eyes to a vast expanse of slightly tanned, smooth, muscled flesh.

*Sweet baby Jesus! Savage is ripped!*

I mean, I've seen him before, in the videos, but this is real life, full living color and flesh right at my fingertips.

Sleeping peacefully on his back, his head is turned away from me, and the arm that was wrapped around me is now sprawled out along the bottom of the pillows, exposing his toned bicep. The crisp white sheet is pulled up just under his pecs, and my hand itches to pull it down so I can examine the rest of him.

*This is creepy. I shouldn't be watching him sleep, thinking about touching him while he is completely unaware. Creepy, right? Predatory?*

I clutch my hands together. Anything to prevent me from giving in to my desire to find out if the rest of his body looks like this. He mentioned he works out every day, but I never imagined he could look like this under all those crisp, perfectly tailored shirts. I don't know what I was expecting, but it wasn't chiseled pecs and arms that look like they belong on a professional athlete, not a strip club owner. The video quality was questionable, but this? This is very real.

The temptation to pull the sheet back grows, and my clit throbs looking at him. I bury my face in my hands and take several deep breaths.

*Just go back to sleep.*

If I can just convince myself I'm in control and slip back down into his arm and against his firm body, maybe I can drift off. I throw my leg over his hip, press my lips to his chest, and relish the taste of his hot skin on my tongue.

*God, he tastes so good.*

Instinctively, I press my bare core against him, searching for relief from my pounding need. The loss of my panties last night should be embarrassing, but it makes it so much easier to seek relief this morning.

*Fuck. That feels good.*

I rock my hips slightly against him, burying my face into his shoulder and chewing my lip against the desire to bite into his hot skin.

With a slight shift, his arm circles me, and I whip my head around to look at him as embarrassment over what I have been doing rushes through me. His blue eyes are on me with laser focus. I shift to move away from him, but he tugs me across his body, centering my very wet pussy over his very hard cock encased in silky sleep pants.

"Were you going somewhere?" His voice is thick, gravelly, and sexy as all fuck. If this is how he sounds in the morning, I want to spend every night with this man, and that is a dangerous thought.

"Um, yeah..." I start to make an excuse, to cover for the fact I had just been trying to rub one out on him while he fucking slept.

*God, I am such a pervert. What was I thinking?*

"No, the only place you need to be is right here, with me."

He shifts beneath me, and even though I can't see it, I can feel his abs flexing against me and I can tell they are just as delicious as I imagined they would be. His cock rubs against my core, and I groan, dropping my forehead against his shoulder and biting my lip again.

"Danika, look at me."

I lift my head. His intent is as clear as the blue of his eyes blazing with heat.

"I need to taste you," he whispers. He takes my mouth in a commanding kiss, sliding his tongue between my lips before I can protest the whole morning breath thing. I try to pull away, but he slides his hand behind my head, holding me in place as he ravages my mouth.

His other hand slides down my stomach, and he reaches under the t-shirt and drags his fingers through my wet core. "Mmmm, I need to taste you here," he murmurs before leaning back and grabbing the hem of the shirt. "You need to lose this. I didn't see nearly enough of you last night."

*Oh, sweet fucking Christ! This man...*

Any reservations or embarrassment I may have felt earlier are replaced by the driving need to have him inside of me. Shifting up onto my knees, I slide my pussy along his thick, hard cock, soaking the silk of his pants with my wetness. He moans and closes his eyes, moving his hands to my hips and digging his fingers into my flesh.

A curse tumbles from his mouth before he grinds his teeth together, and the muscle along his jaw ticks. His fingers loosen on my waist and his eyes open. He moves his hands back to the hem of my shirt and slowly pulls it up over my belly. I grab the shirt from him and yank it up and off, tossing it over the side of the bed and onto the floor.

I'm utterly and completely naked, and as his eyes roam my body, the heat and appreciation I find in his gaze makes my heart race and my need for him scream even harder. A growl slips from his lips before he surges up from the pillow and captures my right nipple in his warm, wet mouth, his dark morning stubble scraping against my sensitive breast.

The palm of his hand finds my left breast, and he tugs and tweaks that nipple in time with the assault of his mouth.

His teeth graze along my flesh, and I cry out, grinding down against his cock and clutching him to me. My nipples are a direct line to my clit, and every tug on them sends a fluttering frenzy and rushing moisture between my legs.

*Delicious torture. That is what this is...torture.*

Finally, I can't take it anymore; grasping his hair, I pull him back from my chest. Heavy-lidded eyes burning with desire meet mine, and he leans up to take my mouth in his. His kiss is soft but full of promise. He pulls away, lies down, and urges me toward the top of the bed.

"Get up here. I need you to come for me." He pulls me forward until my knees are on either side of his neck, my dripping cunt positioned directly over his face. Grasping the headboard for balance, I glance down at him and am not surprised in the least to find a satisfied grin on his face.

"God, Dani, you are so fucking beautiful." He lightly kisses his way up my inner thigh, stopping just short of where I so desperately need him, only to repeat the process on the other side. "Absolutely perfect."

He slowly skims his fingertips along my thighs.

I quiver and drop my head against the headboard. "Please, Savage!"

*You're fucking KILLING me here!*

He chuckles, and his warm breath fans across my mound, causing my hips to instinctively push forward, seeking his mouth. When his tongue finally slides across my aching clit, I cry out, grinding down against him, my entire existence now centered on that tiny pulsing spot.

The glide and swirl of his tongue over and around my clit has my legs trembling, and I know it won't take long for him to push me over the edge. When he slides his fingers into me, I clamp down and roll my hips in rhythm with his thrusting.

I'm right.

The orgasm slams into me like a freight train. My entire body spasms, and I can barely hold myself up against the headboard as fireworks explode against my closed eyelids in time with the throbs of pleasure from my clit.

When the orgasm subsides, my legs become useless, and I sag against the headboard, practically smothering Savage under me. Too weak to even care, I shift back over his chest and slide down his body, only one thing on my mind.

## 15

SAVAGE

She slides slowly down my body. With the taste of her release still on my tongue, I capture her mouth, wrapping my arms around her back and dragging her against me until our bodies are practically one. Her breasts press into my chest, and her nipples pebble against my skin as I grope the globes of her ass and squeeze them.

My dick might explode.

Pressed between our bodies, she grinds her hips against my cock and I almost come. It's like I'm fifteen again, fooling around with Jessica Boswell under the bleachers at the high school football field.

It's been so long since someone but me touched me there, the instant her hand circles me, I'm going to blow.

*Don't lose it, Savage.*

She pulls back from my mouth, pressing her lips to my neck and kissing, sucking, and licking her way across my chest.

I close my eyes, relishing the touch of her lips and hot breath floating across my sensitive skin.

Moving slowly down my body, she reaches my stomach, exploring every groove with her tongue. I'm wound so tight, I'm physically shaking trying to control my reaction to her touch.

It's incredible, and, for a brief moment, I'm able to forget I'm different than any other man, that this is different than every other time I've been with a woman in my life.

But, as her hand slides down to the waistband of my pants, the racing in my heart changes nature, from thrilling and electrifying, to chilling and alarming.

A cold sweat breaks out over my body, and my cock deflates.

*She can't know. What just happened?*

I quickly grab her wrist, stopping her just as she moves to slip her hand beneath the waistband.

Her head jerks up, her eyes searching my face for an explanation. Hoping I can do a good job of concealing my fear, I pull her captured hand to my mouth, pressing my lips to the center of her palm and then offer her a what-I-hope-is-convincing grin.

The question in her gaze is evident.

*Shit, say something.*

"This is about you, Danika, not me. Why don't we make some breakfast?" The look of confusion on her face dissipates, but doesn't completely disappear. She watches me intently, waiting for some further explanation. "Aren't you hungry?"

*Let me change the subject. Please, don't push this right now.*

My heart continues to race while she studies me for what feels like an eternity. Finally, she lets out a resigned sigh and climbs up to press a gentle kiss to my lips.

"Starved." She rolls off my body and climbs from the side of the bed. "I want to hop in the shower quick, though. Do you mind?"

*Oh, thank God.*

Shifting up onto my elbows, I watch her perfect ass shake as she walks toward the bathroom. She stops and turns back to me at the door, waiting for my answer.

"No, I don't mind. You shower and I'll start on breakfast."

She smiles, and the moment the door clicks closed, I drop back onto the bed, pressing my palms into my eyes in frustration.

*What the fuck was that, Savage? A beautiful woman wants to touch your very hard cock and you have to stop her?*

The water starts running in the bathroom, and I try to shake off the momentary lapse of sanity.

*Get your shit together, Savage.*

I grab my t-shirt and yank it on before getting in my chair and leaving the bedroom. Thinking about Danika naked and wet in my shower is going to do nothing to help my blue balls.

Forcing myself to concentrate on putting together breakfast, I don't even notice she's done in the bathroom until I hear her soft footsteps on the wood floor of the living room ten minutes later. She appears at the entry to the kitchen in that damn tiny skirt and another one of my t-shirts.

For reasons I can't even begin to fathom, the fact she had to go into my closet to get it doesn't upset me. In fact, knowing she feels comfortable enough to do that without asking actually makes me insanely happy.

*You have it bad!*

She moves into the kitchen and leans down against the center island. I grin at her and the smile she returns lights up her entire face. "Can I help?"

"If you want to grab the coffee pot and some orange juice from the fridge, that would be great."

"On it." She turns to the fridge and yanks the door open. I curse myself for not keeping the juice on the lowest shelf so she would have to bend over to get it.

She meets me at the table and moans when she sees her plate piled high with scrambled eggs, bacon, and toast. "Oh, my God, this looks so damn good! I'm starving."

"You're hungover."

Glaring at me, she digs her fork into the eggs and takes an enormous bite, another moan slipping from her throat. It's the same sound she makes when I have her pussy against my mouth, and my dick hardens remembering this morning. I reach down and adjust it, discreetly, I hope, before returning to my plate.

We eat in silence for a few minutes, interrupted only by an occasional distracting noise from Danika. She has no fucking clue what she is doing to me with those little sounds.

A shrill ring sounds, and Danika looks up at me in confusion. It rings again and her eyes widen. "Shit, where's my purse? That's my cell."

"On the table by the front door." She jumps from her chair and sprints out toward the living room. I hear her answer the phone and her muffled replies to whomever is on the other end of the line. She reappears with her phone in her hand a minute later and offers me an apologetic smile.

"Sorry, that was one of my contacts for a story I am working on. I really needed to speak with him."

"What's the story?" I set my silverware down on my empty plate.

She hasn't spoken much about her work, but I have been reading her articles religiously since the day she charged into my office. They're good. She's an excellent writer and investigator. She doesn't back down from a difficult story, and she certainly isn't afraid to write things some people may not want to hear. She has ethics, and, in this day and age, that's something almost impossible to find. I do worry, though, that some of the topics she tackles could put her in hot water with some unsavory individuals.

"Oh, just something I've been working on for a while. Not sure where it's going, if anywhere, at this point. This contact is essential to my story, but he's a bit squirrelly."

My heart jumps, and unease overtakes me. "What do you mean squirrelly?"

Sighing heavily, she leans her forearms onto the table and looks up at me, her annoyance apparent. "I can't really get into it, but basically he knows his life is in danger by talking to me, and even though I swore I would protect his identity, he has been waffling about getting me the information I need. I have to go meet with him tonight."

"Life is in danger? What kind of shit have you gotten yourself into? You aren't going alone, are you?" The anger in my voice is a little more prevalent than I intended.

She glares at me and shoves away from the table. "I'm doing my job. I can take care of myself, you know."

*Like you did last night?*

Thankfully, I manage to rein in the desire to point out her state less than twelve hours ago. "I'm sure you can, but is it really safe for you to be meeting with this guy in person? Alone?"

She yanks her plate from the table and storms over to me, her lips pressed together into a fierce scowl. Stopping next to me, she reaches out and grabs my plate, turning to the kitchen without a word.

*Yikes.*

She's fuming mad.

I think we're having our first fight.

The plates clank in the dishwasher, and she slams the door shut, finally looking over at me again. "I managed to make it through the past three years at my job unscathed. I don't need you second-guessing me and acting like my goddamn father."

*Acting like her father? Is that really what I'm doing? Maybe I am overstepping my bounds here.*

Her dad died when she was so young, she's had to take care of herself for a long time. Maybe I'm not giving her enough credit.

"Look," I say, holding my hands up in resignation, "I'm sorry if it came across that way. I'm just worried about you. I don't want anything to happen to you."

She closes her eyes and sighs. When she opens them again, the anger is gone, replaced by something I hope is affection. She circles the counter and walks over to me. Leaning down, she places a quick kiss on my lips before backing away. "I'll be fine. I have to go. I'll call you later, okay?"

"Okay."

She disappears around the corner, and the front door opens and clicks shut. Dropping my head into my hands, I groan.

This morning has already been filled with more drama and mindfucks than I've faced in a long time. I've apparently completely forgotten how to be with a woman without having a mental breakdown or pissing her off. This is not a good way to start things with Danika.

It's like the tiny amount of hope I built is already caving in around me.

---

## DANIKA

"So, what the hell happened?"

It isn't a question. It's more of a whiny demand for information from Caroline. I'd barely set foot in my apartment when my phone rang. Ignoring Caroline is useless. Plus, she has a key to my place, and if I hadn't answered, she would probably show up here demanding the rundown of last night's events.

"Well, I went to the club…"

"Did you wear that mini-skirt?"

*Thank GOD, yes!* Wearing that skirt was probably the best decision I made last night. It certainly made for easy access and, hell, I will never complain about that.

"Yes, now do you want to know what happened or not?" I

drop my purse on the couch and head for my bedroom to get changed for my meeting with Paul. He better show up. I don't have time for his wishy-washy promises and zero results.

She sighs, and I know she's rolling her eyes at me. "Ugh, yes, of course, I just wanted to know what you were wearing. Very important information, you know."

"Well, I wore the skirt and that sparkly top." Which I just realized I left at Savage's when I ran out of there this morning.

Caroline whistles. "Damn, you were really going for it."

"I was, and, it worked. I spent the night with him."

Her squeal is so high-pitched and shockingly loud, I have to hold the phone away from my ear so I don't lose my hearing.

"Was it totally amazing? Was his cock as beautiful in person as it was in the videos?"

*I wish I knew.*

I turn on speakerphone and drop it on the bed so I can change while talking. "Uh, yeah, it was."

*Shit.*

I hate lying, but she wouldn't understand. I'm not sure I understand, but I'm not going to complain after what he did to me.

*FUCK, he has an amazing mouth. And a man who only worries about my pleasure is certainly something new and intriguing.*

"You don't sound very excited."

I hate that she knows me so well, and that I'm such a shitty liar. This calls for my best dodging skills. "I'm just in the middle of something, Care. I have to change and go meet a source, and I don't have much time."

"Fine, but call me when you're done. I want a detailed play-by-play. You know I live vicariously through your escapades, and after all the shit you and Savage have gone through to finally get here, I'm entitled to some deets."

Now I'm the one rolling my eyes while I pull out a pair of jeans and yank them on. "Okay, I'll call you later."

By the time I'm changed and on my way to meet Paul, I'm already fifteen minutes late.

*Shit, shit, shit. I hope he's still there.*

He chose the meeting place and Louis Armstrong Park is another ten minutes from me. When he's already so nervous about what he's doing, keeping him waiting is the *last* thing I want to do, but when I try to call him to tell him I'm running late, it goes straight to voicemail. I try several more times before I finally pull into the parking lot and take off toward the remote corner of the park he indicated.

*Please be here. Please be here.*

I arrive a full half-hour after our meeting time and don't see him anywhere. In fact, I don't see anyone. This area of the park is deserted at this hour, and I can see why he would choose it as a safe location. The chances of us being seen together here are slim.

My heart sinks. *I fucking blew it! All because I wanted to blow Savage...and that didn't even happen!*

I'm not prepared to sacrifice my career to put his worries at ease. He overreacted this morning and, for a minute, I was tempted to storm out still pissed at him. But, the genuine concern in his eyes broke my will to remain defiant, and I can't *really* say I blame him for being apprehensive about me meeting a mysterious (to him) source.

He doesn't know Paul. I do. I trust him. Paul is the guy; I know he can get me what I need. He's been working for Abello for ten years in various capacities. As far as I can tell, he never dirties his hands with anything too bad; Abello has a few right-hand goons who take care of his truly filthy work. But Paul is trusted, and that's exactly what I need, someone on the inside.

A loud cough off to my left draws my attention to a stand of trees. I wander over there, trying to look as casual as possible just in case anyone is watching. Paul is leaning against a large tree, smoking a cigarette and looking around nervously.

"You're late."

"I'm sorry. I got hung up. I tried to call."

He drops the butt and smashes it under his boot. "Turned my phone off. Don't want to be tracked."

*Tracked?*

"You think he can do that?" A shrug is his only response. Silence lingers between us and I finally break it. The less time we are out here, the safer we will be. "Do you have something for me?"

He was supposed to be looking for contracts, messages, anything that would confirm meetings and deals between Dunne and Abello.

*Please have it. I really fucking need this.*

He looks to the ground briefly and he shakes his head. "No, couldn't get into the office without being noticed."

"Shit." Why did he need to meet with me if he doesn't have anything? I glance around again, suddenly wary of being out here alone with a member of the mob. "Um, so why did you want to meet?"

He paces in front of me and pulls a slip of paper from his jacket pocket, holding it out to me. I reach out and grab it.

It's a Post-it note...with my name on it.

My throat constricts, and my knees wobble slightly. "Where did you get this?"

His concern-laced eyes find mine. "It was on the floor outside the office. It must have been stuck to something and fallen off."

"Christ...did you hear anyone mention my name?"

He shakes his head but the worry in his gaze tells me it doesn't matter. The fact my name is there at all is enough for me to essentially have a target on my back.

"So, you don't know what he suspects or if he knows I'm looking into him?"

"No, I don't, but you know what this means. You should back off. This is going to get us both killed."

*Back off? Never!*

I don't care if Abello has my name or suspects what I'm up to. I'm not going to stop doing what I know is right. I just need that information to get Abello out of the picture for good. I chew on my thumbnail and pace in front of him. "Do you think you can still get into the office?"

"What? Didn't you hear what I just said? He has your fucking name!"

"And I know what I'm doing, Paul. I'm not giving this up."

He grunts and curses under his breath. "You're fucking crazy, lady."

*He has no idea.*

I laugh. "Maybe I am. So, can you try again?"

A reluctant sigh seeps from his lips. "Maybe. Dom is gone next week and will be taking a lot of the men with him."

My ears perk up and I stop pacing. "Gone? Gone where?"

"Not sure. All I know is something about going to an important meeting."

An important meeting can only mean one thing—something big is coming. Abello controls New Orleans and the surrounding areas completely, and if he's at a meeting, odds are it's to direct his lackeys in some sadistic plot.

"Okay, see what you can find out about his trip and get into that office. I really need this, Paul."

He stands up to his full height and growls low. I'm sure it's meant to be intimidating, but I don't back down from him.

"You need this? What about me, Danika? I'm putting my ass on the line here, and he already knows something is going on. He's probably already on the lookout for a snitch."

"I know you are, Paul. But you are also doing it for yourself and you know it. You need Abello gone before you will ever be able to walk away, so don't pretend this is altruistic. Just be careful and get me the info as soon as possible. The sooner this is over, the better it is for both of us."

His glare bores into me, but I don't look away. He huffs and reaches into his pocket to pull out a cigarette box. "I'll see what I can do." He ambles away from me, lighting up a fresh stick as he goes.

A week. I just need to wait a week and I should have what I need...from Paul, at least.

# 16

SAVAGE

"Wow, it's HUGE!"

Dani's jaw hangs open, and she turns in a circle to take in all of Minute Maid Park. The drive to Houston took over five hours, but it didn't seem that long in the back of the limo. We made good use of the time. When Dani told me she'd never been to a MLB game, I couldn't resist, even with the distance.

"It is, but there are actually parks that are a lot bigger. This only holds about forty-two thousand. Dodger Stadium holds over fifty-six thousand."

She turns to me and grins. "This is awesome. Thanks so much for bringing me."

"Anytime." I wink. "Let's get to our seats before the first pitch." She follows me over to the wheelchair accessible seating area behind and just to the left of home plate and settles into her chair.

I haven't been to a major league game in probably five years. I forgot how much I enjoyed the energy of the crowd. Baseball had been Mom's response to my discontentment with not being allowed to box anymore after Dad died. And while I never loved it the way I did boxing, there's a familiar feeling of euphoria from being in the stadium.

Dani's knee bounces up and down as she looks around the park and the field. The pitcher is on the mound throwing a few pitches to the catcher while the rest of the team is stretching and throwing around a ball for warm-ups. The smell of popcorn and hotdogs is mouth-watering, but all I can think about is how incredible Dani tastes.

The memory of licking my fingers after getting her off in the limo on the way here is crystal clear, and I can still taste her on my tongue. My cock twitches in my pants and, for once, I'm thankful I'm sitting down and my inappropriately-timed hard-on isn't noticeable to the families wandering around the ballpark.

I can't help it. I can't get enough of her.

She reaches down and grabs the bag from the gift shop, rifling through it until she finds the Astros hat I bought her. She pulls it down over her long hair and turns to me.

*Damn. It's ridiculous how hot she looks in that.*

"How do I look?"

A grin spreads across my face, and I reach out and cup her cheek, urging her to lean in closer to me. "Fucking adorable, actually."

I kiss her gently. She smiles against my lips.

She pulls away slightly and offers me a coy smile. "Oh, really? Then maybe I should wear hats more often?"

I take her hand in mine and squeeze it. "That would hardly be fair."

"Oh, why not?"

"Because I already have a hard time controlling myself around you. If you become any more adorable, I will be in serious fucking trouble."

She laughs and grins at me. "Good answer."

*Christ, how can I be this obsessed with this woman?*

The last week has been a whirlwind. We've both been really busy, but we managed to see each other on Tuesday night and have talked on the phone every night we weren't together. Well, maybe "talking" isn't the right word because, God knows, our chats haven't exactly been PG.

The start of the National Anthem alerts me that it's time to stop daydreaming about Dani and pay attention to what's going on around me. She stands, pulling off her hat and putting it over her heart.

I don't know what I expected to hear, but when she starts singing, I can barely stop myself from laughing. She is truly and utterly awful. There isn't a single note sung on key and yet she plows on, at the top of her lungs.

And fuck if it doesn't make me want her more.

She doesn't care about what anyone thinks, not one single iota. In fact, I'm pretty sure if anyone said anything to her about her lack of vocal skills, she'd probably have some witty retort about how she has other oral talents.

*What I wouldn't give to have those talents used on me.*

It's not from her lack of trying. On Tuesday, when she was over, I managed to avoid the situation completely by just making her come repeatedly. If I never gave her reprieve, she couldn't put me in a position to have Deflate Gate again.

She didn't seem to mind. The constant stream of moans, cries, and grunts as she came all over my face let me know I'm at least doing that right.

The anthem ends, and she sits back down and glances over at me. "What?"

"Nothing."

"Then why do you have that shit-eating grin on your face?"

Apparently, I suck at hiding my reaction to her—on my face or in my pants.

"I was just thinking about Tuesday."

She blushes, and the corners of her mouth tip up as she squirms in her seat.

*Yeah, she's definitely thinking about it now.*

I want her remembering how hot it was. It helps distract from the fact I haven't let her touch me. I just need to get my head in the game and be mentally prepared for it next time.

"Ooh, the first pitch!" Her excitement matches that of the crowd as a roar goes up all around us. Our seats are pretty awesome—one of the few perks of being in a chair is the seating at places like this. Although, if it were an option, I would have her down in the first row, right behind the net, so she could experience having a fast ball flying right at her—it's the closest she'll ever get to being on the field.

For me, the exhilaration of being part of the game was only ever matched by being in the ring. I'm sure a lot of that had to do with the fact that I did it with Dad. I spent every possible minute with him at the gym when he was training. He would put me in the ring and "spar" with me, letting me believe I was actually able to put him down with my eight-year-old punch. It wasn't until after his death that I realized what being in the ring really meant to me. Mom tried to keep me out of competition—and she did, I never fought again—but she couldn't keep me from the gym and the bags. It was my tie to my dad, and there was no way she was taking that from me.

Only the accident could do that.

Dani slides her hand over mine. "Hey, you all right?" She's staring at me, concern in her blue eyes.

"Yeah, just thinking about when I used to play. That's all."

She frowns and squeezes my hand. "I'm sorry. Is this too hard, being here? We can go."

"Fuck no, we aren't leaving. There are a lot of things I've had to deal with not being able to do anymore. This is just part of the deal."

## DANIKA

He sounds sincere, but the sadness in his eyes when he watches the field gives him away. This is hard for him in a way I can never even begin to understand. Even after three years, he's still coming to terms with what happened, what he lost, and things like this are going to continue to mess with him emotionally.

*What the fuck do I do?*

I don't know how to handle this "feelings" shit. Dates, in and of themselves, aren't a typical occurrence for me. Usually, it's meet someone at a bar, go somewhere to fuck, repeat. Maybe I should have stressed to Savage how out of my element I am here. I don't want him thinking I don't care, but I have no fucking clue what to say right now.

Returning my attention to the field, I say the first thing that pops into my head. "More women should come to baseball games. The tight white pants are really doing it for me. I don't think they know what they're missing."

His laugh is music to my ears. He reaches over and cups my cheek, turning me to look at him. "Have I told you how much I love that you have no filter?"

I freeze and try to school my features.

*Love?*

*Holy hell.*

My mind tells me to run screaming but I try to use logic.

*It's just a phrase. Relax.*

*He's not saying he loves you.*

*Deep breaths.*

I manage to plaster a smile on my face before he leans in to kiss me. When our lips meet, I remember why I decided to show up at his club last weekend. The electricity between us is palpable, and I melt when his tongue slides along my bottom lip. The memory of our ride here and his expert hands has me squirming for the second time since we sat down.

How Savage can affect me like this is a mystery. No man has been able to hold my attention for this long, certainly not without sex. Despite Mom and Nora's best efforts, they have been unable to get me to want anything more than a good bang. Maybe my logic for avoiding commitment is flawed, but when Dad died, Mom fell apart, and I was left caring for Nora while Mom spent weeks on end in bed. I can't say I blame her. Dad was an amazing man, father, and husband. She didn't know how to function without him.

I can't imagine loving someone that much. I can't say I've even been with anyone I remotely missed when we weren't together— unless it was missing the orgasms they gave me. But Savage has me second-guessing my stance.

His tongue tangles with mine and a thousand ideas of how we can make use of the five-hour drive back flash through my mind. Images of me straddling him and riding him until his head explodes have me gasping against his mouth.

He pulls away, and his eyebrow quirks up. "Dani, we're in public, remember?"

A cheer from the crowd reminds me we *are* very much in public. I need to keep my libido in check, at least for the time being.

I glare at him for his chastisement. He knew what he was doing when he kissed me. He knows exactly what he does to me. He's been doing it since the moment we met. This week has been no exception. Even though we've only seen each other once, the memory of the multiple orgasms he gave me on the couch while we were "watching" NCIS is still very fresh in my mind.

*God, it had to be at least five times.*

I clench my thighs together against my pulsing clit at the memory and grin to myself like a fucking idiot.

He is so damn talented with his mouth, I swear, it's like a drug and I'm already addicted to this man.

It's not just the sexual attraction either—if that was it, the fact he hasn't fucked me or barely let me touch him would have sent me running, again—he's generous, caring, and makes me laugh. Nora was right, although I refuse to admit it to her.

At dinner on Sunday, Nora called me out in front of Mom about me spending the night at Savage's the night before. I don't remember her seeing me at the club, but then again, I don't remember a whole lot considering the amount I drank. Apparently, being carried out completely passed out did not go unnoticed by my little sister.

"So, are you and Savage a thing now?" she'd asked, looking at me with a strange mix of trepidation and interest.

I hissed at her to shut up, but it was too late. Mom heard and immediately jumped on the interrogate-Dani bandwagon. "Oh, a new guy? Who is this Savage?"

With a not-so-subtle eye roll toward Nora as thanks, I decided the best way to answer was with the truth. "He's Nora's new boss."

The fuck-you glare I got from Nora could have frozen molten lava.

"You have a new job?" Mom had asked, innocently enough.

*Talk about awkward.*

Nora managed to dodge the truth by explaining she's working part time and redirecting the attention to my love life. Mom has no idea Nora quit school, let alone what she's doing for a living now. I had to bite my tongue about a thousand times when Nora answered Mom's questions about her classes. Who knows how long she plans on lying to her, but the truth will come out sooner or later. She will have to face the consequences of her deception.

I only shut Mom up after I finally told her things were too new with Savage to know where they were going. She just smiled and said, "I'm just happy you are giving someone a chance." She feels guilty and responsible for the way I live my life. I don't hide things from her, so she knows my interactions with men aren't designed to lead to love and marriage.

We'd left it at that, along with a note from Nora that she doesn't need me leading Savage on and then breaking his heart. I can't say I blame her; that would make work pretty damn awkward for her. And, as much as I hate that she's stripping, the faith I have in Savage makes the reality of it a little more bearable. I don't want her to have to deal with an angry ex of mine as a boss.

At the same time, I can't let what might happen to Nora affect how I handle the Savage situation. It's new and unusual enough as it is. Looking at him now, with that smug smile on his face, I know I don't regret taking this chance.

*It's worth it.*

I return my attention to the game to avoid thinking any more about Savage's skills and his cock. I'm not up on my baseball. In fact, I only understand about half of what's happening on the field.

"Why isn't the second baseman on second base?" I try to show some interest.

Savage chuckles and seems to realize my ignorance of the game. "Because he needs to cover the area between first base and second base. Just like the shortstop covers the area between second and third."

"That doesn't make any sense. The first basemen stays on his base and the third baseman stays on his. Why wouldn't they just have another short stop for in between first and second?"

He laughs and seems to consider my question. "I haven't thought about it really. It's just how it's always been."

"Well, they should change it."

If I can change, so can baseball.

## 17

**DANIKA**

The click, click, click of my heels on the cement floor echoes in the completely empty warehouse. This place is utterly barren. Only dust and pigeons currently occupy the thousands of feet of space that once housed a bustling car assembly plant.

I glance down at my watch.

7:30.

He should be here by now. Turning in a circle, I search for any sign of Paul. He changed our meeting place, texting me this address an hour ago and telling me to come alone. Like I would ever bring anyone to a meet with him, anyway.

I hate to admit it, but maybe Savage is right. Maybe it's a little dangerous to meet with a source alone, in an abandoned warehouse, where there probably isn't anyone around to hear me scream if something happened. But, this is Paul, and despite his efforts during our last meeting to intimidate me, I don't think he would ever do anything to hurt me.

He's the one who contacted *me,* after all. After our last meeting, he could have disappeared and stopped calling me and there's nothing I could have done about it. But he texted to confirm our meeting today. He said he would try again, and I've been anxious thinking about what he might bring me—photos, recordings, paperwork, anything that can tie Mayor Dunne to Abello by more than just supposition.

I do trust Paul, but the Post-it situation has me on edge. That strange feeling of being watched has followed me since our last meeting. The only time I didn't feel it was when I was at the game with Savage. But I can't let my as-yet unfounded unease stop me from my mission.

*I need this more than I need some quality alone time with Savage. And that's saying A LOT.*

We were both so exhausted after the game last night, we fell asleep on the ride home, quashing any hopes I had of limo sex. The lack of sex is almost as concerning as Paul's caginess. He'd better come through.

A clank on the far side of the warehouse near a line of closed office doors breaks me from my reverie, and I squint into the darkness, looking for the source of the sound. A second later, a shadow emerges, moving toward me slowly.

"Paul?" I take a slow step toward the mystery figure.

"Yeah, uh hey, Danika, sorry I'm late." His voice is quiet and shaky.

"Is everything okay?" He approaches me and, even in the dim lighting of the building, I can see he's nervous. His entire body twitches, and he's in constant motion, looking around the warehouse and twisting his hands together in front of his body.

Shaking his head, he runs his hands back through his hair and paces around me anxiously. "No, I think they're onto me."

*Fuck.*

"Why? What happened?"

He squeezes his eyes shut and grimaces. "Shit. They're going to kill me."

"Paul," I reach out to lay my hand on his arm, "tell me what happened." This is bad. This is really, really bad, but I try to maintain my composure so I don't spook him more.

"I was in the office, going through the files, looking for the documentation you need, and Alonzo came in."

"Shit." Alonzo Mattuci is one of Domenico's high-ranking lieutenants, and, according to rumor, is also his top gun. I heard he has over one hundred kills under his belt. If he caught Paul, it would be a death sentence. "Well, you're here, so obviously he doesn't suspect anything. We both know you would be dead if he had."

Paul nods his agreement and chews on his nail. "He asked me what I was doing and I told him I was looking for a purchase order for one of the truck parts because we needed to replace it with the same part. He seemed to buy it and ended up finding the order for me before shooing me out of the office."

This is particularly concerning, considering the revelations of our last meeting. Abello has my name and now Paul's been caught in the office. Still, we are both still alive.

"Did you get anything before he came in? Did you find anything about the meeting?"

Paul glares at me. Maybe I deserve it, but this story is my career. "Yeah, I did."

He hands me a sheet of paper with the name of one of Abello's construction companies across the top. It's a bid on a construction project downtown—the new offices for the district attorney.

"I don't get it. Why is this important?"

His hand shoots out and snatches the paper back, then he turns it around and points to a line. "See this? Look at the numbers. There's no way they could do this job for that amount of money. They were awarded the contract. Do you know what they ended up getting paid? Almost triple what is on here. Who do you think arranged/approved that?"

There's no doubt in my mind it was Dunne. "But, this doesn't prove anything. We can't prove Dunne did anything to get them the contract or that the overpayment was any form of a payoff."

Paul growls. "Do you really think they would put that in writing?"

"Well, no, but there has to be something! Something with Dunne's name on it. Do you think you can try again?" I know full well the position I am asking him to put himself in. "Please, Paul."

Shaking his head, he paces around me. "I don't know, Danika. It's too dangerous. I just don't know if it's worth it."

*Don't back out on me now! Time to pull out my best logic.*

"Paul, when you came to me, you said you wanted to help me because you know what scumbags Dom and his goons are. You said you wanted to help end him and the corruption going on. I can't do that without your help."

"I know," he says with an exaggerated sigh. "I know."

"What about the meeting? Did you find out what it was for?"

Another clank echoes through the warehouse, and Paul and I both whirl in the direction of the sound, searching in the darkness for any threat.

"I'm outta here." He turns and runs off in the opposite direction before I even have a chance to try to stop him.

*Shit, I need to get out of here.*

I turn and walk as quickly as my four-inch stilettos can carry me toward the door and my car, and I reach into my purse for my keys. Heavy footsteps thud behind me, and I pick up my speed until I'm practically sprinting in my Loubs to stay in front of my pursuer.

*Bad shoe choice for a clandestine meeting, Dani!*

Just before I reach the door, a hand lands on my shoulder and I scream, turning toward my assailant with my keys in my hand as a weapon, just like Dad taught me.

## SAVAGE

*Where the hell is she?*

The clock in the corner of my computer monitor does nothing to ease my worry. I clench my fists for the hundredth time today and try to take a calming breath. Danika was supposed to call me when she was done working today. That should have been two hours ago. It is almost nine, and still no word from her, not even a text.

The bumping bass from the music downstairs rolls through the floor and into my body. Normally, it really doesn't bother me, but tonight, it is adding to the headache slowly building in my skull.

She was supposed to call me when she was done so I could pick her up and we could go to my place. I need another night of her in my bed, in my arms. I crave it more than anything these days, even after only having it once.

A knock at the door startles me and I'm hoping it's her and we just somehow got our wires crossed. "Come in."

The door opens, and Gabe walks in with a nervous-looking Nora, who doesn't seem to want to make eye contact with me. I've done my best to steer clear of her, because, frankly, it's a little awkward to be dating her sister and I'm not quite sure where to draw the line between boss and sort-of friend.

"What's wrong?" I instantly sense the tension emanating from Gabe as he stands behind Nora, nudging her forward toward my desk.

Rolling her eyes toward Gabe, she steps forward and holds out her phone. I reach across my desk, grab it, and read the text message she has up on the screen from Danika.

> Car towed. Need ride. Pick me up at 3535 Florida Ave ASAP

<

"What the fuck?" I slam my fist down on my desk, making Nora jump and shrink away. "Why is she down in the Industrial Canal area? And at this time of night?"

Florida Avenue is the dumps, literally. It runs along the canal that connects the Mississippi to Lake Pontchartrain. After Katrina, it became wall-to-wall warehouses and abandoned houses. Now, it's housing for the homeless and crack addicts. They've been trying to clean it up for years, but with little success.

"I don't know," Nora's voice shakes, "I just saw the text when I got off stage. Looks like she sent it about twenty minutes ago."

"Shit." Gabe gives me a knowing look and brushes past Nora to grab her phone from me.

"Don't worry," he says, handing her the phone, "we'll go get her."

Nora eyes Gabe and me skeptically. "Maybe I should just go get her."

"No," I snap at her, and she recoils at my tone. "Look, I'm sorry, just...let me go get her. Okay? I promise I'll make sure she's all right."

Nora considers me for a moment before sighing and shoving her phone into the pocket of the sweatshirt she has on over what I imagine is nothing on her top. Her legs are bare except for a tiny string thong she wore on stage. "Fine, but make sure you let me know when you have her so I know she's okay."

"Of course." She turns, and with a glance over her shoulder back at us, she disappears out the door.

Gabe turns back to me. He knows me well enough to know I'm fuming. "Are you going to be able to calm down on the way to go get her? Or should I go alone? I don't want you coming along and having to listen to you lecturing her the entire ride back."

Making my way around the desk toward the door, I look back at him. "I promise I'll behave."

His laughing snort is enough response for me to know he knows I am full of shit.

*Seriously, what the fuck was she thinking?*

My entire body is a mass of tense muscles as we drive toward the address on Florida. *What the hell was she thinking, going down there at night?* It's like she has no clue she's a fucking magnificently beautiful woman and there might be people out there who mean her harm.

When we pull up outside a dark, abandoned factory building ten minutes later, Danika stands on the sidewalk next to a man in a black security uniform. She scrunches her lips together in obvious frustration when she sees my car. She probably thought going to Nora meant she could keep this from me.

*Not fucking likely.*

I roll down my window. "Danika, get in."

She glowers at me and storms around the car. When she slides into the backseat next to me, she keeps herself as close to the opposite door as possible. The security officer approaches my window and leans down.

"Your girl here was trespassing on private property. I didn't call the police this time, but I had her car towed before I found her. You can pick it up from Melvin's Towing in the morning."

"Thank you, sir. I appreciate your help." I shake his hand, and we pull away with not a peep from Danika the entire time.

I turn to face her and watch her in profile. Her eyes are narrowed as she looks out the window at the dingy riverside neighborhood.

"Care to explain what you are doing down here, in the middle of the night, alone?" I keep my voice as neutral as I can, not wanting to instigate an argument but needing an answer from her for why she would do something so stupid.

She doesn't respond. In fact, she doesn't acknowledge I've said anything to her at all.

"Silent treatment?"

We turn off Florida on the way back to my condo.

"Gabe," she says, her voice perfectly calm and unwavering, "can you please drop me off at my place?"

*Oh, I don't think so.*

"No, Gabe, take us home."

Her head whips around, and she gives me a blazing look. "Stop it, Savage. I was doing my job. I don't need you to take care of me. Haven't we had this conversation before?"

Swallowing my frustration, I take a deep breath. "Apparently, you do, and you are coming home with me so we can discuss this without an audience."

Glaring at me, she slumps back into her seat and then turns her attention back to the street whizzing past us.

I thought the cold shoulder in the car was bad, but the silence of the elevator ride is stifling. Gabe hasn't said a word and refuses to make eye contact with me. Seems he's just as pissed with me as Danika. When she storms past me off the elevator and flings my condo door open without looking back, I know I'm in for a long night, and not the kind I had been hoping for.

Gabe pauses outside my door, glancing back at me with a raised eyebrow. "You plan on continuing your lecture when you get in there?"

"What the fuck is that supposed to mean?"

He leans back against the wall, crosses his arms over his chest, and smirks at me. "Seriously, Savage? Do you not know what you sounded like back there with her? You were like a father scolding an errant child."

*That's exactly what she said to me last weekend.*

"Bullshit, she knows I'm just worried about her, trying to protect her."

"I'm not so sure she sees it that way. You haven't been together very long, and I get there is this weird chemistry between you two, believe me. I've seen it and felt it, but you can't try to control her, man. She isn't Becca."

Bringing her up is a low fucking blow.

"Of course she isn't. Why would you even mention her?"

"Because it has been so fucking long since you've been with anyone, you seem to have forgotten that not every woman is meek and in need of protection. She was everything Danika is not, and if you don't realize that and start acting like you have some fucking respect for her, you *will* lose her."

With another accusatory look, he turns and opens his door, disappearing without another word.

*Well, fuck. What the hell am I supposed to do with that?*

He's not wrong about Becca. She was always so easy, because she never spoke up, never questioned me, or anyone else for that matter. Until the day she left me, I don't think she had ever done a single thing for herself because she really wanted it, or needed it. I can't fault her for ultimately doing what she felt she needed to do. The way she did it sucked. I mean, really, really, fucking sucked. But, in the end, I was stronger because of it; I am stronger, and so is Danika.

Entering the condo, I'm greeted by silence.

*Where's Princess?*

I check the kitchen first, with no sign of either of them, and then move to my bedroom.

Nada.

Returning to the hall, I pause and listen for any movement. I return to the living room and look around.

*Where the hell are they?*

That's when I notice the patio door is cracked. I make my way over there slowly, until I can see her sitting in the dark on one of the lounge chairs with Princess on her lap.

I slide the door open and approach her with more than a little trepidation.

She knows I'm here. No way she didn't hear the door, but she doesn't react to my presence. Princess, on the other hand, jumps from her lap onto mine the second I stop next to the lounge chair facing Danika. She's facing the water and doesn't even acknowl-edge my arrival.

Sliding my fingers through Princess' silky fur, I take a steadying breath before I start. "Danika, I'm sorry. I didn't mean to be such a dick."

She scoffs, never looking away from the water.

*I'm so screwed here. I just need to tell her the truth.*

"You may not believe me, but I'm just worried about your safety. That's it. It has nothing to do with your capability as a reporter. I think you are fucking brilliant at your job. It's just, I know you have to deal with some unsavory characters at times, and I don't want anything to happen to you."

She finally moves her eyes to meet mine, and I see the anger still lingering there, along with affection, which makes this even worse.

"You have to stop treating me like a child just because you don't have control over everything in your life anymore."

I recoil at her words. The truth fucking hurts, and she has managed to see through my bullshit in a matter of weeks. "I'm that obvious?"

Dropping her head back against the chair, she stares up at the night sky and frowns. "Truth be told, Gabe and I had a bit of a talk last weekend."

*That traitorous asshole!*

"Oh, really? And what did my so-called best friend have to say about me?"

"Nothing I hadn't already figured out for myself. I asked him if you had always been like this."

She doesn't need to explain what "this" is. I get it. I'm a fucking control freak.

"And what did he say?"

Turning her head back to me, she gives me a sad smile. "He said you got worse after the accident."

*Did I?*

There's no denying I'm demanding by nature. I don't settle for second best, in anything. I'll devote any and all of my power to ensuring I get the best out of people, and sometimes, yeah, it makes me come across like a real grade-A asshole. But have I gotten worse since the accident? I don't feel like I've changed, but self-exploration isn't exactly my thing either.

"Well, if Gabe says it, then it's probably true. He knows me better than anyone."

She slides forward in the chair until she is sitting cross-legged in front of me and takes my hand in hers, sliding her warm palm along mine. "He loves you, and he didn't say much, even though I may have pried...a little."

I grin at her admission. "Why were you prying?"

A sheepish smile spreads across her face. "Because I wanted to know everything about you." She stands and reaches down to grab Princess from my lap. After setting her down on the deck, she slides onto my lap and wraps her arms around my neck. "Because I knew I had already fallen in lust with you and I needed to know who you really were, at your core, and he is the best person to ask."

*In lust with me?*

*I'm not exactly sure what that means or what I'm supposed to do with that.*

Her warm breath skates across my ear as her lips skim my cheek. I wrap my arms around her, pulling her fully against me and turn my head to her. "Aren't I the best person to ask?"

"Probably." Her reply barely leaves her lips before I cover them with mine. The need to claim her, to prove to her and myself we are meant to be here, like this, overwhelms me. I need her to realize everything I have said, or done, has been because I care about her, more than I probably should at this point.

She responds in kind, curling her fingers into my hair and sucking my tongue into her mouth to tangle with hers. She's undulating against my very hard dick and moaning in a way that has me almost coming on the spot. I can't get her off the deck and into my bed fast enough, but as I pull away from the kiss to move to the door, Princess jumps up and shoves her way between us.

I drop my forehead against Danika's, both of our breaths coming out in short pants. "Shit, she needs to go out."

She smiles and kisses me slowly before she slides off my lap. "Go quick. I'll meet you in the bedroom in five minutes. I need to take a shower anyway."

"Five minutes...then, you are mine."

Turning back to me from the doorjamb, she grins. "I already am yours."

My heart somehow manages to make it up into my throat.

*Fuck, I hope she means it.*

# 18

## SAVAGE

𝒯he room is dark when I enter. A sliver of moonlight shining on the bed illuminates Danika's perfect body —her perfect, naked body.

My cock reacts, hardening while my heart races uncontrollably. I need to get my shit together. We can't have a repeat of the first night she stayed over.

I've managed to avoid the situation again, too afraid of a repeat performance, or should I say non-performance, to even risk letting her get that close. But tonight, all I want to do is bury myself in her—everywhere.

No matter what I have to do, it's happening tonight.

I can't wait any longer. Jerking off just isn't cutting it anymore.

The moonlight makes her pale skin glow, and she crawls across the bed until she's lying horizontally across it. While I approach the bed, she never looks away from me.

She grins at me, and even in the darkened room, I can see the desire burning in her eyes. I never thought a woman would look at me like that again, that a woman would ever *want* me like that again.

*Thank fucking God for small miracles, or huge ones, in this case.*

"Hurry up." Her whisper carries across the short distance between us, and I realize I stopped moving halfway to the bed.

"Impatient, aren't you?"

She giggles and rolls onto her back, hanging her head over the edge of the bed and looking at me upside down. "Aren't you?"

*Hell yes!*

By the time I make it to bed, she's back on her stomach, watching me with anticipation. She scoots back onto her heels to give me room to join her, and her breasts sway hypnotically. I can barely take my eyes off them as I climb onto the bed. The heat in her stare gives me goose bumps.

*She looks like she wants to devour me and fuck if I'm not ready to let her.*

The moment I settle in bed against my pillows, she's on me, swinging her legs across my hips and straddling me.

I don't even have time to get my clothes off. She hovers with her lips an inch from mine and stares into my eyes. "You're going to stop being so overprotective, right?"

The heat of her core scorches my cock. She rubs against it, and I can't even pretend I'm not on the verge of coming in my pants.

"Huh?"

*Did she ask me something?*

She brushes her lips against mine softly, barely touching them before pulling away.

Her words finally register in my lust-hazed brain and I manage a quick, "Yes, of course," before capturing her mouth in a full-blown, claiming kiss.

I need her to know I'm sorry for being overbearing. Sort of. I won't apologize for being worried about her, but I will try my best to keep my overprotective instincts under control.

I need her to know I'm not going to let her go. I'll do anything to make this work with her.

I need her to know she's mine. I just pray she feels the same way.

While our mouths and tongues thrash together, her fingers deftly unbutton my shirt. She yanks it from my pants and pushes it down off my shoulders. She pulls away long enough to let me free it off my wrists and toss it across the room.

She scrapes her nails down my bare chest and fire blazes through my body.

*Fuck yes!*

Maybe it's because we just had a fight, a real one; or maybe it's because we've waited so long for this moment. Whatever it is, the air is thick with unspoken words and I know tonight is important.

To me.

To her.

To us.

We need this. We need to solidify the relationship in a very tangible way, and it's my fault we haven't already. I'm not stupid. I know she's frustrated with my continued avoidance of her touch. She has to know something's up, but how the fuck can I tell her the last time she tried to grab my dick I fucking deflated like a Macy's parade balloon after it smashes into a power line?

*Stop thinking about it, asshole.*

Her mouth on my collarbone breaks my brief moment of self-doubt, and she slips the button of my pants open before sliding the zipper down. I didn't intend to go commando today, but I forgot to throw my boxer briefs in my gym bag this morning.

Thank fuck I was forgetful. It got me to this moment so much faster. She slips her hand into my pants, and I hold my breath.

When her fingers finally cup my cock, I'm momentarily in nirvana. I barely feel the bang of the back of my skull against the wooden headboard. The only thing in my world is the feeling of her warm hand on my flesh.

She squeezes me gently and hums appreciatively in my ear.

"You have *no* idea how long I've been waiting to do this." Her husky voice is deeper than I've ever heard it, and fuck if it doesn't sound like pure, unadulterated lust. For me.

I don't know how the hell that happened, and now is not the time to question it. Not when I have a woman's hand around my cock for the first time in over three years—my hard cock. *Thank fuck!*

"Jesus!" I bite my lip to keep the string of profanity lingering there from erupting when her gentle squeezes and strokes push me almost to the point of no return.

*There's no way I can have sex with her. I won't last ten seconds.*

I reach down and grab her hand, stilling it just before she's about to slide her thumb across the wet head of my cock. With my other hand, I cradle her face and tilt it up to find the expectant question in her blue eyes.

Before she can ask, I lean down and kiss her, sliding my tongue deep into her mouth and meshing it with hers. She groans and sucks on my tongue while trying desperately to move her hand on my dick. I hold her still and break away from the kiss.

"That's exactly what I want you to do, Dani."

A blow job. I can handle a blow job.

Just thinking about having her wet mouth suctioned around my cock has me throbbing under her palm.

I know she feels it. The grin spreading across her face and the shimmering desire in her eyes confirms she knows exactly what she is doing to me.

## DANIKA

*Oh, thank GOD!*

I'm finally going to taste him, take him in my mouth and work him up into a frenzy like he does to me all the time. And when we're done, I'll give him a little breather before I take what I so desperately need—his cock, inside me, filling and stretching me.

A shudder of anticipation rolls through my body. I scoot down his long frame.

This would be a hell of a lot easier if he didn't have his pants on, but I'm not about to wait.

Something about tonight has my already dangerously impatient libido racing to frantic levels. Maybe it was the argument. I guess this is kind of make-up sex.

I've never had make-up sex before. That would require actually having someone to make-up with. This relationship stuff definitely has its drawbacks. I hate having to second-guess my actions because of what Savage may think—not that I *have* done that. But, after tonight, I kind of get it. I know he cares and worries, and I know I won't be able to get that out of my head.

I care too damn much already.

And I'm going to show him how much.

His cock is hot and hard in my hand, and I stroke it from root to tip, watching as more precum leaks from the slit. My mouth waters, and I lick my lips. I've been fantasizing about what he would taste like since the moment I walked into his office.

But I can't dive right in. That won't do at all.

Fair is fair, and Savage relishes in torturing me with agonizingly slow attentions when he gets me off. There's no way in hell I'm going to let him off that easily.

*Instant gratification is not in the game plan tonight, Savage. Sorry.*

Looking up, I meet his intent gaze. The struggle in his eyes gives me a satisfaction I never expected.

*I'm already getting to him and I've barely touched him.*

*Oh, Savage, you have no fucking idea what you are in for.*

I don't bother to hide my grin from him as I descend on his cock. The tip of my tongue meets the sensitive flesh just below the bulging head. He gasps. His body tenses under me, and he digs his hands into my hair.

*Fuck yes.*

He groans when I slide my tongue down his entire length, wetting it and swirling the tip in slow, methodic circles.

"Christ, Dani..."

His head falls back against the headboard, and his grip on my hair tightens.

My slow torment of him continues as I slip my tongue along first one side, then the other, but never reaching the tip. He shifts slightly under me, and although I know he can feel what I'm doing to him, I wonder if he's capable of thrusting up into my mouth. He hasn't done it, so I'll assume he can't. It must be utter agony to not be able to take control like I know he wants to.

Guilt forms in the pit of my stomach. I can't torture him any more than what he has already suffered.

I lick and suck my way up to the head of his cock and pause momentarily, looking up at the strained cords in his neck.

*Fuck, that's hot. Neck porn at its finest.*

He drops his head down, and his eyes meet mine. He needs this just as much as I do.

Without looking away, I finally take him into my mouth completely, sucking him down as far as I can go.

The sound he makes is more animal than human. It only spurs me on. I slip back up his cock, my tongue gliding along the underside of his flesh the entire way up.

I pause to pay special attention to the sensitive head, sucking at it while his eyes bore into me. With a grunt, he pushes on my head, urging me back down.

His throbbing flesh tastes fucking fantastic, just like I knew it would. I don't fight him. I let him guide me back down his shaft until he hits the back of my throat. I swallow, and a litany of profanity spews from his mouth. He pushes even further, and I tilt my head, opening my throat and accepting all of him.

"Fuck, Dani!"

My name on his lips, in his strangled screams, is like a prayer and I take full advantage. I swallow around his cock and pull back, reaching out and twisting my hand around the wet flesh as it exits my mouth.

I suck and glide along his length—no longer concerned with dragging things out, just frantically needing to witness his release, to finally taste all of him.

His cock swells in my mouth. It won't be long.

"Babe, I'm gonna come..."

I know he's warning me so I can pull away, but there's no fucking way he's coming anywhere but down my throat or in my pussy tonight. I hum around him and he tenses.

"Fuck..." His hands tighten and pull on my hair and jets of cum shoot into my mouth and down my throat while I continue to suck and jerk his cock. I swallow around him, which only seems to draw out his orgasm.

The tug on my hair and look of pure bliss on his face make my clit pulse and the desire to reach between my legs and touch myself is powerful, but I resist.

I would much rather have him there.

And, knowing Savage, he's going to repay this favor in my favorite way—with that gloriously talented mouth of his.

When his cock finally stops pulsing, I swallow what's left in my mouth and slowly lick his over-sensitized flesh to get every last drop left there. He shudders and grabs my shoulders, jerking me up until I am face to face with him.

His glassy gaze is precisely what I've longed to see, what I've longed to be the cause of.

"Jesus, Dani. That was..." He shakes his head, and a grin spreads across his face. "That was fucking incredible."

I return the grin and lean in to kiss him, stopping a hairsbreadth from his lips. "Good. That was the intention."

Our mouths collide. When he slips his tongue along my lips, I open to permit him entry into my mouth, and I know he can taste his release there. It doesn't stop him, and I grind down against his semi-hard cock.

He breaks away and licks his lips, cupping my face between his hands. "Time for me to return the favor."

# 19

## DANIKA

"Tell me again why we're up at the ass crack of dawn on a Saturday to go to the gym?"

*Shoot me now.*

I put the car in park and look over at Nora. She's always so fucking nosy. "Because, I need to get in a better habit of going."

"Yeah, but why so early? You never get up early on weekends."

I'm not going to tell her the real reason. Nora made it very clear she doesn't want to know about my relationship with Savage, and I respect her desire to stay out of it. But I needed someone to come with me, to make my stalking look less obvious. Having a plausible excuse to be here when I know Savage will be here is essential to me maintaining my cool, calm, I'm-in-control appearance when, in truth, I'm absolutely crazy for this man.

In the weeks since the baseball game, I haven't been able to stop thinking about how the accident changed Savage's life. I didn't know him before, and I realized I haven't even bothered to try to find out more about what he does outside of spending his time with me.

From what I've discerned, he was a pretty good athlete before the accident. I know he played baseball as a child and in high school and continued to box, despite his mother's concern. The way he handled himself when the fight erupted at the club a couple weeks ago was clear evidence of his continued athleticism and that got me curious.

After spending last night with Nora, I remembered he would be here this morning for his usual basketball game. Curiosity won out. Nora doesn't need to know we are really here so I can see him on the court and see if him playing is as hot as I think it will be.

"Because, if we are here early, the gym isn't as crowded and we can get through our workouts without being gawked at and annoyed."

*Sounds plausible.*

She rolls her eyes and huffs before throwing her door open and grabbing her gym bag from the back. Savage's car is a few spots down from us, but I doubt Nora notices it. She's probably used to seeing Gabe's car at the club instead of Savage driving, but I know Gabe's out of town this weekend and Savage is riding solo.

I follow her into the building and look around. There's no one at the front desk and, luckily, the place is basically deserted. Of the few people lingering around, no one even looks at us. I hadn't really thought this out. I'm not even a member of this gym. I guess I figured I would ask for a trial membership or something when I got here. This saves me the trouble.

"So, where to?" she asks, looking to me for direction.

There's a large hallway to our right, and I hear yelling and other noises from down the corridor. It looks like the most promising place to find the court. "Um, I'm not sure. Let's go see what's down there."

*Hopefully, it's Savage.*

I want to see him in action.

She looks annoyed but follows me anyway. The closer we get to the end of hall, the more nervous I become.

*Shit, what if he's mad I'm here?*

We reach the open doors to a large gymnasium. I find Savage on the court instantly. He's in a different chair than usual. This one is lower to the ground and the wheels are pitched out at an angle. He flies down the court, while simultaneously dribbling the ball. When he reaches the basket, he maneuvers around another player and easily makes his shot.

The cut-off shirt he's wearing allows me an amazing view of his arms.

*Sweet Lord.*

His muscles ripple and bulge with every move he makes and it's sexy as fuck. Those arms have been wrapped around me, held me in place while he devoured my pussy…

"Huh? Savage is here. Imagine that." Nora's snide comment breaks my momentary lapse into my sexual daydream.

I restrain myself from rolling my eyes at her. "Well, look at that. He is." I lace my voice with as much sweetness and surprise as possible, but I know I'm not fooling her. She knows me too well.

"Did you really drag me here to stalk your boyfriend?"

*Yes.*

"No. Of course not. It's just a happy coincidence that he has his basketball games on Saturday mornings." She narrows her eyes and crosses her arms. She's pissed, and maybe she has a right to be, but there's no harm in watching, even for her. Although, I guess watching your sister ogle your boss could be a tad uncomfortable.

"I'm going to find a treadmill. Enjoy your stalking."

I lean against the doorjamb and watch the game continue. I

don't really understand the rules. Like baseball, I never watched or played basketball, so I'm not really following the game. That's not why I'm here.

My eyes follow Savage.

He's fucking impressive. I never really thought about the upper body strength it takes to do what he does, but it's evident on the court. All the players are surprisingly agile in their chairs and all of them exude a competitive spirit I never expected. I guess I've been naïve and probably a bit uneducated in my belief that people like Savage lose all this with an injury like he has. It doesn't appear to be slowing him down at all. I feel like a real asshole, again, for the way I ran when I found out he was in the chair.

I know he's forgiven me for the way I acted that day. He's more than demonstrated his desire to make this work between us, despite my reservations, and I feel the same way.

Still, we haven't moved any closer to actually sealing the deal, and my frustration is growing, especially when I see him like this. While blowing him is pretty fucking incredible, and he never fails to get me off, multiple times, every time, it isn't enough and I've been avoiding it like the elephant in the room.

Instead of focusing on the problems in our relationship, I've been taking my mother's advice and enjoying the things that do work, which is basically everything else. He makes me happy. The problem is, he also makes me hornier than a dog in heat.

The play on the court ceases. He moves to a row of benches and grabs a towel and water bottle before turning toward the door. His eyes flash when he sees me, and then, a smile spreads across his face.

## SAVAGE

I felt her gaze on me before I saw her. The moment the game ended, my eyes found hers and my heart began racing even harder than it had during the game. I stop in front of her and stare up into her beautiful face.

*How can I miss her so much when it's only been one day?*

"Hey, what are you doing here?"

She smiles and pushes herself up off the jamb. "Oh, Nora and I came to work out."

I let her obvious lie skate. She's a terrible liar, but I don't care why she's really here. I'm just so damn happy to see her.

"I missed you last night." The words are inadequate to describe what I was really feeling at the club. With Gabe gone, I was forced to stay all night. I spent the vast majority of it thinking about Dani and wondering why I was so stupid and told her not to come spend the night. Over the last several weeks, I've grown accustomed to coming home and having her in my bed.

The sense of contentment I feel when I see her under the sheets, waiting for me, is only broken by the unshakable fear that she'll see my scars or I'll have another failure to launch. Keeping her from knowing the truth has been exhausting, and I don't know how much longer I can keep it up.

"Me, too." The sincerity in her reply and heat in her gaze tells me all I need to know. She's no longer fighting this thing between us. She's finally resigned herself to that fact that being in a relationship isn't a bad thing.

"Did you catch any of the game?"

Her eyes spark. She nods. "I did. I have to say, I'm impressed."

*Impressed?*

"Oh, really?"

She leans down and presses her lips to mine briefly before pulling away slightly. "Oh, yes. In fact, it was sexy as hell watching you play. I wish I could join you in the locker room right now."

*Holy shit.*

Never in a million years did I contemplate that her watching me play a simple game of basketball would affect her like this, but her body language matches her words. She wants it. Me. Badly.

"Well, as wonderful as that sounds, and fuck, you have no idea how much I want to take you up on that, we would have an audience." I tip my head toward the rest of the guys who are slowly making their way toward us, and the locker room, and then take a swig of my water.

"I don't see that as a problem."

I choke on the liquid in my throat and cough uncontrollably at her words.

*Christ. Public sex? And here I didn't think she could get hotter.*

She has the audacity to laugh at my reaction, and she doesn't apologize. The guys reach us, and I have to take a deep breath to steady myself before introducing them.

"Guys, this is Dani. Dani, these are the guys." She smiles at them and gives them a little wave and they all do the same before she moves out of the way and they disappear down the hall.

When they're gone, she moves closer to me and leans in. "So, it seems we are alone."

"For now, but I'm sweaty and disgusting and you are here to work out." I grin at her, and she does the same, stepping back from me.

She knows I know she's full of shit about her reason for being here. She came to see me, whether she wants to admit it or not, and that is the biggest fucking ego boost she's ever given me.

"Give me twenty minutes and I'll be ready to go."

"That will be a pretty short workout."

"Better make it count, then," I call over my shoulder as I pass her on my way through the door.

The moment I enter the locker room, they descend on me.

"What the fuck, Savage? How come you never mentioned her?"

They all watch me expectantly. I realize I have no answer to their questions.

*Why didn't I tell any of my friends about Dani?*

Other than Gabe and the family, I haven't spoken to anyone about her and that suddenly seems very odd. I'm sure it's a product of the lingering fear that she'll change her mind and run. It's a lot easier to deal with something like that happening when no one knows about her in the first place.

After Becca ended our engagement and I returned home, the friends who checked in with me always wanted to talk about it, anything to avoid talking about the accident or my injury. How discussing my torpedoed engagement was any better is beyond me, but it was painfully obvious the only way to avoid discussing it was to avoid talking to anyone who knew about it. So my old friends fell pretty much to the wayside and I concentrated on what I could control—my work, the business.

Now, the thought of going through that again, of having to explain to my friends why my relationship failed, seems too painful to comprehend.

"Because it's still pretty new, guys. We've only been together a couple weeks."

"Yeah, but, dude, she's fucking gorgeous!"

*No shit.*

She's fucking gorgeous, funny, sexy as hell, and willing, and yet, I can't get it together enough to actually have sex with her. I should just turn in my man card and be done with it.

"She is amazing. Hopefully it will work out." I don't know how else to respond to them. These guys get it. They know the kind of problems paralysis can cause and I'm sure at least half of them aren't even able to get it up, so I should feel lucky.

But, instead, I feel like an asshole.

I have a sort-of working cock and can't use it. I need a long, cold shower to get my head together before I see Dani again. If I go home with her like this, it will surely be a repeat performance.

Her showing up here was a huge step forward. I can't risk anything setting us back.

## 20

DANIKA

*M*y stomach churns and bile rises in my throat as we pull into the driveway of Savage's mother's house.

Sunday dinner with the Hawkes...somehow it didn't seem so intimidating when he asked me to come a few nights ago, but now, staring at the place he grew up, every potential disaster waiting for me inside is running through my head at Olympic sprinter speeds. Even after being together for months, I don't feel ready to meet the Hawkes.

Savage squeezes my hand from next to me in the back seat.

"You okay? Why do you look like you're about to be sick?"

"Probably because I might blow chunks right here in the back of Gabe's car."

Gabe shifts the car into park and looks at me over his shoulder with a frown. "You better be joking. There will be no chunk blowing in the Mercedes, please."

Savage chuckles and kisses the back of my hand. "She's fine. She's just nervous, although I have no idea why."

"Seriously? No idea? You think meeting the Hawke women isn't just a little bit intimidating?"

Gabe laughs and opens his door. "Well, she's got you there. I'm just glad I'm here for the show." He climbs out, leaving Savage and me alone in the car, and me feeling even worse than I did ten seconds ago.

"Why does he have to be such a prick?"

Laughter fills the car and Savage reaches out to pull my head over to him. He kisses my forehead and then my lips. "Relax. It will be fine. Just remember, Skye will bait you. Don't take it and you'll be fine."

I take a deep breath and nod before I pull away and open my door to climb out. By the time I make it around to the other side of the car, Gabe already has Savage's chair out and Savage has just settled into it.

A bang draws my attention to the front of the house and a woman I can only assume is Mrs. Hawke is practically running down the front walk toward Gabe. He meets her halfway, and she throws herself at him, wrapping her arms around him and burying her face against his chest.

"About goddamn time. Have you been avoiding me, boy?"

She pulls back and looks at Gabe, who offers her a smirk before kissing her gently on the cheek.

"Of course not, Ma, I've just been busy the last month."

*Ma?* I look to Savage, and he shrugs his shoulders before closing the car door.

"He was here all the time growing up. She's really the only mother he's ever had."

My heart aches a little picturing a little blond boy with no mom, but seeing Mrs. Hawke and Gabe together now, there's no doubt he received whatever he needed here, if not at home.

Savage and I make our way up the walkway as Gabe extricates himself from Mrs. Hawke's stranglehold.

"Oh, and you must be Danika!" She steps over to me and embraces me in a tight hug I certainly am not expecting.

*Is this normal? The only people I hug are Mom, Nora, and Caroline...and now Savage.*

"Uh, hi, nice to meet you, Mrs. Hawke."

She pulls back and releases me. "Don't call me Mrs. Hawke. That makes me feel all of my fifty-five years. Call me Antonia." With a smile, she pushes past me and leans down to hug Savage. "I'm so glad you could make it and managed to convince Danika and Gabe to come."

"Me, too, Mom."

Antonia ushers us into the house, and the smell of sautéed garlic hits me, making my mouth water instantly. Whatever she's making smells amazing. I can't wait to taste it, and get my hands on a glass or three of wine. Savage assured me there would be wine. God knows I need it.

The Hawkes' living room is filled with overstuffed furniture and knickknacks on bookcases. It's not exactly what I expected given what Savage's place looks like, but I suppose with his anal-retentive orderly nature, he could never stand to live in a place like this as an adult.

I'm ushered into a chair, and Savage tells me he'll be right back and disappears into another room with his mother. Not exactly sure what to do, I twist my hands nervously on my lap and look around. My eyes land on a row of pictures along the mantle. I get up and move over to them.

They are a beautiful family. The earliest pictures show Savage's dad with all the kids and Antonia. They clearly get their dark hair and olive complexions from their mother and the striking eyes from their father. As I move down the row of photos, Sam Hawke disappears and the kids are older and look even more alike.

The three girls look like they could be triplets in some of the later photos, except one is slightly older and, even though I haven't met any of them, my eyes wander to one of the twins automatically.

*Star.*

I don't know why I know it is her. She looks exactly like Skye, but there's something in her expression, her smile, that is warming and joyful in a way that the other sister's lacks. Savage doesn't talk about her much, and I don't pry. Other than what he told me about the accident and what I managed to pull out of Gabe during our drunken discussion that night at the club, she's still a mystery and one I may never really figure out.

"So, you must be Danika." I turn in the direction of the sharp voice and find Skye standing at the end of the couch with a glass of red wine in her hand. She doesn't smile, and I get the distinct impression she's trying to be intimidating.

*Not gonna work on me, honey.*

Taking a step toward her, I extend my hand. "Hi, and you're Skye, right?"

She looks at my hand but doesn't take it. Instead, she brushes past me to sit in the armchair next to the couch. I drop awkwardly onto the couch and search helplessly for Savage, but he's nowhere to be found.

*Why the hell did he leave me alone? Fucker!*

"So, what's your deal?"

Her question startles me, and I turn back to her. Her icy glare gives me goose bumps, and I rub my arms while I try to figure out what the fuck she's asking. "I'm not sure I understand what you mean?"

She rolls her eyes and takes a swig of her wine before setting it down on the end table next to her. "What's your angle with my brother?"

"My angle?"

"Yeah, are you after his money?"

*What the fuck?*

"Seriously? Why would you even ask that? I don't want a dime from Savage."

Her eyes narrow, and she glares at me with such contempt, I'm tempted to get up and leave the house without bothering to meet the rest of the family.

"You better not hurt him. He's been through enough."

My blood boils, and my skin heats as anger rises. "You think I don't know that? I would never hurt him."

She gives me a look that assures me she doesn't believe me and makes it very clear we aren't going to be best friends anytime soon.

A child's squeal breaks me from her icy gaze, and I turn to find my savior finally arriving.

---

## SAVAGE

"Hello, ladies. What are you two talking about?" With Angelina dangling from my neck, I approach Skye and Danika.

Dani gives me a fake smile, and my heart sinks. I look to Skye, and she widens her eyes as if to ask me "what?"

*Fucking Skye...why can't she ever keep her mouth shut?*

I can only imagine what she must have said to Danika to make her look so uncomfortable. It looks like I'll need to have a private convo with my little sis. After a continued moment of silence, I clear my throat and detangle Angelina so I can turn her to face Dani.

"Angelina, this is my friend, Dani. Dani, this is my niece, Angelina."

Danika gives me a genuine smile and moves from the couch, dropping to her knees in front of me to put herself on the same level as Angelina.

"Hi, Angelina."

She smiles shyly in response before I have a tiny face buried in my neck again. Angelina isn't usually shy around people we introduce her to; maybe it's the tension between Dani and Skye throwing her off.

Someone approaches from behind me, and Angelina giggles.

"Is she being shy all of a sudden?" Storm appears and Danika climbs to her feet. "You look like you could use one of these." Storm hands Dani a glass of wine with a knowing smile before casting a glare at Skye.

"Thank you." Dani reaches out and takes it and then extends her hand to Storm. "You must be Storm."

"I am, and don't let Skye get to you. She's the difficult one in the family."

Skye rolls her eyes and downs the remaining wine in her glass before climbing from her chair and disappearing into the kitchen.

Her attitude needs a serious adjustment. We all cut her some slack, but Dani means too much to me to let her scare her off. Not that I think that would really do it. Dani doesn't scare easily, and I imagine she had some choice words for Skye in response to whatever my sister threw at her.

Things have been going so well since we had our big fight a couple of weeks ago. I don't want anything to get in the way of what is turning out to be a seriously good thing, maybe the best thing that's ever happened to me.

*I won't let this get fucked up.*

Storm shakes Dani's hand and ushers her to sit back down on the couch. She scoops Angelina up off my lap and plops down with her in the chair Skye just vacated.

"So, Savage tells me you're an investigative reporter?"

Relief washes over me when Dani jumps right into an easy conversation with Storm. I knew I could count on the eldest Hawke girl to make her feel welcome.

With Dani in Storm's capable hands, I set out to search for Gabe and Ben. I find them in the backyard, drinking beers on the patio. Skye must have joined my mom in the kitchen. It's probably a good thing she's not back here. I'm not sure I could rein in my anger right now. This is too important to me.

"Hey, man, what's up?" Ben reaches out and shakes my hand. Gabe nods.

"Nothing, except apparently Skye didn't waste any time digging into Dani."

Gabe's lips press into a tight line, and I know he's just as annoyed with her as I am.

Ben chuckles and takes a swig of his beer. "Well, that's just par for the course. If she wants to hang with the Hawkes, she's going to have to learn how to deal with Skye."

I would have loved to avoid Dani's trial by fire, but Ben's right. It was only a matter of time, and Skye doesn't even let up on us, so there's no way she is going to with someone new—especially the first girl I've dated since the accident.

"You think she's gonna last?"

Ben's question is certainly a fair one. After all, he knows about our rocky start. He also knows Becca bailed pretty quickly. It's not out of the question for Dani to still disappear.

Gabe chuckles. "Dude, if you saw them together the way I have, you would know those two are hotter for each other than Texas in August. Plus, she keeps him on his toes, which he needs. She's a tough chick. They will be fine."

I wouldn't have expected Gabe's praises of Danika. It's not that he doesn't like her. I think he genuinely does, but he has been leery of me letting myself get too involved with her too quickly. Maybe that's just being sensible.

Sensible.

I used to be the sensible one...before Danika. Now, I find myself saying and doing things I never would have before. I'm opening myself up to her in ways I never did with Becca, even though we were together for years, not months.

But, on the other hand, I haven't been able to seal the deal with her either.

Not for lack of trying on both our parts.

She walks in the door, looks at me, says my name...just about anything and I'm hard as a fucking rock, but when we get anywhere near going past her gloriously talented cock-sucking, my heart races and I break out into a cold sweat and have to distract her from pursuing it any further.

I don't know how much longer I can put her off without her saying something. She's the most sexually-charged woman I've ever met and, so far, I'm not giving her what she needs.

*And isn't that a fucking bitch?*

The fact she's even lasted this long tells me there's something deeper there between us, that I'm not just imaging or feeling it without reciprocation.

"She's not going anywhere." I say it with more conviction than I feel, but I also don't feel like it's a lie. She's not going anywhere —if I have anything to say about it.

Ben tilts his beer toward me and smiles. "Good. You've definitely been less of an asshole since she came around."

Gabe spits out his beer and coughs through his laughter.

"Gee, thanks, Ben."

He holds his hands up in surrender. "Hey, I'm just calling it like I see it."

After regaining control of his lungs, Gabe takes another drink before his face takes on a somber look. "Did your mom tell you about Stone?"

*Fuck. What now?*

"No, what about him?"

Gabe's eyes flicker over to Ben before coming back to me. "Well, apparently he blew a deadline for some brief he was supposed to be writing or filing or something."

*Sure sounds like something Stone would do.*

"Shit. Did they fire him?"

He shakes his head. "Not yet. They are apparently putting him on 'probation' and giving him another chance."

"Jesus, that kid can't even make it a couple months without blowing it, can he?" My frustration over Stone never really goes away, but things like this make it flare to epic proportions. He just can't get his shit together, and I have no fucking clue why.

The door slides open behind me. I turn to find Skye watching us with another glass of wine in her hand. "Mom says dinner is ready."

*This should be fun.*

## 21

DANIKA

"So, was it as bad as you thought it would be?"
Caroline quirks an eyebrow at me and takes a bite of her salad while she waits for my response. We somehow managed to sneak away for a late lunch, which is basically unheard of on a Tuesday. For some reason, Tuesdays are a total nuthouse at the paper and we often end up eating protein bars and downing Diet Coke to keep ourselves going. Mondays are worse, which is why we haven't had a chance to discuss the big dinner yet, but Tuesdays are definitely a close second.

I have to think about my answer for a minute. I genuinely don't know how to feel about my Hawke family dinner experience.

Antonia, Storm, and Ben were just as wonderful and welcoming as Savage assured me they would be, but Skye's disdain and attitude threw me for a loop, despite being fore-warned by Savage and Gabe.

It's not like I don't understand her desire to protect Savage. I get it. I really do. The stuff he went through, physically and emotionally, would leave most people fragile and easily taken advantage of. But Savage is different. He's one of the strongest people I've ever met—on all levels—and he's smart enough to know what he wants and what's good for him.

"It was good. I guess. His youngest sister, Skye, is a bit of a bitch, but I can deal with her."

"Is that the one whose twin died?"

"Yeah, so they tend to cut her a little more slack than anyone else, but she was distinctly hostile toward me all night. Thankfully, Gabe helped the Hawkes tame her."

Caroline's eyes light up at the mention of Gabe. "Ooo...sexy special forces man was there?"

I roll my eyes and take a bite of my sandwich. Caroline has developed a rather unhealthy crush on Gabe, even though they've only met twice and only briefly. The last thing I need is for her to be another notch in his belt. That would make for a lot of awkwardness in the future for both me and Savage.

"Yes, Gabe was there. But leave it alone, Caroline. He's not the guy for you. He would fuck you and leave you miserable the next day."

She scoffs and has the balls to try to look offended by my concern. "What are you? My mom? Maybe I just need a good lay and don't mind being tossed like a used condom!"

My stomach tightens at the sex reference. It has been months, and still, no sex. Savage is a fucking animal in bed, never satisfied with pleasuring me once, sometimes making me come so many times I don't think I will ever be able to move from that bed again when he's done.

I squeeze my legs together at the delicious memory, but, still, he deflects all my attempts to consummate our relationship, and my vagina is starting to develop cobwebs. I've barely been able to get him to let me blow him. He lets me, but there's always something dark deep in his eyes that I just can't read.

It's not that I don't think he wants to fuck me. I'm positive he does, but something is stopping him and I have no fucking clue what it is.

"Seriously, Dani, I'm a big girl, and I can take care of myself. Just because you get to snuggle with Savage after you fuck doesn't mean I need that to have a good time with Gabe."

I cringe, and the guilt about not revealing the sex situation to Caroline creeps up. After all, she is my best friend, and usually, my sex confidant. But, for some reason, what goes on with Savage is something I want to keep to myself. I have absolutely zero desire to share it with her, and I don't care to examine why right now.

*Turn it back to her.*

"I'm sorry, Care, but I can't not warn you. He's the definition of a player. You should see the string of women who stagger out of his condo in the morning."

She grins and winks at me. "If they aren't walking straight, then he's definitely doing something right."

*Can't argue with that logic.*

"True...look, do what you want, just don't say I didn't warn you."

After sticking her tongue out at me in the most adult way possible, she laughs. "Yes, Mom. I have been duly warned and I appreciate your concern for my sexual wellbeing."

"Anytime."

We finish quickly and head back to the office. Both of us need to bust our asses this afternoon if we are going to get out of here before seven tonight.

And I *really* need to get out of here on time. I have something special planned for Savage tonight. There's no way I'm postponing to polish off another article about the inaccurate parking meters and how they're leading to excessive parking tickets.

The lingerie I bought is absolutely perfect. Slutty and sexy. If this doesn't work, then I'm at a complete loss as to what to do.

A girl can only go without dick for so long. And God knows, it has been *way* too long for me. This is literally the longest I've gone without a good fuck since I still had my virginity, and my body is screaming for it.

Mouth, tongue, fingers just aren't going to cut it anymore. Savage has a dick as beautiful as he is, inside and out, and I need it—inside me.

*What if it doesn't happen tonight?*

The question has been rattling around in my head for weeks and it's always the same answer—I'll deal with it when the time comes.

But when does the time come? How many times am I going to let him distract me with his oral talents and avoid actual body-slamming sex?

Deep down, I know the answer. I just don't want to admit to myself, let alone anyone else. Hence, my reluctance to discuss anything with Caroline.

I already love him.

Somehow, someway, I fell for him.

Hard—like jump off the Hoover Dam and smack into Lake Mead hard.

It was something I never thought I needed. Something I *had* never needed before.

Savage is everything every woman dreams about—funny, caring, generous, sexy as hell—and he's mine. I don't want to lose that. I won't. Not for anything.

---

## SAVAGE

I know something is up the moment I enter my condo. It was a late night at the club, and Dani sent me a text asking what time I'd be home. That, in and of itself, isn't unusual, but the smell of scented candles drifting down the hallway from the bedroom alerts me that she's been waiting, and with something very specific on her mind—the same thing that's been on my mind since the moment I met her.

Sex.

She needs it. I need it, but fuck if I know how to actually achieve it. It's hard enough keeping my shit together when she blows me.

*Christ, I can't believe I actually have to give myself a pep talk to let my girlfriend suck my dick.*

*Man card revoked!*

As I make my way down the hall toward the flickering light visible from my open bedroom door, I wonder if all my mental prep has done any good. I keep telling myself to relax, that everything will be fine. My cock works, and that's a lot more than most men in my situation can say.

*Just roll with it, Savage. Let it all go and let her guide you.*

I'm surprised to find an empty room. Candles offer a soft glow and illuminate the bed. I don't know what I expected, but an empty room wasn't it.

"Dani?"

The door to the bathroom opens just as I reach the side of the bed. I turn toward the sound.

My breath catches in my throat. My heart beats a rapid tattoo in my chest.

*Well, fuck...*

Dani went all-out tonight—for me.

Black silk hugs her tight curves—the barely-there panties emphasizing her long legs and the bra pushing her chest up to the fucking ceiling with every breath she takes. The vast expanse of exposed skin on her stomach is taut and absofuckinglutely perfect in the soft candlelight. Her eyes lock on mine and never waver. I've never seen her look so determined. It's clear she's on a mission.

*Shit.*

My girlfriend thinks she needs sexy lingerie in order to get me to fuck her. Dani should never have to question how much I want her, need her. The fact she went to these lengths only assures me I need to get my shit in order and now.

She approaches me slowly; each step she takes closer has my heart racing more.

*Jesus, she's a fucking goddess.*

When she reaches me, she doesn't say anything, just grins before she leans down to kiss me. I'm expecting something hot, deep, and probing, but I get the opposite. Her lips barely graze mine before she pulls back and turns to crawl up on the bed.

She stretches out, and I turn my chair so I'm facing her.

"You going to join me up here?" Her voice holds promise and expectation.

Tonight's the night.

This needs to happen now. I've pussed out long enough. Time to man up.

I try to keep my trepidation off my face as I join her on the bed. She watches me closely, and as soon as I'm settled, she reaches for my belt. A laugh bubbles up from my chest, and her eyes flip up to meet mine in question.

"What's so funny?"

I run my hand up her arm and push her hair back from her face. "Is there something you want, Dani?"

Her lips drop into a slight frown and she glares at me. "Are you really going to make me say it?"

I chuckle and bring her face to mine, pressing my lips to hers to silence her protest and take the frown away. When I pull away, I smile and nod. "Yes."

She scowls and returns to her task, yanking my belt from my pants and tossing it on the floor beside the bed before going in for the button and zipper.

The room is dark enough I'm confident she won't see much if

I let her fully remove my pants and if we're really going to do this tonight, I don't have much of a choice. I shift and help her slide my pants off, leaving me in my boxer-briefs and button-down shirt.

Instead of reaching up to start unbuttoning it, she grabs the lapels and yanks, hard. Buttons go flying across the room as they're ripped from the fabric.

"Damn, Danika, impatient for something?"

She swings her leg across my waist and leans in until her mouth is against my right ear. "You want me to say it?"

I nod.

"Fine, I'll say it. You. I'm desperate for you. I need to feel you inside me. Having you in my mouth isn't enough. I need your cock inside my pussy, now."

*Sweet fuck. Her dirty talk practically has me ready to blow.*

I'm hard as granite.

*Maybe I can really do this.*

Her tongue slips along the rim of my ear, and I tremble, my fingers digging into her hips. She slides her right hand down over my stomach and under the elastic of my boxers until she finds my engorged flesh. She grasps me and her tongue dips into my ear, sending me even closer to the edge of control. I want to be inside her even more than she wants it, I can guarantee that.

Nothing is going to stop this tonight. I've got this under control.

Her hand strokes my cock and then squeezes around it. "I need to feel this big cock of yours pounding into me until I can't take it anymore."

## 22

DANIKA

*H*e stills under me and turns his head away with a quick jerk.

"Savage? What's wrong?"

His hand finds my wrist, and he yanks me off his cock while his eyes avoid mine.

*Oh, no...I am NOT getting rejected again.*

"Savage?" I pull my hand from his grip and move to turn his face to mine, but before I can, he grabs my waist and lifts me off him, setting me on the bed to his side. "Whoa, what the fuck?"

*Is this seriously happening?*

"Sorry." He glances back at me over his shoulder as he lifts himself back into his chair. "I'm not feeling well all of a sudden. It must be something I ate."

Before I can formulate a response, he's across the room and the bathroom door slams shut, effectively preventing any further questioning.

*Did he actually pull the "I have a headache" excuse?*

I slump down onto the bed and grab the nearest pillow, pulling it down over my face so I can scream into it without making Gabe think Savage is murdering me in here.

It feels good.

Cathartic.

When I bring the pillow away and take a deep breath, the cool air helps calm me, but only marginally.

I just don't fucking get it. Five hundred dollars of La Perla and it got me exactly nowhere! He couldn't get away from me fast enough.

Is this some game for him? Some way to still exert his dominance? He strings me along but doesn't seal the deal?

What does he want? For me to beg? Because, hell, I'm ready to beg and then some.

*How has it come to this? Me...actually needing to beg for sex. Something is quite seriously fucking wrong with the world if it has come to me begging.*

I hurl the pillow across the room, and it hits the bathroom door silently. I'm tempted to throw something else, something that will give me a satisfying bang or crash, but even as angry as I am right now, I don't want to ruin any of Savage's things.

Despite how I feel at the moment, Savage has his hooks in me, and now I'm wondering if he really is sick.

*Shit. I'm such a bitch. I should check on him.*

I slide off the bed and hustle to the bathroom door. I don't hear anything. No water running. No tell-tale sounds of Savage praying to the porcelain god.

"Savage? Are you all right?"

The toilet flushes, and I spend several awkward moments standing with my ear up against the door, waiting for his response. I watch the doorknob turn, and I take a step back, almost tripping on the damn pillow.

*Crap.*

I bend down and grab it just as the door opens and Savage

appears. He certainly doesn't look sick, and he avoids making eye contact with me as he rolls past me and directly for the bed.

Without even glancing my way, he moves into bed and tosses his shirt onto his chair. "I'm exhausted and feel like shit. I'm just going to go to sleep. You might want to go home tonight in case whatever I have isn't food poisoning. I don't want to get you sick."

*You've got to be fucking kidding me.*

*Go home? He's actually telling me to leave!*

I don't think I've ever felt like such a pile of shit. Honestly, I thought tonight would be different, that maybe all he needed was a black silk nudge in the right direction. I guess I was wrong. What he needs is me to go home and leave him the fuck alone.

Well, I can certainly accommodate his request.

"Feel better." The words come out as icy as my heart feels right now—cold and dark in my chest. This is what I get for opening myself up to a relationship. Rejection.

I slip my jeans and t-shirt on over the useless expensive fabric and grab my overnight bag and purse. When I reach the bedroom door, I pause to look back at him. The candles are still lit. I should probably blow them all out before I leave—I don't want the place to burn down—but right now, I just want to get out.

"Don't forget to blow out all the candles." My words are met with silence. I bite my tongue to prevent myself from saying something I'll regret later.

Making my way to the front door, I fish around in my purse until I find my phone. I call Nora, and she picks up almost immediately.

"Hello?"

"Hey, I'm coming over." I know she didn't work tonight and is probably on the couch with a pint of mint chocolate chip.

"Why? Is everything okay?"

I let out a deep sigh and press the button for the elevator. "Of course it is, my boyfriend just rejected me and told me to go home."

"Shit, Dani, you know how weird it is for me when you talk to me about Savage. I have to see him at work, you know?"

She doesn't know the half of it. I've managed to keep my personal shit with Savage just that, personal. Even Caroline doesn't know what's been going on. But, Nora's right. It isn't fair for me to put her in an awkward position with her boss.

"I promise I won't talk about him anymore tonight. I just want to come spend some time with my baby sister, all right?"

"Of course. I'll see you soon."

The elevator dings just as she hangs up, and I enter the car and lean against the back wall, my ego utterly deflated. I'm out of ideas here. Maybe it's time to give up trying and admit I was right to avoid getting emotionally tangled with someone like this.

---

## SAVAGE

When I left for the gym this morning, I didn't think it was possible to be more frustrated, but I was wrong.

I stare up at the bar, which is weighed down with three hundred fifty pounds again, and I know, without even trying, I won't be able to lift it today.

*Fucking pussy.*

*Yeah, I know.*

What happened with Dani last night won't stop playing in a loop in my head, and it's throwing me completely off my game. She didn't even respond to my good morning text.

I can't say I blame her.

What I did last night might land on the top of the "unforgivable" list.

"Fuck." I drop my forearm over my eyes and resign myself to the fact I won't get anywhere with my workout today—at least the weight-lifting part.

"What the hell is wrong with you today?"

I move my arm, and Rick is looking down at me with both concern and frustration.

"Nothing, I'm just...tired, I guess."

"Bullshit." He holds his hand out, and I grasp it, letting him help pull me to a sitting position. "I've known you for three years, and I've seen you tired. I've seen you in pain. I've seen you sick. This is none of these. So, spill."

I search the immediate area for Gabe but don't see him.

*Good. The last thing I need is him hearing this shit. He already thinks I'm a huge pushover for her.*

"It's Dani."

"I should have guessed. Only a woman could make a man look so miserable."

*Ain't that the truth?*

I move into my chair, and Rick follows me back to the gymnasium where the heavy and speed bags are ready and waiting. It's been a while since I've used them. They used to be my go-to form of stress-relief. After Dad died, Mom forbade me from fighting professionally. At ten, I never questioned her edict, but I also loved boxing and continued to train and spar despite the look of disdain I got from her when she found out.

It was different after the accident, though. I couldn't get my release on the bag anymore.

Now, it calls to me in the way it used to, and the urge to wrap my hands and pummel it is unshakable.

Rick grabs the tape and wraps and begins preparing my hands without me even asking. When he's done, he points to the heavy bag without a word.

He doesn't need to coach me. I probably know more about boxing and throwing a good punch than anyone in this gym, and he knows it. He also appears smart enough to give me some space to pound it out.

The first crack of my right against the leather of the bag is more satisfying than words can describe. The vibration and slight sting in my hand is like coming home without ever knowing I had been gone.

*Home.*

When I used to think of home, it was Mom's house, or my condo. Now, when I think of home, all I see is Dani's flowing blonde hair, loving blue eyes, and dazzling smile directed at me.

*I. AM. SO. COMPLETELY. FUCKED!*

The combinations my father drilled into me as a child come back easily. I demolish the bag, pounding it until my arms and shoulders drop helplessly to my sides.

Maybe I should have given this a bit more thought. I still need to actually move in my chair today.

Rick moves from behind the bag and eyes me. "You want to talk about it now?"

"Fuck! Seriously?"

He unwraps my hands and tosses everything to the side. "Yes, seriously. You don't have the energy to kill the bag again, and it looks like it hasn't done anything to ease your frustration. So, talk."

*Shit.*

I run my shaking hands back through my sweat-soaked hair and clench my eyes closed. "I just feel like I'm failing miserably at the whole relationship thing with her."

The responding chuckle from Rick only angers me more. "Dude, you excel at everything you do. I'm sure it's the same with Dani. You are probably overreacting."

*Am I?*

He wouldn't be saying that if he knew everything, but fuck if I'm about to admit my inability to fuck my girlfriend to him, or anyone else for that matter.

"Yeah, maybe." I don't know how else to respond. I know he means well, but he's not going to get anything out of me today.

"If you're looking for a nice date night for you two, you should come to my sister's show."

"What kind of show?" I vaguely recall Rick telling me his younger sister is some kind of artist, but I've never been much of an art fan so I didn't really pay much attention.

I follow him toward the locker room, my arms and shoulders screaming in protest with every move.

"She's being featured at a gallery next Saturday. Her whole new collection will be displayed. There will be food and wine. It should be a good time."

*An art gallery might not be a bad idea.*

"Okay, sounds interesting. I think Dani would enjoy it."

"Great, I'll make sure to put you on the list, and I'll text you all the details tonight. Margaret will be thrilled you're coming. She's terrified no one will like her work and she'll be stuck there all night with people giving her dirty looks. A few friendly faces will be greatly appreciated."

*I know the feeling. I sure as hell hope Danika's face is friendly the next time I see her.*

## 23

SAVAGE

*S*itting on the side of the bed, I lean down and slide my shoes on. I sense movement in front of me, and when I sit back up, I find Danika leaning against the doorjamb, watching me. Her four-inch cabernet-red stilettos make her already-mile-long legs look never ending. The shortness of her black sequin dress only adds to the effect.

Her blonde hair cascades in ringlets around her face, stopping just at her shoulders, and as she glides slowly toward me across the hardwood floor, it swings around her. Somehow, she has managed to match her lipstick to her shoes perfectly. How women do that, I will never understand.

The corners of those perfectly-colored lips tip up as she looks me over. Thank God the freeze out of the last week has thawed. She was pissed—rip off my balls if I would let her near them pissed—since the whole lingerie/rejection incident. I don't blame her, I really don't, but we also never talked about it.

It's been simmering beneath the surface, and I've been

waiting for things to erupt. I don't know what's been holding her back from confronting me about it, but I know why I haven't mentioned it—fear.

I am utterly terrified she will leave me if I tell her the truth— if I even can. I don't even know what I would say...how I would tell her...

"Well, you clean up nice." She stops in front of me and looks down at me with a grin. I tilt my head back, taking her in as she towers over me in her heels.

I spent my entire life towering over people. At six foot three, most men didn't come eye-to-eye with me. It sounds petty, and vain, but being bigger and stronger than everyone always gave me a sense of pride and confidence in everything I did. Literally looking down on everyone—everyday—can certainly give someone a superiority complex, but it wasn't like that for me. It was just a sense of knowing my own power.

Until you lose it, you never realize what being on the same level with someone, what looking at them eye-to-eye, actually means. It's something I still can't get used to, which is why I spend most of my time behind my desk at the club and I let Gabe and my various restaurant and bar managers handle all the day-to-day operations.

Danika drops to her knees in front of me and pushes my knees apart so she can slide between them. Somehow, she knows exactly what I need in this moment. She reaches out and grabs the ends of my bowtie, tugging on them gently before sliding her hands up to cup my face.

"There," she kisses me then pulls away with a grin, "now you are perfect."

"Hmm, I don't know about perfect." I push her hair back from her face, tucking it behind her ear.

"Well," she gets to her feet without ever taking her eyes off me, "perfect for me, then."

I catch her wrist as she turns to walk away. Glancing back

over her shoulder, she raises her eyebrow in question. "You look amazing tonight. I'm not sure I want you going anywhere public in that dress."

She grins and turns to bend down and kiss me again. "Don't worry, you are the only one who will be able to see up it."

*Thank God! I would murder anyone else who even tried to get a peek.*

I burst out laughing as she turns and disappears into the bathroom. She's probably right. "I'll meet you by the door." I slide into my chair and head to the living room.

The click of her heels tells me she's right behind me, and she appears at my side, her clutch tucked under her arm. "Ready?"

"Yep, let's go."

The ride to the gallery is short, less than ten minutes through the light drizzle falling over the city. Our driver for the evening is a guy I've used before. He's always prompt and very professional, which I appreciate when Gabe isn't accompanying me somewhere. Frankly, I'm glad he had plans with one of his bimbos tonight, because I don't want to do anything but focus my attention on Danika and making sure she has a wonderful evening out.

*I owe her that...after everything.*

We pull up outside the gallery, and I usher Danika inside in front of me, trying to prevent her from getting too wet as the drizzle increases to a steady rain. As soon as we enter, Rick and his sister, Margaret, greet us near the door.

"Savage! So glad you could make it!" Maggie bends down and gives me a hug before turning to Danika. "And you must be Danika. I've heard so much about you from Rick. Apparently, Savage talks about you constantly at the gym."

*Shit.*

"Oh, really?" She glances down at me. "And just what does he say?"

Rick looks momentarily stunned. Then, he smiles and winks at me. "Only good things, of course. It's nice to finally meet you."

They hug briefly before someone grabs Maggie and drags her off into the gallery. She waves a quick wave goodbye to us.

Rick waves her off. "Sorry, she's being pulled in a hundred directions tonight, but I guess that's good. I have to greet some more people. I'll find you guys later."

We say goodbye, and I follow Danika over toward the right wall of the gallery, where a large canvas is hanging, bright spotlights framing it in a white glow. We stop in front of it and examine the painting. A waiter strolls past and offers us champagne, which we both grab, before returning our attention to Maggie's work.

"Is it just me," Danika glances down at me, "or is that a giant vagina?"

I almost choke on my champagne. Coughing to clear my windpipe, I take another sip and return my eyes to the painting. Now that she said that, I can't see anything but pussy.

"Uh, yeah, vag all the way."

The reds, pinks, and peaches on the canvas melt together in a vertical, oblong oval.

She laughs, rubbing her hand on the back on my neck. "Do you think it was intentional? Is Maggie some big feminist or something?"

I shrug. "Who knows? I've only met her a couple times, and I can't say she ever seemed to have any sort of agenda, at least not one she discussed with me. But, I don't think there is any way you can paint something like that and not see it looks like a crotch."

"Agreed," she squeezes my neck gently, "let's go see another one and see if the pussy theme continues."

I chuckle and follow her to the next painting, currently being examined intently by someone I know very well.

"Andrew! I didn't expect to see you here. It's been a while." He turns toward me, and I can't miss the surprise in his eyes when he sees me.

He looks around the room nervously. "Savage," he shakes my hand, "it's, uh, good to see you. You're looking good."

His eyes dart away from my face and over my shoulder, and he shifts side to side.

"Thanks, you too. This is my girlfriend, Danika."

He smiles at her and shakes her hand, but his unease doesn't sit well with me.

"Nice to meet you." His eyes aren't even on her. He's looking around the room again.

*Why so nervous, old friend?*

I realize Danika has no idea who he is and that I'm doing a terrible job at introductions. "Andrew and I were roommates in college," I explain, "but we haven't seen each other in over three years."

"Three years?" His brow furrows. "Has it really been that long?"

*You know exactly how long it's been.*

I smile despite my annoyance at him playing dumb. "Yep, we haven't seen each other or even spoken since right before the accident." I watch his smile falter, now that I've called him out and drawn attention to his shitty idea of friendship.

"Oh, yeah, I, uh, guess so." He runs his left hand back through his hair, and the overhead light glints off a gold band on a really important finger. I'm just about to ask him about it when I hear a sudden intake of breath behind me.

"Savage?"

I know that voice.

I know that voice all too well.

*What the hell is Rebecca doing here?*

She slides into view, her hands, holding a bottle of water and a glass of what I imagine is whiskey, shaking visibly. My eyes immediately drop to the very obvious baby bump accentuated by her skin-tight dress and then shift over to the giant diamond on her ring finger.

Andrew avoids eye contact when I look to him. He grabs the whiskey from her trembling hand, taking a long drink before wrapping his arm around her waist protectively.

*Jesus fuck!*

"Becca." I try to keep the disdain from my voice, but Danika's supportive hand on my neck alerts me I probably failed miserably.

"You, uh, look good." Her voice shakes as badly as her hand, clenched to white knuckles around the bottle of water.

"Looks like I missed something big here. How long have you two been married?" I watch as they look at each other uncomfortably and then the floor—anywhere but at me.

Andrew is the one who finally has the balls the answer. "About two and a half years."

Two and a half years. She didn't even wait a year after leaving me to marry one of my best friends.

"Wow, you don't take long, do you, Becca?" This time, I don't even bother to try to contain my anger. The tension in the air is as thick as a London fog. Danika squeezes my neck again and then steps toward Becca.

"Hello, Becca, I'm Savage's girlfriend, Danika. I've heard so much about you. I wish I could say any of it was complimentary, but, I'm sure you already know that."

My heart may have just stopped; my breathing certainly has.

*Where the hell did that come from?*

I don't know, but I've never been more ecstatic Danika doesn't have a filter than I am at this moment, seeing the look on Becca and Andrew's faces.

Turning to me, Danika raises an eyebrow and smiles. "Let's go enjoy the exhibit."

I nod and move around a speechless Andrew. Becca, on the other hand, has started that damn whimper that always began before she started to cry. How I ever found her, or that, attractive, is beyond me.

Danika strolls to the far side of the gallery and drops down onto a bench facing another large, vaginal masterpiece. I stop next to her, afraid to look at her after the way I lost my shit in front of my ex.

"No," she says firmly, "turn around and look at me."

I sigh and follow her command. I expect to see anger, annoyance, even jealousy in her eyes, but all I find is compassion and understanding.

"So...your ex seems like a raging cunt."

I drop my head into my hands and laugh, and it feels really fucking good. Danika is a genius at pulling me from my darkest moods with her smart mouth. I look up at her and find her smiling at me, watching me expectantly. A waiter passes next to us and she stops him, grabbing two more glasses of champagne.

"We need these." She hands me one and I drink half of it in one gulp, while she does the same.

That had to be uncomfortable for her, no matter how much she's trying to be supportive. "I'm sorry..."

"No," she sits forward toward me, "you don't apologize for those assholes. Let's just forget they exist and get back to enjoying all the lovely pussy art."

Grinning, I lean forward until we are a breath from each other. "You're pretty incredible, you know that?"

She bats her eyelashes coquettishly. "I do."

"Good." I kiss her, intending it to be sweet and gentle, but she slides her arms around my neck and crushes her mouth against me, twining her tongue with mine.

When she pulls away, she smiles at me and stands, draining her champagne before walking over to the painting. "So, what do you think of this one?"

## DANIKA

The sexual tension in the elevator on the ride back up to Savage's place is palpable. We didn't see Becca and Andrew the rest of the evening. I imagine after our encounter with them, they fled the gallery as quickly as possible. Somehow, we managed to forget the awkwardness and tension of the confrontation and still have a wonderful evening together.

Maggie definitely loves vagina. I don't know if she's a lesbian or not, but she definitely has love for the female anatomy. There's simply no other explanation for the walls upon walls of paintings depicting female genitalia. The snickers and looks from the other patrons at the event make me confident we were not the only ones to notice a theme. That being said, the woman has talent. A lot of talent. If I were a gynecologist, I would have bought one of the pieces for my waiting room. It would certainly be a conversation piece.

Staring at vaginas and flirting with Savage all night, not to mention the four or five glasses of champagne we both drank, left me wet, hot, and needy by the time we climbed into the car. Savage must have sensed my distress, because almost as soon as we got on the road, his hand was sliding up my thigh and between my legs.

The moment his fingers found my wet core and clit, I almost cried out in relief. Somehow, I managed to bite my lip and control myself so the poor driver didn't have to sit and listen to us fooling around in the backseat like horny teenagers.

*Two fucking times. He made me come twice during that short ten-minute ride. God, that man's hands...*

Now, this elevator ride is never-ending. The need coiled inside me is driving me to the brink of madness. It has been months, and I still haven't felt Savage inside me. The man is hung like a horse—I've seen, felt, licked, and sucked the evidence.

His desire for me is clear.

But still...no sex.

I'm trying not to read too much into it, but something has to give. When he flat out rejected me after I threw myself at him in the sexiest lingerie I could find, I almost lost it.

Frustration isn't strong enough of a word to describe how it felt, how it feels. I gave him the silent treatment for a couple days, but ultimately couldn't bring myself to cut things off. Not when he sent me his now-signature white roses.

The ding of the elevator breaks my train of thought, and I follow Savage down the hall to his door. I open it for him and Princess jumps up into his lap as soon as we walk in.

"Do you need to take her out?"

"No," he picks her up and lets her lick his face, "Gabe sent me a text about fifteen minutes ago telling me he already took her when he got home."

"Wow, Gabe beat us home? That's gotta be a first." I laugh and run my hand back through his hair. "Let's go to bed."

He tilts his head into my touch and looks up at me with clear understanding burning in his eyes.

*Thank God he needs this as much as I do.*

"Excellent plan," he pulls my hand from his hair and kisses it. He orders Princess to go to bed, and she scampers off across the living room to her bed in the corner. He follows me down the hall to the bedroom.

He disappears into the closet to get out of his tux while I slip off my dress and head to the bathroom.

My heart races in anticipation of tonight. I've never been nervous for sex—ever. But tonight, with Savage, it's different. It actually *means* something, and that is fucking terrifying. I don't know how I know it will be tonight, maybe it was the run-in with Becca, but deep in my gut, I know he knows it's time.

Several deep, steadying breaths later, I emerge to find him already in bed waiting for me, a storm of desire in his gaze. I move toward the bed slowly, watching him watch me. The way his eyes roam my naked body sends a shiver of anticipation down my spine and causes my already needy body to cry out for his touch.

"Have I ever told you how fucking beautiful you are?"

I slide under the covers and press my body along his. "Once or twice."

He drags me from his side until I am lying completely on top of him before he takes my face in his hands and angles his mouth over mine in a possessive kiss. He devours me, sliding his hands from my head down my sides until he firmly grips my ass, pulling me tightly up against his hard cock.

Our gasps mingle with our breaths as the kiss deepens further, and I can't seem to get close enough to him. I want to crawl inside of him, become part of him, let him become a part of me, even more than he already has.

I can't imagine not having him, not having this, in my life. I thought I was happy before. I thought great sex was enough, but I was wrong. I need this. I need someone who wants me to be their everything. I need Savage.

His hand slips between our grinding bodies and glides down my belly until he finds my throbbing core.

"Oh, God, please!" I gasp into his mouth as he lingers against my flesh, barely skimming the surface, doing nothing but stoking the desperate need coiled inside me.

"Please, what? Tell me what you want, baby." His husky voice vibrating against my lips resonates through my body.

My clit pulses against the palm of his hand. I roll my hips against him, grinding against his palm, urging him to move and put me out of my misery.

"You," I manage to gasp out as he slips his fingers inside me. *Finally.*

I clench around them and he groans against my mouth.

"Fuck, you're so wet." He slowly slides his fingers out, then thrusts them in again, beginning a steady rhythm I match with my hips. His palm grinds against my clit, and he increases the pace. My entire body heats, my skin flushing and my head spinning, signaling my impending orgasm. Hot breath floats across my neck as he kisses his way to my ear, grazing his teeth over the lobe and finally sends my body spinning into an explosive orgasm.

His hand and mouth never still until I collapse onto him, panting against the damp skin of his chest. He nuzzles in my hair, pressing his lips against my head and gently rubbing my back. His hard cock pushes against my belly, and, as I regain my senses, I reach between us to grasp it, craving the hot flesh in my hand.

Just as my thumb slips across the wet tip, he grabs my wrist and rolls me onto my back. "I'm not done with you yet."

I groan in frustration as he shifts me up against the headboard so he can drop his head between my legs. I comply, simply because he leaves me no other choice. His strong arms hold me down as he teases his tongue along my swollen and overly-sensitive flesh. I shudder and grip his shoulders, digging my fingers into the firm muscles as he probes inside me.

He doesn't go easy on me, even though I know he is more than aware of how sensitive I am after I come. He draws my clit between his lips and sucks in time with my undulating hips. I grip his hair, tugging on it and pulling him closer, frantic for another release.

This one comes so quickly, it blindsides me, my world spinning out in a shattering of stars and flashes of light. I cry out his name, smashing myself against his face, riding out the orgasm until I'm so sensitive I have to push him away and beg him to stop.

I collapse against the headboard, and he nuzzles my stomach, kissing his way up to lavish attention to my breasts. His hot breath across my nipples makes me shudder against him, craving him inside me more now than I ever have in the past.

"You okay, baby?"

I manage to nod as he presses his lips to mine, the taste of my release still there.

Sliding my tongue along his bottom lip, I suck it into my mouth and he groans. He wraps his arms around my back and rolls onto his back. I slide down and straddle him, drag my drenched pussy against his cock, and rock my hips.

His eyes roll back into his head, and he digs in his fingers into my waist. I roll my hips again and his eyes fly open, raw need emanating in the blue depths. I lean down and kiss him, pouring my need for him into the act.

*Yes. This. We both need this.*

I shift forward until the head of his cock is resting against my core and rock against him again, catching his groan in my mouth.

He sits up so we are face-to-face. Reaching down, I grasp him and moan in appreciation at the thick, hot flesh in my hand. His cock bucks against me, his fervent kiss continuing while I position him at my entrance.

His heart races against my chest, and his skin feels cold and clammy. He's no longer returning my kiss and is taking short, jagged, gasping breaths.

I pull back and find his eyes squeezed shut. His cock deflates in my hand, and I move quickly to capture his face between my palms.

*Something is seriously wrong here.*

"Savage, what's wrong?" He doesn't open his eyes. He doesn't respond. He doesn't move, other than to take rapid, shallow breaths. His entire body shakes violently. His arms tighten around me as he clings to me like a lifeline and his breathing nears hyperventilation.

*Holy shit, he is having a full-blown panic attack.*

# 24

## DANIKA

*H*e latches onto me, burying his face against my neck. I hold him close, and his chest heaves. The cool clamminess of his skin against mine is unnerving. I've never seen someone like this.

*Jesus, what the fuck do I do?*

"Savage, baby, it's okay, just breathe." I try to soothe him, but I have no fucking clue what's happening, what brought this on, and he's completely unresponsive.

*How the hell do I get through to him?*

Asking him what's wrong does nothing, and he fights any attempts for me to pull away. So, I hold him, murmuring reassurances to him for what seems like an eternity while my mind races with every scenario that might have brought this on.

When I finally reach the answer, my heart freezes in my chest.

*Sex. It's sex.*

Every single time I've tried to take it past fooling around and oral, he makes some excuse or distracts me. I had him practically inside me this time, and he's having a meltdown over it.

*Why? What did I do?*

I search every moment we've spent together over the last three months for any explanation but find none.

Eventually, his breathing slows, and his body stops shaking. Even then, he maintains his iron grasp on me and refuses to respond to my increasingly concerned questions.

"Savage, what's wrong? Baby, please talk to me." I try to pull away again, but he clutches me tighter, preventing me from seeing his face. I don't need to see it to know he's crying. My skin is soaked from his tears rolling down from my collarbone onto my breast.

A man like Savage doesn't cry. At least, not in front of someone. Whatever this is, it's killing him. I've never felt so fucking helpless. There's absolutely nothing I can do because I don't even know what the problem is.

Minutes tick by with complete, unnerving silence in the room. His pain hangs heavy in the air, but I can't seem to bring him back from wherever he is.

*Come on, Savage. Talk to me.*

I beg. I urge him to tell me what's going on. I try everything with no response.

When he finally shifts, slowly releasing his grip on me and leaning back, relief floods me.

*Finally.*

His eyes are vacant, red, and puffy, and he doesn't seem to focus on me, rather, some place behind me in the room.

I take his face in my hands, turning him until his empty eyes meet mine. "Savage, tell me what's wrong."

He shakes his head and drops onto his back, resting his forearms over his eyes without a word.

*Seriously?*

Despair and anger create a volatile mix inside me. I slide off his hips and kneel next to him, taking a deep, cleansing breath before I try again.

"You aren't going to tell me what's going on?"

No response.

His arms remain draped over his eyes, his body motionless, except for the now-steady slow rise and fall of his chest. I watch him, waiting for him to acknowledge me, acknowledge anything, but he doesn't, and it becomes abundantly clear to me he has no intention of talking to me about what happened.

*Why, Savage? What can't you just fucking talk to me?*

The realization has me clutching my chest against the pain of my heart being torn open. I bite back the sob that threatens to escape. Tears slide down my cheeks before I even realize I'm crying.

"Savage, please talk to me." I sob. "I need you to talk to me."

He doesn't budge, and as the pain of knowing he can't confide in me overtakes me, I shift back on the bed, away from him. I slide off the mattress onto shaking legs and have to grab the bedpost to stop from falling forward as another sob echoes in the too-silent room.

"I'm sorry."

The words are so quiet, I'm not even sure I really hear them. Wiping my eyes, I turn back to the bed and find him in the same position, but his arms have moved up, revealing his red-tinged, hopeless gaze. He looks completely lost, but he won't take the lifeline I've repeatedly offered him.

"Why won't you talk to me? Please, tell me what's wrong." I beg, not even bothering to try to hide my distress.

*What does it matter at this point?*

He closes his eyes and takes a deep breath. When he refocuses on me, I know I won't get an answer. Gone is the Savage who always promised to be an open book, who always said he would be honest with me. All that's left is a brick wall of silence.

"I'm sorry...I just...can't," he whispers.

I drop my head, close my eyes, and try to breathe through the heaving of my chest. When I finally look back at him, a single tear slides from his eye and rolls back down his cheek to his pillow. I know what I need to do, but the pain of actually following through with it may kill me.

My eyes lock on his. I brush aside what my heart is begging me to do and decide it's time to listen to my head for once. "Then, I need to go."

He flinches but otherwise doesn't move and doesn't respond.

"I don't know what is going on with you. I can't believe I'm actually going to say this, but if you told me we couldn't have sex because of something that happened with the accident, that would be okay. It wouldn't be a deal breaker...because I love you. I don't need...that...but this, this isn't physical Savage, and you won't fucking talk to me, so how the hell can we ever fix it? You not talking to me...that *is* a deal breaker."

His vacant stare never wavers, and I turn to the bathroom, confident I'm doing what I need to do, while, at the same time, sure I am making the biggest mistake of my life. I feel his eyes on me, but I don't look back.

Looking back would break me further, and what is happening isn't healthy for either of us.

*Why the hell did I ever let myself fall in love with him?*

I close the door behind me and slide down it until the cold tile of the floor hits my naked skin. I drop my face into my hands and give in to the relentless agony of what I've done.

---

## SAVAGE

I watch her disappear in the bathroom and hear her fall apart the second the door clicks shut. The sound of the latch falling into place might as well be a gun firing, because I'm pretty confident I just killed the best thing that ever happened to me. Even though my heart is no longer racing like I ran a marathon, my body continues to shake, and I scrub my hands over my face to try to clear my head.

*Fuck.*

I can't be here when she comes out. I can't face her after that, after I completely fell apart in front of her, after I literally withered in her hand.

Getting out now is my only concern. I dress quickly in sweatpants and a t-shirt and grab Princess, who is waiting at the closed bedroom door. I cross the hall and pound on Gabe's door. I know better than to open it without knocking, even though I know it's unlocked. I have inadvertently walked in and seen his naked ass riding whatever girl came home with him that night. I love the guy, but love only goes so far.

He doesn't answer so I pound on the door again, anxious to get gone before Danika tries to leave the condo. Finally, the door opens, and a very haggard looking Gabe glares at me.

"What the fuck dude? It's 3:30 in the morning."

"I know," I hand Princess to him, "but I need you to come to the gym with me."

He pets her and lets her lick his face before he gives me an annoyed look. "The gym? Now?"

"Yes, right now. Go get changed and let's get out of here. Leave Princess at your place. You don't have someone here with you, do you?"

He rolls his eyes and sets her down. I follow him into his place.

"No, she left an hour ago. Want to tell me what's going on? You look like shit."

*Fuck no, I don't want to tell you what's going on. That's the last thing I need right now, my best friend knowing I'm a fucking failure in bed.*

"No, please, just go change."

He throws up his hands in resignation and disappears down the hall, Princess following closely at his heels. I know she'll settle in, probably in the middle of his feather bed, and sleep until we get back.

*At least that's one female I know I can please.*

*Fuck.*

I run my hands back through my hair and squeeze my eyes closed, trying to shut out the vivid image of the look on Dani's face when she told me she loves me...and that it's over.

It doesn't help, but maybe banging the weights or hitting the bag will.

Gabe reappears, looking just as annoyed as he did a minute ago, and grabs his gym bag and the keys.

We ride down in the elevator in silence. I know he's dying to ask me what's going on, but he keeps his mouth shut, probably sensing he would lose his head if he asks again. I pull myself into the passenger seat, and he puts my chair in the trunk before we set out in continued silence.

Halfway through the ride to the gym, I finally can't take him glancing over at me anymore.

"She told me she loves me."

He jerks and swings his head to look at me, then quickly returns to looking at the road. "What? Well, that's great, isn't it? Why are you so upset?"

I pause before answering, trying to figure out how much to tell him. "Because I blew it."

"Shit. How? What did you do? What did you say?"

I release a deep sigh and slouch down, resting my temple against the cool glass of the window. "Nothing."

"Nothing?" The surprise in his voice is more than evident, and I can only imagine what is running through his head right now. "What the fuck, Savage?"

"I know. I fucked up everything." An unfamiliar tightening in my chest has me reaching up and rubbing it.

*What if I can't fix this? What if it's too late?*

We pull into the parking lot of the gym, and Gabe throws the car in park, turning to look at me. "Do you love her?"

My head snaps around to face him. "Of course I do. She's the best thing that ever happened to me."

"Then why didn't you tell her that?"

The million dollar question. Why didn't I tell her anything? Why, in that moment when the only thing keeping me here, keeping me together was her, couldn't I tell her? "Because, I'm so fucked up, Gabe. I don't know what to do."

"What happened?"

My mind races through the evening, how much fun we had at the gallery, despite the run-in with Andrew and Becca. The car ride home, my fingers buried in her heat when all I wanted there was my throbbing dick. The way she tasted when she came against my mouth, screaming my name. The almost-painful throb of my cock as she pressed her wet pussy against it and started to slip it inside. Then, the pain and tightness in my chest, suffocating me while my mind spun out of control.

"I panicked."

His brow furrows. "You panicked when she said 'I love you?'"

"No," I close my eyes against the memory and shake my head, "I panicked when she tried to have sex with me."

I chance a glance at him. I can practically see the cogs of his brain spinning.

"What? I don't understand. You two have been together for like three or four months..."

*The greatest months in my entire fucking life.*

"Yeah, we have. We just haven't been 'together' together."

He drops back against his seat, his eyebrows furrowed in confusion. "Is this because of the accident? Can you not...you know?"

I groan. "No, that's the fucking point. I have no problem getting hard when I'm with her, or when I am alone for that matter, but I haven't been able to 'seal the deal,' so to speak. It has never been this bad though, the panicked feeling. This time, I completely lost my shit."

"What did she say?"

Dropping my head back against the headrest, I stare at the ceiling of the car, wishing everything was just a bad dream instead of a very real-life nightmare. "That's when she told me she loved me, and I just laid there and said nothing. It was like I was completely numb and mute. I couldn't say anything."

He sighs and turns off the car. "You know you need to get your shit figured out so you can fix this, right? Danika is fucking perfect for you. You belong together."

"Like I don't know that." I snap glare at him.

"Hey, man, I'm your best friend. It's my job to call it like I see it."

"Yeah, well, right now, I need you to be my best friend who shuts his trap and helps me burn off all this crap I have built up right now, all right?"

He nods his agreement, shaking his head in disbelief shortly thereafter. "Hope you're ready to get your ass kicked."

The door slams, and he moves around the back of the car.

*An ass-kicking sounds good right now.*

"I deserve it."

## 25

DANIKA

*M*y phone rings just as I stumble into my
apartment, grocery bags hanging off my arms.
Who am I kidding? I might as well call them liquor bags, since all
I bought was three bottles of Prosecco and two of Stranahan's
Colorado Whiskey.

Thankfully, Caroline is on her way over. Otherwise, I might
feel like an alcoholic.

I set the bags on the counter and scramble for my phone,
digging in my purse until I find it. I groan when I see the
caller ID.

*Why did I give Skye my number?*

*Because Savage thought maybe there was a chance to smooth
things over that has never come.*

She's the last person I want to talk to right now. Well, that's
not true. Savage probably is.

*How can I want to hear from him so badly, yet dread it so
completely?*

Maybe because the way we left things yesterday felt so cold and final. When I managed to drag myself up off the bathroom floor and take a quick shower, I returned to find the bedroom, and the condo, empty. Even Princess was MIA, and I still haven't heard from Savage.

The ringing stops, and I let out a sigh of relief, setting my phone on the counter to unpack my bags and get the Prosecco chilled. No sooner do I close the door to the fridge when the shrill ringing starts again.

She'll just keep calling.

"Hey, Skye." I try to put some cheer in my voice, but it sounds fake, even to my own ears.

"Danika, what the hell is going on?"

*Crap. What did Savage tell her? Time to play dumb.*

"What do you mean?"

"Savage says he's not coming to family dinner tonight. He sounded off, but not sick. Something is going on, and Gabe is keeping his mouth shut. I figured you're the only one I can get the truth out of."

The truth? The truth is not something I want to discuss with Savage's nosy little sister. "Everything's fine. Savage is fine. He's probably just tired."

She sighs loudly. "Whatever. I know you are all keeping something from me. Savage never misses Sunday dinner. I'll figure it out sooner or later. Thanks for nothing."

*Click.*

I look down at my phone. Her abruptness and attitude shouldn't surprise me. Not after that family dinner and her warning.

A knock at the door startles me. I almost drop the bottle in my hand.

*Geez, I'm jumpy.*

"It's open." I pop open the bottle of Stranahan's.

Caroline makes her way to the kitchen. When she sees the

bottles on the counter, she frowns. She hasn't even seen the ones in the fridge. Maybe I shouldn't mention the Prosecco. She doesn't say a word, just walks to the fridge, opens it, sighs, and closes it.

She turns to face me. "Did you have to buy the whole store?"

Pouring myself a double, I nod. "Yes."

"Better pour me one, then." She makes making her way into the living room and drops down onto the couch. "So, you going to tell me what happened? You were very vague earlier."

I had been intentionally vague. *How the hell do I tell her Savage and I have never had sex? How do I tell her I confessed my love for him and he just laid there, silent?* She's my best friend, but that doesn't mean she'll understand. In fact, her knowing me so well makes me think she won't understand this, not at all.

I pour her a drink and drop down into the opposite end of the couch, facing her, with my knees pulled up to my chest. Taking a long sip of my whiskey, I savor the burn and sweetness as it slides down my throat.

It's better to get this done quickly, like ripping off a Band-Aid.

"Savage and I have never had sex."

She jerks up, her eyes wide, her mouth hanging open. "What? How the hell is that even possible? You have been together for months!"

*No shit.*

"I know. It's hard to explain. I wanted to, believe me, but, he always managed to divert me from it. He is so damn good at distracting me, I never actually thought about why he was doing it. It was frustrating, but I never thought anything was seriously wrong."

She nods and sips her whiskey. "Are you sure he can? I mean, it doesn't have to do with the accident, does it?"

"No, believe me, he is very capable."

"So, what happened last night?"

I start with the gallery, describing our run-in with Andrew and Becca.

"Whoa! You're right. She sounds like a total raging cunt. She abandons him when he needs her the most, and then runs off to marry his good friend right away. Talk about heartless."

"No shit."

"So, was he a total prick the rest of the night after that?"

I smile, remembering the way his eyes shimmered with joy and laughter as we made our way around what we dubbed "The Hall of Vagina," not bothering to attempt to hide our giggles until Maggie saw us. Then, we sobered up quickly. "No, actually, he was pretty fucking perfect once we left that bitch behind."

Caroline leans forward and shakes her head. "So, what went wrong? I don't get it."

Images of last night flit around in my head, the feeling of helplessness I had then starting all over again. I take a large gulp of my whiskey, letting the burn of the liquor replace the memory of the burn of my eyes with my own tears. "He freaked out. I mean, full-blown panic attack that lasted something like half an hour."

"Freaked out how?"

I drop my head and stare into the half-empty whiskey glass. I attempt to describe what went down the best I can, but finding words to accurately portray the turmoil of the night proves impossible. I stumble through my description of Savage's break-down, finally sucking up the courage to lift my head and see Caroline's reaction.

She stares at me, completely dumbfounded. "Whoa, so that sounds like it was pretty intense."

"Intense doesn't even begin to cover it. I've never been so terrified in my entire life. There was nothing I could do, nothing I could say, to pull him from whatever bottomless, black abyss he fell into."

Setting her glass on the coffee table, Caroline reaches out and yanks my glass from my hand, downing the rest. "Sorry, your story is enough to make me need more of this, and I wasn't even there! I can't even imagine what a mind-fuck that must have been for you."

I run my hands back through my hair, fighting the tears threatening to escape as I mentally relive every fucking second, because every second had felt like an eternity.

"I was helpless, and he refused to talk to me."

"So, what did you do?"

I bark out a mirthless laugh. "Well, fucking genius that I am, I told him I loved him and then left him when he probably needed me the most."

She stands, disappears into the kitchen, and returns with the bottle. She pours two generous fingers into each of our glasses and holds one out to me. "You told him you loved him?"

The disbelief and concern in her expression has me practically chugging down the potent whiskey. I hiss against the burn, burying my face against my knees. "Yep."

"Did you mean it?"

My head snaps up. "Of course, I meant it. You think that's something I throw around? Just toss out there to any guy who makes me come?"

"No, Danika, in fact, I'm shocked as shit you told him. Part of me wondered if you were even capable of the commitment loving someone requires."

"Wow, harsh much?"

She rolls her eyes. "Dude, come on, I don't call you 'slut' just because you're prettier and thinner than me. You and I both know, until you met Savage, you only had one use for men— good, old-fashioned, sweaty, dirty, nasty-as-hell sex!"

I cringe.

She isn't wrong.

I made my mind up long ago that men were put on this Earth to pleasure me, period. I was never one of those girls who needed to be wined and dined. Frankly, you were much more likely to get laid walking up to me at a bar and asking me to fuck than if you spent hours schmoozing me and making me feel like a princess.

My stomach churns and bile rises in my throat. *Would I have used Savage as just a fuck buddy? Would I have had mind-blowing sex and walked away without looking back if it had been an option from the beginning?*

"Shit." I scrub my hands over my face and reach for my glass, downing the rest. "I guess I wasn't exactly looking for love and a white picket fence. But, that doesn't mean I don't love him."

"Honey, I just want you to be happy. Savage is a great guy, but, this is your first real relationship, and, sometimes I wonder if you subconsciously see him as some kind of project, something to fix?"

"Fuck you, Caroline, how can you honestly think that?"

She holds her hands up and backs away from me on the couch. "I'm just playing devil's advocate, Dani, take it or leave it. Just be sure you know what you are doing before you sit here and pine for someone who may never be able to give you what you need."

"You have no idea what I need, Caroline. How could you? I didn't even know I needed it until I met Savage."

---

## SAVAGE

I stare at the empty pizza box and beer bottles on the coffee table, and my stomach churns, already revolting against the cheesy goodness and empty calories I scarfed down. Gabe reclines next to me on the couch, flipping aimlessly through channels, just like he has been for the last two hours, with Princess snuggled on his lap.

Glancing at my phone, I groan when I see twenty-three

missed calls. I scroll through the call log, and I'm not surprised to see most of them are from Skye—one from Mom, one from Storm, but the other twenty-one, all Skye. I knew she didn't believe a word I said when we spoke earlier today. I've never been a good liar, and Skye can see through bullshit better than anyone I've ever met, probably because she's so good at spewing it herself.

*Twenty-three fucking calls and none of them are from Dani.* The churning storm starts again in my stomach.

I just couldn't bear family dinner tonight. Everyone would be asking about Danika, wondering why she didn't come along again, and, as aforementioned, I'm a shitty liar.

Gabe stops on *Naked and Afraid*. It appears this week's participants are fulfilling their death wishes in Uganda. Why anyone would want to put themselves, or their bodies, through this for twenty-one days is beyond me, but it does make for entertaining television.

Groaning and stretching his arms back, Gabe glances over at me and frowns before dropping his hands back onto his lap and petting Princess. "Are you going to sit there and mope all night?"

"Probably."

He sighs and rolls his eyes. "Seriously, dude, just fucking call her!"

"And say what? Sorry I had a meltdown and ignored you when you told me you loved me?"

He cracks a smile and shrugs. "Well, maybe not in those words."

"That's the point. I have no idea what the hell to say, how to explain any of it, when I don't even understand it."

Gabe stares at me, and I can tell he wants to say something more, but instead, he hands Princess off to me and stands, grabbing the pizza box and piling the empty beer bottles into it.

"Where are you going?" I turn to watch him disappear into the kitchen and re-emerge sans garbage.

He pauses at the door, his back to me. He looks like he's contemplating something. It isn't like Gabe not to just say whatever is on his mind, and, quite frankly, it's disconcerting.

Glancing over his shoulder at me, he offers me a half-smile and opens the door. "I have something I need to take care of tonight, before it gets too late."

He's lying. I know it, and he knows I know it. But, I don't call him on it. Whatever is on his mind, he doesn't want to share it, so I will give him his space.

"See ya tomorrow, then." He waves over his shoulder and disappears into the hallway.

Princess stands on my lap, looking up at me expectantly. "What do you want?" She jumps down next to me on the couch and slips under my hand. "You want me to pet you? You women are so demanding."

I return my attention to the dumbasses in the savanna and manage to forget how badly I blew things with Danika for an hour. Well, not forget, but push it to the back of my mind long enough to have a few laughs at the expense of these suckers.

*Actually, disappearing into the African wilderness sounds pretty awesome right about now, though I doubt it's handicapped accessible.*

My phone vibrates, signaling an incoming text message. I grab it and prepare to be bombarded by more questions from Skye I have no intention of answering. But, it isn't Skye. It's Gabe.

*What the hell? He couldn't just come across the damn hall?*

> Dr. Anna Cochran (504) 205-1289 <

< What? Who is that? >

> She's a shrink. She helped me. Call her. <

*A shrink? Since when does Gabe see a shrink?*

We've been best friends basically our entire lives, and I've never once heard him mention going to therapy. Even after he was discharged, he never said anything to give any indication he was seeing someone, or that he needed to.

I always assumed Gabe told me everything. I guess because I

never keep any secrets from him. It's hard to keep secrets from the person I depend on for so many things, someone I'm closer to than my own actual brother.

*But, a shrink?*

I've never really believed in that shit. It's for people who are weak, who can't get their shit together, and that has never been me. After the accident, my doctors sent in a therapist to talk to me, and I practically barked him out of the room. I put what was left of my former life back together just fine on my own.

Still, the events of the last night run through my mind—the way Danika looked when she told me she loved me, when I didn't respond.

*Fuck!*

I may have thought I had my shit together, but the last twenty-four hours certainly have me rethinking that belief.

< You really think she can help? >

> I do. <

I sigh and run my hand through Princess' soft fur, the feel of the silky strands through my fingers soothing my frayed nerves. "It can't hurt to try, right, girl?" She looks up, tilting her head to the side as if she actually understands what I am saying to her. "Yeah, that's my thought, too."

Staring at the litany of unanswered text messages and phone calls from Skye, another text comes through. I know I have to respond before she shows up, unannounced, on my doorstep.

< Skye, leave it alone. I'm fine. I'll talk to you tomorrow. It's almost midnight, go to sleep. >

The three little dots show up instantly.

> You're fine, my ass! You better call me tomorrow morning or I will come down to the club. <

She will, and she won't leave until she squeezes every last painful detail from me. She's even more brutal in person than she is digitally.

< I promise. Goodnight. >

> Goodnight. Get ready to spill. <

I slip my phone into my pocket and look down at Princess, who is lying on her back with her tiny little paws in the air, begging for a belly rub. "It's time for bed, girl. Let's get you outside."

After a quick pit-stop, I climb into bed, emotionally exhausted. The soul-crushing loneliness of an empty bed hits me immediately.

*What if she never comes back? What if that was the last time I'll have the woman I love in my bed?*

My phone sits dark on the nightstand. I stare at it—for an inordinate amount of time—hoping, praying, she will call, or text...anything to tell me she's thinking about me, and we aren't over.

But, she won't call, or text, because I've given her no indication we aren't over. My action, or inaction, only confirmed to her that I didn't want to fix whatever is wrong between us, and that can't be further from the truth.

Grabbing my phone, I open the last message she sent me, right before she arrived at my place to head to the gallery opening.

> Be there in ten! Can't wait to see you in a tux...and out of one ;) <

*Fuck.*

I take a deep, cleansing breath, and try to shake off the fear making my heart race just thinking about talking to her.

*Suck it up, you fucking pussy!*

I start typing, not even sure what I am going to write.

< I'm sorry. I know that in no way begins to make up for what happened last night, but I don't know what else to say. I'm fucked up, Danika, in ways you can't even imagine, ways I didn't even realize until recently. It isn't fair to you to put you through this. I need to figure my shit out, and I am going to try to do that. But I don't know when, or if, I'll ever be in a place to be with you again.

I just need you to know that I'm trying, and that I love you. I'm sorry I didn't, couldn't, tell you last night, but I need you to know that. >

Staring at what I wrote, my finger hovers over the green "Send" button. Once I send it, there's no taking it back. Maybe it's wrong to tell her I love her. It certainly isn't the most romantic thing in the world to do it via text message, but I need her to know. I need her to understand this isn't about her.

Clicking "Send" feels like pulling the pin on a grenade. Once it's done, there's no going back. It could explode in my hand.

I close my eyes and drop my head back against the headboard, staring at the bright moonlight shining across the off-white ceiling. When my phone vibrates in my hand, I jerk up and scramble to open the message.

> Figure it out. I will be here. <

Seven words. But those seven words speak volumes to me about Danika, and who she is. She hasn't given up, and that's all that matters right now. That's all I can ask of her, all I can expect after what I put her through.

I just hope it's enough.

# 26

SAVAGE

*I* fucking hate that brown chair. The leather creaks every time she moves, and it's like nails screeching on a chalkboard, giving me a fucking migraine every single time I'm here. She moves a lot, constantly crossing and uncrossing her legs, adjusting her glasses, taking a drink of water. For a shrink, she clearly has some issues of her own if she can't sit still for an hour-long session.

Three weeks of this has driven me almost to my breaking point.

"Savage? Did you hear me?"

Shifting my eyes up from the arm of the chair, I find her watching me intently, eyebrows raised. "What? Sorry."

She smiles. She isn't an unattractive woman, not really my type, but pretty, in that nerdy librarian way some men drool over. But the only woman I care about is tall, blonde, and not currently speaking to me, by my own choice.

"It's all right. I said that you have been coming here twice a week for the last three weeks, and I still feel like I know nothing about you."

I internally roll my eyes at her. If I actually did it, she would call me out on it. I'd end up getting talked in circles about why her comment annoyed me.

"What do you mean? I told you all about myself."

She smiles again, but it doesn't reach her eyes and she jots something down on her notepad. "You've told me about your work. You've told me all about your relationship with Danika. You've told me about it, in great detail. I feel like I know Danika extremely well. She sounds like a wonderful woman. What I don't know, is anything about you outside the relationship, and you haven't told me why you are here other than that you said you 'blew things' with her."

*Shit.*

She's right, of course. I've spent weeks telling her how I met Dani, how we started dating, how our relationship progressed, but I never actually told her what happened. I've danced around the subject just like I've avoided talking about me and my family when she's asked.

"So," she continues, "today, you are going to tell me about you, and then you are going to tell me what went wrong with Danika."

I hate talking about myself—truly. I'm sure there are people who love it, those vain people who get off on the attention, but I'm not one of those people, never have been. But, I guess if I really want to figure out how to fix things, I need to play along.

"What do you want to know?"

She smiles again. "Everything. Start by telling me about your family."

I launch into the family tree, giving her the run-down of my parents and siblings as quickly and succinctly as possible. No need to volunteer too much information.

"You mentioned one of your sisters passed away. Can you tell me about that?"

My chest tightens. I should have expected she would ask. It's only natural for her to wonder about that, and I should have been prepared to talk about it. She hasn't asked about the chair either, probably waiting for me to mention it.

"Um, well, it was a car accident, three years ago. I was with her."

"Is that how you were injured?" She leans forward slightly in her chair.

*Creak.*

I cringe. "Yes."

*Don't volunteer information.*

"I can see you're uncomfortable talking about this, but sometimes the things we're most uncomfortable discussing are what we really need to."

*Well, shit. Sense. Why does she have to make sense?*

I take a deep breath and begin talking. I tell her about the accident. I tell her everything. I tell her the truth, the truth I've never told anyone—not Danika, not Gabe, not my siblings, not even Mom. By the time I'm done, I can't see anything through my tears.

I fucking hate crying. There's no other way to say it. I'm not a crier. I can count on one hand the number of times I've cried in my life, and now, I am a blubbering idiot.

Something pushes against my hand, and through the veil of tears, I realize it is a box of tissues.

*Jesus, I am such a pussy.*

I grab one, blow my nose, and wipe my eyes quickly to destroy the evidence.

When I look back up at her, she's watching me intently—no doubt analyzing me in ways I can't even imagine.

She offers me a kind smile. "Tell me about after the accident. Tell me about the hospital."

*Wow, she isn't taking it easy on me, is she?*

I talk, and talk, and talk, until I tell her all—every damn doctor, every surgery, every sleepless night, everything.

This isn't so hard. Its clinical. It doesn't rip my heart out the way talking about Star does.

When I finish, she simply nods. "Looks like we have a little time left. Do you want to talk about what happened with Danika?"

*Jesus Christ, woman! Give me a fucking break!*

I look at my watch. *How could all of that only taken half an hour?* Maybe because she didn't say much, just nodded and gave me a lot of sympathetic looks. But I don't want her sympathy. I want her to fix me.

"I kind of had a meltdown."

"Meltdown? Explain what you mean by that."

The night is all too clear in my head. "Well, the night started out great. Then it got weird..."

I tell her about the gallery, the run-in with Andrew and Becca, and everything else.

"When you say you froze, what does that mean? Tell me how you felt physically and what was going on in your mind."

The answer to her questions isn't readily apparent to me. "I don't know exactly. My heart started racing, and not in a good way, my skin felt all tight, like it was shrinking all over my body, and I broke into a cold sweat. I felt like I was suffocating and couldn't breathe."

She nods and urges me to continue.

"I don't think I was really thinking anything."

She eyes me skeptically. "What was the last thing you do remember thinking before you had the panic attack?"

"I guess I was thinking how much I loved her, and how I just wanted her to be happy."

"Was that all? Try to put yourself back in the moment, and tell me if you remember anything else."

I close my eyes and remember the feeling of her skin against mine, her breath against my face and neck, her mouth on mine, her hand on my cock, easing it into her wet heat...

*Shit. Getting a hard-on in the shrink's office is not a good idea.*

"Um, I guess I was thinking about what sex with her was going to be like."

"What do you mean?"

*What the hell do I mean?*

All the fantasies I've had over the last four months of fucking Danika flood my brain—her against the wall while I slam into her, her pinned to the bed while I fuck her from behind, all the things I want to do and know I never can.

"I mean, I was wondering how I was going to, you know...do it..."

She leans back in her chair and nods. "Have you been with anyone sexually since the accident?"

*What the fuck does that have to do with anything?*

"No."

"Have you tried to be with anyone else?"

I shake my head. "No."

"How did Danika react when you froze?"

Dropping my head into my hands, I squeeze my eyes shut and try not to picture the look on her face before she turned her back on me and walked away. That will only lead to more tears.

"She was worried. She tried to calm me down, but I don't think she had any idea what was happening." The fear in her eyes is crystal clear in my mind, although I wish it was something I could forget.

"Did she say anything?"

I groan. "She told me she loves me."

"You say that like it isn't a good thing."

"It is a good thing. I love her, too. She's the best thing that ever happened to me. But..."

She waits for me to continue but breaks the silence when it's clear I won't. "But what?"

I look back up at her when I hear the creak of the leather. "But I can't give her what she needs."

Dr. Cochran nods and leans toward me. "What is it you think she needs?"

"Fuck." I pull my hair back and clench my eyes, remembering her words, her tears. "She needs someone who is fucking whole."

"Did she say that?"

I shake my head but avoid any eye contact with her.

"Savage. Please look at me."

I finally look at her, and she smiles. "Did she say that?"

"No."

"What did she say?"

*As if I could ever forget her words.*

"She said it wouldn't be a deal breaker if I couldn't have sex, but that it was a deal breaker that I wouldn't tell her what was going on."

Doc relaxes back in her chair and watches me. "Hmm."

"Why are you 'hmming?'" My annoyance level has reached nuclear levels. Talking about this isn't helping. All it's doing is making me relive the worst fucking moments of my life.

"Well, you told me Becca left you after the accident..." I nod in agreement. "Why do you think she left?"

"How the fuck would I know?" I spit the words at her. "I never even spoke to her about it. All she told Storm was that she 'couldn't do it' and then she fucking disappeared from my life."

*She left me when I needed her. She left me when my life had fallen apart.*

"Just because she didn't tell you doesn't mean you haven't speculated or thought about it. Tell me why you think she left."

Her inability to see the obvious has my blood boiling. I am about an inch away from leaving and not coming back. "Why the hell do you think? Because I was a fucking wreck! I was in the hospital and had no idea how I was going to live like this, what it was going to mean...she couldn't deal."

"Any chance you are projecting your perceptions of Becca's feelings onto Danika?"

I hear the words, but they don't process. They are a jumble of sounds in my mind, mixing in with all the shit already floating in there. I shake my head, trying to clear away everything else, concentrate on what she said, but I can't.

"Savage?"

"What?" I snap, but she doesn't recoil.

She watches me for a moment before continuing. "Is it possible you are projecting the way you think Becca felt onto Danika? It seems to me, based on what she told you, that she loves you, and isn't going anywhere, no matter what."

*Is that what I have been doing? Have I been ignoring everything Danika has said and done and let my own mind create problems that don't exist?*

If that is what I have been doing...how the fuck do I stop?

---

## DANIKA

The flashing lights and bumping bass make it impossible for me to stand still. I toss back the last of my drink and move to the dance floor to find Caroline. She has her ass ground against the crotch of a very attractive blond man in tight jeans and a white button-down shirt. His hands are all over her.

I grin at her as she winks and holds her hand out to me. I grab it and let her pull me to her.

Our hips bump together, and she leans in, pressing her lips to my ear. "Thank God! You have returned to the land of the living. If you sat at the table for five more minutes, you might have grown roots. Let's see you get this thing going!" She smacks my ass and blondie behind her laughs and nuzzles against the back of her neck.

*Looks like someone is getting laid tonight.*

*Shit.*

I don't want to think about sex. In fact, I have intentionally avoided anything sexual for weeks. Thinking about sex means thinking about Savage, and the fact I haven't heard from him since he told me he loves me, in a fucking text message. I told him I wasn't going anywhere, and he disappeared on me —completely.

He's okay. I know that. Nora has, somewhat reluctantly, provided me some tidbits of information. She says he has barely left his office but always smiles and says hello to her. It has to be awkward. He probably assumes I told her everything, but I didn't. I couldn't. I could never betray him like that. Yes, I told Caroline, but that's different. Caroline is Caroline. Nora is his employee.

Caroline yanks on my hips, bringing me back to the present as she grinds her pelvis against mine, sandwiching herself between me and her new friend. I try to lose myself in the music, in the beat, in the sway of my body against hers.

Maybe this is exactly what I needed—time to unwind and forget the stress of the Savage situation and my dead story. Paul has disappeared again, and this time, I've given up hope of ever hearing from him. He made his choice—he chose the bad guys. Either that, or he is dead in the bayou.

That thought sends chills down my spine but does nothing to discourage me from continuing. I'll just have to find another source for my story.

At least that gives me something to keep me occupied. I've been trying to make new contacts and find new sources over the last couple weeks, but people around Abello are tight-lipped. It certainly won't be easy, but I'm up for the challenge.

Someone sidles up behind me—a hard, tall body plastered

against my back. Something I haven't felt in weeks grinds against my ass, and I stifle a moan.

*Shit.*

I glance over my shoulder and find a dark-haired stranger grinning at me as his hands come around my waist.

"Hey," he drops his mouth to my ear, "you know, you are the most beautiful woman out here tonight. I love the way you move."

Any other night, well any other night pre-Savage, that probably would have worked. I would have been out the door with him in ten minutes and fucking him within twenty. But the moment the words leave his mouth, I pull away from him and bolt toward the back of the club.

Someone grabs my wrist, halting my retreat. "Dani, where are you going?" Caroline's wide-eyed gaze searches my face for an answer, but right now, I just need air and to get away from the hot, hard bodies, and my guilt.

"Caroline," I plead, "please, let go."

"No," she gets in my face, "what happened back there?" She points toward the dance floor, where her blond partner is watching her expectantly and motioning for her to come back.

"Nothing. I just, wasn't feeling it, and I have to pee."

She eyes me, clearly not buying the bullshit I'm putting out. She knows me too well and isn't going to let this go.

"Fine. I'm coming with you, then."

"What about blondie back there?" I look back to the dance floor, and he's still watching Caroline intently, although the dark-haired man with the raging hard-on has disappeared.

She waves to him and points to the back. He nods and turns around, disappearing off the far side of the dance floor.

Surprisingly, there isn't any line for the bathroom. I enter a stall and take care of business, relishing the few seconds of privacy, because I know as soon as I step out, Caroline will be all over me again.

I flush and open the door.

She's leaning against the counter, her foot tapping in time with the music. "You going to tell me what really happened?"

After dropping my purse on the counter, I wash my hands and turn to her. "He used some cheesy pickup line on me, and it reminded me how much I *hate* the club scene, and the men here."

"Oh really?" She smirks. "Since when? You used to love coming here."

Sighing, I reach into my purse for my phone. "Since you know when. Now, drop it. Please."

My heart lurches into my throat when I see Savage's name on my screen with a new text message. After weeks of nothing, finally, he's reaching out to me.

*Some fucking timing.*

I shudder thinking about that guy touching me and with shaking hands, I swipe the screen and open the message.

> I miss you. It probably isn't fair for me to be contacting you like this, when I'm still not in any place to try to fix things. But, I can't stop thinking about you and wondering if you are okay. I can't stop missing you. I need you to know I love you and I am really trying to make things right. I hope you can forgive me. <

"Danika? What is it?" Caroline leans in over my phone and reads the message. "Oh." She slinks back and drops against the counter again. "So, what are you going to do?" The disapproval in her voice does not go unnoticed.

Turning to her, I glare. "What's your problem?"

"You. You are my problem. You haven't been *you* in a long time, Danika, ever since you met Savage. At first, I thought that was a good thing. You were maturing, settling down, but now, I think this guy is just wrong for you, and you won't let it go."

*Wrong for me?*

"No, I won't let it go. Because I love him—"

"Sometimes love isn't enough, Dani. He's your first relationship, like *ever*, and you jumped into it without having any concept of what it means. You've been nothing but miserable since you met him and you've changed, and not in a good way."

"Jesus, Caroline, how can you actually think that? Savage is the best thing that ever happened to me."

She huffs and rolls her eyes at me. "Bullshit! You went from being happy and carefree, completely enjoying your life, to crying and being depressed, unless you were angry at him for something. A healthy relationship shouldn't be like that."

"Like you would know what a healthy relationship is. When was the last time you had one?"

The glare she gives me could melt the polar ice caps. "This isn't about me, Dani, it's about you and Savage."

"Exactly! It's about me and Savage, so you have absolutely no say in it. God, why can't you just be happy for me?"

"I would be happy for you if you were *happy*, Dani. But you're not."

I can't deny she's right about that, I haven't been happy the last couple weeks, how could I be? But to say Savage isn't good for me, that this relationship isn't good for me, couldn't be more wrong.

"Care, you need to stop butting into my life. It's none of your fucking business what goes on between me and Savage."

"It is my business, Dani. I can't stand by and watch you be miserable any more. You were happier when you were just being a slut."

My hand whips out, and my palm smacks across her cheek before I even realize what I'm doing. The sting of my palm connecting with her flesh and her shriek of surprise makes me shake my head and take a step back. I've never struck someone out of anger before, ever.

She looks at me with wide, confused eyes and presses her hand to her reddening cheek. "Jesus, Danika! You need to remember who your friends are."

She turns and flees the bathroom, and I turn and stare at myself in the mirror.

*Where the hell did that come from?*

Caroline has called me a slut thousands of times, and I've never been offended, not even once. Hell, I've called myself a slut more times than I can count. So, why did it set me off and turn me into the raging Hulk this time?

*She's just trying to look out for me, right? Am I deluding myself in thinking Savage and I will be able to work things out?*

Savage.

He's why that word made my blood boil.

For the first time in my life, I wasn't with a man just to get off. Despite my bone-deep aversion to romance and relationships, I fell in love with him and being separated from him—even though I know it's the right thing—has been excruciating. If we can't make this work, I don't know how I can ever go back to my old life of meaningless sex. Because, let's face it, Caroline hadn't been saying anything that hadn't been true before Savage.

I grab my phone again and reread the message. I take a moment debating my response. After not speaking for so long, there are a thousand things I want to say, but none of them seem appropriate via text message.

< I miss you, too. I'm not going anywhere. I love you. Tell me what you need. >

Those damn little dots appear, and knowing he has been waiting for my response warms my heart.

> You. I just need you. I need you to believe that we can figure this out. <

< I do. >

> I'm sorry I'm not ready yet. <

< It's okay. >

A desperate desire to get home overwhelms me. Being in this place feels dirty, and guilt weighs heavy in the pit of my stomach.

*What the fuck was I thinking? Why did I let Caroline talk me into coming here? This isn't my life anymore.*

I bolt out of the bathroom and make a beeline for the front door. I can't get out of here fast enough. I hail a cab and don't look back. My phone buzzes, and I look down.

> I'll talk to you soon, I promise. <

< You better. >

> I will. <

I smile and clutch my phone to my chest. Maybe there is a chance. Maybe there's still hope for us. But maybe Caroline is right. I just don't know.

## 27

## DANIKA

*T*his day won't end. I stare at the words on my screen, but they all blur together. Relaxing back in my chair, I scrub my hands over my face and groan. Two more agonizing weeks, and still, nothing. No resolution of my story, no resolution of the Savage situation.

"What's your problem?"

I spin my chair to face the door to my office and find Caroline leaning against the frame, arms crossed over her chest.

"Nothing, I just want to get the hell out of here." She walks in and slides up onto my desk, crossing her legs and folding up like a pretzel.

She shrugs. "So leave."

"I can't yet. I just sent my article about the closing of the Spring Street Library to Doug, and he hasn't sent it back to me yet."

She lets out an annoyed sigh and rolls her eyes. "What does it matter? You would just be going home to watch Netflix anyway, and you know it. Why don't you hang around until I'm done and we can go grab dinner and some drinks instead?"

I hate to admit when Caroline is right, but she is. As soon as I walk in the door, I will be slipping into my sweatpants and returning to my *White Collar* marathon on Netflix. Matt Bomer is so damn hot. That dark, wavy hair, those piercing blue eyes...

Without even realizing it, the image of Matt morphs into Savage in my head.

"Hello? Earth to Danika..." Caroline waves her arms frantically in front of my face.

Knocking them down, I huff. "Stop it. I'll go, okay?"

She grins and clasps her hands together. "All right, I should be done in about an hour. You want to go to Maxine's?"

Maxine's is a trendy martini bar and tapas restaurant right down the street from the paper. We used to frequent it before I started spending so much of my time with Savage. I haven't been there in ages. Just thinking about their French onion soup has my mouth watering and stomach growling.

"Sounds good, now go finish up so we can get out of here."

She smacks me upside the head as she slides off my desk.

"What the hell was that for?" I watch her walk to the door.

"In case you were thinking about bailing, I feel like I need to remind you I have a very violent nature." She grins and disappears around the corner into the hallway.

Things have been strained between us since that night at the club. We didn't even talk for three days, which is an eternity for us. When I finally sucked it up and called her to apologize, she made me grovel and admit that she was just looking out for my best interests, even if I disagree with her.

Things aren't the same, but they're getting there. Slowly.

Spinning back to my desk, I check my email again for a reply from Doug. Nothing yet. I open my internet browser and start aimlessly reading celebrity gossip sites. Just because my life is boring as fuck doesn't mean I can't live vicariously and gain entertainment through their misguided life choices.

My phone beeps, indicating an incoming text.

Savage.

> I'm ready to talk. Can I see you tonight? <

The telltale burn of tears starts in my eyes, and I squeeze them closed. No way I'm going to cry before I even hear what he has to say. I've cried too much as it is. Still, my stomach churns and my heart races at the thought of seeing him again, of sharing space with his imposing presence, of the possibility that this meeting may be our last, that we may say goodbye.

With shaking hands, I quickly shoot him a reply text.

< Yes. I can be there by 6. >

> See you then. <

I turn to my computer and am relieved to find the email I've been waiting for from Doug. I open it and groan. He wants some changes before he approves my article. I glance at the clock at the bottom of my screen. It's already 5:10. I told Savage I would be there by six, and it will take at last half an hour to get there this time of day. I better work fast. I open the article and scan the suggested changes. These shouldn't take too long.

"You almost ready?"

*Shit. Caroline. How the hell did I forget about her?*

I spin around and find her at the door again, a grin on her face. "I busted through my work like a madwoman so we could get out of here."

"Crap. Caroline..."

Shaking her head, she steps into my office, hands on her hips. "Oh, hell no, you are not bailing on me tonight."

I sigh, running my hands back through my hair. I know this is going to be a fight no matter what I say. She still isn't completely over what happened at the club, and even though we smoothed things over after the blowup, we are still on a bit of shaky ground right now. "Savage sent me a text. He wants me to come over so we can talk."

Her anger-laden face relaxes slightly, and she drops her arms to her sides and mumbles something to herself. "You know how I feel about this whole situation with Savage, but you need to talk to him, so go. I'm not mad."

"Really?"

"Yes," she steps into me and wraps her arms around me in a much-needed, comforting hug, "you need to sort your shit out with him, and it needs to happen sooner rather than later, for all our sanity's sakes."

I grin against her shoulder and squeeze her tight. "Thanks, Caroline. I owe you a night out."

"You do." She pulls away and smiles at me. "Now go sort out the clusterfuck that is your relationship."

"I need to finish some quick edits, and then my ass is outta here."

"Get 'er done!" she yells as she walks out the door.

That went better than expected. I return to my desk and quickly set to work on the edits. I'm racing through them like a madwoman, desperately trying to appease my editor while my mind is one hundred percent on Savage, not my work.

I get them done in record time and, just as I am shutting my computer down, my phone rings. I grab it, thinking it is probably Savage, but I see a "No Caller Info" message flash across the screen.

It isn't unusual for me to get calls from blocked numbers. Most of my sources don't want their identities revealed, and, even if they trust me not to reveal them, there's always the risk of my phone records being subpoenaed and inadvertently outing them.

"Hello?"

I hear rustling on the other end, but no answer.

"Hello?" I ask again.

"Danika, it's Paul. I need to see you."

"Paul! Where the hell have you been? I've been looking for you for weeks. Is everything okay?"

I've searched high and low for him, using every contact I have to try to determine if he was still with Abello, left town, or checked out permanently. If he got caught, we both knew he would pay with his life. Abello isn't someone who knows the meaning of the word "forgiveness."

"I'm fine, I just had to lay low for a while. I got what you need. Meet me at the Olde Market."

"Shit, right now?" I begin haphazardly throwing stuff into my purse.

"Yes, right now. I'll meet you in twenty."

*Click.*

The line goes dead before I have a chance to respond.

*Fuck, fuck, triple fuck!*

I'm supposed to meet Savage in half an hour. I've been waiting weeks for him to say he wants to talk. But I've been hunting down this story for almost a year, and it could make my career.

I grab my bag and race out of my office.

When I pass Caroline's office, I wave.

"Good luck with Savage tonight." She walks out into the hallway and follows me down to the bank of elevators.

"Oh, thanks, girl, but I'm not going over until later." I push the down button and wait anxiously for the car to come all the way up to the twenty-fifth floor to get me.

She recoils. "What? Why not? Why are you racing out of here like crazy then?"

"My contact on that big story just called. I need to go meet him."

"Wait, the one who basically disappeared for weeks?"

"Yeah."

"Wow, well, good luck!"

Ding. The doors slide open and I race in, pressing the lobby button and grinning at her.

"Thanks! This is going to be huge!" The doors slide closed, and I begin my descent.

I grab my phone and pull up Savage's number, hitting "Call" the second the doors open and I step into the lobby. It rings, and rings, and rings as I race across the shiny marble floor and out the revolving doors into the murky waning light of early evening.

"Come on, Savage, pick up." I stop at the crosswalk and wait for the traffic signal so I can make it across Main Street to the parking structure.

"Hello, you have reached Savage Hawke. Leave a message."

*Shit. Why the hell isn't he answering his phone?*

"Savage, it's me. I know I said I would be there by six, but something came up. I have to meet with someone first, but I will come over as soon as I'm done, I promise. I'll call you when I am on my way. I can't wait to see you."

I climb into my car and peel out of the parking structure, making the twenty-minute drive to the Olde Market building in less than fifteen, despite the traffic. Good thing I didn't see any cops along the way. I probably would have lost my license for reckless driving. The thought that I might be finally getting the information I need to blow this story wide open has my heart and mind racing. Knowing I'll also be seeing Savage tonight has my stomach churning. I have no idea what this means, but, good or bad, it needs to happen. Living in limbo is killing me.

I pull up to the curb outside the Olde Market on Riverside which, appropriately enough, runs along the Mississippi River and used to house a bustling harbor. In the last ten years, the shipping business has migrated more to trucks than boats, and slowly, the businesses along the river have closed. The Olde Market used to be a busy fish and produce market. It was the best place in town to get fresh-caught seafood and had the freshest fruits and vegetables you could find. That ended four years ago, when it closed its doors for good. The building was pretty well known. The giant, red tomato on top of the warehouse used to light up and spin, making it visible from almost anywhere in town.

Dad used to bring Nora and me here every Saturday morning, if he wasn't working. We would pick up what we needed for dinner that night. It was just Dad and us girls, and I looked forward to it all week. Any time I spent with Dad was special, but for some reason, leaving Mom at home and coming out here as a kid to meander among the stalls felt like something truly spectacular.

Looking at it now, you would never guess it used to have thousands of customers coming and going all week. The once clear and shining glass windows of the building are now all grimy and shattered. The infamous tomato is no longer lit or turning, its red facade covered in dirt and dust.

*God, it's depressing.*

I glance at my phone. It's almost six. Grabbing my purse, I climb out of the car and walk up to the chain-link fence surrounding the property. Looking up and down the length of the fence, there doesn't appear to be any opening to gain entry onto the property.

*How the fuck does Paul expect me to get in there?*

Continuing down the sidewalk to the south, I come across a portion of the fence pulled away from the pole enough for someone to slip through it.

*You've got to be fucking kidding me.*

I look down at my floaty, mid-thigh length dress covered by my trench coat and my pumps, and curse Paul. If I tear this dress or break a heel, I will kill him. I don't care how much I need this information.

The wire fencing pushes back easily, and I slip through the opening. Managing to emerge unscathed, I check my phone to make sure I didn't somehow miss a return call or text from Savage but find nothing. I look around the vast parking lot, but nothing is moving except for a plastic bag blowing across the wasteland toward the dumpsters by the far corner of the building. At least it's headed in the right direction.

*Let's make this quick.*

I hurry across the parking lot toward the closest side of the building, where I can see a door is slightly ajar. As I approach, my phone begins to buzz in my hand, and I look down to find Savage calling.

"Savage..."

Just as I answer, the door flies open, and Paul grabs my arm, pulling me inside the building with a quick jerk. I almost drop my phone and am about to tell Savage I can't talk, when I see who else is here.

Slipping my phone into the pocket of my trench coat, I pray the call stayed connected and Savage can hear what's going on.

---

## SAVAGE

"Hello? Danika?"

I just got out of the shower and found a message from her telling me she would be late. I don't care, as long I get to see her, but I wanted to find out if she had already eaten or if I should have something ready for her, so I called her back right away.

Rustling noises and footsteps echo in the phone, but she isn't responding.

"Ms. Eriksson, so nice of you to join us." The male voice is somewhat muffled, but it's familiar.

*Who the fuck is that?*

"What's going on?" That voice I would know anywhere— Danika. She sounds muffled, too. Her phone must be in her purse or something.

*I wonder if she knows it's still connected?*

"Don't play dumb, Ms. Eriksson. It doesn't suit you. You know precisely why we're here."

The voice, I know I recognize it. I've heard it before, and it's dancing around in the back of my mind, just out of reach.

I listen, straining to hear anything else, but all I get is more rustling and garbled words.

"Get your fucking hands off me!"

My hand clenches around the phone. *Dani. She's in trouble.* I press "Mute" and turn on speaker phone.

I head for the front door and race across the hall to Gabe's.

"There's no need to be so rude, Ms. Eriksson. We're just here to have a little chat."

Without knocking, I open the door and find him sitting at the kitchen counter, a spoon halfway up to his mouth. "What the fuck, dude?" He raises an eyebrow and drops the spoon into his bowl.

"Danika's in trouble." I set my phone on the counter next to him.

"Bullshit," she says, her rage evident even through the muffled connection, "the people you have 'friendly chats' with are usually never seen again."

Her words turn my blood to ice in my veins as I finally make the connection to the voice. Matteo Cortesi—Abello's right-hand goon.

*What the fuck is she doing with him?*

"Shit, Gabe, she's with Matteo Cortesi."

Gabe shoves his stool back and drops his bowl into the sink. "Where is she?"

"I don't fucking know. She said she had to meet someone before she came over here, and then I called her back and I heard she was in trouble."

"Shit, do you think Caroline would know?"

"Maybe." I've been listening to Danika's conversation with

Matteo while I explain what's happening to Gabe. So far, a reference to someone named Paul and an article are all I've been able to make out, nothing useful to us.

Gabe disappears down the hallway toward his bedroom, and I continue to listen, my entire body screaming to get the fuck out of here and to find her.

"...he didn't tell me anything. I don't know anything that could hurt Mr. Abello."

*Fuck, why didn't she tell me she was doing a story on Abello?*

I would've warned her off, made it very clear he wasn't someone to be fucked with.

"You really expect me to believe you don't have anything damaging on him? Nice try, sweetheart, but Paul already confessed everything he told you. The only question now is who else you've told."

"I haven't told anyone anything..."

Gabe reemerges in black cargo pants and a tight, long-sleeve black t-shirt, his rifle case over one arm and two handguns strapped into the holster around his shoulders. His phone is pressed to his ear, and he nods. "Okay, got it. Thanks, Caroline."

"Did you find her?"

He sets the rifle case on the coffee table and unzips it, pulling out his .300 Win Mag and quickly checking it over. Gabe rarely discusses his time as an Army Ranger sniper, but I know he was good enough to receive two silver stars for his service. Knowing he's backing me up on this should ease my tension and fear, but it doesn't, not when Danika's life is in danger.

"Yeah, Caroline said she was going to meet a source, but she didn't know where. I asked her if Danika had the 'find my phone' app. Turns out she does, and Caroline was able to guess her password. The phone is down on Riverside Drive at the Olde Market building."

"Shit, it will take us at least ten minutes to get down there."

"Let's go." He repacks the rifle and grabs his keys. "I'll call the police. You keep listening so I can give them an update on what's happening."

Gabe drives like a Formula 1 racer, weaving around other cars, blowing past them like they're barely moving. Danika and Matteo continue to argue about how much Paul told her and what her editor at the paper knows. She stands her ground, and despite my fear and anger at her for getting into this situation, I'm actually proud of her.

"I told you," she replies for the tenth time. "I never told anyone about the story, and Paul never told me anything."

"Well, we already know you're lying about Paul, so why should I believe you about anything?" Matteo's voice grows louder. The thought of that man getting closer to Danika makes my skin crawl.

I vaguely hear Gabe telling the police we are three blocks from the Olde Market.

*Three blocks.*

It might as well be three miles. He tears around corners at warp speed, slamming me into the door as we pull onto Riverside Drive. He stops the car several yards behind Danika's.

"Why does it matter what you believe?" Dani's voice stays strong and steady, even though she's no doubt terrified. "You're going to kill me anyway."

Gabe's head whips around when he hears that, and he jumps out of the car, grabs his rifle, and tosses me his cell phone. "Keep the police updated. They should be right behind us."

I nod and watch him disappear into the darkness. I don't know what he's going to do, but I know it's something I can't even fathom. As long as it gets Dani out of there safely, I don't care.

"What makes you so sure we're going to kill you?" Matteo asks.

I can picture the sneer on his face as he taunts her.

"You didn't lure me to an abandoned building, show up with

two of your goons, and interrogate me about my story just to let me walk away."

*Two goons? She's telling us how many men there are.*

I get on Gabe's phone and relay the information to the dispatcher just as two squad cars and a SWAT vehicle pull up behind me.

Matteo's maniacal laugh pours from the phone. "You're smarter than you look, Ms. Eriksson. I shouldn't be wasting all our time."

*Boom.*

A single gunshot rings out, the blast echoing through the phone and going straight to my heart.

## 28

DANIKA

*M*y heart stops.

The piercing ring of the gunshot reverberates in my ears and through my chest.

Matteo only fired a shot in the air—a warning shot or maybe to try to scare the shit out of me—but it could just as easily have been in my head.

I have no clue why he didn't just kill me, but the smile on his face tells me he enjoyed scaring me almost as much as he would have enjoyed leaving my dead body here.

*Sadistic fuck!*

Somehow, I manage to school my features—letting this man know he terrifies me would be a colossal mistake.

"Now, Ms. Eriksson, let's stop dancing around the issue and get down to business. You and I both know that I need to know what sort of documentation you kept regarding your meetings with Paul, where those notes are located, and who has access to them. You may be telling me the truth about not telling anyone

about your story, but we both know you wouldn't start investi-
gating a story like this without meticulously documenting every
single thing your source revealed."

*Shit. Matteo is smarter than I gave him credit for.*

I figured he was just another goon, another meathead Abello
used for muscle and intimidation. Apparently, he has some intelligence. It must be why Abello trusts him so much.

My eyes flicker between the two other men standing behind
Paul, just to the left of me. Now, these two, who haven't spoken a
word, are clearly just muscle, but not Matteo.

Maybe I can appeal to his intelligence to buy more time. I
know if that call stayed connected, Savage will come for me. He
has to.

*Stall.*

"All right, if I tell you everything Paul told me, and where you
can find my notes, will you let me go?"

*Of course they won't.*

I know that. But, I need to keep him talking and I'm not above
playing the blonde bimbo if I need to.

He smirks at me, and the evil glint in his eyes reminds me of a
cat toying with a mouse caught under its paw. He knows he has
the upper hand, but he enjoys his job too much to end this
quickly. He's also too smart to kill me before he's sure he has
every single piece of evidence relating to his boss.

"If I did let you go, what sort of guarantee would I have that
you won't immediately run to the police, or the media, and reveal
everything anyway?"

"You would have my word."

Matteo drops his head back, and his dark laughter echoes
throughout the empty warehouse. The two goons join him,
though I doubt they have any idea what he's laughing at.

"Oh, Ms. Eriksson, it really is too bad we had to meet under
these circumstances, because, frankly, I think I really like you."

*Use it.*

"I agree. Another day, another time, things might have been different." I take a step closer to him. Maybe he's dumb enough to fall for it, and maybe, just maybe, I can get my hand on his gun before I end up dead.

He eyes me suspiciously and steps to the side, closer to Paul and his goons.

*Why the hell does he have to be the only smart evil henchman in history?*

"Unfortunately, Ms. Eriksson, I have my orders, so let's not make this any harder than it has to be. Give me what I need, and I will end this quickly. If you don't, I'll have to make this very unpleasant for you."

"I can handle pain," I say with fake boldness, but my body is screaming for me to run. I'm sure Matteo knows ways to inflict pain I can't even imagine, and there's no way I want to find out. But revealing information from a source is also not an option.

I never thought I'd actually be in this position. My stories aren't the kind someone receives death threats for, let alone ends up with a maniacal asshole pointing a gun at them. Paul should have stayed away. He should have trusted his gut and put as many miles between himself and the Abello crew as he could. But he came back, because of me, because I pushed and pushed and pushed and made promises I couldn't fucking keep.

*Why did I have to push so hard to break this damn story?*

If I had never started my probe into Mayor Dunne and discovered the apparent Abello connection, none of this would be happening. So what if Dunne took some bribes and gave away some contracts? So what if he may have had some help from Abello in disposing of unwanted rivals and inconvenient speed bumps to his political climb?

None of it directly affected me. None of it interfered with my ability to live my life and do my job. Damn me and my ambition. Damn the journalistic integrity that prevented me from turning a blind eye to the apparent corruption. I thought I could make a difference; I thought I could actually change things.

All I've managed to do is put my life, as well as Paul's, in danger, and I still don't even have any actionable evidence.

*Complete. Utter. Miserable. Failure.*

Matteo barks out another laugh at my false bravado and steps closer to Paul, who has remained silent, shaking near me. "Well, maybe you need a little reminder of what I'm capable of."

In a split second, his gun goes from down at his side to the back of Paul's head, and he fires.

---

## SAVAGE

I cry out when the second shot rings out through the phone and in the air outside. The first time Matteo fired, I swear my heart stopped.

Everything I had dreamed of for my future, everything I had dreamed of for a future with Danika, disappeared in a millisecond.

Until I heard Danika's voice again, I thought for sure we were too late. It had apparently just been a warning shot, but Matteo just said he wanted to remind her what he was capable of...

Images of her lying in pools of her own blood, her eyes wide and lifeless flash across my vision, mingling with the memories of Star's death. That's been happening a lot lately, ever since Doc got me talking about the accident. The visions, the nightmares, things I had somehow managed to push out of my head after the accident—all of it came crashing down like a tidal wave.

And now, I might lose Danika.

*No. I can't.*

The officer standing outside my open door says something to me, but I don't hear it over the rush of blood in my ears. I'm listening for anything over the line, any indication at all of what has happened, but the line is dead.

"Oh, God!" I scream and toss the phone on the seat next to me, dropping my head in my hands as the tears stream from my eyes. I can't do this. I can't.

Three sharp cracks ring out, and I turn my head to the officer who has turned back to look toward the building. His walkie squawks and garbled words race out in an indistinguishable stream. He responds and starts to walk away from me toward one of the police vehicles.

"No," I grab his arm, "what's happening? Is Danika all right?"

He pulls my hand from his arm. "She's okay. Your friend really knows how to take care of business."

His words don't immediately register. All I hear is that Dani's okay, and, at this moment, that's all that matters. Then I realize he said something else.

"What? What do you mean?" The officer doesn't answer me and turns to speak with another officer, putting his back to me. I look past him toward the warehouse and see several dark figures moving around. A flood light spills out from the SWAT vehicle parked behind me, and in the bright florescent lights, Gabe emerges from the building with someone cradled in his arms.

*Danika.*

My heart beats out of my chest, and I can't seem to get any oxygen in my lungs as I watch Gabe stride across the parking lot toward the parade of vehicles along the street. The flashing lights of the squad cars, ambulances, and fire trucks paint strange colors across his stern face. Every step he takes seems to last for an eternity.

I've never felt more helpless in my entire life. Not even when I was lying in that hospital bed being told I lost the use of my legs. Nothing compares to the agony of watching and waiting, knowing there's nothing I can do.

The closer he comes, the more anxious I get.

I should have been in there. I should have been the one who saved her.

*She has to be okay.*

As they approach the fence-line, I notice her tan trench coat is streaked in something dark.

*Blood.*

*She's not okay...*

My vision blurs, my head swims, and I struggle to keep my shit together. Gabe moves through the opening the police cut in the fence and makes his way toward the car.

Her arms are wrapped around Gabe's neck, and her face is turned into him, obscuring my view and preventing me from seeing her like I need to. The officer who has been standing near the car steps away to make room, and Gabe steps into the open door next to me.

"Savage."

I know he's talking to me; I hear his words. But answering him is out of the question. My voice is caught in my throat.

*She isn't moving. She's covered in blood and she isn't moving.*

"Savage, snap out of it." He nudges my shoulder, and I shake my head, trying to clear the fog of panic that has overtaken me. "She's okay," he leans into the car with her, "it's not her blood."

*Not her blood.*

I should have known that. If she'd been hurt, the paramedics would have taken her immediately. Apparently, logic flies out the window in these situations.

He starts to lower her into my lap, but she cries out and grips his neck, clinging to him. "No, no, please don't...please..."

Her cries make my heart shatter all over again. She's clinging to Gabe for comfort—not me. And why shouldn't she? He's the one who saved her, who risked his life to make sure she was safe.

*While I sat here, fucking useless...*

Gabe pulls his head away from hers and cups her face in one

of his palms. "Danika, look, it's Savage." He turns her to look at me, and her wide, red eyes meet mine.

She practically leaps from his arms trying to get to me. He helps lower her into the car, and she climbs into my lap, latching her arms around my neck and sobbing against my shoulder, her whole body violently shaking with each breath she tries to take.

"Shh, baby, it's okay. You're safe." I run my hand up and down her back, trying to soothe her, but nothing I do seems to help. Her despair is complete; she's inconsolable.

I hold her for what feels like an eternity before an officer approaches and tells Gabe he needs to talk to the sergeant. Gabe nods to me and disappears.

Another officer approaches almost immediately.

"Mr. Hawke, we need to take Ms. Eriksson to get checked out by the paramedics."

She stiffens in my arms, her grip on my neck tightening.

"Can that wait?" I ask.

He shakes his head. "I'm afraid not, sir. They need to see her right now."

"Danika, baby, you need to go..."

"NO!" She screams and finally pulls back from my neck, allowing me to see her face fully for the first time in almost two months. Fear overpowers her beautiful features, her eyes so wide and terrified, I can't see any of the stunning blue that normally gazes back at me. "Please, no, don't leave me."

I capture her face in my hands and smooth my thumbs over her blood-spattered cheeks. "Danika, baby, they need to look at you to make sure you're okay. I am not going anywhere. They will bring you right back to me."

She shakes her head vigorously, tears streaming down her face, her fingers digging into my shirt and clutching at it frantically. "No, please, don't make me go."

I glance over at the officer, who gives me a sympathetic look, but it's clear she has to go, no matter how much she might protest.

"Can I go with her?"

She buries her face against my neck, sobs racking her body again, and I know no matter what the answer is, I can't leave her again, not for anything.

He nods. "I'm sure that won't be a problem."

"Thank you. Can you get my chair from the trunk, please?"

He looks momentarily confused, then glances down at my legs and back up to my face.

"Oh, uh, sure." He disappears around the back of the car. I pull Danika's face away from my shoulder. Her bottom lip trembles and tears still stream down her cheeks, but her breathing has returned somewhat to normal.

"Baby, I am going to go with you, okay? But you need to go with the officer, so I can get out of the car."

Her eyes are glazed over, and I'm not one hundred percent sure she understands what I'm saying, but she nods anyway. When the officer returns, she allows him to help her out of the car. The second I'm seated in my chair, she lunges at me, curling herself back into a ball on my lap.

The officer just points in the direction of the ambulance, and I follow him over there, Danika seemingly oblivious we are even moving.

She's in shock.

*How could she not be, after what just happened?*

We go through the same routine when the paramedics try to get her off my lap to do their exam. I finally convince her to get onto the gurney, but only because I promise to not move and hold her hand the entire time.

She has several scrapes along the right side of her face, but no other visible injuries. I hear the paramedics say something about shock, but I concentrate on squeezing her hand to let her know I'm here.

When the sergeant approaches and tells us we need to go the station to give a statement, she collapses into a fit of hysterics again.

I want nothing more than to bring her home and just hold her, show her I am not going anywhere, but there's no way we are getting out of going to the station. She cries against my neck the entire ride there, her body shaking and her breath hitching with every sob. My already-pummeled emotions are running wild, and I can barely keep myself in check. The only thing keeping me from completely falling apart is knowing Danika needs me.

## 29

SAVAGE

The interview at the police station drags on for four agonizing hours. Listening to Danika recount her ordeal in excruciating detail had my stomach roiling and my hands stinging from clenching them throughout her story.

When she described Matteo blowing off Paul's head and his body falling onto her, knocking her to the ground and pinning her under him, I could barely stop myself from grabbing her arm and pulling her from that room to end her distress.

I know they needed to know what happened—every gory detail—but watching her in so much anguish killed me. Now, as we finally approach my building, she's once again clinging to me, her warm breath puffing across my neck and cheek. I know she isn't asleep. I can feel her lashes fluttering against my skin as she blinks away her tears.

No one has said a word since we left the station.

They let Gabe go.

*Thank God.*

Anyone else who shot three people in the head with a sniper rifle would probably spend several days in jail while there was an investigation, at least, and may be prosecuted, at worst. But with Gabe's background, family connections, and the circumstances, I can't say I'm surprised it was easy for him to get released immediately.

His eyes lock with mine in the rearview mirror, and I see the same darkness there I remember from when he returned from one of his many deployments. He doesn't like killing, and I know he suffered when he had to do it.

In the past, he's always been very good at hiding it from people—everyone except me. I don't know how I didn't know he was seeing a shrink. I guess I just figured he was dealing with his demons in his own way, but I'm glad he did. Otherwise, he would have ended up even more fucked up than he already is.

We pull into our building's underground parking. The moment the car stops moving, Danika shifts in my arms and leans back, looking around to see where we are. "We're home, baby," I whisper, pressing my lips to hers gently.

*Home. My home. Not hers.*

*Fuck, I want it to be her home.*

I want her here, with me, where she belongs. Here, where I can love her, and protect her.

This isn't over with Dom, not by a long shot. No way he's going to just walk away knowing she's still alive, knowing what she knows, what she could do to him, knowing she caused the death of his right-hand man and two others. But, I will deal with that tomorrow. Tonight, tonight is about taking care of her, making sure she realizes she is safe, giving her whatever she needs.

Her unfocused, red-rimmed eyes search my face, but she doesn't respond. Gabe opens the back door and helps her climb out, but as soon as I slide into my chair, she lurches to climb back into my lap. I don't blame her. She's terrified and still in shock.

The silence continues on the elevator ride. Gabe holds the door to my condo open and Princess races out, jumping at me and then at Gabe's legs. He scoops her up and nods as he heads across the hall to his place. No words are necessary. Not now.

*Hell, what would I say, anyway? Thanks for murdering three people to rescue my girlfriend?*

I head straight for the bathroom. While the medical staff did the best they could to somewhat clean her up, there's still blood spattered and smeared on her cheek and in her hair.

*Thank God she hasn't been able to look in a mirror.*

Stopping next to the glass door of the massive shower, I nudge her.

"Baby, let's get you out of these clothes and cleaned up."

She looks at me with vacant eyes and my heart breaks just a little more.

I give her a fake, reassuring smile and capture her face between my palms. I don't want to leave her for a moment, but I need to grab something for her to sleep in. "Can you get undressed while I run to the closet?"

Terror flashes in her eyes, and she shakes her head in my hands vigorously, mumbling about me not leaving her.

"Shh, baby, I'll be right outside. I'll be back in a minute. I promise."

She whimpers but relaxes slightly, finally letting me help her stand. She wobbles slightly and grabs the edge of the counter with her free hand to help steady herself.

"I'll be right back," I reassure her.

She nods and reluctantly releases her death grip on my hand. I grab a t-shirt from my closet and return to her as quickly as I can. The two minutes I'm away from her are agonizing for me. I can't even imagine how they are for her.

She hasn't moved. Her entire body is tense. She stands with her back to the shower, her eyes locked on some unknown spot on the tile floor.

I set the shirt on the counter and capture her hand, bringing it up to my mouth and pressing my lips to soft skin on the back. "Come on, let's get you in the shower."

Her gaze flickers over to mine, and she nods in agreement.

The silence is deafening.

Danika is always alive with chatter, filling those voids with her bubbly personality, inappropriate comments, and witty retorts. Now, she's just a shell of the woman I know and love.

*Come back to me.*

Moving agonizingly slowly, she removes her dress, her coat long since gone, as it carried the most evidence of Paul's death. After pulling it off over her head, she lets it fall to the ground, then slowly removes her bra and panties, letting them drop without ever looking at me.

After months of not seeing her, to have her standing here, beautiful and naked in front of me, and to feel nothing but regret and fear, tears my soul apart. She's broken—beautiful, but broken —and there isn't anything I can do to make this easier for her. I would take all her pain if I could, wipe away the memories of everything she saw and experienced tonight. I would do anything for her.

Using the touchpad on the wall, I turn on the shower jets and usher her to the stall. Steam fogs the glass and the temperature in the room rises rapidly.

I urge her to enter the stream of hot water. She pauses before she steps in, turning to look at me. "You aren't leaving, are you?" Her voice is faint and shaky, and I fear she's on the verge of another meltdown if I refuse her plea.

She's never seen me completely naked.

It was never a conscious decision, but now that I've spent so much time talking with Doc, I realize I've intentionally prevented her from seeing all of me. My fear of rejection surpassed the overwhelming desire I've always had for her touch me.

Right now, she needs me. That's all that matters. My mental shit isn't important.

"I'm right behind you."

She nods and releases my hand, stepping into the shower and moving under the hot spray.

I undress, dropping my clothes on top of Danika's before I move onto the bench along the rear wall of the stall. She has her back to me, her face turned up into the water which cascades down over her shoulders.

It should be sexual, but all I can picture is that vacant look in her eyes, the way her body shook against me as she sobbed.

She reaches down and grabs the shampoo bottle, pouring it into her hand and massaging it into her hair before turning around and dousing her long, blonde curls under the spray. The red-tinged water swirls down her body and into the drain.

*Shit.*

I cringe, again thankful she never looked in a mirror to see the horror coating her. I know she knows I'm here, even though she hasn't acknowledged my presence verbally. Her shoulders relaxed the moment I entered. Knowing I might have helped relieve some of the distress, even a little, is at least something.

Her head drops, and she opens her eyes, fixing them on mine. The vacant look is still there, but underneath it, I see a glimmer of my girl, giving me hope she will get through this.

*Please, baby, let me help you.*

She reaches down and grabs the bar of soap off the ledge, closing her eyes again as she runs it over her body, the suds rolling over her pink flesh and down the drain.

When she's done, I reach up and turn on the spray above the bench seat, drowning myself in water that's almost too hot. She steps toward me, placing her taut belly right in front of my face. I reach out, wrap my hand on her hip, and draw her to me, my mouth finding the flat expanse of her stomach. "I love you, Danika."

I don't know if she hears me over the rushing water, and it doesn't matter. I don't need to hear her say it back.

Her fingers weave into my wet hair, nails scratching my scalp. She sobs, her body pressing against mine as she breaks down, collapsing onto her knees on the tile. I should have expected her to fall apart again, but seeing her like this, naked and vulnerable, throws me. It's so different from the Dani I know.

She wraps her arms around my waist, pressing her face against my chest, her tears mixing with the water cascading around us. I hold her, burying my face in her wet hair. I hold her until our skin prunes and there's so much steam in the room I can barely see two feet in front of me.

"Baby?" I gently pull her face away from my chest, cradling her in my hands. "Let's go to bed."

She nods and slowly gets to her feet, never looking away from me. Sliding the door open, she slips out around my chair and grabs two towels from the warming rack. She wraps one around her body, hands me one, and turns to the counter, wiping the steam from the mirror. I watch her out of the corner of my eye as I dry off. She stares at her image, unmoving, until I finally make it to her side, placing my hand on her arm.

Jerking slightly at my touch, she tenses before letting out a deep breath and closing her eyes. When she opens them again, she gives me what I think is supposed to be a smile. She takes her toothbrush from the holder and hands me mine. We finish getting ready for bed in silence. She pulls my t-shirt over her head and disappears into the bedroom.

I follow her into the room. The faint moonlight flowing in through the blinds and curtains falls over her form, which is already huddled under the covers in my bed.

*Our bed. Or, at least, it will be.*

I climb in and slide behind her, pulling her against me and wrapping her in my arms. She whimpers and pushes back against me, closing her hands over mine across her chest.

She can't get close enough to me, and I completely understand the feeling. If I could find a way to stay like this forever, and never let her go, I would do it without a second thought.

The emotional and physical exhaustion of the day overwhelms me, and I start to drift off. I snap my eyes open, not wanting to sleep if she needs or wants to talk, but I feel the steady rise and fall of her chest and know she's sleeping. I let myself go, both relieved and thankful to finally have her here in my arms and terrified of what tomorrow will bring for us.

## DANIKA

Paul's brown eyes bore into mine, accusations in his stare...*I got him into this.* He's right. I never should have pressed him. I did this. I brought this monster down on us.

The click of the trigger reverberates in my head, and then the side of Paul's head explodes, blood splatters my face, and I scream...

"Shit, Danika! Wake up!"

Strong arms wrap around me, shaking me gently, and my own scream echoes in the room. Hot tears pour down my cheeks. My chest is so tight, I can't seem to get oxygen into my lungs.

"Baby, you're okay. It was just a dream. You're safe."

*Savage.*

He pulls on my shoulder, forcing me onto my back as he hovers over me.

Even in the dim moonlight, I can see the fear and concern in his eyes. He searches my face, brushing the tears from my cheeks and kissing my forehead. "You're okay, Danika."

I shake my head, digging my fingers into his ribcage in frustration. "No, I'm not okay. He killed him, Savage. He killed him, because of me. He blew his goddamn head off."

A noise I don't even recognize rips from my chest. Savage pulls me into his body, pressing his face into my neck.

His warm breath fans over my ear as he holds me through my meltdown. "No, Danika, it wasn't your fault. Paul made his own choices. He knew what he was getting into when he agreed to help you."

None of this would have happened if I hadn't insisted he keep trying. He was ready to walk away. If I hadn't been so damn determined to break this story and advance my career, he would still be alive.

*Why the hell did I go meet him alone? Why didn't I insist on him coming to me, somewhere safe?*

I close my eyes, but all I see is the side of his head exploding, blood, and the shock and fear in his eyes before he collapsed onto me. Unnatural sounds continue to emanate from somewhere deep inside of me, and Savage continues to murmur reassurances I know aren't true.

"Everything is not okay!" I scream, pushing at his heavy body.

*He doesn't understand!*

"You have no idea what it's like to look in someone's eyes as they die.... You can't possibly understand.... Things will never be okay..."

He lets me push him away, rolling onto his back while maintaining his hand on my hip. I feel the tension in his body, and I realize I'm being a total bitch when all he is doing is trying to help, but if he tells me things will be okay one more time, I might punch him in the nuts.

I stare at the ceiling, watching the shadows cast by the moonlight. I can't look at him, not now.

Savage jerks up and flicks on the lamp on his nightstand, momentarily blinding me.

"What the hell?" I cover my eyes and roll onto my side, turning my back to him and the offending light.

"You're wrong..." His usually strong, sure voice breaks and quivers slightly, enough that I roll back to face him.

I see him waging an internal struggle, and my stomach knots, my fears over the last six weeks about the future of my relationship mingling with the intense emotions leftover from the night's events. "Wrong about what?"

He runs his hands back through his hair, rubbing the back of his neck and staring at the ceiling. The tension in his body sets my heart pounding and brings bile up my throat.

"I do know, what it's like to watch someone die."

My heart stutters in my chest, and my mind races trying to process what he said. "What...what do you mean?"

Sighing, he drops down onto his back and turns his head to face me. "I was going to tell you tonight.... It was one of the things I needed to explain to you."

Sliding closer to him, I press my hand on his chest, and his heart races under my palm. "Savage, what are you trying to tell me?"

He closes his eyes briefly and when he reopens them, they shimmer with unshed tears. "I know I told you I would never lie to you, that I was an open book, but, I did...I lied to you, I lied to everyone, about the accident."

*The accident?*

We haven't discussed the accident since the first night he told me the story. It isn't exactly something I would bring up, and he doesn't like talking about it, for obvious reasons. But, I remember every single detail he told me that night.

"What do you mean?"

"Shit..." He grinds his palms into his eyes before returning his gaze to me. "I didn't tell anyone the truth. I thought I was protecting them, making it easier."

"Savage, I don't understand..."

He slips his arm around my back and rubs his hand down my spine, and I shiver at his touch.

"I know. I'm sorry. This is just...fuck...a lot harder than I thought it would be. It was so much easier to tell Dr. Cochran."

"Who's Dr. Cochran?"

"My shrink."

I hope my face doesn't show my shock at finding out Savage has been seeing a shrink. He never seemed the type to lay on a couch and vent. He's always so strong, and sure...I can't imagine how hard it must be for him to open up to a total stranger and show any vulnerability.

"You're seeing a psychiatrist?"

He nods, the corner of his mouth turning up slightly. "I know, hard to believe, isn't it?"

I return his half-smile. "Kinda. So, tell me about the accident. What do you need to come clean about?"

He takes a deep breath, letting it out in a rush. "I told everyone I was unconscious almost immediately and don't remember anything about the accident. But, that's not true. I was awake, very much awake, until just after the rescue personnel finally got me out of the car."

Somehow, I manage to get my hand over my mouth to stifle my gasp. *He was awake? The entire time?* Envisioning the pain he must have been in, the terror he must have felt, makes my stomach churn and I have to swallow down the bile threatening to rise.

"After the car rolled, I was disoriented for a minute, but when I finally came around, I realized the car was on a strange angle and my legs were crushed beneath the dashboard, my seat twisted around toward the window. I yelled out for Star, but she didn't answer me. The position I was in, I could barely move, but I turned my head and looked over my shoulder...and I saw her..."

He trails off and it finally clicks, what he said...*"I know what it's like to watch someone die."*

"Oh, my God." I can't stop the words from tumbling from my

mouth as the tears well in my eyes, spilling in hot trails down my cheeks.

He brushes them away with his thumbs and a sad smile forms on his face. "She was still alive. I told everyone she died instantly, because I didn't want them to know she suffered. She was crushed. I couldn't see anything below the middle of her chest. I reached my hand out, searching for her, trying to touch her. I said her name, begged her to talk to me. Her eyes found mine, and I knew she knew she wasn't going to make it..."

His voices breaks, and he clears his throat, taking another cleansing breath before he continues. "I finally felt her hand, and I grabbed it. She squeezed back so lightly I almost didn't feel it. I told her she was going to be all right. She shook her head and said my name. It was so soft, I barely heard it...and when she spoke..."

A sob breaks free, his chest seizing under me, and I press my lips to his cheek, totally clueless how to comfort him.

"When she tried to speak, blood poured from her mouth... and I knew...I clutched her hand and talked to her, kept telling her we were going to be okay. I knew it was a lie. I knew she wasn't going to make it, and I knew there was a good chance I wouldn't either. The pain was overwhelming, but I also realized I couldn't feel my legs, and, knowing they were crushed and I should be feeling something, I knew..."

I can barely see him through my tears. I fight the sobs continuously rising in my throat, but eventually, they erupt, and he pulls me against him, bringing his face next to mine, pressing his lips to my temple.

"Don't cry, baby," he murmurs, his hand slowly sliding up and down my back.

*Don't cry? He can't be serious...*

"She died within minutes. I watched the life drain from her face, her lifeless eyes staring at me...so, baby, I know it's not exactly the same thing, but I need you to know, it does get better, easier. Eventually, you won't see it every time you close your eyes. It never goes away, not totally, but it does get better."

I want to believe him, want to believe the images in my head will eventually fade, but right now, that seems impossible. I pull back from his chest, now wet with my tears, and I wipe his from his face.

He gives me a sad smile and leans up to kiss me gently. "I'm sorry I didn't tell you the truth from the beginning."

I shake my head, brushing his hair back from his forehead. "It's okay. I understand why you didn't tell me, why you didn't tell your family."

"Do you think I should tell them?"

"No." I answer quickly, and he looks surprised at my instant reaction. "There isn't any reason to put them through that, is there?"

"No, I guess there isn't. But, I'm glad I told you, and I'm glad Dr. Cochran made me realize I needed to talk about it."

The relief is apparent in his voice, and the darkness swallowing me lightens knowing he found a way to deal with whatever was going on with him, whatever was keeping us apart. "You like him then?"

He tenses under me and glances away before returning his eyes to mine. "Um, her, and yeah, she's good."

*Her? His shrink is a woman?*

The thought of him revealing everything about himself to someone else, when he couldn't to me, is hard enough, but learning it's a woman...

*Rip my fucking heart out why don't you?*

I see the trepidation in his gaze, and I know he's concerned with my reaction. As much as the gaping hole in my chest hurts like a bitch, I'm somehow rational enough to realize it doesn't matter who he is talking to, as long as it means he talks to me in the end.

I swallow my jealousy and kiss him, letting my actions say

what I can't with words, that it's okay. Pulling away, I smile and wipe the last of his tears from his face. "I love you."

"I love you, too."

He reaches over and shuts off the light and then I settle into his side, burying my face against his shoulder. "We still need to talk tomorrow," he presses his lips to my forehead, "but try to get some sleep. It will get easier, baby."

I want to believe him. I want to believe that it does get better, but right now, when I try to close my eyes, all I see is Paul, and it is hard to believe that will ever go away.

# 30

## DANIKA

*I*'m awakened by bright light hitting my eyelids. I cover my eyes with my hand, groaning in annoyance as I roll onto my other side, turning my back on the offending light.

Reaching out with my free hand, I search for Savage, wanting to bury my face against his chest and ignore the daylight. My palm finds a warm plane of hard flesh, but I realize immediately something is different. The smooth, hot skin is lacking the sexy light mat of hair Savage has spattered across his chest.

My eyes fly open, and I lower my protective hand from my face to find him flat on his stomach, his arms tucked up under his pillow, head turned away from me.

Savage doesn't sleep on his stomach. Ever.

I never asked him why. I guess it never occurred to me to ask, but now, seeing the vast expanse of skin and tight muscle, I curse myself for having not begged to see it sooner.

My fingers itch to touch every inch of him, and I shift closer, watching the steady rise and fall of his back under my palm. I run it across his upper back and shoulders; he groans and shifts slightly. I still, waiting for him to wake, but he almost immediately returns to the steady breathing of sleep. Sliding my hand lower, I finally reach the sheet, resting across the middle of his back.

I don't even think before I do it. I just slowly drag the sheet down, exposing the rest of his back, and the crisscrossing myriad of scars.

My breath catches in my throat and tears pool in my eyes. I cover my mouth to keep from making any noise that may wake him. I knew he would have scars. The number of surgeries he had was mind boggling, but looking at them, seeing the physical evidence of all the anguish he went through, makes it so much more real.

Wiping the tears from my face, I reach out and brush my fingertips down the biggest scar, running from the center of his back down to the base of his spine. The red, straight line is raised from the skin slightly and is smooth under my touch. Just as I reach the base of the scar, his body jerks and, I yank my hand from his skin, whipping my head up to his face.

His wary blue eyes meet mine as he watches me over his shoulder. Propped up on his elbows, he stares at me, and I feel like a teenage boy who has been caught going through his dad's porn collection.

"I...I'm sorry..." Words fail me as I try to construct a valid excuse for my actions.

He shakes his head. "No, don't apologize. Go ahead."

Even as he encourages me to go on, I see the trepidation and unease in his gaze. I know this can't be easy for him, but the fact he's willing to let me do it anyway gives me hope we can really work through whatever barriers he'd put up between us in the past. He turns his head and buries his face in his hands on the pillow.

I reluctantly reach out, gliding my fingers down his back

again, from the top of his spine down to just above his ass. His body bows up into my touch, and he releases a strangled groan.

"You okay?" I lean in so I can see his profile.

He nods, his eyes still clenched closed.

"Do you want me to stop?"

He shakes his head but offers no verbal response.

The need to touch and know every part of him draws me into him again and I reach out, sliding my fingers across another scar, this one bisecting the large one down the center of his back. Craving the taste of his skin on my lips, I lean down, pressing them to the top of the scar and slowly kissing my way down its length.

He moans and arches into me again, his body tensing then relaxing as I move across each scar, giving it the same attention and treatment.

I don't know how much of this he can actually feel, or if his reaction is just from knowing I'm doing it, but by the time I'm done, his entire body is shaking, his face still buried in his hands. He hasn't spoken a word since he urged me to continue, and I'm suddenly overwhelmed by fear as I remember the painful silence of his panic attack and his inability to talk to me.

I kiss my way across his shoulder blades until my face is against his arm. His eyes are clenched shut, and my fear spikes as I reach out and run my hand through his hair. "Baby, are you okay?"

Slowly, he turns his head until he locks eyes with me. I expect to see fear, but instead, I'm met with a fire and intensity I've never seen before.

"Savage?"

He rolls onto his side and pulls me in to him, pressing his erect cock against my stomach, the thin t-shirt I wear doing nothing to dampen the heat of his body. Burying his hand in my hair, he guides my mouth to his, capturing it in a devastating kiss that renders me completely immobile. There are no soft preliminaries. His tongue glides across my lips, begging for entrance. I comply and respond in kind, tangling with him as I push my body against his, wanting, needing to be closer.

Abruptly, he pulls away and rolls onto his back, scrubbing his hands down his face before pushing himself up and sitting back against the headboard. "Shit, I'm sorry...I shouldn't have...I just..."

I slide my leg across his hips and straddle him. Capturing his face in my hands, I tilt his head back, forcing him to look at me. "Oh, no, don't you dare apologize for anything." Reaching between my legs, I grasp his erection and brush the head of his cock through my wetness, eliciting a groan from him. "Baby, do you want this?"

His shimmering eyes hold mine momentarily before he presses his forehead to mine. "You know I do, but..."

"No," I shake my head, "no buts. This is about us, right here, right now. Nothing else matters right now, as long as this is what you want." I press my mouth to his, letting him taste my need for him, my need for him to make everything else disappear, even if only for a few moments.

*Please, Savage...*

His hands cradle my head, and he consumes me with his mouth. I slide my wet pussy along his length, coating him in my arousal and letting him feel my need. When I rock my hips against the head of his cock, he groans into my mouth, moving one hand down and finding my clit.

I cry out at his touch, my throbbing clit needing the contact almost as much as my clenching core needs him inside me right now. "Savage," I gasp, "please..."

His hand slides from my clit down to his cock. He positions himself at my center, and I slide down.

SAVAGE

She engulfs my cock, her wet, clasping heat gripping me and making my head spin off in a thousand directions. Inch by inch, she takes me into her, stretching her tight walls that clench around my throbbing flesh.

"Sweet fuck." The words tumble from my mouth as stars flash in my vision. The pain of her nails digging into my shoulders brings me back. She gasps when she impales herself fully on my dick, rocking against my pelvis.

For the thousandth time since the accident, I thank God I can feel this. It isn't like I remember it, it never will be, but it's everything I need it to be.

Leaning forward, she captures my mouth as she tightens her pussy around my cock. My gasp mingles with her groan and she smiles against my mouth.

"I love you," she murmurs against my lips.

I kiss her deeply. "I love you, too, baby."

She grins and leans back, locking her eyes on mine, sliding up and down my cock, grinding herself against my pelvis on every down thrust. My hands slip under her t-shirt to find her hips, helping her set a slow, steady rhythm.

*Sweet glorious fuck...*

Finally being inside her, finally feeling us come together like this, is so overwhelming, it's hard to believe it isn't a dream. How this amazing woman could be here, like this, with me, after the shit I've put her through, makes no logical sense to me, but somehow, she is here, and she loves me.

She rolls her hips, changing the angle of our connection and pleasure shoots up my spine. Dropping my head back, I close my eyes and savor the glide of her body moving on mine.

My entire body tingles and warms, warning me of my upcoming release. I open my eyes and watch her—head tilted back, eyes closed, mouth hanging open as she moans in ecstasy, her clasping pussy tugging at my cock with every retreat. She reaches down and grabs the hem of the t-shirt, quickly lifting it up and over her head, freeing her breasts.

I won't last much longer. Not with her riding me like this. Leaning forward, I capture her nipple in my mouth, sucking gently while she continues to roll and grind her hips against mine. Her breathing is nothing more than urgent pants and moans, and I pray she's as close as I am. I move to her other breast, grazing it lightly with my teeth.

She cries out, her eyes rolling back into her head as her pussy ripples and clenches around me with her orgasm.

Watching her come, seeing the absolute bliss when she reaches her peak, combined with the relentless grinding along my cock sends me spiraling off into the most intense orgasm of my life.

*Jesus...*

Collapsing against me, she buries her face in my neck, her breath coming in rapid pants against my heated skin. Our heartbeats race against each other, and I clutch her to me, unwilling to let go of her for anything.

I never thought I would have this.

When I built and enforced the wall between us, I thought I had ruined everything, maybe beyond repair. I was convinced of that just days ago. The talk I had planned to have with her last night, before I almost lost her forever, wasn't going to fix things. I knew that it was too little, too late. I hurt her too badly for things to ever be okay. I was ready to let her go, to tell her that I did love her, but that loving her was only going to hurt her.

Now, I have hope, and hope is a dangerous thing.

Because, there's still so much I need to tell her. There's still so much she doesn't know, and, after last night, she may never be able to forgive me for it.

I hold her until our heartbeats return to normal, running my hand through her hair and down her back, her smooth skin warm under my palm. Her steady, even breathing tells me she has dozed off, and I can't blame her. After what she went through yesterday, and the near-sleepless night we both had, my eyelids feel heavy as lead.

Resigning myself to the fact that the things still left to say can wait, I close my eyes and let the rise and fall of her chest against mine lull me to sleep.

My phone chirps on my nightstand and startles me awake. I reach out and grab it, turning off the alarm. I silenced my calls and texts last night, but forgot to turn off the 8:30 a.m. alarm I set to remind myself of a meeting at 9:00 a.m. with a supplier. Glancing at my phone, I sigh, seeing fifty-six missed calls and twenty-three new texts messages from various members of my family, employees, and numbers I don't recognize.

As I swipe to read the message, a text from Gabe appears.

> Morning news. You're on it. <

I curse and fire off a response. It makes sense they wouldn't have mentioned Gabe. I'm sure the police don't want it publicized that a retired Army sniper took out three mafia hitmen before the SWAT team could even get set up.

< Can you please deal with my family? I need some more time with her. >

> Of course, anything you need. <

< Thanks, man. >

Sliding the phone back onto the nightstand, I nudge Danika awake. "Baby, wake up."

She groans and snuggles against me, turning her face into my shoulder.

I chuckle and nuzzle my mouth against her ear. "Time to wake up, love."

She squirms on my lap, my cock, still embedded inside her, starts to harden again. Moaning in approval, she squeezes my flesh and slowly raises her head, a grin spreading across her lips. She reaches up and brushes the hair out of my face and smiles at me. "You better be waking me for a good reason." She purrs, clenching around me and eliciting a groan from somewhere deep in my chest.

"Hmm, well, baby, I hate to do it, but we need to get up, get something to eat, and then talk."

Her smile fades into a frown, and she shifts her body forward, her swollen wet pussy tightening on my cock. My semi goes to a full-blown raging hard-on in a second. I grip her hips, trying to steady her and prevent her from further distracting behaviors. "Danika..."

She pouts and leans in, kissing me deeply. When she pulls away, she smirks and rolls her hips despite my best efforts to keep her still. "Come on, Savage, ten minutes."

The mischief and joy on her face make it impossible for me to ignore her request. Even if I could physically stop my reaction to her, which God knows I can't, the fact she can be so happy and free-spirited after what she went through last night means I can't possibly deny her. Not when reality is waiting for us.

I groan my resignation and capture her face in my hands, releasing her waist, which immediately rolls on my cock. She moans into my mouth, sucking on my tongue in the same rhythm she sets with her hips. I slide my hands down her sides and under her ass cheeks. She squeezes them in my hands as she tightens her walls around my dick.

She moves like a woman on a mission, her hips rocking and slamming against mine vigorously as she gasps and moans. I kiss my way up her neck until I reach her ear, sucking the lobe between my teeth and scraping it gently. She bucks, her breath catching in her throat before she cries my name, redoubling her efforts.

My body burns, my love and desire for her mixing with pure unadulterated need as we both race for our release. Sliding a hand between us, I find her swollen, wet clit and tug it between my fingers. She gasps, and her eyes fly open, finding mine. "God, yes..."

She leans back, placing her hands on either side of my legs, and looks down. My eyes slide down the smooth expanse of flawless skin until I finally see where our bodies are connected. I continue to roll my thumb over her clit and watch in awe as my cock disappears into her wet pussy, only to reappear a second later coated in our earlier release and current arousal.

My chest tightens. My entire body is engulfed in flames as I watch her ride my cock with reckless abandon, pulling me closer to orgasm.

"Oh fuck," she drops her head back and shoves herself against my hand on every upward thrust of her hips, "I'm gonna come."

*Thank God. I won't last another minute.*

"God, I fucking love you." I slide my other hand off her hip and up to her breast, twisting her nipple at the same time as her clit. She screams my name, bowing up and exploding in erratic jerks on my cock.

Watching her find her release pushes me over the edge, and I let go; my body detonates and lights flash behind my eyelids.

"Fuck..." she mumbles as she collapses, panting against my chest. I wrap my heavy arms around her and kiss her hair.

"I think we just did."

She laughs against my skin, pressing her lips to my collarbone and sliding her tongue up my neck to my mouth. She slips it along my lips. I open for her and return the slow, sensuous kiss, relishing the afterglow.

When she tries to bury her face against my neck again, I capture her hair, tugging gently to pull her head back. "Oh no, you don't. No falling asleep again. We need to eat and talk." I try to sound and look stern, but her little pout is so adorable, I end up grinning and kissing her again.

Eventually, she pulls away with a sigh and climbs off my lap with a groan as my semi-hard dick slides from inside her. She disappears into the bathroom. I hear the toilet flush and running water before the door opens. She approaches, carrying a wash-cloth in her hand.

Stopping next to the bed, she glances down at my cock. I follow her eyes to the mess we managed to create on my lap. She laughs and hands me the wet washcloth. "You need this."

I take it from her and begin wiping off the remnants of our morning when I notice her eyes traveling farther south. I know what she's seeing, and I try to calm my racing heart as I watch her examine my legs. She hasn't seen them before, and now that she's seeing the scars, the muscle atrophy, all of me in all my glory, my stomach twists and my chest tightens painfully. She reaches out and runs her finger up the scar along my left shin before her eyes flick up to mine.

"Compound fracture. There are three more on my right leg. They were both crushed by the dashboard collapsing when the car rolled."

She looks at my right leg and traces the scars slowly before turning to me, leaning in and giving me a quick kiss and taking the washcloth from me. "I'm going to take a quick shower. You start breakfast."

I watch her walk away from me in awe. I don't know what I was expecting when she saw all of me, but it certainly wasn't that. Maybe Doc is right. I haven't been giving her enough credit, but that still doesn't mean there aren't things waiting for an opportu-nity to devastate us.

## 31

SAVAGE

*W*hile she showers, I slip out of bed and pull on a t-shirt and boxers before heading to the kitchen to start breakfast. The condo is always so eerily quiet and empty feeling when Princess isn't here. I'll bring her home after we finish our talk, assuming Danika hasn't killed me once she hears everything.

I shudder picturing her reaction.

*How the fuck do I tell her? She is going to freak, completely lose her shit.*

Attempting to focus my attention on breakfast, I pull out eggs, bell peppers, onion, and cheese to make omelets.

As soon as I crack the eggs, she appears at the end of the kitchen island, in nothing but one of my t-shirts, her damp hair falling in loose curls to her shoulders. Her freshly-showered skin has a pink hue and she smiles at me, completely oblivious as to what is to come.

*I wish I could put it off, avoid telling her and just let her have a few hours of calm after everything she went through.*

"That was fast."

She travels around the island and gives me a quick kiss on the cheek, followed by a knowing grin.

I know she wants to make a "that's what she said" joke. I can practically see her restraining herself, and I can't help but laugh.

"What's so funny?"

"You." I wrap my arm around the back of her thighs and pull the t-shirt up, confirming my suspicion she is completely naked underneath. My well-worked cock hardens. I'm tempted to pull her down onto my lap for another round right here, right now.

She glances down and smiles as I press my lips to the smooth skin on the side of her ass. She shrugs. "I don't have any clothes here."

"I'll have Gabe go over to your place and grab some of your things today." I brush my lips across her skin, making my way to her stomach.

She steps away, letting the shirt fall back into place. "Why can't I just go?"

Somehow, I knew this was going to be a fight. I just hoped we could hold off and save all the combat for after breakfast. I'm fucking starving, and my head is starting to pound due to a lack of sustenance.

"Look, we will talk about it later. I'm going to go take a quick shower. Will you make the omelets?"

She scowls at me, her annoyance at my delay evident. "Fine." She grabs the knife off the cutting board and one of the peppers.

I retreat to the master bathroom and shower as quickly as I can. When I return to the kitchen, she is just placing plates with the omelets on the table. She grabs the pot of coffee and sits next to my spot, pouring herself a large cup.

"You want some?" she asks with some definite attitude in her voice.

*Shit.*

She pours me a cup without waiting for my response and sets the pot down on the table.

"Yes, please." I take my place and watch as she adds cream and sugar to her cup before taking a sip and moaning in appreciation. I much prefer when she makes that sound because of me, and who the fuck knows when that will happen again. The way I anticipate this morning going, I won't hold my breath.

We eat in silence for several minutes, but I watch her out of the corner of my eye. The tension she carries is evident in her posture and I know she has to be exhausted—physically and mentally. Knowing I'm going to make things worse as soon as we finish this meal makes me quickly lose my appetite.

I push away my half-eaten omelet and sit back, watching Danika scarf down her breakfast like she hasn't eaten in days. I'm relieved. Part of me was terrified she would slump into some sort of depression, but she seems okay today, more than okay.

I always knew she was a badass bitch, but I know she was affected by what happened last night. There's no way a human being couldn't be. The nightmares are evidence enough. I just hope she doesn't do something stupid, like try to ignore it, the way I did.

She drops her fork to the plate with a clank and turns to me. "You done?"

I nod and she scowls. "What? You didn't like it?"

"No, it was great. I'm just not that hungry, I guess."

She gives me an incredulous look and grabs our plates, taking them to rinse in the sink before placing them in the dishwasher. I head into the living room, knowing she'll follow me when she's done.

Besides, I need a few seconds alone to figure out what the fuck I'm going to say to her. My alone time in the shower did me no good. All I could think about was how fucking incredible it felt to be inside of her. How fucking amazing I felt watching her come apart in my arms.

*Shit. Shit. Shit.*

I head to the couch and pull myself into the corner of it to wait for her. She appears in the archway, with more than a little trepidation in her gaze.

Holding my hand out across the back of the couch, I motion her over. "Come here. Come sit with me."

She eyes me warily and slowly crosses the room. She stops in front of me, climbs into my lap, and leans back against my chest, resting her head against my shoulder. "You going to tell me what's going on now?"

I press my lips to her temple, holding them there as long as I can and savoring the feeling of having her in my arms before she gets annoyed at my non-answer. She turns her head to look at me expectantly.

"Shit, this is harder than I thought it was going to be," I run my hand back through my hair. "I don't even know where to start."

"Well, what did you want to say last night when you asked me to come over?"

I guess that's as good a place to start as any. Truthfully, it's best we have that conversation right away, because after I tell her about Abello and the rest of it, she may run before even giving me a chance to explain.

"I wanted to talk about us."

Tilting her head back, she locks her eyes with mine, and I see a hundred questions, and fear. "What about us?"

"I've been trying to figure things out."

Her eyebrow quirks up. "Did you?"

"Some of them. I need you to know, I love you. That never could and never will change."

"Why do I feel like there is a 'but' coming?"

I sigh, burying my face in her partially-damp hair. "Because, I don't know if this morning changes anything."

She turns across my lap and takes my face in her hand, forcing me to look at her. "What would this morning have changed?"

Having to look into the eyes of the woman you love, more than anything, and tell her you aren't sure you can satisfy her is probably the most fucked up, torturous thing a man can do. I haven't even said anything and already my chest feels like it has been ripped open and battery acid poured inside.

"That night, when you left..."

She nods, urging me to continue.

"...that wasn't the first time that happened."

She takes my hand in hers and squeezes it gently. "The first time what happened, baby?"

"That I had a panic attack. The other ones just weren't that bad."

"When did they start?"

I knew she would ask. That question was inevitable. So is giving her the answer I know will hurt her no matter how I say it.

"When I met you."

She freezes, her entire body tensing as she processes my words.

"Danika, listen to me. This isn't about you. You did nothing wrong. This is about me, and how fucked up I am in the head without ever realizing it." The tears pool in her eyes and threaten to fall, clinging to her bottom lashes. "Please don't cry. Let me explain."

She nods. I wipe the tears from her face.

"You know I haven't dated anyone since the accident. What I never told you was that for almost eight months after the accident, I wasn't sure if I would ever be able to be with anyone again."

Her eyes widen and I know she understands what I'm trying to say.

"You mean...?" I nod and she glances down at my crotch. Natural reaction to telling someone you were impotent, I guess. "So, what happened?"

I shrug. "Eventually the surgeries were completed, and the swelling finally went down. My body was able to recover and some of the nerves regenerated. Let me tell you, I've never been so happy to have morning wood as I was that day."

"Oh, my God! Do you think that's why Becca left?"

Danika always has a way of getting right to the heart of the matter, and then kicking you in the balls. I should have known she'd see right through me.

"I don't know, maybe. I'm sure it was part of it. We didn't know what was going to happen, or what our lives would be like. She couldn't handle it, and honestly, I don't blame her."

"She was a total cunt."

I can't stifle my laugh, and I drop my head back before kissing her. "I won't disagree with that. The truth is, I never realized what all that, and her leaving, did to me emotionally. I put so much into just getting stronger and getting back to my business, I never really let myself consider anything else."

"Until I came along..."

I squeeze her hand and bring it to my mouth, brushing my lips across her knuckles. "Until you came along."

"So, every time I tried to have sex with you, you were freaking the fuck out, and I was essentially instigating a panic attack?" Her tears begin again.

I sigh. "No, baby, don't think about it that way. It wasn't anything you did. It was what I was doing to myself. Dr. Cochran made me realize what I've been doing, and how unfair it was to you."

The way she looked at me that night, standing beside my bed, completely broken, I'll never forget that as long as I live. I never want to see her like that again, especially because of something I did.

"I never meant to hurt you," I continue. "I just didn't understand what was going on, or why, and I didn't know how to deal with it."

She watches me silently. For someone who is constantly talking, the silence from her is deafening. I know she's just processing what I said, but I fear she is over-thinking. Finally, she clears her throat.

"So, all this distance you put between us, it was because you thought you couldn't have sex with me?"

"It isn't that simple."

"Oh, no? Well, I think this morning proved it is that simple."

Not that simple, not by a long shot. She didn't know me before. There's no way she will understand. My frustration grows. I'm trying to figure out a way to make her comprehend my real struggle. "No, it really isn't."

She lets out an exasperated sigh and drops back against the couch. "Then explain it to me. I'm not understanding what the problem is here."

*Oh, fuck it...*

"The problem is I don't know how to have sex."

She bursts out laughing until she realizes I'm not joking. "Wait, you're serious? Baby, did we not have sex twice this morning?"

I scrub my hands down my face in frustration. "You didn't know me before. That was not how sex usually went with me before the accident. In case you haven't noticed, I am a bit of a control freak."

She rolls her eyes and smirks at me. "No shit. So, what, you were a Dom?"

"What? Fuck no, nothing like that. I just like to be in control in the bedroom, and everywhere else in my life, and now, I don't know what to do, because I lost that."

She looks at me, confusion written in her furrowed brow and the twist of her mouth. "What makes you think you lost that?"

"Seriously?"

"Yes, seriously. I'm not following you here."

"Jesus Christ, Danika." My anger and frustration finally boil over. "I can't use my fucking legs. How the hell am I supposed to fuck you?"

---

## DANIKA

I want to slap him—just haul off and smack my hand across his beautiful face. I want to scream at him and shake him and rage until he realizes how fucking ridiculous he is, how totally, completely, utterly crazy he sounds at this moment.

But, instead, I take a cleansing breath, slide down his lap, and throw my leg across him, straddling his pelvis and squeezing his hips between my knees.

Taking his face in my hands, I force him to look at me. "Stop. Just, stop."

"Danika..."

The exhaustion he's feeling is written all over his face and, even though I know he doesn't want to hear it, he *is* going to listen to me.

"No, now you're done; now you are going to listen to me." He starts to protest, but I press my hand over his mouth and shake my head. "No."

He glares at me, but when I remove my hand, he presses his lips in a tight line and raises his eyebrow in question.

"Baby, did you really think I don't know you have some dominance and control issues? The moment I walked into your office, you radiated power, confidence, control. You exude it, whether you intend to or not. You were the epitome of everything I always sought out, a man who would pin me against the wall and fuck me blind whenever I wanted it."

He freezes beneath me, his eyes going cold at my words.

I know that probably hurt him, but he needs to hear what I have to say, all of it. "Hard and fast was the way I always lived my life, and preferred my sex. I never wanted a relationship. I never wanted love. I never wanted anything more than great sex, and I was happy with that. Or so I thought. You want to know why I came to the club that night, after I had left like a fucking asshole? I came back because I barely knew you and I already wanted something more than I ever wanted with anyone before. I wanted you for more than your cock."

The corner of his mouth quirks up slightly, and he tilts his head to the side. "I'm not sure if I should take that as a compliment or an insult?"

I kiss him gently and shift closer to him. "It is definitely a compliment. Look, I'm not going to lie. When I found out, I was confused as hell and not sure what I was going to do. Then, when I was in D.C., I kept waiting for you to call or text me like a fucking high schooler waiting to see if her crush is going to ask her to prom."

He chuckles, squeezing his hands around my waist.

"I'm serious. I wasn't even like that in high school. This has been a completely new and utterly terrifying experience for me."

"Being with me is terrifying?" he asks jokingly. He leans in to nuzzle my neck.

"No, being *in love* with you is terrifying. I'm afraid I'm going to lose you and won't know how to live without you."

He pulls back, his love-filled gaze filling me with a warmth only he can provide. "Baby, you won't lose me, ever. The last couple months have been torture for me, trying to stay away from you."

*Ditto.*

"Then, why are you trying to push me away again?"

He recoils slightly, confusion in his eyes. "I'm not."

"Then stop talking nonsense. Baby, I'm not worried about our sex life."

"How can you possibly say that?"

"Well, there have to be a thousand different ways to have sex. The Kama Sutra alone has sixty-four positions."

He groans. "I don't want to know how you know that. Seriously."

I roll my eyes and continue, "My point is, we try and figure out what works. And if all else fails, I don't care if I have to ride you like Seabiscuit."

His laughter fills my ears and eases the tension in my chest. "Really? Seabiscuit? You need to update your analogies. American Pharoah, baby, American Pharoah."

"Shut the fuck up." I pull his face to mine and attack his mouth with my own. All this talk of sex is making me horny as hell. I rock my hips against his, pressing down on his hardening cock. His arms come up around my back, tugging me closer until our chests touch, our hearts already racing against each other.

Thank God I don't have any underwear on, because I can feel the heat of his cock on my flesh through the thin material of his boxers.

"Fuck," he groans, "you're wet already."

I shrug, kissing my way to his ear. "What do you expect? I've been imagining riding you like a racehorse."

He chuckles in my ears and pulls down on my hips, pushing my clit against his hardness.

I growl in his ear. "Take these damn boxers off. Now."

"God, yes."

I slide down to his knees, grabbing the waistband of his boxers and yanking them down to his thighs, letting his erection spring free.

His fingers dig into the flesh of my hips as he yanks me back toward him, capturing his cock between our bodies and crushing his mouth to mine. His all-consuming kiss steals my breath. I let myself go, completely losing myself in him—his kiss, his touch.

Rising up onto my knees, I grasp him, positioning the broad head against my wet core. He groans into my mouth. I slowly lower myself down onto his length, his cock stretching and filling me in a way only he can.

*Sweet Christ...YES!*

I always believed sex was just sex, but with Savage, it isn't sex. It's connecting on a level I never knew existed. As I begin to move, taking him into me over and over again, I can't fathom living my life without him, without this.

Everything else is forgotten when we are together. His hands are everywhere—my face, my breasts, my clit. I can barely keep track as my orgasm builds, preventing any form of thinking from being even remotely possible.

All feeling; no thinking.

Exactly what we both need—reaffirmation of us, of our future, of our love.

The silence of the room is broken only by our moans and the sounds of our flesh colliding in our race for release.

I finally pull away from his mouth, gasping for air as my body heats and the telltale tingle of impending orgasm starts in my core. "Oh fuck, I'm gonna come," I cry out and slam down on his dick, grinding against his pelvis, taking him as deep as possible.

He slides his tongue along my neck, then sucks my earlobe between his lips. "Come for me," he whispers, his voice shaking with his body, and I know he is fighting his own release.

I whimper and cry out his name when my orgasm washes over me like a tsunami. Wave after wave of pleasure course through my body, my head spinning and my rhythm falters. He catches my mouth as my orgasm wanes, and sucks my tongue into his mouth, tangling it with his own.

Rising above him and slamming down, he groans into my mouth. I repeat the move, swirling my hips, and he gasps, his eyes rolling back into his head and his release explodes in my pussy in hot pulses.

He collapses back against the arm of the couch, dragging me with him and wrapping his arms around me, cradling the back of my head against his sweat-dampened t-shirt.

I relax and just let him hold me, praying this isn't just some cruel dream.

# 32

## SAVAGE

*I* clutch her close to me, not wanting even an inch of space between us. I know we both needed that, need this connection after everything that has happened.

That I'm going to have to fracture this beautiful reverie with the truth about Abello breaks my heart. She doesn't deserve this bullshit, but she has somehow found her way here, in the middle of a shit storm she doesn't know the half of.

She stirs against me and her sleepy eyes meet mine, a small smile spreading across her face before quickly vanishing as she looks at me. "Hey, you look worried. What's wrong?"

I brush the hair from her face and kiss her, hoping to momentarily delay the inevitable. "There's something else I need to tell you."

Sitting up, she eyes me warily. "What now?"

There is no way I'm having this conversation with my dick still inside her. "Why don't you go get cleaned up? Then, we'll talk."

She makes an adorable growly noise, different but no less sexy than the one she makes when I'm deep inside of her. "Fine, two minutes."

As she slides my cock from her warm body, we both groan. I pull my boxers back up, and she disappears down the hallway toward the bathroom.

When she reappears, so does the wariness in her gaze. She stops next to the couch, watching me suspiciously. "So?"

"Sit back down." I pat my lap and she sighs, reluctantly dropping down onto it. I plant a quick kiss on her temple before getting down to business. "We need to talk about last night."

She stiffens immediately, and I sense a wall coming up before I can even say another word. "I don't want to talk about it right now."

"I understand, baby, and you don't have to talk. You just need to listen. There are things you don't know that you really need to."

"Fine."

I run my hands through my hair, a bad habit I have when I'm nervous and have never been able to break. "Um, first you need to understand I would have told you all of this a long time ago if I'd known what you were working on. I understand why you didn't tell me, but once you hear all this, you will know why things might be a lot different if you had known, if I had known."

"Jesus," she turns on my lap so she can see me, "you're really starting to freak me out here. Out with it."

*Here goes nothing...*

"I know Abello."

She doesn't say anything, watching me as if she is waiting for something. "So? Everyone knows who he is."

"No, I don't just know who he is. I actually *know* him. He is kind of my uncle."

"What?" She flies up off my lap before I can grab her. She looms over me, surprise and anger evident in her quivering mouth and clenched fists at her sides. "What do you mean, he is 'kind of your uncle?'"

*This is going well.*

"Shit, baby, please sit back down."

"No." She takes two steps back from the couch, intentionally putting herself out of my reach. "Talk."

"He isn't my real uncle. We aren't related. But, he grew up on the same block as my mother and my dad was in his class in school. They all knew each other since, like, grade school. My mom's best friend growing up was his little sister, Maria."

"You have to be fucking kidding me." She groans, rubbing her hands over her face before turning back to me. I would do anything to spare her the pain I know this is causing her, but I can't stop now. She needs to know everything.

"When I was little, he was kind of just around a lot. He and my father were friends, and we called him Uncle Dom. When my dad died, he was around even more, constantly checking on us and my mom, making sure we were okay financially or whatever. It wasn't until I was in high school that I discovered who and what he was. I tried to distance myself from him, and I did, for a long time."

"But," she interjects, "I know there is a 'but.' There's always a fucking 'but.'"

I sigh and then take a deep, cleansing breath. "But, when I graduated from college, I couldn't get a loan to open the bar. I didn't have any credit."

She sneers. "So, you went to Abello."

"No, of course not, but my mother told him about my struggle finding financing, and one day a check from him just showed up. I called him and told him I didn't want his money, but he insisted, said my father would have wanted me to have a chance to prove myself as a business owner. He said he had faith in me and would give me five years to pay back the loan, without interest."

"Damn."

"Yeah, so I took it. I knew I shouldn't have, but I did. I paid it all back in less than two years and went on with my life and my various business ventures, trying to forget I had ever had ties to him. But, he started asking for favors."

The nervous look returns to her face, and I can only imagine what horrific things she's imagining Abello may have asked me to do over the years.

"No, never anything like that," I reassure her. "It was always innocuous stuff, like wanting to use the backroom at the bar for a meeting, or reserving the champagne room and entertaining one of his high-profile guests. Never anything illegal, as far as I could tell."

"That doesn't make it okay," she retorts. "He is evil incarnate! I can't believe you ever let yourself get involved with him."

"You think I don't know that?" I clench my hands into fists so hard I think my palms may be bleeding. I think of the position both Danika and I are now in with Abello. "You think I like being tied to a fucking mafia boss for the rest of my life?"

"Fuck!" She screams and begins pacing back and forth between the couch and the coffee table. She's already freaking out and I haven't even told her half of it yet. I'm afraid she'll go nuclear when she finally knows everything.

*Deep breath, Savage. Then get it out.*

"There's more."

She pauses and turns to face me. "You have to be fucking kidding me. What more could there possibly be? You're basically related to the man who tried to have me killed last night. What the fuck more can there be?"

Her voice rises several octaves as she borders on hysteria, but it does no good to withhold this from her. It's like ripping off a bandage. Best to get it done quickly.

"When you were researching the mayor, what do you remember finding about his family?"

She closes her eyes briefly before she returns to pacing, alternating between squeezing her hands into fists at her sides and chewing on her nails. "Um, Mayor Dunne's wife died giving birth, and everyone kind of lost track of his son after he graduated from high school. I think his name was Anderson. The mayor never talks about him."

Bomb dropping in three...two...one...

"That's because they haven't spoken in over ten years."

She stops in front of me, hands on her hips. "And how the hell would you know that?"

I take a deep breath and attempt to prepare myself for her epic meltdown. "Because Gabe is Mayor Dunne's son."

A gasp escapes before she shakes her head. "No, no, that's impossible. Gabe isn't a Dunne."

"His mother's maiden name was Anderson. They named him Anderson Gabriel Dunne. When he was eighteen, he had his name legally changed to Gabriel Anderson. He enlisted, and he never spoke to his father again."

She stops and collapses onto the other end of the couch, dropping her head against the back and closing her eyes. "This is like some sick fucking joke."

"I know, but, baby, I need you to understand how dangerous this is. Abello is not going to let the killing of his right-hand man and two of his lieutenants go unanswered, and by now, he knows not only that you are alive, but that you and I are involved."

When she turns her head to face me, I see the tears shimmering in her eyes and hold my hand out to her, urging her to come over. She resists momentarily but eventually grabs my hand and lets me pull her up against me.

She buries her face in my chest, and her warm tears splash against me, drenching my shirt.

"Don't cry, baby. It's going to be okay. We're going to figure this out."

"How?" She sobs so hard, she practically chokes herself.

"How the hell do we get a mobster to stop trying to fucking kill us?"

"Shh." I try to comfort her, but, frankly, I don't have a clue how I'm going to convince Abello to let this go. There's no way he can let Danika live with a chance she might publish the story, and he will assume both Gabe and I are involved and helping her at this point. "Danika, was what you told Matteo true? Does no one else know about your story?"

She sniffles and looks up at me with her red-rimmed eyes. "Yes, I never told anyone what I was working on."

My mind races, and a plan begins to form. "What about your notes? Where are they?"

If I can get my hands on them, maybe, just maybe, we have a chance at keeping ourselves alive.

"At my place, I keep them in a notebook. It's probably on my desk."

I nod and kiss her head, holding her close to me as I run through the plan mentally.

I'm a lunatic. It's the only explanation for why I think this might actually work, but, right now, I feel like there aren't really a lot of options. The police can't keep us safe from someone like Abello. He has so many men on his payroll; he has people in every precinct of the city. Even if we left town, where the hell would we go? Would we really be able to leave our families behind? He would find us anyway. With his connections, it wouldn't even be hard.

"I need to go talk to Gabe. Are you going to be okay here alone for a little bit? I'll be right across the hall."

She nods weakly. "Yeah, I need to call Nora and my mom anyway. They will be freaking the fuck out by now."

I kiss her again, taking my time to show her through actions what I can't in words. I will fix this.

## DANIKA

Savage heads to Gabe's with a promise he'll return as soon as he can and an order not to leave the condo unless it's to come to Gabe's because I need something.

I agree, reluctantly. Even though I know it would be dangerous and stupid to leave the building, the thought of being cooped up here for God knows how long while Gabe and Savage try to figure this out is giving me cabin fever already.

Wandering back to the bedroom, I climb onto Savage's bed and recline against the headboard, staring at my phone in my hand. I have multiple messages from Nora, Caroline, Mom, Doug, and pretty much everyone I have ever met asking if I am okay. I barely listen to them before I hit the "Delete" button. I don't want to have to discuss what went down with everyone. If I did, I'm not sure I could maintain the level of calm and control I have managed so far today.

The only reason I'm not currently in a corner sobbing and generally becoming a mental patient is because of Savage. His strength and reassurances have grounded me, and the break-through we had concerning our relationship has cemented us in a way I didn't think possible. All the magnificent hormones racing through my body from the multiple orgasms can't hurt either.

Taking a deep breath, I mentally prepare myself for the call with Mom and Nora. I'm doing this three-way; no way in hell I am going to do it twice.

As soon as the phone starts ringing, I feel like I'm going to vomit. I need to tell them right off the bat I'm not getting into details with them. There's no way I would survive discussing that, especially without Savage here.

"Danika? Oh, my God! Are you okay?" Nora screeches into the phone.

"Yes, I'm okay. Hold on, I'm going to get Mom on the line."

"No, don't call her. I'm at her house. I'll put it on speaker." She screams for Mom, and I can picture her running down the hallway in Mom's tiny ranch house at breakneck speeds just like when we were kids. Rustling follows, and then, Mom screams when Nora tells her I am on the phone.

I groan and drop my head back against the headboard, squeezing my eyes shut and enjoying my last second of peace and calm before the inquisition begins.

"Danika! Are you okay? What the hell happened? We got a call from Gabe saying you were okay, but..."

"Mom..." I interject, the tension between my temples swelling infinitely.

"...then this morning on the news we saw pictures of you and Savage and you were covered in blood! They said something about three dead..."

"Mom! Stop." I don't mean to snap at her. Really, I don't, but she never stops. She never listens, and if she starts drilling me about what happened I know I will lose it. I can't lose it. I can't. I'm too strong for that.

*Keep it together.*

After a sharp intake of breath, Nora whispers something to Mom before responding. "Are you okay, really?"

I sigh, pressing on my temples to try to ease some of the pressure. "Yes, I'm fine. I'm at Savage's and will be here for a while, I think, but I'm fine. I promise."

Nora tells Mom she will be right back and I hear her footsteps and a door slam. "Sorry, I needed to get away from Mom. You're at Savage's? What's going on? Are you two back together?"

"Yeah, we are. We talked, and things are good."

I don't know how else to explain it to her. I have no intention of giving her any of the salacious details. It's awkward enough having my sister work for my boyfriend. The last thing that needs to be tossed in that mix is her having knowledge of our deep, dark secrets.

She releases a sigh. "Thank God. You two were miserable the last couple weeks. I swear to God, if you didn't figure this shit out soon, Gabe and I were ready to lock you two in a room and leave you until you got your stuff together."

"Gee, thanks, sis." I slide off the bed and make my way to the bathroom. A long, scalding-hot bath sounds amazing right now. I grab what I need and walk down the hallway to the guest bathroom and its enormous whirlpool jet bathtub.

"I'm just being honest. It was awful watching both of you torture yourselves. It was clear neither of you wanted this breakup, or whatever it was. I'm just happy you worked it out. I could have done without the heart attack I had when Gabe called to tell us what happened and then we saw you on the news."

"Yeah, sorry about that." I switch on the water and sit on the side of the tub as the steam rises around me. The eucalyptus bath salts sitting on the edge of the tub look beyond inviting so I dump some in as the tub fills.

"What are you doing now? You need me to come over?"

"No, Savage is over at Gabe's for a bit. I am going to take a long, hot bath and just try to relax."

"Okay."

I hear the disappointment in her voice

"But let me know if you need me."

I know she wants to be here to support me, and I love her even more for it, but I'm too on edge right now to deal with her. Especially when she doesn't, and can't, know the whole story.

"Maybe tomorrow, Nora. I'll call you."

"Okay, I love you."

"Love you, too." I hang up and slide my phone onto the counter before I strip and step into the tub. The hot water sears my skin, almost to the point of intolerability, but I sink down into it anyway, letting it continue filling around me.

Dropping my head back against the headrest, I close my eyes and try to concentrate on the sound of the rushing water. Maybe it will wash away the images in my head, the ones that, even after what happened with Savage this morning, I can't seem to shake.

He promised things would get better. He said it gets easier, more bearable.

I hope he's right because the thought of going to bed and closing my eyes, being with my thoughts and the vivid memories all night, terrifies me. It's different in the daylight, easier to make it through with distractions like Savage. But nothing will ever get better if he and Gabe can't find a way to deal with Abello.

The cops told me they didn't have enough on him to arrest him, just like I didn't have enough to write my story. So, Savage is right. They're useless as far as protecting me is concerned.

But something inside tells me not to underestimate Savage, or Gabe, for that matter.

They'll figure something out. They have to.

## 33

SAVAGE

*G*abe stares at me from across the coffee table. "You want to do what?" HIs jaw drops open in disbelief. "Are you fucking insane?"

His response shouldn't surprise me, I guess. My plan isn't exactly foolproof, but I can't think of any other feasible way to get out of this clusterfuck.

"You have a better plan?"

"Than blackmailing the head of the fucking mob and then relying on him to keep a promise not to come after us? Yeah, I think I can come up with something better than that, Savage. For fuck's sake, you can't trust this guy. You, of all people, should know and understand that."

"Oh yeah, and what's your plan? Take him out with your damn rifle?" As soon as the words leave my mouth, I regret them.

He recoils and presses his lips together in a tight line as his green eyes go ice-cold instantly. It wasn't fair, and I know it.

*Low blow, Savage. Nice work.*

I know what a toll his job took on him. Maybe I don't understand the full extent. I doubt he will ever open up enough to talk
to me about what went on over there, but just knowing it got bad
enough he went to a shrink tells me all I need to know. A good
friend doesn't throw something like that in your face. I'm such an
asshole.

"Gabe, I'm sorry. I didn't mean that."

He drops back in the sofa and leans his head back, effectively
avoiding any eye contact with me. "Yeah, you did."

The silence lingers between us, and I try to determine something, anything to say. I could deny it, but I would be lying. As
much as I hate that what I said hurt him, I also know he's good,
really fucking good at killing. And whether he likes that fact or
not, it's still true, and it would still solve all of our problems.

He scrubs his hands down his face before finally returning his
leery gaze to me. "I can't kill him, Savage," he murmurs, his voice
barely loud enough to hear.

Gabe doesn't break. Ever. He's been my best friend, my
brother, my rock, since I was too young to realize how important it was. He's been with me through the hardest days of my
life, and risked his own life to save Danika's. And I know he
would do it again, without me ever asking. He doesn't break,
but he is bent right now, after what happened last night, so far
I'm afraid anything I say may push him over some invisible
edge.

"I know you can't. I didn't really mean that was an option. I
just meant it might solve our problem."

He nods slowly, then reaches for his beer on the table and tips
it back, draining what's left in the bottle. "You really think it could
work?"

"What? My plan?"

"Yeah."

I've been thinking about this nonstop since we rescued
Danika. A hundred different ideas have battled around in my

head, and I've rejected every single one of them. This is all I have, all we have, our only chance at surviving this.

"If I was just some random guy off the street whose girlfriend got in over her head? No. Not for a fucking second do I think it would work. But, Abello knows me. He knows I don't fuck around, and he knows my word means something. And I know him. I don't think he wants to hurt me, either directly, or by going after Danika or you. I think if I presented this option, another way to him, he will take it rather than face the consequences of taking us out."

Just the thought of him coming after Danika or Gabe makes me so angry, my skin heats and my heartbeat races. "I'm not going to let him fuck with us, Gabe. It took me too long to get to where I am, to finally be happy, I'm not going to lose it now."

"What about my dad? You know he won't just let this go if Abello follows through with your plan."

Hearing Gabe refer to Dunne as his dad makes my skin crawl. Dad was more of a father to him than that self-centered asshole ever was. The only good thing Dunne ever did for him was to let him spend most of his time with us and basically let him go when he turned eighteen. Now, this shit with Abello may not only bring down Dunne, but it may also out Gabe's true identity, something he has worked very hard at concealing for over a decade.

"I know, but he is the lesser of two evils here, and we can deal with any blowback from him down the road."

Gabe sighs and leans back on the couch. "I guess we don't have much of a choice."

"Not really."

"Then call Dom, get the meeting set up, and let's get this done."

I make the call, with my heart in my throat. Dom doesn't answer, but I manage to arrange to meet at Angelo's on Friday night through one of his goons. Now, all I can think about is getting back to Dani. Even though she's just been across the hall, and I've only been away from her for two hours, it already feels like an eternity.

Princess follows me across the hall to my place, and the darkness and silence immediately set me on edge. "Dani?"

She doesn't respond.

*Where the hell are you?*

I follow Princess down the hall toward my bedroom and when I pass the guest bath, the unmistakable smell of eucalyptus wafts from the open door. She must have taken a bath.

*Good, she needs to relax.*

My bedroom is dark. Dani pulled the curtains closed over the blinds so no light would get in but I know she's there, in my bed. Even in the darkness, her form stands out and calls to me. I approach the bed and the steady sound of her breathing tells me she's finally getting some much-needed sleep.

*You should leave her be.*

Despite every fiber of my being calling out to climb into bed with her and take her in my arms, I don't. Instead, I turn and head back toward the living room, with every intention of letting her sleep.

"Savage?"

Her voice is soft, and it floats across the room to me. I turn back toward her and see she's leaning up on one arm, facing me. The darkness can't hide the need emanating from her, or the fact that she's naked.

"Hey, sorry, I didn't mean to wake you."

She doesn't respond, just pulls back the covers on my side of the bed, silently asking me to join her.

*Like she needs to ask.*

## DANIKA

He moves onto the bed, and I lie back down, turning my back to him so he can wrap me in his arms and hold me like I need him to right now.

Just feeling his weight shift the bed behind me quells some of the anxiety I've been feeling since he went to Gabe's.

*Did they figure something out? Or am I going to be looking over my shoulder the rest of my life because of Abello?*

His arms slip around me, and he pulls me back against his chest. I never bothered to put on any clothes after my bath. Exhaustion hit me so hard, all I wanted to do was sleep. Thank God I didn't, because his naked skin pressed against mine is utterly divine and just what I need right now.

"Mmm..." The low, rumbling of contentment sounds from somewhere deep in his chest and vibrates along my back. "You smell amazing."

"I took a long bath after I talked to my mom and Nora."

"How did that go?"

"Pretty much what I expected. How did it go with Gabe?"

His warm breath flutters against the hair on the back of my neck and he sighs. I shift even closer against him, pressing his semi-hard cock against my ass.

He groans and tries to push away from me slightly, but I don't let him.

"You know, it makes it a little hard to talk, let alone think when you do that with your ass."

I chuckle and rock back against him again. "I know. Look, I don't need to know the specifics right now, but I just need to know you have a plan."

He answers without hesitation, "We have a plan. I won't let anything happen to you."

"I know." I turn my head to the side and look at him. His blue eyes are blazing in the dark room, and I know he would die to protect me. Despite everything that has happened, lying here in his arms, I actually believe everything is going to be all right.

My lips find his and instantly, a fire ignites between us. I try to turn in his arms but he stops me, holding me firmly in place and breaks away from our kiss. "Dani, no."

*What? Is he seriously going to deny me sex right now?*

"Savage..." I start to protest, but he silences me with another kiss and pushes on my shoulder until my chest is flat on the bed.

*Sweet Jesus, if he's thinking what I think he's thinking...fuck yes!*

A shiver of anticipation rolls through me, and I flatten myself completely on the bed, my head turned to the side, and wait while he shifts his body across my back until his dick is pressed between my ass cheeks. My pussy clenches, and I stifle a whimper.

His massive arms support his weight, and he leans in until his lips are a hairsbreadth from mine. I look up at him and see the mix of love, lust, and trepidation there. There's no doubt in my mind he's terrified of even attempting this. His need to control a situation he's unfamiliar with must be absolutely killing him right now. But he's doing it.

*For me.*

I kiss him and reach back, wrapping my hand around his cock and squeezing it firmly. He groans into my mouth, and I grin against his lips while I arch my back and rub the head of his cock against my wet core.

"Fuck!" He gasps and shifts first one hand, then the other, up onto the top of the headboard, the weight of his lower body still pressed along mine.

"Can you kneel?"

He nods. "As long as I have the headboard to support me."

I scoot forward and push up onto my hands and knees, giving him room behind me. He pulls himself up until he's kneeling, and I reach back, angling his cock so it just barely presses into me. The wood creaks under his grasp and his entire body vibrates behind me.

With a little shifting of my hips, I'm able to push back and take his cock in, inch by inch, slow and steady.

*Damn...he feels even bigger this way. I didn't think that was possible.*

I work my way back until he has completely filled me. Another shudder rolls through my body, and his teeth nip at the side of my neck.

"Fuck, Dani, you feel so incredible."

My response is something between a whimper and a moan and I move forward, slowly easing myself off his cock. The headboard creaks as he pulls against it, meeting my backward thrust. He's using the headboard for leverage...

*I sure as hell hope it doesn't break.*

We find a rhythm—me sliding back against him and him pulling himself forward as much as he can. Our gasps and moans echo through the room and that, combined with the sound of our skin slapping together, has me nearly orgasming.

Teeth sink into my shoulder, and I cry out, contracting and squeezing him through the next several thrusts. My knees are quivering and so are his arms—the veins bulging in his massive biceps. Our combined sweat drips down my back, and if I don't come soon, I know he will beat me to the punch.

I slide my right hand down to my swollen clit and rub against it furiously—needing to come more than I need air right now. He grunts in my ear and stills behind me just as my body begins pulsing with pleasure.

"Dani..." He gasps my name as he comes.

My head falls to the pillow, and his name comes from my lips, garbled. I collapse onto the bed, his cock slipping free. He moves his hands down off the headboard and slides behind me, pulling me onto my side and up against him.

His panting breath tickles my ear, and he presses his lips to the sensitive skin just below it. "God, I fucking love you."

I manage to catch my breath and turn in his arms until I can look up at his face. "I love you, too, Savage."

The corner of his mouth quirks up before he leans in and presses a gentle kiss to my lips. I hold his face in my hands and pull away, making sure he keeps his eyes on mine.

It's terrifying how much I love this man, how much he has come to mean to me and my life.

*I can't lose him...ever. I can't let whatever goes on in his head ever get between us again.*

"Don't ever forget, I'm not going anywhere. This is where I belong...where we belong."

# 34

SAVAGE

*S*itting across from Abello at the back booth of Angelo's, I wonder what the fuck I was thinking when I decided this was a good idea. There are probably ten guns on me right now and another ten ready and willing if they are needed.

Abello glares at me, his hands folded together on the table in front of him. He's absolutely still—nothing moves, not even his chest. The man is a fucking statue. I can't even tell if he's breathing.

He's been like this for five minutes, or at least it feels like five minutes. Gabe sits next to me stoically. I don't dare turn my head to check on him. Breaking eye contact with Abello is tantamount to admitting defeat. His cold, brown eyes continue to bore into me as I fight the urge to shift in my seat under his scrutiny.

Finally, a ghost of a smile crosses his lips, and he clears his throat. "I have to hand it to you, Savage. I didn't think you had it in you. When I learned of your connection to Ms. Eriksson, I never imagined you would come out swinging in her defense. You never did have your father's fight in you."

I smirk and reach out to grab my glass of Scotch, taking a long sip and savoring it, giving me a chance to compose myself. "If it surprises you I would do anything to protect the woman I love, then you haven't been paying much attention to me the last thirty years."

He returns my smirk and leans on his forearms toward me across the table. "Oh, I know all about you, Savage, more than you could ever imagine. I just never thought you would stoop to blackmail. Your mother raised you better than that."

"You didn't give him much fucking choice, did you?" Gabe interjects, his voice vibrating with his effort to maintain self-control. Undoubtedly, he's just itching to lunge across the table and strangle the life from Abello with his bare hands.

Abello laughs—a cold, empty sound that can't camouflage the darkness and hatred in his eyes. "Everyone has choices, Mr. Anderson, or should I call you Mr. Dunne?"

*Shit.*

Of course Abello knows Gabe's real identity. They were both around our house all the time when I was growing up, but hearing him actually say it is something else. It's an unspoken threat to out Gabe. It's the least of our worries, but it's a very personal attack.

"Fuck you," Gabe spits back at him, his hands balling into fists on the tabletop. I move my hand over onto his wrist in warning. This is not the time, the place, or the person, to antagonize. He will not hesitate to kill us, all three of us, unless he believes what I just got done telling him.

Abello returns his attention to me.

I release Gabe when I feel him relax slightly. "Let's just end this now, Dom. Do we, or do we not, have an understanding?"

He grabs the manila envelope off the table. It contains a copy of Danika's notes, our only bargaining chip. He reclines in the booth, shaking the envelope in his hand. "I'm expected to believe you, your little girlfriend, and Mr. Dunne here are going to keep your mouths shut, indefinitely?"

"We have no reason to talk, Dom, not unless any unfortunate accidents befall any of us. Like I said, we keep our mouths shut, you agree not to move against any of us, and, if you do, the original notes go to the FBI and the two other copies to the local police, and the media."

I know there isn't enough there to actually arrest him. Most of it is stories and speculations, but it could lead to new sources of information, and ultimately, maybe a legit prosecution. My hope is that he doesn't want to risk that.

I'm also relying on the fact that he cares for Mom. He now knows how much Danika means to me, and by association, my family. Men like Abello don't have loyalty to much, but family is the exception, and as far as he's concerned, we are family.

The corner of his mouth twitches up. "You forgot the part where I somehow convince Mayor Dunne to resign and never run for public office again."

"And that." I grin at him as I down the rest of my Scotch. Glancing at Gabe, I find his usual stoicism has returned. That man has ice in his veins, at least that's what I always believed.

Abello rubs his chin and examines the envelope as if he has x-ray vision and can see its contents. When I handed it over to him at the beginning of our meeting, he opened it and glanced at its contents, then shoved them back in as if he couldn't care less. Now, he looks at it like he holds the construction plans to Fort Knox in his palms.

After a moment of contemplation, he nods and gives us another fake smile. "You have a deal, gentlemen. But, don't push me. I'm not a man you should fuck with, and I would really hate to upset your mother, Savage."

The veiled threat does not go unnoticed, and I bite my tongue to avoid setting him off. This was it, this was all we had, our only plan, our only chance to get out of this with Danika's safety assured. I couldn't fucking care less about my safety, and I know Gabe feels the same way, but neither of us could live with ourselves if we played a role in bringing her into the crossfire, again.

"Good evening, gentlemen." He slips from the booth and is immediately surrounded by his entourage of armed goons.

I release the breath I've been holding for so long my chest aches and drop my head into my hands. Gabe calls for our waiter and orders us another round of Scotch.

"No, man," I turn toward him, "I need to get home to Danika."

He smacks me on the back as the waiter sets the tumblers of amber liquid on the white fabric tablecloth. "No, you need to drink this and relax. If you go home to her all jacked up on adrenaline like you are right now, it will not end well. Trust me, I know from experience."

I nod at him and pick up the glass, swirling it around with my hand. Maybe he's right. I do need to calm down before seeing Danika. This is the end, of all the lies, all the bullshit, all the drama, and it's a new beginning for us. Some decompression time is a good thing.

Gabe drops his elbows to the table and drains his glass in one swallow. Imitating him, I tip the tumbler back and savor the sting of the liquid flowing down my throat as I drain it.

I twist and spin the empty tumbler on the table, the candlelight reflecting off the facets, sending flashes of rainbow colors across the white tablecloth. I make my decision then and there and pull my phone from my jacket so I can call Danika.

"Savage? Where are you? Are you all right?" The panic in her voice makes me regret waiting even the two minutes it took to have another drink.

"Baby, I'm fine. Everything is fine. It worked."

She releases a massive sob, and I can picture her crumpled up on the couch with Princess, crying and shaking. I should be there with her, and knowing I'm going to delay my return even more is a knife twisting in my gut. "Shh, don't cry. I'll be home soon."

She sniffles, and rather than being disgusting, it's somehow adorable. "Please come home to me."

"I will, baby. I love you."

"Love you, too."

## DANIKA

"Where the hell is he?" I ask Princess as I pace the floors of the condo for the hundredth time chewing on my nail so badly I'm starting to bleed. "Shit," I yank my finger from my mouth, "he said he was coming home over an hour ago. He should be here by now."

I finally force myself to sit on the couch, and I stare at the door, willing it to open, willing him to come through it. Princess jumps onto my lap and I run my fingers through her silky fur, trying to push myself to take deep breaths and telling myself not to cry again.

*He's fine.*

*He called.*

*He's fine.*

Images of fiery crashes and Paul's head exploding before my eyes race through my head. The tears start again. Fucking Abello, he's a psychopath. The coldest of the cold, ruthless and unforgiving. Will he really let us all walk away unscathed? Did he agree only to give Savage and Gabe a false sense of security before taking them out the moment they left Angelo's?

My heart races and the tears increase. I become a sobbing mess. Princess stands on my lap, leaning up to lick at my face and offer me what comfort she can.

Pulling my phone from my pocket, I check for the millionth time for a call or text from Savage, but, nothing. I shoot off a text.

< Where are you? >

I wait anxiously for a reply, but when none comes, I call. Straight to voicemail.

My worry is now bordering on hysteria as I move from the couch, set Princess on the floor, and begin to pace again.

I call Gabe. Same result.

Frustrated, I almost chuck my phone at the wall, but no one will be able to get a hold of me if I destroy it.

*Deep breaths.*

*In. Out. Repeat.*

I'm so focused on keeping myself breathing, I don't even hear the door open.

"Danika."

His voice snaps me from my neurotic pacing, and I whip around to face the door. It shuts behind him just as Princess jumps up onto his lap. He absently runs his hand down from her head to her back before shooing her off.

I assess him, making sure he is okay before I rush to him, climbing onto his lap and throwing my arms around his neck, clutching him to me. He wraps his arms around me, embracing me and holding me to him while I sob against his neck.

*Thank God.*

Finally, I'm able to catch my breath and I pull back, my eyes finding his. I can see a storm of emotions in their blue depths.

I smack him on the shoulder. "Where the hell were you? I was freaking the fuck out. You said you would be home over an hour ago."

Capturing my face in his hands, he kisses me gently. "I'm sorry, baby. I didn't mean to make you worry. I had something I had to take care of."

"And you couldn't have called?" I bark, shoving at his chest. "I thought something happened to you. You weren't answering your phone."

He frowns and reaches into his breast pocket, removing his phone and glancing down at it. "Shit, the battery died and I didn't even notice."

I scowl at him, crossing my arms over my chest as he gives me an apologetic half-smile. He slides his phone back into his pocket and once again takes my face in his hands.

"I'm sorry. Really, I am."

The sincerity in his voice weakens me and the tirade I was about to unleash on him goes out the window. We are finally free of the Abello threat. "So, it's really over?"

He smiles and nods, brushing my hair back behind my ears. "It's really over." Dragging my head down, he takes my mouth with his.

I pour all the anxiety and turmoil of the last week into our kiss.

His tongue slides along my bottom lip, urging me to open for him. Permitting him access, I suck him in as I slide my legs to the side, straddling his hips. The kiss deepens and a low groan emanates from him.

He bites my bottom lip and my clit throbs in response. I grind my hips against his, pushing my core against his erection. He moans and releases my lip with a pop.

My eyes meet his and I see the same lust and love there I hope he can see in mine. I reach for his belt and yank it off. I fling it across the room, a loud bang sounding as the metal clasp strikes the wood floor. He chuckles against my neck and licks his way up to my ear as I work the buttons and zipper of his pants. My hands shake, making the task ridiculously difficult.

Finally, I'm able to slip my hand in and wrap my palm around his cock. He hisses against my ear as I stroke his length, sliding the pad of my thumb across the head of his cock, spreading the pre-cum.

"Shit, baby, I need to be inside you..." he growls in my ear and slides his hand up under the t-shirt I'm wearing. His eyes widen when his fingers find my wet core. "No panties?"

I shake my head when he strokes my flesh, his thumb swirling around my clit, causing my hips to buck against him.

*Fuck.*

"You, inside me...now."

He moves his hand, and I guide the head of his cock inside of me before slamming my hips down, impaling myself on him.

He catches my gasp in his mouth, kissing me deeply while I squeeze around his hot flesh. I rock against him, riding his cock hard. I slam down on him with so much force, his chair actually shifts on the floor. Neither of us care.

I'm completely consumed by him. He is my everything, and I know I can never live without him, without this in my life.

Sliding his hand between us, his long fingers find my clit and I press against them as he rolls and pinches it in the way we both know is certain to quickly send me over the edge. The fire in my core builds and I drop my head back, his free hand finding my breast under the shirt and tugging at my erect nipple.

"Fuck! Yes, baby, just like that...please..."

He groans in appreciation and kisses his way up my neck. I tilt my head down, allowing my mouth to meet his as the inferno rages inside me, about to explode.

One more twist of my nipple and my orgasm slams into me, my entire body rolling and bucking uncontrolled on his cock. My walls squeeze against him. He curses and drops his forehead to mine as he comes, pulse after pulse of heat coating my core.

I collapse on him—wrung out emotionally and physically. Our panting breaths mix until I can't tell what's his or what's mine. The aftershocks of my orgasm cause random muscle spasms and shakes in my body. His arms surround me, and he kisses me gently.

"I love you, baby. I'm so sorry I worried you."

The reminder of my earlier anger registers, and I pull away from him. "Yeah, where the hell were you, anyway?"

He grins and mischief sparkles in his eyes.

"What?" My annoyance grows at his nonchalance regarding my earlier distress, caused solely by him.

*Douchebag. Does he have any idea how frantic I was?*

He leans in to kiss me again, but I retreat, shaking my head. "Oh no, don't you dare try to distract me."

A resigned sigh puffs from his lips as they curl into a little half-smile. "Reach in my inside right jacket pocket."

Sliding my hand between his shirt and jacket, I find the interior pocket and reach down, my fingers connecting with a small, velvet box.

*Holy shit. Holy shit. Holy shit.*

My heart thuds in my chest, and a loud rush floods my ears as I squeeze my eyes closed and try to catch my breath.

"Danika?" He takes my face in his hands and lifts my head up toward him. "Baby, look at me."

I open my eyes and find his concerned ones staring back at me.

"Take a deep breath and pull it out."

Seems easy enough.

In through the nose, out through the mouth. Breathe. Breathe.

Finally, the rushing sound in my ears dissipates and I can once again feel the box at my fingertips inside his pocket. I curl my hand around it and pull it out, opening my hand so the black box sits on my palm.

He reaches up, takes it from my hand, and flips it open, turning it to face me.

My breath catches again when I see the ring.

A beautiful solitaire. Simple. Perfect.

"I was going to ask you tomorrow night at dinner, but I don't want to wait anymore. I don't want to wait for anything with you. We've waited long enough."

I couldn't agree more.

I throw my arms around him, clutching him to me as the tears pool and streak down my face. He chuckles. "Is that a yes?"

Pulling away, I nod, because I won't even bother to try to speak right now. Tears shimmer in his eyes and he pulls the ring from the box and slips it on my finger.

He kisses me softly and then pulls away, taking a deep breath through his tears. "When I met you, I found me—the real me, not the one I tried to be after the accident, but the one I actually *am* now. I can never thank you enough for that."

For once, I don't have any words. How could anyone respond to that? I want to tell him he did the same for me—that he helped me find who I'm really supposed to be, but words completely fail me.

"This is the start of our forever," he whispers against my lips. I kiss him deeply, clenching my pussy around his semi-hard dick still buried deep inside me.

*Our forever.*

He's right. This is the start of it, the start of something I never thought I'd have, and certainly not with the pussy peddler I set out so determined to hate. But, Savage is it. The moment we collided in his office, I knew I would never be the same. He's proven to me that he's the best decision I've made in my entire life.

I lose myself to him and his kiss again. There's nothing and no one who will be able to destroy what we've built and fuck them if they try.

# EPILOGUE
## SIX MONTHS LATER

### SAVAGE

$\mathcal{H}$er knee bounces up and down furiously next to me in the exam room. I would love to tell her there isn't anything to be worried or nervous about, but that would be a lie. I've spent enough time in hospitals and doctor's offices over the last couple years to give me a healthy dose of anxiety whenever I find myself in another one of these white, sterile rooms, where the smell of antiseptic inevitably seeps into my nostrils.

This room is just like the others. I wonder if they are specifically designed to make you uneasy. I'm sure that isn't the case. In fact, I remember reading some article about paint colors and how hospitals and doctor's offices use light greens and blues because they are supposed to be soothing colors. Well, the barely blue, basically white walls of this room are doing nothing to calm me, and sure as shit are doing nothing to calm Danika.

I reach out and lay my hand on her knee.

Her head snaps up and she looks confused. "What?"

Smiling at her, I move my hand and, taking her hand in mine,

I bring it to my mouth, pressing my lips to smooth skin on the back. "You were driving me crazy with the leg thing."

"Oh, sorry," she squeezes my hand, "I didn't realize I was doing it."

"I know, baby." She never does. It's one of her nervous habits, along with pacing and biting her nails, and I can't blame her for being nervous today. My own stomach is churning, and the familiar taste of acid begins working its way up my throat.

It hasn't exactly been an easy year for us, and the shit with Abello was just the culmination of months of dancing around our issues. But, that's over now. I don't hide things from her anymore, and I don't think it's possible for her to hide anything from me—she's too damn honest and has proven time and time again that she lacks a filter.

Things have been relatively smooth sailing since the day we got married almost three months ago. She knelt next to me at the altar and promised to be with me through better or worse, and I couldn't help but wonder if it was possible for things to ever be worse than what we'd already experienced. It's not like most couples have mob bosses trying to kill them.

The fact that Abello has left us alone has just as much to do with my threat as it does with Danika's ability to get back to work and pretend that tossing the story under the rug doesn't eat away at her every day. If she hadn't been able to do that, I don't know where we would be. Things are still tense and a bit unsettled with Gabe's father. After his resignation, he began his campaign to win us over by reinitiating contact, probably in hopes he could convince us to back off the edict we laid out for him. But right now, that's the least of my worries.

Today, it would be easy to let go, let myself fully feel the trepidation I've been trying to keep at bay, but I have to be the strong one today. If it's bad news, Danika won't handle it well. I'm used to receiving bad news in doctor's offices, and I know how to take it in stride. Danika, on the other hand, is far too invested to take it if it's bad news.

*Shit, who am I kidding? I won't take it well either.*

Still, it's up to me to be strong for her today.

I press my lips to her temple, letting them linger there. I can never get enough of feeling her smooth skin against my mouth, my hands, everything. How I ever managed to be here, with her, like this, is beyond any comprehension even now. I've lost a lot of things in my life, but I found the one thing that mattered, and I will do anything to ensure she is happy.

"Where is the damn doctor, anyway?" She jumps up from her chair and paces back and forth in the small exam room, chewing on her finger nail. I try to hide my smirk behind my hand. She's so adorably predictable sometimes. "It must be bad news. Why else would he keep us waiting like this?"

"Because he can, babe. Don't assume it's bad news." Holding out my hand, I motion her over to me. "Come here."

She rolls her eyes and huffs before taking my hand and allowing me to pull her down onto my lap.

She immediately buries her face into my neck, her hot breath fluttering up around my ear as she snuggles against me. I gently rub my hand up and down her back and take her left hand in mine. My finger idly spins the ring on her finger back and forth, round and round. The tension is radiating off her, and I wish there was something I could say to make it better for her, something I haven't already thought of over the last six months.

Burying my face in her hair, I inhale the lavender, bergamot, and peppermint scent of her shampoo. I start another attempt to calm her when the door flies open and Dr. Rudolph strolls in, smile on his face, clipboard tucked under his arm.

"Mr. and Mrs. Hawke, thank you so much for waiting. I apologize for the slight delay." He sets the clipboard down and leans back against the counter, crossing his arms over his chest. "How are we doing today?"

Danika shifts on my lap, turning toward him. "Nervous, Doctor. Please, tell us what the tests said, tell us what's wrong."

Leave it to Danika to get right to the point. I squeeze her hand, hoping the small gesture might offer her some reassurance. She squeezes it back, but it is far from gentle as she apparently puts all her worry and frustration into crushing my fingers.

Dr. Rudolph smiles kindly and glances between us. "Why are you so sure something is wrong, Mrs. Hawke?"

She lets out an annoyed sigh, and I have no doubt she's gearing up to give the poor doc a tongue-lashing. I'm not brave enough a man to interrupt her, so I bite my tongue and wait for the show.

"Why? Because we have been trying to get pregnant for six months and it isn't working!" she yells. "That shouldn't happen! Teenagers get knocked up having sex once. We fuck like rabbits and nothing!"

I cover my smile with my free hand, and Dr. Rudolph gives me a sympathetic look.

Yes, we fuck like rabbits, and that is a good thing for any man; but I also have to deal with her sharp tongue on a daily basis, and I sense the doc may have experience with a similarly strong-willed woman given the smirk on his face.

"Four months," he stands and grabs the clipboard off the counter.

"What?" we ask in unison.

Looking up from his clipboard, he stares Danika down. "You tried for four months."

He barely has the words out of his mouth before she retorts, "No, it has definitely been six months."

He chuckles and, even though Danika continues to appear clueless, the realization of what he just said sinks in and my heart skips a beat. I try to get her attention by tugging on her shoulder. "Baby, listen to what he's saying instead of jumping down his throat."

She glares at me, then returns her attention to the doctor. "Look, Doctor, I don't know..."

He holds up his hand, silencing her mid-sentence. "Mrs. Hawke, I'm trying to tell you, if you would let me...you're pregnant."

---

## DANIKA

I hear the words, but they don't register immediately. Not until Savage takes my face between his shaking palms and turns it until I'm looking into his crystal-blue eyes. They shimmer with unshed tears.

Savage isn't a crier, not really. I've only seen it a handful of times in the last year. Considering what he's been through, what we have been through, that says a lot about how strong he is. But right now, that strength seems to have momentarily vanished.

"What?" The word comes out as nothing more than a whisper. If I wasn't sitting on his lap, my mouth mere inches from his, I doubt he would have even heard it.

"You're pregnant," he says, grinning. "We are going to have a baby." He pulls me to him and kisses me before I can even respond, stealing my breath with his excited passion. Our lips move together slowly as we savor this moment.

When he finally pulls away, I take a moment to steady my breathing and racing heart before I turn to the doctor. "How? I mean, I know how, but I haven't had any symptoms and I had my period last month."

Smiling, he crosses his arms again and leans back against the counter. "As many as twenty-five percent of women never experience morning sickness, and it isn't unusual for some women to have spotting throughout their pregnancy that can appear to just be a light period. We will do a pelvic exam and ultrasound to make sure everything is progressing as it should."

I shake my head, bewildered. "But you're one hundred percent sure I'm pregnant?"

He nods. "Your HCG levels are over ten thousand. You are definitely pregnant, and those numbers suggest you are about two months along."

My mind spins as I try to recall the last two months.

*Two months? Two fucking months! How the hell could I be pregnant for that long and not know it?*

Granted, things have been a little hectic recently. Savage opened a new restaurant and the second gentleman's club, and I've been chasing down a local real estate mogul who is basically a slumlord hiding behind a dozen layers of subordinates. But still, two months?

I feel like an idiot. The last two months have been difficult for us, and not just because we've been so busy, but also because of the emotional strain of not being able to get pregnant. I've been a total wreck, crying constantly and I'm sure making Savage miserable. Looking back, all the crying and breakdowns were probably pregnancy hormones, but it doesn't make me feel any less bad about how I have been acting.

"Danika? Baby, you okay?" Savage grabs my chin and gently turns me to face him, nothing but love and concern in his eyes.

My eyes burn as the tears form and I nod. "Yeah, I'm okay, just...shocked."

*We deserve this. We deserve some good news. We deserve to have everything we've ever wanted.*

I realize I'm shaking when Savage pulls me to his chest and holds me tight. "Shh, don't cry."

*I'm crying?*

Apparently the shaking is accompanied by sobbing I didn't even hear and tears streaming down my face I didn't even feel. These hormones are a fucking bitch. I didn't even cry this much on our wedding day and that was a day I never thought I'd ever see in my lifetime, let alone to Savage after all the shit that went down.

I thought we had our happily ever after when we got married, but today, it feels like that's only half of it. The Hawkes are going to freak out when they find out about the baby.

Since the minute we announced our engagement, the entire family has been pestering us about starting a family. I often have to remind them that Savage is only thirty-one and I am only twenty-six, but that doesn't seem to faze them. Even Skye has gotten in on the action, constantly checking in with me on how things are going.

We aren't friends. I wouldn't go that far, but I think marrying Savage finally convinced her I'm not some whore gold-digger out to take advantage of her big brother.

"Mrs. Hawke..."

I had completely forgotten Dr. Rudolph was still in the room. After quickly wiping my face, I turn to him. "Sorry."

He smiles and nods. "No need to apologize. I am going to go get the nurse and have them set up the room for the exam and ultrasound."

"Thank you, Dr. Rudolph."

I'm glad Savage said something, because I am still having trouble forming coherent thoughts and sentences. The doctor leaves and I turn my attention back to Savage.

He grins at me and kisses my forehead. "So, we're having a baby."

"Apparently, we are." I smile back at him and then inexplicable giggling overtakes me and I throw my arms around his neck. "We're gonna have a baby."

"It better not be a girl."

I jerk back and glare at him.

*Why the hell would he say something like that? Asshat.*

"What the fuck, Savage?"

He chuckles and pinches my side playfully. "I'm just thinking it will be really hard to explain that her daddy is a pussy peddler —might be easier with a boy."

I hope you enjoyed *Savage Collision*! Click here to get an exclusive BONUS SCENE with Savage and Danika on Valentine's Day! https://BookHip.com/CZAWXNX

# ABOUT THE AUTHOR

Gwyn McNamee is an attorney, writer, wife, and mother (to one human baby and two fur babies). Originally from the Midwest, Gwyn relocated to her husband's home town of Las Vegas in 2015 and is enjoying her respite from the cold and snow. Gwyn has been writing down her crazy stories and ideas for years and finally decided to share them with the world. She loves to write stories with a bit of suspense and action mingled with romance and heat.

When she isn't either writing or voraciously devouring any books she can get her hands on, Gwyn is busy adding to her tattoo collection, golfing, and stirring up trouble with her perfect mix of sweetness and sarcasm (usually while wearing heels).

Gwyn loves to hear from her readers. Here is where you can find her:

FB Reader Group: https://www.facebook.com/groups/1667380963540655/

Newsletter: www.gwynmcnamee.com/newsletter

Website: http://www.gwynmcnamee.com/

Facebook: https://www.facebook.com/AuthorGwynMcNamee/

Twitter: https://twitter.com/GwynMcNamee

Instagram: https://www.instagram.com/gwynmcnamee

Bookbub: https://www.bookbub.com/authors/gwynmcnamee

# OTHER WORKS BY GWYN MCNAMEE

Billionaires of New Orleans:

The Hawke Family Series

*Savage Collision* (The Hawke Family - Book One)

He's everything she didn't know she wanted. She's everything he thought he could never have.

The last thing I expect when I walk into The Hawkeye Club is to fall head over heels in lust. It's supposed to be a rescue mission. I have to get my baby sister off the pole, into some clothes, and out of the grasp of the pussy peddler who somehow manipulated her into stripping. But the moment I see Savage Hawke and verbally spar with him, my ability to remain rational flies out the window and my libido takes center stage. I've never wanted a relationship—my time is better spent focusing on taking down the scum running this city—but what I want and what I need are apparently two different things.

Danika Eriksson storms into my office in her high heels and on her high horse. Her holier-than-thou attitude and accusations should offend me, but instead, I can't get her out of my head or my heart. Her incomparable drive, take-no prisoners attitude, and blatant honesty captivate me and hold me prisoner. I should steer clear, but my self-preservation instinct is apparently dead—which is exactly what our relationship will be once she knows everything. It's only a matter of time.

The truth doesn't always set you free. Sometimes, it just royally screws you.

AVAILABLE AT ALL RETAILERS:

books2read.com/SavageCollision

*Tortured Skye* (The Hawke Family - Book Two)

She's always been off-limits. He's always just out of reach.

Falling in love with Gabe Anderson was as easy as breathing. Fighting my feelings for my brother's best friend was agonizingly hard. I never imagined giving in to my desire for him would cause such a destructive ripple effect. That kiss was my grasp at a lifeline—something, anything to hold me steady in my crumbling life. Now, I have to suffer with the fallout while trying to convince him it's all worth the consequences.

Guilt overwhelms me—over what I've done, the lives I've taken, and more than anything, over my feelings for Skye Hawke. Craving my best friend's little sister is insanely self-destructive. It never should have happened, but since the moment she kissed me, I haven't been able to get her out of my mind. If I take what I want, I risk losing everything. If I don't, I'll lose her and a piece of myself. The raging storm threatening to rain down on the city is nothing compared to the one that will come from my decision.

Love can be torture, but sometimes, love is the only thing that can save you.

AVAILABLE AT ALL RETAILERS:

Books2read.com/Tortured-Skye

*Stone Sober* (The Hawke Family - Book Three)

She's innocent and sweet. He's dark and depraved.

Stone Hawke is precisely the kind of man women are warned about— handsome, intelligent, arrogant, and intricately entangled with some dangerous people. I should stay away, but he manages to strip my soul bare with just a look and dominates my thoughts. Bad decisions are in my past. My life is (mostly) on track, even if it is no longer the one to medical school. I can't allow myself to cave to the fierce pull and ardent attraction I feel toward the youngest Hawke.

Nora Eriksson is off-limits, and not just because she's my brother's employee and sister-in-law. Despite the fact she's stripping at The Hawkeye Club, she has an innocent and pure heart. Normally, the only thing that appeals to me about innocence is the opportunity to taint it. But not when it comes to Nora. I can't expose her to the filth permeating my life. There are too many things I can't control, things completely out of my hands. She doesn't deserve any of it, but the power she holds over me is stronger than any addiction.

The hardest battles we fight are often with ourselves, but only through defeating our own demons can we find true peace.

AVAILABLE AT ALL RETAILERS:

books2read.com/StoneSober

*Building Storm (The Hawke Family - Book Four)*

She hasn't been living. He's looking for a way to forget it all.

My life went up in flames. All I'm left with is my daughter and ashes. The simple act of breathing is so excruciating, there are days I wish I could stop altogether. So I have no business being at the party, and I definitely shouldn't be in the arms of the handsome stranger. When his lips meet mine, he breathes life into me for the first time since the day the inferno disintegrated my world. But loving again isn't in the cards, and there are even greater dangers to face than trying to keep Landon McCabe out of my heart.

Running is my only option. I have to get away from Chicago and the betrayal that shattered my world. I need a new life-one without attachments. The vibrancy of New Orleans convinces me it's possible to start over. Yet in all the excitement of a new city, it's Storm Hawke's dark, sad beauty that draws me in. She isn't looking for love, and we both need a hot, sweaty release without feelings getting involved. But even the best laid plans fail, and life can leave you burned.

Love can build, and love can destroy. But in the end, love is what raises you from the ashes.

AVAILABLE AT ALL RETAILERS:

books2read.com/BuildingStorm

*Tainted Saint (The Hawke Family - Book Five)*

He's searching for absolution. She wants her happily ever after.

Solomon Clarke goes by Saint, though he's anything but. After lusting for him from afar, the masquerade party affords me the anonymity to pursue that attraction without worrying about the fall-out of hooking-up with the bouncer from the Hawkeye Club. From the second he lays his eyes and hands on me, I'm helpless to resist him. Even burying myself in a dangerous investigation can't erase the memory of our combustible connection and one night together. The only problem... he has no idea who I am.

Caroline Brooks thinks I don't see her watching me, the way her eyes rake over me with appreciation. But I've noticed, and the party is the perfect opportunity to unleash the desire I've kept reined in for so damn long. It also sets off a series of events no one sees coming. Events that leave those I love hurting because of my failures. While the guilt eats away at my soul, Caroline continues to weigh on my heart. That woman may be the death of me, but oh, what a way to go.

Life isn't always clean, and sometimes, it takes a saint to do the dirty work.

AVAILABLE AT ALL RETAILERS:

books2read.com/TaintedSaint

*Steele Resolve (The Hawke Family - Book Six)*

For one man, power is king. For the other, loyalty reigns.

Mob boss Luca "Steele" Abello isn't just dangerous—he's lethal. A master manipulator, liar, and user, no one should trust a word that comes out of his mouth. Yet, I can't get him out of my head. The time we spent together before I knew his true identity is seared into my brain. His touch. His voice. They haunt my every waking hour and occupy my dreams. So does my guilt. I'm literally sleeping with the enemy and betraying the only family I've ever had. When I come clean, it will be the end of me.

Byron Harris is a distraction I can't afford. I never should have let it go beyond that first night, but I couldn't stay away. Even when I learned who he was, when the *only* option was to end things, I kept going back, risking his life and mine to continue our indiscretion. The truth of what I am could get us both killed, but being with the man who's such an integral part of the Hawke family is even more terrifying. The only people I've ever cared about are on opposing sides, and I'm the rift that could end their friendship forever.

Love is a battlefield isn't just a saying. For some, it's a reality.

AVAILABLE AT ALL RETAILERS:

books2read.com/SteeleResolve

*Then check out the Billionaires of New Orleans: The Hawke Family Second Generation Series to meet the children of the original characters!*